RAVE
MARL
AND

DON'T LET GO

"4 Stars! Another winner in a top-notch series! . . . Four different plot threads are delicately woven together, each resonating with emotional overtones of loss and rebirth."
—*Romantic Times BOOKreviews Magazine*

"An exhilarating thriller . . . Readers will enjoy this fine family drama as Ms. Melton provides a strong tale."
—*Midwest Book Review*

"A rich read . . . multilayered characters . . . I recommend you find *Don't Let Go* . . . you'll be glad you did."
—*RomRevToday.com*

"Melton delivers another suspenseful tale that you will never forget." —*BookCoveReviews.com*

NEXT TO DIE

"A romance that sizzles." —*Publishers Weekly*

"There is a lot of action and suspense . . . a work that is as exciting as it is heartwarmingly riveting."
—*Midwest Book Review*

Dam Neck Naval Annex

more . . .

Book #6

"A fast and fulfilling read . . . filled with emotion and suspense. The characters are finely drawn and the plot well crafted."　　　　　**—RomRevToday.com**

"Riveting suspense."　　　　**—OnceUponARomance.com**

"Fast-paced thrill and challenging romances make this a winning story."　　　　**—HuntressReviews.com**

"Melton brings her considerable knowledge about the military and intelligence world to this Navy SEAL series. You'll enjoy this peek into the world—and love the romance that develops between Joe and Penny."
　　　　　　　　　　—FreshFiction.com

"Another pleasing chapter in Melton's highly addictive Navy SEALs series . . . Joe and Penny are both very appealing characters and their romance is rich and involving."　　　　　　**—BookLoons.com**

TIME TO RUN

"Melton . . . doesn't miss a beat in this involving story."
　　　　　　　　　　—Publishers Weekly

"Melton's compelling protagonists propel the gritty and realistic storytelling . . . Excellent!"
—*Romantic Times BOOKreviews Magazine*

"This book will twist all of your heartstrings . . . you won't be able to put *Time to Run* down . . . a must-read."
—**FreshFiction.com**

"Exceedingly riveting . . . enthralling . . . you'll find yourself racing through it from one exciting scene to the next . . . my favorite."
—**RomRevToday.com**

"An exciting tale starring a fine lead couple . . . fans will enjoy this wonderful thriller."
—*Midwest Book Review*

"Exciting and emotionally moving . . . gripping."
—**Bookloons Reviews**

"Edgy contemporary romantic suspense . . . emotional fireworks as well as some fancy sniper shooting."
—**Booklist**

more . . .

IN THE DARK

"Fantastic . . . keeps you riveted . . . will keep you guessing . . . Well done!"   **—OnceUponARomance.net**

"A strong thriller . . . Action-packed . . . will keep the audience on the edge of their seats."   **—Blether.com**

"Hooked me from the first page . . . filled with romance, suspense, and characters who will pull you in and never let you go."

—Lisa Jackson, *New York Times* bestselling author of *Absolute Fear*

"Packed with action from the first page to the last . . . a must."   **—*Novel Talk***

"[A] hard-charging romantic thriller as warm and heady as a Caribbean sun-soaked bay."   **—*Bookpage***

"Picking up where *Forget Me Not* left off . . . danger, passion, and adventure."

—*Romantic Times BOOKreviews Magazine*

FORGET ME NOT

"Refreshing . . . fine writing, likable characters, and realistic emotions."   **—*Publishers Weekly***

"An intriguing romantic suspense . . . Readers will take great delight." —*Midwest Book Review*

"The gifted Melton does an excellent job building emotion, danger, and tension in her transfixing novel." —*Romantic Times BOOKreviews Magazine*

"Entertaining . . . moving and passionate . . . with plenty of action and suspense . . . *Forget Me Not* is a winner; don't miss it." —*RomRevToday.com*

"A wonderful book, touching at all the right heartstrings. I highly recommend it!" —**Heather Graham**, author of *Dead on the Dance Floor*

"Amazing . . . fantastic . . . a riveting plot, engaging characters, and unforgettable love story . . . not to be missed." —**NewandUsedBooks.com**

"A thrilling romance." —**TheBestReviews.com**

"Riveting . . . you'll definitely want to pick this one up." —**RomanceJunkies.com**

"Wonderful, thrilling . . . loved it!" —**RomanceReviewsMag.com**

Also by Marliss Melton

Forget Me Not

In the Dark

Time to Run

Next to Die

Don't Let Go

ATTENTION CORPORATIONS AND ORGANIZATIONS:
MOST HACHETTE BOOK GROUP USA books are available
at quantity discounts with bulk purchase for educational,
business, or sales promotional use. For information,
please call or write:

**Special Markets Department, Hachette Book Group USA
237 Park Avenue, New York, NY 10017
Telephone: 1-800-222-6747 Fax: 1-800-477-5925**

Melton, Marliss.
Too far gone /

2008.
33305216781470
la   11/24/08

MARLISS MELTON

TOO FAR GONE

FOREVER

NEW YORK   BOSTON

This book is a work of fiction. Names, characters, places, and incidents are the product of the author's imagination or are used fictitiously. Any resemblance to actual events, locales, or persons, living or dead, is coincidental.

If you purchase this book without a cover you should be aware that this book may have been stolen property and reported as "unsold and destroyed" to the publisher. In such case neither the author nor the publisher has received any payment for this "stripped book."

Copyright © 2008 by Marliss Arruda
All rights reserved. Except as permitted under the U.S. Copyright Act of 1976, no part of this publication may be reproduced, distributed, or transmitted in any form or by any means, or stored in a database or retrieval system, without the prior written permission of the publisher.

Cover design by Dale Fioricco

Forever
Hachette Book Group USA
237 Park Avenue
New York, NY 10017
Visit our Web site at www.HachetteBookGroupUSA.com

Printed in the United States of America

Forever is an imprint of Grand Central Publishing. The Forever name and logo is a trademark of Hachette Book Group USA, Inc.

First Printing: November 2008

10 9 8 7 6 5 4 3 2 1

This book is dedicated to the memory of
Navy SEAL Petty Officer 2nd Class, Michael Monsoor,
who saved his comrades' lives by jumping on a hand
grenade in Ramadi, Iraq, on September 29, 2006. He was
posthumously awarded the Medal of Honor for his
sacrifice and the Silver Star for previous
heroic acts. In his lifetime, his valiant service
earned him the Bronze Star, the Purple Heart,
and the Combat Action Ribbon. May he ever
be the recipient of our humble gratitude.

Acknowledgments

For the citizens and natives of Savannah, Georgia, please forgive any insinuation that corruption rules your beautiful city. With the release of *Midnight in the Garden of Good and Evil*, Savannah became the prototype setting for a story involving intrigue and mystery. I have used that circumstance to my benefit and greatly appreciate your forbearance.

As always, writing a story is never an act completed in isolation. Many people contributed to the project, some without ever even realizing it. My thanks go to the hospitable folks at Old Town Trolley Tours in Savannah; to my editor, Michele Bidelspach, for giving me the time I needed for revisions; to retired FBI Special Agent Kevin McPartland for answering all of my annoying questions; and to officer Mark Kearney for answering my questions about getting arrested and going to jail.

My assistant, Janie Hawkins, deserves untold recognition for enduring the agonies of labor pains as we birthed this baby together. Bless you, Janie, for loving Sean and Ellie as much as I do and for sharing your time and talent to help me tell their tale.

TOO FAR
GONE

Prologue

✦

Carl Stuart thrust his way out of the smoky, port-side bar a good sight more sober than he wanted to be. He had no more money to spend on liquor, not a dime. The sultry Savannah air closed around him like the warm swamp waters of his Mississippi home, except that the air in this touristy town was filled with succulent odors emanating from the many restaurants on River Street. The laughter of visitors seemed to mock him as he shrugged around them and skulked along the ballast-paved streets of the historic waterfront.

Heading toward the shadows of the east end, he entertained the fantasy of falling into the glinting river tonight to end his sorry-ass life.

He'd come all this way for nothing. The construction job that had enticed him to Georgia had proven too arduous. The foreman hadn't cut him any slack and had finally plain-out fired him. And just this morning, Tammy'd booted him out of their apartment, calling him a good-for-nothing. He hated being called that. That's what Ellie used to say.

Carl had nursed those words all day, growing increasingly belligerent. Tonight he'd haunted several bars, hoping to join in a bar fight, one bloody and painful enough to take his mind off his woes, but no one else was in a fighting mood, apparently.

The soles of his dingy shoes struck the stone street with a hollow sound. Like the saying went, *Life's a bitch and then you die.* He could've been somebody, if only . . .

He walked with his head down, tantalizing himself with images of nothingness—the relief that would come once the warm waters claimed him.

A woman's sudden cry startled him, forcing his head up. "Help!" she wailed, gesticulating. "That man took my purse!"

Carl's gaze flew to the shadowy figure fleeing away from her, heading toward stone steps that led up to Bay Street, forty-two feet above the riverfront. With a grim smile, Carl answered the call, glad for an excuse to exorcise his rage.

"Thank you!" cried the handsome woman as he tore past her.

The youth with the purse threw a startled look behind him. He staggered up the stairs, clumsy in his haste, tripping over his feet and rising up again. He was no match for Carl, who'd been an all-star quarterback in high school, back before Ellie had stolen his future. That had been over a decade ago, but Carl was still quick and agile, capable of tackling a man to the ground and delivering a good ass-whooping when he had a mind to.

Tonight he wanted to really hurt somebody. With a roar that chilled his own blood, he tackled the boy's ankles and brought him down hard. He scrambled up and over him, only to rear back when a blade flashed in the youth's hand. With a swipe of his arm, Carl knocked the knife free. As it clattered down the steps, he clenched his fist and plowed it into the youth's jaw.

Crunch! The grip on the purse went slack; still, Carl rained down punishment, pummeling the boy's face until it bled. Then he snatched up his prize and looked down at the woman.

She stood at the base of the steps, her jewelry glittering under the flame of the ancient navigational beacon overhead. The purse in Carl's hands felt heavy, fat with money and credit cards. It was his for the taking. All he had to do was step over his bloody victim and flee up the rest of the stairs.

Temptation nipped at him. But by now the lone woman had gathered a gaggle of well-groomed friends about her, all of whom peered up at him expectantly. *Shit*.

With a shudder of disappointment, Carl hefted the purse and carried it heavily down the steps. The woman rushed up to him, eyes shining with gratitude. "Oh, thank you so much!" she gushed, reaching to take her purse back.

Aware that her friends were hovering protectively, Carl grudgingly parted with it. A sullen, angry feeling filled his heart. Life was so fucking unfair.

Turning back to her friends, the woman waltzed off with them, clearly in high spirits. As they left him standing there bereft, he overheard her offer to buy them a round so they could celebrate her good fortune.

"Ungrateful bitch," Carl muttered, glancing down at his bloodied knuckles.

* * *

Within the spotless interior of a Bentley Arnage parked nearby, Owen Dulay turned his head to catch his lawyer's speculative eye.

"He did the right thing," remarked Lynwood Spenser with surprise.

"I thought he might," countered Owen with mixed relief and satisfaction.

"Though he needn't have bludgeoned that boy half to death," Lynwood pointed out.

"The boy will be compensated. What matters is that he gave the woman what was hers," Owen insisted. "He has the heart of a Centurion." At least, that was what he'd been hoping to convince himself.

"That's not what the foreman on the job site says," muttered the lawyer.

Owen flashed him an impatient glare. "He's all I've got, Lynwood. You know the law."

"I advise you to consider a trial period," the lawyer suggested, "before making such a critical decision."

"That won't be necessary," Owen assured him. "I will mold him into the man he needs to be."

As Lynwood Spenser heaved a skeptical sigh, Owen Dulay stepped out of his vehicle to issue Carl Stuart an offer he couldn't refuse.

Chapter One

◆

With the rain coming down in sheets outside her minuscule rancher and with her two older sons chasing each other wildly through the rooms, Ellie Smart was on the verge of pulling her hair out. "Boys!" she snapped, glaring up from the biology book in her lap. "I've had enough. Go to your room this instant and find a game to play or a book to read!"

"I don't have nothin' new to read, Mama," protested ten-year-old Christopher.

"I hate readin'!" Caleb, his younger brother, declared.

Ellie set her book aside and rose ominously from the couch. "Then we'll just have to practice math," she threatened, skirting the baby who crawled into her path. Caleb's performance in second-grade math was a matter of great concern to his teacher and, of course, to Ellie, who never found enough time to help him.

Sacrificing her own studies, she snatched up the practice cards she had bought at Wal-Mart and ordered him to sit on the couch. He thumped down on the sofa with a rubber ball in hand, knocking her textbook to the floor.

"Careful!" Ellie scolded, hating the note of frustration in her voice. Being a single mother was the toughest job a woman could have, short of living in a dingy trailer by a swamp in Mississippi with a no-good, lying, cheating, loser of a husband named Carl.

"Chris," she requested of her ten-year-old, "kindly take the baby to your bedroom."

"Yes, Mama," said Chris with a sigh.

Positioning herself in front of Caleb, Ellie readied the cards in her hand and began to drill him. "Twelve," she corrected him when he got the answer wrong. "We just did that one, remember?" It was hard to tell if Caleb had a problem remembering or if he was being intentionally obtuse. Either way, she stood on the verge of a nervous breakdown.

The vision of a white Chevy truck pulling into her driveway startled an exclamation out of her. Well, look who was back from God-knew-where.

Caleb shot to his knees to see what she was looking at. "Yay!" he shouted. "Mr. Sean's back!"

"Stay put!" Ellie ordered when he made to jump off the sofa.

As Sean darted from his truck to her front stoop with a plastic sack in one hand, Ellie went to open the door, aware that her heart had started racing.

Chief Petty Officer Sean Harlan was her landlord. The day she'd met him ten months ago, she'd realized he was dangerous—not because he was a SEAL and a sniper, but because of his charm. He was bald and muscular, with twinkling blue eyes and a killer smile. She had recognized him then for exactly what he was: a ladies' man, with no more staying power than a butterfly on a lilac bush.

When Ellie and her boys were new to Virginia Beach, keeping clear of Sean hadn't been easy. He'd hung around her little rental house, one of several he owned and leased, putting on the finishing touches. He'd built a sandbox in the backyard for her boys and brought them bicycles. But then, for the last six months, he'd been overseas, and life had settled down into a grinding but stable routine.

She'd forgotten how unsettling his presence could be.

"Hi." With that killer grin and rainwater clinging to his eyelashes, his sex appeal rolled over her like hot oil, completely visceral yet utterly undesired. "Are the boys here?" His eyes seemed even bluer, set against a suntanned face.

Lord have mercy. "Of course," she said, her voice huskier than usual. "Come in." She stepped back, and he eased past her, causing the walls of the little house to shrink inward. His shoulders seemed broader than ever, his bare calves below the khaki shorts sleek and powerful. The faint scent of citrus always seemed to cling to him. She swallowed against a suddenly dry throat.

"Mr. Sean!" Caleb launched himself off the couch to tackle him at the waist.

With a mock roar, Sean collapsed onto the couch and pulled him into a bear hug.

"You're back!" exclaimed Christopher, hurrying out of the hallway with the baby to grin down at them.

Sean shot to his feet, rubbed his knuckles over Chris's head, and took the eleven-month-old baby from his arms. "Holy smokes, little guy," he exclaimed, dangling him up at eye level. "Watcha been eatin'?"

Colton grinned, showing off his four front teeth.

"Pretty much everything he can get his hands on," Ellie explained.

"Oh, yeah?" he said. As he glanced over at her, his gaze dropped briefly to her breasts.

Her nipples tingled as if he'd actually caressed them. "Caleb was practicing his math facts," she informed him, holding up the cards as evidence.

"Oh, sorry," he said, not sounding at all contrite. "I brought you guys a present." He lifted the bag looped over his arm.

"What is it?" Caleb's face lit up with excitement.

Santa Claus is back, Ellie thought with a roll of her eyes.

As Sean handed her the baby, the heat of his strong fingers seemed to scorch her. He glanced at her sharply as if surprised by the awareness sparking between them. Delving into the bag, he pulled out a tin cylinder and gave it to the boys. Caleb and Christopher tore into it, falling to their knees. "It's a magnet set. Cool!" Chris exclaimed.

Sean smiled down at their blond heads. "Got it at the airport. This is for the little guy," he said, pulling out a stuffed monkey and handing it to Colton. The baby grasped it, staring with amazement into the monkey's plastic eyes.

"Thank you," murmured Ellie. "You don't need to bring them gifts, you know. They're just happy to have you back."

He gave her a long, searching look. "What about you?" he demanded unexpectedly.

The soft challenge drove the breath from her lungs. "I wouldn't have a home without you," she retorted, aware that her legs were trembling. What was wrong with her? He was gone just six months, yet her body seemed to come alive in his presence. He probably had that effect on all women, young and old alike.

Ellie tucked a strand of golden brown hair behind her ear. The soft, curly texture heightened her awareness of her femininity. What was she thinking, allowing hormones to rule her thoughts? Men were trouble, and her friends had warned her about Sean—first Solomon in his terse, no-nonsense way and then his wife, Jordan, who just came right out and told her to ignore Sean if he flirted. Even her neighbor Belinda had made some comments about Sean being a love-'em-and-leave-'em type if ever there was one. Having been bitten by one man, you'd think she had the sense to be twice shy.

"So, listen," said Sean, sounding a little uncertain of himself, "do you think I could take the bigger boys right now to Fun Zone?"

Caleb jerked his gaze up from the magnet set. "Fun Zone!" he cried.

Chris's gray eyes swiveled up at her. "Can we go, Mama? Please?"

Ellie heaved an exasperated sigh. "Caleb has to practice his math facts," she reminded Sean.

"No problem," he said, glancing at the cards in her hand. "Addition is our mission. By the time I bring 'em home, Caleb will know how to add anything up to . . . ?"

"Twenty," Caleb supplied, surprisingly astute.

Ellie raised a dubious eyebrow. "How are you going to teach him that at Fun Zone?" she demanded, picturing the boys and Sean clambering through tubes and coasting down slides. She almost wished she could go, too.

"Now, Miz Ellie." Sean sent her a long-suffering look, but the way he drawled her name in his resonant baritone made her insides quiver. "Not all boys learn math like you girly girls with books and cards and all. We learn by doing, ain't that right?" He glanced at Caleb for corroboration.

"Yep."

"I can learn by reading," Christopher piped up with a worried look.

"That's 'cause you're smart," Sean countered, "like your mama."

Ellie's insides quivered again.

"Chris is a girly boy," Caleb taunted.

Sean cut him a frown, and Caleb's mouth snapped shut.

He sure has a way with them, Ellie thought. She wondered if he was going to let them down the way their daddy had. Sean's absence these past months had been hard enough, only it hadn't been his decision to leave. He'd had a job to do.

"So, can we go?" he asked. He seemed more antsy than usual, but then his muscles had always thrummed with an energy level she could only envy.

"I don't have any money," she stalled, angling her chin higher.

"No problem. I've got free tickets." He patted his back pocket. "MWR was giving them away."

MWR had to be some kind of perk for the military. Ellie threw her hands up. "Go ahead. It's not like I can tell them no now." Besides, she could use the reprieve to study for her upcoming finals.

Sean grinned at the boys. "Come on, fellas. Put your shoes on."

"Yay!" As they dashed off in search of their shoes,

Ellie played with Colton and his monkey. She could sense Sean's gaze focusing intently on them both.

"I should have gotten you something, too," he said with an apologetic grimace.

She looked up at him, surprised. "No, you shouldn't," she retorted definitively.

"You deserve something," he argued. "When's the last time someone gave you something?"

"'Bout nine months ago," she answered honestly, "when you gave me this house to rent and kept me and my boys from living in my car on the streets."

"Ellie." He inhaled, expanding his already immense chest, and shook his head. "You have no idea—"

"Mama, where are my new shoes?" Caleb's cry from the back of the house cut him off. Ellie hurried to help him, both frightened and excited by whatever Sean was going to say.

"They're right here, honey," she said, kicking them out from under his bed.

Jamming his feet into his sneakers, Caleb ran for the door. "Okay, I'm ready," he declared. Chris followed right behind him.

"I'll have them home by suppertime," Sean promised. He sent both boys ahead of him with, "Run! The truck's unlocked."

He and Ellie remained in the cramped hallway. Ellie clutched Colton to her chest like a shield, her heart beating irregularly. "I hope you get some studying done," Sean said gruffly, proving he hadn't overlooked her textbook on the floor. "You should be proud of yourself," he added, "going back to school and all."

She'd received so few scraps of encouragement in her

life that his words seemed to lift her right off the floor. Was that what he'd been about to tell her earlier? "Just doing what I have to do," she murmured with a pinch of disappointment.

"Well. See you," he said, and with a wink and a smile, he was gone.

She watched him jog through the rain to his truck, where the boys tussled inside, fogging up the windows.

His beat-up Chevy shot out of her driveway backward, reversed direction, and disappeared. The house seemed suddenly too quiet. She wished she'd been invited to go along with them. Sean's presence was like a sunbeam on a cloudy day.

You fool, scolded a voice in her head. Not every itch needs scratching. Her attraction to Sean would only distract her from the goals she'd set for herself: to get a degree in nursing with the aim of becoming a certified midwife. Mooning over a man would get her nowhere. Hadn't she learned that lesson from marrying Carl?

Putting her weight against the door, Ellie tried to ignore the throb of desire that left her feeling needy and unfulfilled. She was a woman, after all, in the prime of her life. She wasn't a naïve sixteen-year-old anymore, stupid enough to think the all-star, high school quarterback was her salvation from years of foster care. Oh, no. She was her own woman now. And an affair with Sean Harlan spelled nothing but disaster for her and her boys.

"Daddy, you wanted to see me?" Skyler Dulay slipped through her father's office door and shut it quietly behind her.

She caught him putting the key that opened his file

cabinet back in the box he kept hidden in the back of his drawer. Over the years, she'd realized that was where he hid it. He did so now with precise and methodical movements, sending her a smile that failed to reach his dark, enigmatic eyes. The grandfather clock in the corner ticked off the seconds, and Skyler's anxiety escalated.

Her father slowly stood. At well over six feet and always impeccably dressed, he cut an intimidating figure. She scarcely breathed as he rounded his desk. "Yes, I have a matter to discuss before you leave for the shelter today," he imparted in his deceptively gentle, Southern drawl.

She glanced at the clock, her heart thudding heavily. News that was shared in her father's study was never welcoming. "I'm already late," she pointed out.

"This won't wait," he said, coming to stand before her, his smile now gone. He put out his hands, palms up, indicating she should lay her hands over his. She did so and was, as usual, overcome by a sudden sense of helplessness. At twenty-three, she still felt like a child.

"As the daughter of a Centurion, I'm sure you understand your obligations," he began with an omnipotent glint in his murky eyes.

Skyler's insides cramped. "Of course," she murmured, terrified of what might come next.

"You've known for years that you would marry Ashton Jameson. He and I have decided to move up the wedding date."

Skyler's heart seemed to stop, then start up at an erratic pace. "Up to when?" she asked as the blood rushed from her cheeks.

"The end of this month," he replied. His dark watchful eyes dared her to defy him.

"But, why?" she protested. "I have Mama to look after."

His grip tightened. "You are not a son," he said, reminding her of the Centurion laws forbidding daughters to inherit. "Without my wealth, you have nothing."

Wrenching her hands from his, she walked to the window to hide her dismay. Below her, Carl, their gardener, snipped back the shriveled stalks of dead lilies, his lanky hair falling over his eyes. "I don't want your wealth," she dared to admit, clutching the heavy silk drape in one hand.

With a harsh grip, her father dragged her around. "Rubbish," he declared. "You've no idea what it means to go without."

"I work at a homeless shelter," she reminded him, her cheeks flaming with indignation.

"And you come home to a mansion with servants," he articulated with a nasty smile.

"Jameson is fifty years old!" Skyler cried, coming to the heart of her protest.

"Exactly," hissed her father. "And one day, not too long from now, he'll die, leaving you a wealthy widow, still young enough to pursue your silly little dreams."

Chilled by his prediction and offended that he had belittled her aspirations, Skyler dug her nails into her palms for courage. "I am a grown woman," she insisted, though her voice quavered. "I should get to choose who I'm going to marry."

The look that crossed her father's face struck fear in her heart. "Tonight, Jameson is giving you a ring," he warned, scarcely above a whisper. Dismay smothered Skyler's brief rebellion. "If you even think of refusing him, I'll put you where you should have been all these years."

A shudder wracked Skyler's slender frame. He held

her fate, her terrible secret, like a trump card in the palm of his hand. "Now, have a good day," he added, releasing her with a genteel nod and a steely smile.

Feeling as though the breath had been knocked from her lungs, Skyler fled to the door and pushed through it, careful not to let it slam. Her father abhorred unseemly displays.

At just past midnight, Sean swung into Ellie's driveway, wary of the message that had summoned him here. Sure enough, every light in the house was out, just like her voice mail, left on his cell an hour ago, had advised him.

Nothing's working—not the switches or the outlets. There must be a problem with the main breaker in the electric box, she'd surmised in her husky drawl.

He loved the way she talked, liquefying short little words into long, molasses-smooth ones. He'd wondered, though, if she was telling the truth. Or was her call just a ploy to get him to drop by, late at night when the boys were sleeping? It wouldn't be the first time a woman tenant with ulterior motives had summoned him.

The possibility that Ellie had something like that in mind heated his blood.

Candlelight flickered faintly behind her drawn blinds. With a tingle of excitement and an equally strong dose of wariness, Sean knocked lightly on her door.

The snap of a twig out back and the barest whisper of a footfall made him step back and listen. *What was that?*

But then the door eased open, and suddenly all of his attention was caught up in the vision of Ellie in a soft, worn nightgown with ragged lace at the neckline. His suspicions spiraled straight to his groin. Why else would she greet him in her nightie if not to lure him to her bed? But she was clutching a candle before her, holding it up like a weapon. Maybe sex wasn't the first thing on her mind—too bad.

He swallowed hard. "Sorry it took me so long to come over. I had duty tonight."

"Honestly, it's fine. I'd given up on you coming at all." She seemed nervous about his timing. "This can wait till morning. It's awful late."

"But you're up," he pointed out.

"I've got finals this week," she admitted. She did look tired, her eyes red with strain and rimmed with dark circles.

She must have been waiting tables earlier, he surmised, since her hair was still braided. Soft-looking curls straggled out of the single French braid and framed her face like a halo. Her skin looked creamy and flawless. Wide gray eyes skittered over his battle dress uniform and webbed belt to the gun holstered at his waist. He saw her swallow, noted the faint, fast flutter of her pulse in the hollow at the base of her throat.

The mid-May air seemed suddenly thick and damp, making it harder to breathe. "Why don't I check it out while I'm here?" Sean suggested, praying, hoping she wouldn't make the first move. If she did, he was toast. After six months in a godforsaken desert, he'd come home ready to get laid, and Ellie looked mighty fine at the moment.

Her eyebrows drew together, betraying her misgivings. "All right," she relented, and slowly opened the door.

The minute he stepped inside, he realized he could smell her. She'd showered off the scent of food and perspiration that clung to her after waiting tables. Now she smelled of clean woman and fresh cotton, an alluring blend that had him digging deep to keep from reaching for her.

"Why do you lock it?" she demanded, making him realize that while his mind was on sex, hers was on more practical things.

"What, the electric panel? I don't."

"Well, it's locked now, or I'd have thrown the switch myself."

"Hmm." With a frown, Sean stalked down the short hall to the kitchen. The electric panel was mounted on the wall over her washer and dryer—two ancient appliances bought at a garage sale. He tugged at the metal door and found it stuck. Giving it a hard jerk, it popped open. A paperclip clattered onto the dryer.

Sean picked it up. "The door was jammed," he said, peering at the control panel. Sure enough, the main switch had been thrown. He popped it on again, and light flooded down on them from the recessed fixture overhead. Shutting the little metal door, he picked up the paper clip and showed it to Ellie like a piece of damning evidence.

"Well, I didn't do it," she protested, holding a hand out as she extinguished her candle.

"One of the boys maybe?" Their fingers brushed, sparking that same reaction he'd felt the other day. His breath caught, and his gaze jumped to where her nipples, firmly erect, jutted through the fabric of her gown. *Holy hell.* "I'd better go," he rasped, brushing past her to escape to the door.

At the doorway, he glanced back, catching a look of unguarded desire that she quickly concealed by lowering her lashes. "Ellie." He gripped the doorknob hard. "If things were different, you'd have trouble getting rid of me right now."

Her spine stiffened even as her eyes flared with surprise. "Different how?" she demanded.

He realized she'd misunderstood him. He changed direction, walking up to within six inches of her, close enough to inhale her scent. "You have no idea how amazing you are, do you?" he demanded, wishing to God he could press her back against the wall and show her what she did to him. The image of her against the wall, him against her, *inside her,* almost undid him.

She looked up at him, suspiciously puzzled.

"Look, it isn't you. I just don't date women with kids," he explained to her gently, regretfully. "That's all. It's just . . . not a good idea, trust me."

Ellie reeled with mortification. Was she that transparent that he simply *assumed* she wanted to sleep with him? Shame and self-directed anger made her ears burn. "No, it's not a good idea," she agreed. "And just so you know, that's just fine with me. What makes you so cocksure I even want a man in my life? You may be good with my boys, Mr. Harlan," she choked out fiercely, "but I can get along just fine without you."

"Is that right?" he murmured, his eyes glinting at the challenge. He gave her mouth a scorching look.

"Damn right it is," she blurted, appalled by the quaver in her voice, dying for that kiss she just knew he was imagining, and thinking, *Just shut up!* Only she couldn't. "What's a man good for when all he does is take up room in the bed, thinking he's all that and a bag of chips? Carl couldn't even watch his own kids without calling it babysittin'. And forget about changing diapers! You think I want a man when all he does when the going gets rough is run off with another woman . . . or off to war?" she choked out hoarsely.

The sudden wail of the baby told her she had awakened Colton. With a stamp of her foot, she whirled toward his bedroom, muttering, "Kindly let yourself out." God, what had she been thinking going off on him like that?

To her consternation, he followed right on her heels. She plucked up the baby, realized his diaper was soiled, and turned toward the changing table. The atmosphere in the cramped little room seemed to crackle. As she popped the snaps on Colton's sleeper, fingers trembling, the silence seemed to swell.

Suddenly, Sean edged her aside, startling her back. With a challenging look, he wrested the wet wipes from her hands and reached for a fresh diaper.

With movements that were brisk and certain, he pulled back the tape to release the smelly diaper and eased it aside. Then he wiped the baby's bottom, sealing the wipes and diaper into a tidy ball. In another three seconds, he had girded Colton in a fresh diaper.

By the time he'd snapped Colton's sleeper, the baby was grinning up at him in full approval and Ellie was trembling with humiliation and dread. "You got him?" Sean asked, striding into the bathroom across the hall to wash his hands.

With her heart racing, she swung the baby back into his crib and waited to face the music.

Now she'd done it. All her life, from her earliest memories of following her mother from one man's home to another to the day her beloved Granny Annie had died and she'd been handed over to social services, Ellie's life had been a series of uprootings. Not even Carl had thought twice about selling that shabby old trailer out from under her and her boys. How could she be so stupid as to offend her landlord, just when things were settling down for them?

He loomed suddenly at the door. Ellie swallowed hard, gripping the crib rail as she scrounged for the apology she owed him, but Sean was the first to speak.

With a mocking smile and a glint in his eyes, he said quietly, "Never challenge a SEAL, darlin'. There isn't anything we can't fuckin' do." With a wink that took the edge off his boast, he disappeared from the door.

A second later, she heard the front door open and close quietly. His truck engine roared and he pulled away.

Ignoring Colton's wail of protest, she crossed to his door and turned the lights out. "Night, night, sweetpea," she choked out. She went straight to her darkened bedroom and sprawled onto her stomach across the bed, feeling heartsick.

Well, at least it's over, reasoned a voice that sounded like Granny Annie's. *You can bet Sean won't be sniffing 'round your skirts no more.*

For some reason, that realization only left her feeling worse. She'd be lucky if he didn't throw her out of his house on her ear. She'd never find a rental half as nice or affordable.

Chapter Two

◆

Drake Donovan regarded the mysterious lump of meat on his tray with revulsion and asked himself, *Why did I volunteer for this again?* Being an undercover special agent for the FBI was anything but glamorous. From the moment he'd skulked into this homeless shelter in Savannah, Georgia, his dignity had been shredded too many times to count, and his stomach had rumbled with digestive problems.

He was four months into his assignment, and what he'd learned about the Centurions and their leader, Owen Dulay, could be written on one side of a Post-it note. But it wasn't too late to change tactics. The time had come to befriend Dulay's daughter, Skyler. Tray in hand, he made his way over to her now.

With a halo of short golden curls and wide blue eyes, Skyler Dulay looked every bit like the angel of mercy she was reputed to be. But looks could be deceiving, as Drake knew well. For months now, he'd played the part of a runaway teen. With his slight frame and baby face, he'd spent most of his two years in the FBI masquerading as a high school student in efforts to uncover drug dealers and gang leaders.

Who really knew what secrets lurked behind Skyler's wide blue eyes? After all, her father, the object of FBI scrutiny, had probably been using charities like this one to launder money for years, and yet no one had managed to prove it. Some at Quantico put the number of his Centurion followers into the tens of thousands. It was believed they'd infiltrated the topmost levels of government, where they now protected their own.

Having watched Skyler for some time, Drake hadn't made up his mind yet whether she was what she seemed. Gracious and poised, she won the hearts of the pathetic creatures who ambled in, searching for a warm meal, a smile, and a place to lay their heads. Could a woman that selfless really exist?

As he slid his tray onto the table beside her, she gave him a startled look. "Mind if I sit here?" he asked.

"No, not at all." She sent him a fleeting smile and directed her attention back to the Vietnam vet who was busy regaling her with tales of his heroism.

"Sorry to interrupt," Drake murmured. Nibbling his mystery meat, he reviewed what little he knew of Dulay's daughter. She'd graduated with honors from the Savannah School for the Arts but still lived with her father. Her mother, once heralded the beauty of Savannah, now lay bedridden with Alzheimer's at Savannah's Hospice House, and Skyler divided her time between caring for her mother and rehabilitating homeless men.

She seemed entirely selfless in her devotions. But if she had even a clue of her father's illicit dealings, and if he could persuade her to tell him, Drake would know more than he did now. It was certainly worth an effort.

As the veteran picked up his tray and left, Drake made his presence known. "Hi," he said, grinning like the eighteen-year-old he pretended be.

"How are you?" she replied. Her smile revealed dimples in both cheeks but failed to reach her eyes.

For months, they'd done nothing but watch each other across the busy hall.

"Drake, is it?" she asked.

"Yes, very good." He chased down the taste in his mouth with a swig of milk. "You doing okay?" he asked her earnestly.

His question seemed to catch her off guard. "Of course," she said brightly. "I'm surprised you're still here. It's almost summer now. You do landscaping, don't you?"

It amazed him that she could keep everyone straight. "I did," he said with a shrug. "I've applied everywhere, but no one wants me."

"Not even Bushwhackers? I thought they always needed help."

"Oh, yeah, but they . . . uh, they heard about my former habit."

"Oh." She assessed his worn T-shirt gravely. "Are you still attending the group sessions?" she asked him gently. The shelter offered free drug counseling every other afternoon.

"Oh, yeah," he reassured her. "I've been clean for weeks, but, you know, it's hard to shake a reputation." In fact, having a supposed drug addiction might even keep her from befriending him—damn. Too late to change that tune now.

"Don't let that dissuade you," she urged. "Someone will hire you eventually. You're young and strong." Her gaze flickered to his muscular biceps, then back to his face, and she frowned. He wondered if she could see the tiny lines fanning the corners of his eyes, betraying his real age.

"So, I noticed you're wearing an engagement ring," he prompted, startling her into meeting his gaze.

For a split second, his remark seemed to devastate her. Her lashes fell as she glanced at the immense diamond on her left hand and swiftly hid it in her lap. "It feels too decadent to wear here," she muttered, firming her lips.

"Who's the lucky guy?" he asked, intrigued by her lack of enthusiasm.

She glanced at him briefly, managing the false smile. "His name is Ashton Jameson. He's a friend of my father's."

Several seconds ticked by before Drake managed to read between the lines. "Wait a minute, you mean this is like an arranged marriage? Not that it's any of my business," he added with a searching look. "But is it?"

His incredulous concern managed to penetrate the invisible buffer between them. "I've known Ashton all my life," she replied, not really answering his question.

"What does your mother think?" he asked, knowing perfectly well the answer to his question.

With a stricken look, she touched the pendant dangling from the silver chain at her neck. "My mother has Alzheimer's," she informed him quickly. "She doesn't even know me."

He was struck by an overwhelming urge to take her into his arms. Jesus, was she really this vulnerable? "I'm sorry," he murmured, focusing on the pendant as she stroked it. "Did she give you that?" he asked softly. It looked like a key.

"When I was younger," Skyler confirmed. "It's the key to her heart," she said, clearly repeating what her mother had told her. She sent him a heartbreaking smile.

Drake swallowed hard to remind himself of his agenda. "So . . . you love him, this Ashton guy?" he asked.

Her downcast gaze and sudden silence supplied an obvious answer. This time he wanted to throw her over his shoulder and run like hell.

"You know," he growled, wondering what kind of surreal existence she lived, "I had a dad who used to run my life."

She nodded but didn't look up.

"He's the reason I ran away from home," Drake added, hating that he was lying, but in a way it wasn't all that much of a lie. His father was his boss, the special agent in charge of the undercover division, and—sadly—he still wielded a powerful influence over Drake's life. "I've never looked back," he added, wishing his words held more weight.

Skyler finally looked at him, eyes suspiciously shiny. "If you'll excuse me," she told him hoarsely. "I have to go. My mother's waiting."

"Oh, sure." He jumped up, pulling back her chair.

She rose with a curious but grateful look.

"Be careful," he added. "It's raining out there."

As she headed to the locked coat closet to retrieve her purse and keys, he couldn't keep his eyes off her. Gathering her belongings, she prepared to dash into the late spring shower. She sent him one last glance, and their gazes locked. A warm feeling skittered through Drake.

He told himself he was glad to have found an informant.

"If you pussies can't complete this course in less than four minutes," Sean bellowed at the dozen or so young men scrambling up the wall of the obstacle course, "you're going to be here all fucking morning!"

The junior SEALs glanced at him quizzically but quickly picked up speed.

"What in God's name has gotten into you?" demanded Senior Chief Solomon McGuire, who stood next to Sean, their backs to the building.

It was a brisk fifty-five degrees with the sun just edging over the Atlantic Ocean and a chill breeze blowing in off the dunes at Dam Neck Naval Annex, but Solomon, who hailed from Maine, stood in his PT shorts and T-shirt, while Sean shivered in his sweats. Solomon's cheeks were still ruddy from an early morning jog on the beach. He looked so freaking content that Sean wanted to punch him in the nose.

"Nothing," he snapped. He could feel his friend watching him through his pale, all-seeing eyes.

"Nothing, my ass. You've been surly ever since you got back from Afghanistan."

Sean shot him a quelling glare.

"And normally you're a pushover on Mondays." The senior chief smirked, his black mustache lifting. "What's the matter? Haven't you been laid yet?"

"Mind your own fucking business."

Solomon's eyebrows shot toward his hairline, which

was as thick and black as his mustache, except for a streak of silver that hinted at his maturity. "You haven't!" he surmised. "What happened to that blonde at the NCO club Friday night, the one with the pierced nose?"

"Claudia," Sean supplied.

"I thought you got her phone number."

Sean shrugged. He had, so what? He hadn't called. "I don't want Claudia," he muttered. Since Ellie had gone off on him the other night, stating all the reasons why she didn't want or need a man in her life, he'd done nothing but think about proving her wrong, which was the worst damn notion he'd had in a long time.

He didn't date women with kids.

"Then who do you want?" Solomon demanded in that terse, bossy way of his that made it evident he wasn't going to quit nagging Sean until he had an answer.

Why not tell him? Solomon's reaction might be just the antidote he needed to his unwanted obsession.

"All right," said Sean, pivoting to face him. "It's Ellie. I thought about her the whole time I was in Afghanistan. And now that I'm back, I'm thinking about her more. I can't get that woman out of my mind."

Solomon's thunderous expression might have been funny under different circumstances. He went nose-to-nose with Sean. "Leave Ellie the hell alone," he growled, in danger of crushing the paper coffee cup that steamed in one hand. "She is not yours to fuck with."

If Sean didn't know better, he'd say Solomon was jealous. But Solomon's world revolved around his lovely bride, Jordan, and their growing family. Ellie was Solomon's first wife's stepsister, who for the past three years had raised Solomon's son, Silas, until last summer when

Ellie's desperate finances had forced her to seek out Solomon and return his son to him. Her efforts had earned her his lifelong gratitude. Ever since Ellie had followed Silas to Virginia, Solomon had helped her in any way she'd let him—not just because he felt he owed her, but because he admired her courage and grit, much the way Sean did.

"You wanted to know," Sean pointed out, swinging back to observe the SEALs' progress on the obstacle course.

Solomon glowered at him. "What are you going to do about it?" he demanded.

"I don't know," Sean admitted. He crossed his arms over his chest as a shiver rippled through him. "Gibbons, go back and help your teammate, for Christ's sake! This isn't fucking *Survivor* series."

"You'd better do something soon," Solomon warned him, "or you're going to blow a gasket. I say you take time off, hook up with one of your regulars, and screw her brains out."

Sean grunted. He couldn't think of a single other woman who turned him on right now.

Solomon rubbed his mustache. "What about that golf pro, the one with all the sex toys?" he suggested.

"Oh, yeah, Tiffany," Sean murmured, picturing the feisty little brunette with a faint stirring of interest. "I wonder if she's around."

"Call her," Solomon exhorted, finishing off his coffee with a long swig. "And stay the hell away from Ellie," he added, stalking toward the Spec Ops building.

Sean glanced at his watch. "Time's up!" he roared, causing the men on the course to cease their efforts with groans of defeat. "My little sister can move faster than you pansies. Now, start over!"

A shadow fell over Carl as he wormed a finger into the soft soil, intending to uproot a dandelion weed. The crooked little smile on his face faded, and a cool sweat beaded his brow as he recognized the silhouette folding over him.

Mr. Dulay must have been watching through the window. Since offering him a gardening job and a place to live ten months ago, Carl had been conscious of his employer assessing and monitoring his every action. He must have seen how Carl had leered at Miz Skyler just now as she hastened from the garage to the rear entrance, hiding under her umbrella like a turtle in its shell. Only she couldn't hide those shapely calves coming out of plaid capris, and those legs had inspired an appreciative whistle, which his employer must have overheard.

Scrambling to his feet, Carl prepared to answer for his crime. "Sir?" he squeaked.

"I'd like a word with you," Owen Dulay announced, his gaze as dark and fathomless as a well.

"Sure," said Carl with a careless shrug and a twitch in his cheek.

Dulay gestured with a hand. "Let's take a walk."

Together they passed along the walkway between the three-story mansion and the carriage house where Carl lived, entering the private garden surrounded by ten-foot sandstone walls. Carl had labored several months in this charming little garden, pruning branches, raking leaves, coaxing exotic shrubs to bloom as the weather warmed. Trailing his employer toward the fountain of a griffin spouting water, his anxiety rose with every second that Dulay remained quiet.

At last the man turned, slipped his hands into the pockets of his golfing trousers, and with watchful eyes announced, "I've located your children, Carl. The ones you claimed you couldn't find?"

The announcement was so unexpected that Carl froze, his mouth hanging open. "My children?" he squeaked.

"Christopher, Caleb, and Colton?" Dulay prompted, supplying the names that on very rare occasions gnawed at Carl's conscience. He'd sooner just forget about them.

"The brotherhood wouldn't approve of the way you've washed your hands of your obligations, Carl," Dulay added, his voice redolent with disapproval. "Any man who fathers children is responsible for their welfare."

"But Ellie took 'em from me," Carl insisted. "I wanted to pay child support, honest." He was so frightened by the Centurions' opinion of him that tears sprang to his eyes, lending credence to his assertions. "I've looked everywhere for those boys," he added, his voice breaking with emotion. "Where'd you find them?"

"It doesn't matter where," Dulay replied, glancing up at the windows of his Federal-period home. "What matters is that you've sworn, as a Centurion, to protect your progeny. And while our daughters help propagate our own kind, it is our sons who are our greatest treasure and legacy," he added, sending Carl that strange, piercing look he'd seen before.

Carl nodded in agreement.

"Soon your boys will be returned to you," Dulay added, making Carl's blood run cold. To him? How was he going to look after them? He barely made enough to support himself.

"They'll remain at a boys' home just outside the city," his employer continued, "until you find the means to look after them. Once I find a gardener to replace you, I'll employ you as my chauffeur. The pay is more, which should accommodate you a higher standard of living in order to support your sons."

Carl nearly wilted with relief. He was off the hook for a while longer, thank goodness. "W-what about Ellie, my ex-wife?" He simply couldn't envision Ellie relinquishing her boys.

"Don't concern yourself with her," Dulay advised, a malicious glimmer in his eyes. "She'll get what she deserves for keeping them from you."

A chill rippled down Carl's spine. Dear God, was there nothing this man couldn't do?

"Doing right by your sons is the only way you'll be one of the Elite," Dulay added, his gaze darkly compelling. "I need you to trust me implicitly in all things, Carl."

Carl swallowed against a dry mouth. "Oh, I do, sir," he reassured him. "I do."

"Well, then," said Dulay with a dismissive nod, "carry on." Turning his back on Carl, he strode arrogantly toward his mansion.

Sean was proud of himself, damned if he wasn't. Thanks to Solomon's suggestion, he was firmly in control of his libido. The CO hadn't even batted an eye on Monday when he'd asked for Thursday and Friday off, leaving him with a four-day weekend in which to dissipate his lust. Tiffany Hughes, an ever-willing playmate from his past, had agreed to let him tag along as she headed up to Williamsburg to compete in the LPGA. By the time he returned to work on Monday, he'd be so sated, he wouldn't even be able to think about Ellie, no, sir.

Yet, as he pointed his car toward Tiffany's condo, where they would rendezvous and head out, he envisioned Ellie escorting Chris and Caleb to the bus stop, dropping Colton off at her neighbor's, and heading off to class, and a sense of longing swamped him. She'd said she had her final exams this week, he thought, recalling how she'd studied by candlelight. Damn, he admired her! But admiration and desire weren't enough for a woman like Ellie. And Sean had never been, would never be, a one-woman man.

Gunning the motor of his 1969 Pontiac GTO, the car he drove when he wasn't working, Sean roared past Ellie's exit and kept right on going. The morning sun shone brightly in a flawless blue sky. He was as free as a bird to fly, yet thoughts of Ellie still kept him captive.

Knocking at Tiffany's condo door several minutes later, he ignored the voice inside him that insisted he didn't want to be here. And when Tiffany opened the door wearing nothing but an apron, he was glad he'd ignored it. "Well, hello," he exclaimed, drinking in the vision she presented. The frilly little apron failed to cover her pert breasts, which peeked out on either side of the bib. The hem fell to her thighs, hiding the dark pubic hair she kept neatly groomed.

"Come on in, big fella," she purred with a come-and-get-me grin. Turning away, she sashayed down the hall with nothing covering her naked backside but a tempting little bow.

With a quick glance behind him, Sean stepped inside and shut the door.

"Caleb, quit," Ellie begged, reaching over the back of her seat to put a calming hand on Caleb's knee. "Leave the baby alone!"

The blare of a horn jerked her gaze forward, giving her just enough time to slam on the brakes as a white delivery van pulled out into the street ahead of her. Dear Lord, had she just run a stop sign and nearly killed them all?

Startled, adrenaline tingling in her extremities, she scolded herself for not paying more attention. She was punch-drunk from lack of sleep. She'd taken her biology exam this morning, after studying last night until dawn. Then she'd gone straight to work waiting tables till supper time.

Then, picking up the boys from Belinda's, she'd headed back to the junior college instead of home in order to submit an extra-credit assignment she had hastily written on her break at work. The exam had proven tougher than expected, and without some extra-credit work, she was afraid her grade in the course would kill her GPA, which, in turn, would ruin her hopes for an academic scholarship for next semester.

"We're almost there," she added, speeding along the narrow rural road, a shortcut to the college. The van in front of her seemed in no particular hurry to get anywhere. She peered around it, hoping to pass, but the double-yellow line, plus the tall, dark pines and ditches filled with evening shadows dissuaded her. "Come on," she muttered in exasperation.

She glanced at her watch, not altogether certain her instructor would still be there to take her assignment.

Fishing her cell phone from her purse, she divided her attention between the keypad and the road, calling Professor Sloan to tell him she was running late. "I'll be there in five minutes," she promised, hearing impatience in his reply.

The brake lights on the van flared, and Ellie braked abruptly, laying the phone on the seat before it caused her to get into an accident. "Christopher, how much homework do you have tonight?" she asked, wondering at the odds of tucking in early. God, she was tired!

Through bleary eyes, she watched in puzzlement, scarcely hearing Chris's reply, as the rear doors of the van opened right in front of her, and two strangers leapt out and circled around either side of her car.

It wasn't until her front doors opened simultaneously and her dome light illumined their menacing faces that reality penetrated Ellie's haze of exhaustion. Shock pegged her to the seat as the stranger on Christopher's side hauled her son against him and thrust a gun to his head. "Get out, woman," he growled with an ugly snarl, "or this is the first kid to die."

In the same instant, a thick arm coiled around Ellie's neck, hauling her against a sweaty frame. The barrel of a gun gouged her temple. "Out with you," he muttered, tugging her from the car.

Ellie grabbed the steering wheel. Her senses expanded to take in everything at once: the pocked face of the stranger grasping her son, his deep Southern accent, the nauseating odor emanating from the arm encircling her neck, Christopher's pinched and breathless expression of horror, Caleb's complete stunned silence, and Colton's soft sleepy snores.

She saw and heard and felt everything.

"No," she wheezed as the stricture about her neck tightened, and the stranger tugged harder, pulling her upper body out first.

With the Impala still in gear and her foot on the brake, Ellie groped for the shifter and knocked it into reverse. At the same time, she jackknifed her hips, straining to reach the accelerator, but the man holding Christopher lunged across the seat, twisting the key in the ignition. The engine died before her car even rolled a few inches.

"That wasn't very smart, bitch. Take her out," he snapped at his companion. "We gotta go." With that, he thrust Christopher deeper into the seat and got in beside him, slamming the door shut.

Palms coated in sweat, Ellie's grip slipped as her assailant tugged her violently free, choking her in the process. *No!* she screamed in silent denial as he dragged her, kicking and clawing, from the driver's seat. With equal violence, he flung her out into the oncoming lane.

Ellie's cheek struck the rough pavement. Dazed by the impact, she rolled sluggishly to her knees, gaping with disbelief as the man hurled her purse at her and leapt into the seat she'd just occupied.

Ellie staggered to her feet. "No!" she cried, lurching toward the car. He slammed the door in her face, muting the sound of Christopher's and Caleb's cries. Ellie beat on the window. She reached for the door handle but not before the lock engaged. Even as she screamed for them to stop, both the van and her car began to pull away.

Desperate to reach her crying children, Ellie clung to the door handle. She refused to let go, screaming hoarse demands, peering through the shadows to memorize the driver's face. As the car sped up, she broke into a sprint, her gaze now fixed on the fat fingers gripping her steering wheel and the ink stamped over his first knuckle.

Her legs wheeled beneath her, her feet scarcely touching the ground as the car pulled her forward. For several seconds, she managed to keep pace. Then, with a roar, the car shot forward, tearing the handle from her grasp, spilling her with bone-jarring force onto the rough pavement, where she rolled and skidded to a stop.

Stunned by the impact, the breath knocked clean out of her, all four limbs abraded and bleeding, Ellie stared in silent horror as the blurred taillights of her vehicle grew smaller and dimmer, then disappeared altogether.

Chapter Three

✦

Colty was crying again. The man in the passenger seat up front waved the gun that glinted in the dark and said to Caleb, "You'd better find a way to shut that baby up."

Chris usually took care of Colty when Mama was busy, but Chris was stuck up front, squashed between Ugly Man and Sweaty Man. Caleb spared a glance at Colton's red, wet face. He couldn't afford to take his eyes off the road right now.

He'd been memorizing the way for hours now. But with all the rights and lefts they'd just taken, still following the van, he really needed to concentrate. Paying attention to your *s'roundin's* was important, 'cause then you could never really get lost. At least that's what Mr. Sean had taught him.

"I can help the baby," offered Chris, and the two men shared a look.

"What do you think?" Ugly Man asked Sweaty Man.

"His diaper's just wet," Chris added quietly.

Mr. Sean used to say that Chris was a good negotiator, 'cause he used his words.

"We're almost there," said Sweaty Man. "We'll put 'em all in the back of the van."

Almost where? Caleb wondered. Then he wondered if his mom would be able to catch up to them. Thinking about her running beside the car, yellin' and cryin' and beatin' on the window made his stomach hurt worse than when he knew he had to go to school.

The car's headlights shone on a sign that read JONES LAKE STATE PARK, and they slowed down to turn in, driving into woods that were pitch-black and scary. Suddenly, Caleb had to pee real bad. These men weren't gonna kill them, were they?

Sweaty Man drove past a playground that looked creepy in the dark, then a picnic shelter. Starlight twinkled on the surface of what looked like a lake. "Stay in the car," said Ugly Man, and both men got out.

Slick as a snake, Christopher scrambled over the front seat, taking Caleb by surprise. "Take this," he whispered, thrusting something cold and hard into Caleb's hand as he started unbuckling the baby from his car seat.

It was Mama's cell phone! Caleb looked down at it in amazement. "Hurry, Caleb. Go out that way," whispered Chris, "and run for the trees. You call nine-one-one while I carry Colty. We gotta hide while they're busy!"

Flashing him a grin, Caleb shoved the door open and made a run for it, his little legs pumping hard to escape.

But Chris wasn't so fast. Looking back, Caleb saw Sweaty Man grab his brother by the collar and yank him back.

Caleb ran faster. Dodging the sharp branches, he pushed 9 and 1 on the cell phone. Then he pushed 4 by mistake.

Dang it! He could hear Ugly Man crashing through the woods behind him.

Ugly Man grabbed him by the hair.

Ouch, that hurt!

"No!" Caleb swung around with his fist. Ugly Man shoved him, and he ended up lying on the leafy ground, kicking. One of his shoes fell off, but he still had the cell phone. Ugly Man slapped him hard across the face, and blood spurted from his nose. Caleb brought up his arm to protect himself, and that was when Ugly Man saw what he had. He snatched the phone away, hauled Caleb to his feet, and marched him back to the others with just one shoe on.

He was shoved into the van they'd been following. Chris was already in the back holding the baby on his lap. He took one look at Caleb's nose and started crying.

"Don't cry, Chris'fer," Caleb told him fiercely. "It ain't gonna help nothin'!"

Chris handed him one of Colton's wet wipes.

Hearing a motor rev, they both peered outside as their old car rolled away from them.

Sweaty Man got into the back of the van and pointed a fat finger at them. "Don't you give us any more trouble, you hear?" he growled.

In the distance, Caleb heard a mighty splash.

Ugly Man jumped into the front of the van, breathing hard. "Let's go," he said to a third guy, the driver.

They peeled out of there, bouncing back onto a paved road. "What'd you do with the cell phone?" Sweaty Man called up to his friends.

"Tossed it into the woods," said Ugly Man.

His companion gave a worried grunt.

"How much farther?" Ugly Man asked.

"'Bout four hours."

Caleb heard Chris sniffle. His big brother had tried and failed to get them out of this mess. It was up to Caleb now. He'd just have to think and act like Mr. Sean.

When he grew up, he was gonna be just like him, and no one was going to mess with his family.

Sean ignored his phone as much as possible when he was on leave. He avoided the television and radio, anything to keep from hearing that the world was falling apart without him holding the line, killing the bad guys. By day three, he had no idea what kind of bad shit was going on where, and it was starting to nag at his conscience.

He needed to come up for air.

"Hey, Tiff," he said as they sat at an outdoor table of a restaurant overlooking the James River. "I think I'm gonna head back today."

She barely glanced up from the roster that listed her tee-off time. "Sure, whatever," she said with a shrug.

He spent a second comparing her self-absorption to Ellie's selflessness in giving her boys a better life. "Good luck," he said, laying a twenty on the table to cover the check. "You're a good sport," he added, bending down to give her cheek a parting kiss.

His comment drew a quizzical look from her, but he was already striding away, heading to their unit to pack his stuff. Then he jogged down to the parking lot, relieved that they'd driven separate cars.

The pampered life Tiffany led was fun to escape to now and then, but real life, as Sean knew, was a world filled with hardship, duty, and honor. Meals Ready to Eat didn't come with room service, and his personality was too dynamic to stay cooped up in a series of hotel rooms and trendy hot spots like this one.

It wasn't that he missed Ellie and her boys. Nah. He just had the habit of checking up on things, was all. Hell, he needed to drive by his other rentals while he was home, too.

As he slipped into his sun-warmed GTO, he reached for his cell phone and discovered the battery had died. No problem, he'd just charge it on the way home. He turned on the radio, only to be driven crazy by the endless chatter of commercials. Popping in his favorite CD, he departed Kingsmill Resort, driving just over the speed limit to get the one-hour road trip behind him.

As he neared his home in Virginia Beach, Ellie's exit came up on him, daring him to test his newfound self-restraint. He wasn't in any danger of doing something inappropriate, so why not? Besides, he was curious to see how she and the boys were spending their Saturday.

But as he pulled into her driveway moments later, he realized her car was gone. No one was home.

Well, shit. Disappointment left him sitting gloomily in his seat. It was then that he noticed all the blinds on her windows were drawn. Usually she only covered her windows at night, preferring by day to let the light stream in. An uneasy premonition skittered through him, prompting him to push out of his car to investigate.

Knocking at the door, he listened to the anticipated silence, found a key to her house on his key ring, and let himself in. Normally, he wouldn't dream of marching right in, but his gut churned with uneasiness, which he needed to put to rest.

The scent of stale milk was the first thing to hit him as he crossed the threshold. His disbelieving gaze lit upon the overturned sofa cushions, the toys strewn across the carpet, and Ellie's scattered schoolwork. "Ellie?" he called out as the realization that something awful had transpired yanked his scalp tight.

He raced to her bedroom, terrified he'd stumble across a body or something equally awful. At her door, he drew up short, astonished to see her mattress ripped from its frame; drawers were yanked from her dresser, their contents thrown helter-skelter about the room. Even her ragged nightgown lay in a mangled heap. "What the hell?" Sean breathed.

Reeling, he returned to the living room to haul open the drapes. Bright spring sunshine flooded in. His gaze went straight to Belinda's car, parked next door.

Belinda would have answers, he thought, abandoning the house to jump the fence between the properties. He rapped on Belinda's front door, breathing hard.

Her stricken countenance as she opened the door confirmed his worst fears. "What happened?" he demanded.

Belinda's red-rimmed eyes puddled up. "Ellie's at the jail," she replied, clutching her two-year-old daughter. "Her boys were snatched from her Thursday night. It's all over the news. She says two men pulled her from her car and took off with the boys, but now the media's sayin' that maybe she killed them," she added, her double chin quivering. "But I know she didn't."

Stunned, Sean could only stand on her front stoop and stare over at Ellie's house and the empty driveway. "No," he rasped. Those boys were her life. How could this happen to her?

Without a word, he swiveled and ran for his car, revving his engine before he'd even shut the door. He shot backward out of Ellie's driveway, calling up the people who would care most if Ellie found herself in a crisis: Solomon and Jordan McGuire.

"Why the hell haven't you answered your phone?" Solomon snarled in his ear in lieu of a greeting.

"The battery died. I just charged it," Sean replied. "Where's Ellie? What's going on?"

"She's at the police station on Leroy Drive. She's been staying with us at night. The police haven't arrested her but they're keeping her there all day."

Sean gripped the steering wheel harder. *Shit!* Ellie had to be out of her mind. "I went by her house just now," he confessed. "Belinda told me everything."

"It's all over the radio, dumb ass. Every news station in town is covering the abduction of three little boys, and you're too busy fucking around to notice?"

Solomon was clearly too irate for Sean to point out that taking leave was his idea. "I'm heading to the station to be with her right now," he grated, stopping at a red light. "What's this about the media trying to say Ellie did it?"

Solomon made a sound of disgust. "That's ridiculous. She was thrown out of her car on Harper's Road by two guys who drove off with the boys." In the background, Sean overheard the distinctive wail of an infant.

"I suppose Jordan's pissed at me, too," Sean surmised. "You didn't tell Ellie where I was, I hope?"

"I said you were on leave, and I couldn't track you down."

Sean pinched the bridge of his nose. To think all this time she'd been going out of her mind. He could not believe that her boys had been kidnapped. Who would do such a thing? It was fucking unreal.

He gunned the accelerator as the light switched to green.

"By the way, the police want to question you, too."

"What?"

"They want to know where you were the night the boys were taken."

"Christ," Sean muttered, slowing his approach to the police station. He could see it up ahead, an American flag flying on a pole out front.

"If I were you," Solomon advised, "I'd get a hold of your lawyer friend before walking into a police station. I've tried to get Ellie to seek counsel, too, but she says innocent people shouldn't need lawyers."

Sean swore. In his opinion, Ellie couldn't afford *not* to have an attorney right now. The urge to rush to her side was overpowering, but if the police honestly thought he had anything to do with her boys' abduction, he'd be far better off armed with legal counsel. "You're right," he decided, executing a swift U-turn at the next intersection. "I'll call Reno Silverman. And I'll pay for him to represent Ellie, too."

"Thank you," Solomon bit out with irony.

Sean heaved a sigh and hung up. His timing sucked. Taking off with Tiffany Hughes might yet prove to be the worst mistake he'd ever made.

*   *   *

Ellie wanted to die. Since Thursday night, she'd kept nothing down. She was exhausted. All she wanted to do was jump into a car and go looking for her missing boys, but the police had brought her back to this room with the two-way mirror in order to ask her the same damn questions they had asked her yesterday and the day before. Why couldn't they remember her answers?

At first, they'd seemed helpful. On the night her boys were taken, as she'd lain in the hospital being treated for shock and multiple abrasions, they had put out a preliminary BOLO for a Chevy Impala. They'd dispatched an officer to her house to pick up photos of her boys and had disseminated the photos to the media. At midnight, the hospital had released her to Solomon McGuire, who'd been summoned to take her home. He'd brought her to his new house instead, a refurbished rambler overlooking the Lynnhaven Inlet.

There she'd spent the interminable hours till dawn staring into the dark, her heart frozen in disbelief. Every wail of Solomon's infant daughter had torn at her heartstrings as she wondered if she would ever hear her children cry again.

The next day, the police had picked her up. They'd driven her to her home and talked her into signing a Consent to Search document. In addition to providing the DNA samples they needed, police thought they might find something she couldn't recall because of her trauma.

She'd watched in disbelief as they'd overturned every box of toys, every drawer and mattress, in total disregard for her feelings. "Why are you doing this?" she'd cried. They'd assured her they were looking for clues, something to explain why her boys had been snatched from her.

Only, they hadn't found any.

They'd driven her back to the station, where they'd proceeded to question her more thoroughly. Where was she from? What had brought her from Mississippi to Virginia?

Ellie had answered with utter candidness, praying that her replies would point to whoever had kidnapped her boys. But with no sleep the night before, her recollections grew less distinct. Like an impressionist painting, the details of the abduction seemed undefined when analyzed in isolation.

The heavyset officer, whose chair creaked under his weight, had asked several times, "Why would anyone want to steal an eighty-four Chevy Impala?"

She'd had no answer for him.

"Why didn't they take your purse?" he'd asked again and again.

"I don't know. They threw it at me." She'd pawed through it after her car disappeared, looking for her cell phone; only it wasn't in there. She'd left it on the car seat.

"Why didn't you put it back in your purse?" he'd asked.

"I told you," she'd replied, rubbing her burning eyes. "I used it to call my professor, to ask him to wait for me because I was running late. Caleb was in the backseat, causing a stir. I had to come to a sudden halt. I must have just put it down."

"Sounds like you were pretty stressed," Sergeant Peyton had observed.

Ellie, who was beyond exhausted and could see no point in being questioned any further, had laughed hysterically. Her? Stressed?

She'd laughed until she'd cried, and then, finally, with the sun setting on the second day, they'd released her to Solomon and Jordan, who'd brought her, too dejected to speak, back to their home.

The police, despite Solomon's protests, had picked her up again this morning, escorting her to the same horrible room with its two-way mirror. It was then that Ellie suffered the bone-chilling suspicion that she'd become a suspect in the abduction of her own sons.

As Sergeant Peyton rubbed the prickles on his jowly jaw, the signet ring on his right hand gave a wink. "Tell me about your ex-husband," he exhorted.

She was relieved that his focus was, for the moment, on Carl and not on her. But the idea of Carl kidnapping her boys was ludicrous. She'd already explained how Carl had made no fuss whatsoever over her bid for custody, how he'd washed his hands of his obligations. "I really don't think he took them," she insisted dully.

Peyton shook his head. "Well," he said, skewering her with a sharp look, "tell me more about your landlord, then. He's sure been lying low."

With an enigmatic scowl, Solomon had explained that Sean had taken leave. The police were hoping to question him; only he wasn't answering his calls.

"He's been overseas," said Ellie, squashing her resentment that Sean had yet to come to her defense. "He needed time off." What was she to him, anyway, but another tenant?

"According to your neighbor, Belinda Cartright, he's

more than just your landlord," Peyton offered with a suggestive lift of his eyebrows.

Ellie choked on her protest. "I don't know where she got that notion," she retorted, her face growing hot.

He shrugged, looking down at the notepad in front of him. "Says right here his truck was parked at your house last Sunday, 'long about midnight."

Ellie stared at him in disbelief. "He came by to fix the lights. Our electricity went out."

"At midnight?" drawled the officer with disbelief.

"He's in the military. He had to cover the watch that night. He couldn't come any earlier," Ellie insisted. "He's just my landlord. It could never be more than that."

Peyton's eyes sharpened. "And why is that?"

Too late. With a feeling that she had just stepped into a hornet's nest, Ellie tried to explain. "Sean Harlan's a Navy SEAL. He's not the kind of man who settles down and has a family. Besides, I don't need or want a man in my life."

Peyton sent her a patronizing smile. She could tell he didn't believe her. "With three boys, I imagine it's tough to have any kind of social life. I know how it is. I've got two of my own, you know."

The design on his ring was that of a dragon or a griffin, a hideous creature just like him. Repulsed by his demeanor, Ellie hugged herself to quell the shuddering that wouldn't stop. "You should count yourself lucky," she told him, bristling.

"Oh, I don't know. I'd like to strangle 'em both sometimes."

His cell phone vibrated, a loud humming that startled

Ellie. Noting her shot nerves, Peyton kept his eyes on her as he took the call.

The fear that she was no longer in this room to be helped coalesced into a knot of anxiety. Peyton's thick lips took on a cynical twist as he listened to his caller.

"That was my partner," he relayed as the call ended. "Professor Sloan says he didn't hear any children in the background when you called the other night. Wonder why that is? Why wouldn't he have heard your kids in the background, Ms. Stuart? You said that they were acting up."

Ellie gripped the arms of her chair, outraged. "You think that *I* did something to my boys?" she demanded, willing herself not to shriek, not to lunge at him and tear his eyes out.

"Now, calm down, Ms. Stuart. It's my job to consider everything. You did just say you and Mr. Harlan could never be more than friends. What would change that?" he wondered out loud.

Ellie could only stare at him, aghast, her mouth hanging open.

"Maybe he'd want you more if you weren't strapped with three mouths to feed," Peyton suggested helpfully.

A red haze filmed over Ellie's vision. She clung tighter to the arms of the chair to keep from flying at him. "I love my sons!" she choked out, tears gushing from her eyes. "No man in the world could ever come between me and my boys! Don't you *ever* tell me that I did something to my children. They're my life. My whole life, goddamn you!" By the end of her tirade, she was standing, quaking from head to toe as she loomed over Peyton like an Amazon queen.

A brisk knock at the door curtailed her outburst.

Peyton shot her what was meant to be a reassuring look as he rose to answer the summons. "Yes, what is it?"

Ellie dragged air into her tight lungs. The police actually believed she could have done something horrible to her very own children! She'd heard of mothers like that—women who'd drowned their children in the bathtub or locked them in their car seats and drove them into a lake. How dare he lump her into that category? Her knees threatened to buckle, but she locked them and forced herself to remain standing. She had to find a way out of here. Whatever it took, she would find her boys and prove him wrong!

"Sir, Miss Stuart's lawyer is here. He wants a word with you."

Peyton shot her a look of surprise. "You have a lawyer?"

Befuddled, Ellie could only stare in confusion as a slim gentleman with a pleasant and professional demeanor stepped into the room. "Reno Silverman," he announced himself, handing Peyton his business card. He rounded the table and placed a reassuring grip on Ellie's elbow. "Is my client under arrest?" he inquired mildly. "Or is she merely being detained for questioning?"

Peyton hooked a fleshy thumb over his belt. "We were just making progress," he replied, his mouth pursed with disappointment.

"Then she hasn't been arrested," Silverman deduced. "We'll be in touch," he added, drawing Ellie toward the door. "I'm sure she could use some time to herself."

Ellie went with Silverman, amazed that she'd been offered a way out without having to resort to violence. The lawyer opened the door for her and hustled her out. "I can just leave?" she asked, her legs quaking unreliably.

He drew her down a bright hallway, where the sunlight outside told her that it was close to noon. "I'm sure they didn't tell you that," he answered grimly as he opened one of the double glass doors.

The flawless blue sky filled with winging seagulls struck Ellie as incongruous. How could the sun even shine with her boys stolen and gone? None of it seemed real.

Suddenly, individuals toting cameras and microphones thundered toward them, firing questions at her. "Have you heard any news about your children, Miss Stuart?" they asked, thrusting microphones into her face.

"No comment," the lawyer replied for her, drawing her past the reporters and across the parking lot to a well-used silver Chevy Tahoe. As he opened the door, Ellie hesitated, asking, "Why did you do that? I mean, why are you helping me?"

"This isn't the place to have an attorney–client conversation, Ms. Stuart, trust me," he said with a glance at the reporters. "Please, get in and I'll explain once we're on our way."

Ellie didn't move. "I can't afford a lawyer, Mr. Silverman. I mean, I will pay you, but I'll have to make installments over time—" She grabbed the open door as the ground whirled beneath her feet. "I just want my boys back!" she cried.

"I promise to help you find your sons, Ms. Stuart," he said, trundling her into his SUV. "Don't worry about the money. Your bill's already been paid." Closing the door on her stunned confusion, he rounded the vehicle and slipped behind the wheel.

"Are you a court-appointed lawyer?" she asked as he started the Tahoe. "Are they going to arrest me?"

"No and not yet," he replied, backing up. "Let's get you safely to Sean's house and then we'll talk."

"Sean," she repeated, realizing with mixed feelings that it was Sean who'd sent Mr. Silverman to rescue her. What had taken him so long? she wondered, tamping down her resentment, which was coupled with gratitude that he'd sent his own lawyer to save her.

Where had he been these last few days that not even Solomon could get hold of him?

Chapter Four

✦

Even in her misery, Ellie was ashamed of her appearance as Sean helped her out of Mr. Silverman's SUV. She'd never wanted him to see her this way, battered and skinned, her hair unkempt and tumbling loose. Mostly she didn't want him seeing the desolation and despair on her face that revealed the depth of her vulnerability. Life had taught Ellie that it didn't pay to appear weak or less than able.

"Jesus, Ellie," he rasped, putting an arm around her as he escorted her to his front door. The comfort of his touch and his familiar citrus scent brought tears to her eyes. "I'm so sorry," he apologized quietly. "I ignore my phone whenever I take leave," he explained. Hearing the self-blame in his voice, it was easier to accept his help, to lean into his strength.

Every ache and pain that came from striking the pavement seemed to ease now that he was with her. Only the ever-constant ache in her chest remained.

"Reno"—Sean caught his lawyer's eye—"thanks, man. Come on in so we can talk."

As he drew Ellie up the two steps to his driftwood-gray contemporary, his gaze dropped to the raw, healing skin on her forearms and hands. His eyes flashed and his mouth firmed. Once within his foyer, he turned her to face him, examining her wounds and realizing her knees were in worse shape. His ears turned a dull shade of red. "Fucking bastards."

"I wouldn't let go of the car," Ellie explained. "They were going pretty fast before I fell off."

Sensing his horror, Ellie relived the awful moment when the door handle had slipped from her grasp and she had flown to the ground, tumbling and skidding to a bone-jarring stop. Self-pity strangled her abruptly, and her composure fled.

With a muttered curse, Sean gathered her to him and gently rocked her. With a whimper of relief, she wallowed in his comfort, welcomed the sense of finally being completely sheltered.

"I'm sorry," he repeated. "Ellie, I'm so sorry."

Tears sprang to her eyes, but she immediately blinked them back. She couldn't waste time crying, not when her boys needed her to find them. "It's not your fault," she choked, withdrawing reluctantly. "I just want my boys back."

Sean glanced helplessly at Reno. "Come on in the living room," he invited them both.

Sean's living space was all hardwood floors and immense, comfortable couches set before a widescreen TV. "You want a drink?" he offered them both. "Iced tea? Beer?"

"I'll have an iced tea," said Mr. Silverman, making himself at home on one end of Sean's couch.

"Ellie?"

"Water, please." She sat on the edge of the overstuffed armchair, unwilling to get too comfortable.

Bringing the lawyer his tea and Ellie her water, Sean hovered protectively. "Are you cold?" he asked Ellie, who sat there hugging herself.

"No," she said. She just couldn't get herself to stop trembling. "The police think I killed my boys," she blurted, unable to help her accusing tone as she added, "You shouldn't have come over so late the other night. Now Belinda thinks we're lovers, and the cops think I killed my boys so I could be with you." Again her eyes filled with hot tears. She willed them dry.

The stupefied look on Sean's face dispelled her misplaced anger. How could he ever have guessed what would happen to her boys? He'd been looking after her in his spare time, just doing what landlords did when tenants called with problems; that was all. "It's not your fault," she added again with a miserable shake of her head.

"Tell me what happened," Sean exhorted, his expression the grimmest she'd ever seen it.

As he stood there, growing increasingly rigid, she recounted the episode as she had a hundred times now, including every detail she could think of, trembling all over again as she relived her shock.

"Did the police make composite sketches of these men?" Mr. Silverman inquired.

"Yes," said Ellie. The energy it had taken to describe the kidnappers' features had left her exhausted. "One of the sketches looks just like the guy. The other one not so much."

"Who are these guys?" Sean wondered out loud.

"I don't know," said Ellie wearily. She wanted to crawl into a hole and die; only she imagined she could still hear her children calling for her.

"I mean, they obviously planned this in order to pull it off," Sean mused, pacing toward the kitchen and back again. "It's not like some random kidnapping. And you haven't had any calls for ransom money, have you?"

"My cell phone's gone," Ellie replied. "I left it in the car." She had to talk through clenched teeth to keep them from chattering. "And I don't have a home phone."

Sean drew up short, shooting her a thoughtful look. "What about your ex-husband?" he inquired. Seeing her shiver, he fetched a burgundy throw from the end of the couch and draped it over her shoulders.

"Carl never wanted the boys," Ellie retorted. The warmth of the blanket helped to quell her shudders, but the feeling that her world had ended had her wilting into the chair cushions, curling her knees to her chest.

With his heart in his throat, Sean watched Ellie quietly fold. It amazed him that she'd kept it together this long. Shooting Reno a silent message to stay put, he bent over and scooped her up into his arms, ignoring her feeble protests.

"You need to sleep, Ellie," he told her, knowing for a fact that she hadn't slept a wink, not with her boys' lives in danger. Again ignoring her protest, he carried her up the steps, past his utilitarian guest room to the master suite, where his California king sprawled under a black and gold brocade comforter. His matching curtains were designed to blot out the sunlight, even at high noon.

Letting her feet slide to the floor, he felt Ellie sway against him as he pulled the comforter and sheets back.

She was already half-asleep, but she was still fully dressed. "Here, sit down," he murmured, lowering her to the mattress. "Let me find you something to sleep in."

He pulled a light blue chambray shirt from his closet. Ellie remained trancelike as he crossed to the windows to drop the curtains, muffling the sunlight.

All he could make out was her silhouette as he returned to her side. "Let's put this on," he suggested. "You want help or . . ."

"I'll do it," she murmured, taking it from him.

"I want you to take a sleeping pill," he started to suggest.

"No," she said, cutting him off.

"Try to sleep," he said with a sigh. "I'll be right downstairs with Reno."

As he moved to the door, he heard her draw her knit top over her head. He couldn't resist a quick look back. How ironic that Ellie, whom he'd dreamed of undressing a thousand times, was now undressing herself in his bedroom and sleeping in his bed, all alone.

Shutting the door with a soft click, he made his way downstairs, where Reno had turned on the television.

"Check this out," Reno said, waving him over. "They found her car."

Standing beside the sofa, Sean braced himself for the news that the boys' bodies had been found.

"The pings of Ellie Stuart's cell phone drew state police to Jones Lake State Park in North Carolina," announced the pretty copper-haired reporter, "where minutes ago, her 1984 Chevy Impala was pulled from the lake behind me. The bodies of ten-year-old Christopher Stuart and his two younger brothers, Caleb and Colton, were *not* inside." The knots in Sean's abdomen eased. Thank God, they hadn't been found dead!

"Divers continue to search the lake for clues that might indicate the children's whereabouts," the young woman added as the camera flashed to men in wet suits. "Stuart's cell phone, stained in blood, might also offer clues. But until DNA tests can be processed, it remains unclear whether the blood belongs to her children or to someone else. While police have released these composites of the suspected kidnappers, Stuart herself remains a person of interest."

The screen flashed to the computer-generated drawings of two men. Sean took a good hard look at them. The first had broad, distinct features, a square jaw, and pocks on his face. The other was a fat man with beady eyes and indistinct features.

"This is Ophelia Price, for Channel Ten news."

"Hey, I know that chick," Sean realized as the program flashed to a different story. "That's Vinny DeInnocenti's fiancée. She'd better not be insinuating that Ellie's lying." Vinny was a petty officer second class and a close friend on Sean's SEAL Team. He'd proposed to the pretty, older journalist a while ago.

"Don't worry about the media," Reno advised, ever calm, ever rational. "The law won't charge Ellie without probable cause."

Sean heaved a troubled sigh. "What would that look like? Give me an example."

"Bodies," said Reno with an apologetic shrug. "If they find the boys dead and it looks like their mother killed them, then they'll arrest her. Also, if they find a murder weapon with her prints on it, or if a witness steps forward claiming to have seen something, then they might arrest her. But then the clock starts ticking, and they have a set amount of time to find the evidence to convict her. For now, she's just a person of interest."

"Yeah, well, then, so am I," Sean concluded. He scrubbed a hand over his smooth, shaven head. "The neighbor told the cops that we're lovers," he mused.

"Are you?" Reno inquired blandly.

Sean looked him straight in the eye. "No," he said clearly.

Reno's mouth quirked. "Well, that's a first," he quipped, taking a sip of his tea.

"Ellie deserves better than me," Sean added, crossing to the kitchen to pull a beer from the fridge. "Her boys are great," he added, tossing back a swig. Picturing Christopher's solemn face, Caleb's cocky stride, and the baby's smile, tears stabbed at his eyes. "Fuck!" he exclaimed, shaking his head at the magnitude of what had happened. "Damn it, Reno. No one loves her boys the way Ellie does. She doesn't deserve this."

Reno regarded him with an odd light in his eyes.

"What?" Sean prompted.

The lawyer waved a hand. "Nothing," he said. "So assuming she's innocent—because I've never known you to be wrong about people's motivations—who would have abducted Ellie's boys? You mentioned her ex-husband."

"His name's Carl," Sean replied. He had nothing but contempt for the man, given the scars on Ellie's heart that made it so hard for her to trust. "From what I've gathered, he left Ellie for a cocktail waitress last year."

"Where was this?"

"Mantachie, Mississippi."

Reno studied his steepled fingers. "Fastest route to Mississippi wouldn't take you through North Carolina, would it?" he pointed out.

"So? Maybe they dumped the car there to throw people off," Sean replied. "We have to think of something," he insisted. "We can't just sit on our asses and let the media have a feeding frenzy—which they will, as soon as they hear that a Navy SEAL is Ellie's *lover*."

Reno sat back, crossing his legs at the ankle. "What do you want to do?" he said, putting the ball back in Sean's court.

"I need to talk to my commander," Sean answered grimly. "You mind hanging out here a couple of hours while I go to Spec Ops?" he asked, standing up. "Who's watching your kids?"

Reno's wife had died of cancer, leaving him with six young children.

"My brother," Reno reassured him, reaching for the remote. "Go ahead. I'll fend off the cops when they show up to question you."

Sean hesitated. "You think they're going to show up today?" he asked, his stomach knotting.

"Yep."

Shit. He really didn't want to explain where he'd been when Ellie's boys were kidnapped. Especially not in front of Ellie. "I'll be back soon," he promised, carrying his half-finished beer to the sink. Grabbing his truck keys this time, he headed to the door.

No cops yet. He hoped to stay one step ahead of them.

* * *

Sean knocked quietly at his commander's open door. Lieutenant Commander Joe Montgomery glanced up from his desk and blinked in surprise. "Chief," he said, "I thought you were still on leave. Come in."

Sean marched front and center to stand at attention. "I'm on leave till Monday, sir, but I'm hoping to request more time off. An emergency's come up."

The CO's dark green eyes narrowed slightly at Sean's terse announcement. "Have a seat," he suggested.

Sean lowered himself stiffly into one of the two leather seats facing the commander's desk.

Eighteen months had passed since the CO had gotten that scar on his face, a scar that might have ended up on Sean, if his future commander hadn't pulled him off a reconnaissance op and taken his place. That was back in Afghanistan. Whoever heard of a lieutenant commander heading to the field, anyway? But Joe Montgomery, aka Monty, had been gung ho back then, and when Sean spiked a fever, Monty had gone in his stead, leading Sean's squad into the worst disaster in SEAL history.

Amazingly, Monty had survived, but Sean's three closest friends hadn't. Sixteen more men swooping down in a rescue helicopter had also perished when an RPG struck their helo.

Initially, Sean had blamed Monty for the fiasco, going face-to-face with him at Bagram Air Base. He'd basically said if Monty hadn't pulled rank to take his place, things might have turned out differently, lives might have been saved. His pain had been too raw for him to hold back.

Since then, he'd realized Monty had more than paid for his decision. Not only would he have to carry that scar around for life, but he'd also have to contend with survivor's guilt.

One of the first things Monty did upon taking command of Team Twelve was to request Sean to join his team, a dream come true for a man who'd spent two solid years in a hot zone. But Team Three still wanted a piece of him, which was why he'd had to go back to Afghanistan recently.

"What's going on, Chief?" his commander asked him now.

Where to start? Sean wondered. "I need to help one of my tenants find her kids. They were kidnapped on Thursday," he summarized briefly.

"This is the same woman who's been staying with the senior chief," the CO surmised.

"Yes, sir," said Sean, heartened Monty had heard of the situation. "Her car was just found in North Carolina, but the kids are still missing."

"You think you can help find them?" asked the CO dubiously.

"I have some idea of where to start," Sean replied.

Montgomery drummed the surface of his desk with a long-fingered hand. "You know, your personal life isn't supposed to interfere with your professional obligations," he observed in a neutral tone.

Here it comes, thought Sean. He'd been waiting for this for months. An officer like Joe Montgomery wasn't going to be dressed down by a chief petty officer and not eventually get even.

And yet the CO's next words didn't fit the picture. "How much time do you think you need?"

"Like a week?" Sean hedged. Was that enough time to locate three boys who could be just about anywhere?

"A whole week," Montgomery mused with an inscrutable gaze that had the power to make grown men squirm.

"Seven days," Sean added helpfully.

A glint of humor pierced Monty's dark eyes. "Is it?" He reached for a pen. To Sean's growing surprise, he jotted a note on his sticky pad. "Leave this on Veronica's desk," he instructed, tearing it off. "She'll type up a leave chit on Monday, and I'll sign it then."

Sean had broken out in a light sweat. That was it? He wasn't going to get the reprimand he'd felt he had coming? "Thank you, sir."

"One more thing," the CO added. "You might want to call Lieutenant Lindstrom. His wife's with the FBI, you know."

"Yes, sir. That's a good idea, sir."

"Dismissed," said Montgomery with an enigmatic gleam in his eyes.

Sean jumped to attention and practically ran for the door. That had gone far better than he'd anticipated.

But then he spied Vinny disappearing into a supply closet, and his frustrations resurfaced.

Vinny took his job as the corpsman of Echo Platoon ultra-seriously, which was why he inventoried medical supplies every Saturday morning, ensuring his men would never be caught without morphine, tourniquets, or syringes when they needed them most.

At the sound of approaching footsteps, he leaned out of the supply closet and grinned to see his chief and good friend Sean Harlan bearing down on him. "Harley, you're back."

"Yeah. We need to talk," Sean announced, making it clear he wasn't going to kiss Vinny on both cheeks today, a habit he'd acquired to harass Vinny, especially since Spec Ops was full of macho guys.

"What's up?" Vinny asked, tossing a box of bandages back on the shelf.

"Do you know where your fiancée is?" Sean asked with a glitter of anger in his blue eyes.

"Er . . . sure." Vinny thought back to their phone conversation this morning. "She's following a news story down in North Carolina. Some kids went missing, and the car they disappeared in was found at the bottom of a lake." He was disconcerted to see Sean's jaw muscles bunch and flex. "Why?" he asked with sudden dread. What had Ophelia done now?

"Those kids," Sean explained, "are the sons of Ellie Stuart, who rents one of my houses. And despite what your fiancée may want to imply in her reports, Ellie Stuart would never fucking kill her kids or drown them in a lake. I want you to call her, now, and warn her not to go there. Got it?"

Vinny felt his swarthy face blanch even as he watched Sean's fairer complexion turn a ruddy red.

Vinny didn't involve himself in Lia's business. She was the one with a nose for corruption. She could sniff out drama in a heartbeat, and he admired her doggedness when it came to cornering her quarry. "Sure," he said with more confidence than he felt.

"And while you're at it, you'd better explain that I am

not Ellie Stuart's lover, and if she tries to take that angle, I'll sue Channel Ten News for slander."

"Okay." This was definitely not where Vinny explained that Lia did her own thing and that he made a point of never getting in the way. "Yeah, sure, I'll talk to her," he promised, then fell back on the more comfortable role of confidant. "Are you okay, Harley? You seem pretty stressed over this."

Sean just gave him an impatient glare. "You have no idea," he said, stalking away.

"Where are you going?" Vinny asked as his friend headed for the exit.

"To find the sons of bitches who took those boys," Sean called back.

"No!" Jerking awake, Ellie found herself seated in a bed in a darkened room, her heart hammering in the wake of her nightmare. She dragged in a cleansing breath, fighting to shake off the vision of her car sinking into water with her three boys' faces plastered to the rear window.

It was only a dream. Her boys weren't dead; they'd just been taken away. At the memory of their abduction, she kicked off the damp sheets in a panic. She couldn't afford to just lie here. But where was here? Oh, yes, Sean's room.

Through her haze of despair, it hadn't escaped her that he'd put her in his house, in his room, in his bed, wearing a shirt that smelled like him.

Hearing voices, she tiptoed across the room and slipped into a hallway filled with late-afternoon sunlight.

Her heart raced with residual fear as she started down the stairs, her ears tuned to the discussion under way.

One voice was Sean's, and the other belonged to . . . Sergeant Peyton! She froze, afraid to take another step, terrified he'd come to arrest her.

"After what you did to Ellie's house?" Sean's tone was incredulous. "You're gonna have to come up with a warrant to do that, Sergeant."

"I'd be more worried about how it looks *not* to let us look around," Peyton warned.

"Like I said, if you have any more questions, you can call my lawyer," Sean insisted. "I think we've chatted long enough. Why don't you take off and do something more productive, like find Ellie's boys."

"That's exactly what I'm doing, Mr. Harlan."

"*Chief* Harlan," Sean corrected him. "And from what I understand, the FBI has taken over the investigation since the car was found out of state."

"The FBI," Peyton retorted, his tone dripping with scorn, "can't keep us local boys from doing our job. By the way, you can tell Miss Stuart that her cell phone turned up under a pile of leaves."

"Whose blood was on it?" Sean asked.

Cell phone? Blood? Something had happened that Ellie didn't know about. Her knees folded beneath her, and she sat abruptly on the sixth step.

"Dunno yet," Peyton replied. She could picture the sergeant squinting up at Sean, weighing his words with care. "Maybe you could tell me. Just where were you the night the boys were taken?"

The air seemed to freeze like glass, then split and crackle.

"You need to leave," Sean said in a voice Ellie had never heard before—a voice that sounded dangerous. It pulled her from her own fears.

"Are you threatening a police officer, Chief Harlan?" Sergeant Peyton boldly countered.

"What do you think?" she heard Sean murmur. His cold, menacing tone sent goose bumps skating over Ellie's skin.

"Hmmph." She could picture Peyton taking a swaggering step backward, pretending Sean's bristling didn't faze him. "We'll be in touch," he promised. She heard him retreat down off the stoop. His car throttled and pulled away, and only then did Sean shut the door.

For a long minute, the house remained completely quiet. All Ellie could hear were her own shallow breaths. Just then, Sean slid silently around the partition, his bright blue eyes pinning her with a look of dismay. "How long have you been there?" he asked.

"Long enough," she whispered hoarsely. "Where'd they find my car?" she demanded, trembling from head to foot.

"Come on down," he urged, pulling her gently down the rest of the stairs.

Ellie spared the slightest thought for what she was—or, rather, wasn't—wearing. Sean's soft shirt hung to her thighs, and all she wore beneath it were her panties. Fortunately, Mr. Silverman was gone.

"Where was the car?" she demanded again. Sean's silence only fed her fear.

"Sit." He swung her around the side of his sofa and pushed her gently onto its plush cushions. "They found the car in North Carolina," he stated, hunkering before her. He kept his hands on her wrists, as if feeling her pulse. "Someone drove it into a lake at a state park."

Just like her dream. The room started to whirl. "The boys!" she heard herself cry. *They were dead. She knew it.*

"The boys weren't in it."

"They were in it?" The blood was roaring in her ears too loudly for her to hear.

"They were *not* in the car, Ellie. No one's found your boys yet."

His words penetrated her despair, and Sean's handsome, worried face came abruptly into focus. Ellie's relief was equally sharp. Alive! Not dead. To her chagrin, she burst into tears.

With a sound between a groan and a mutter, Sean pulled her head to his shoulder. "It's okay, sweetheart," he reassured her.

But it wasn't okay to cry, because her boys still needed her. She drew a shuddering breath and pulled away. "Let's find them," she replied, dashing the wetness from her face. "Let's go right now."

Sean could only marvel at Ellie's strength. If she were any other woman, she'd be sobbing uncontrollably. Instead, her tear-filled eyes gleamed with determination. A touch of color bloomed in her cheeks, relieving her stark pallor.

"It might not look good for us to leave the area," he replied. "The wife of one of my lieutenants works for the FBI. She's going to call me and tell us what to do."

Ellie nodded, reluctantly amenable. "Okay."

"I think we should look for Carl," he added.

The fight in her eyes abruptly dimmed. "He didn't take them," she refuted with a shake of her head.

"How do you know that?" Sean demanded. "We can't afford to ignore the possibility. Where is Carl? Do you even know how to get a hold of him?"

The police had asked her the same thing. She'd been down this road a dozen times. "No," she said tiredly. "His mama died last year of cancer, so I can't ask her. I've already called Turley's Show Bar where he used to hang out. Marty, who runs the place, said he got a job off in Savannah, Georgia, but didn't leave a forwarding address."

"What about the woman he ran off with, the cocktail waitress. Did she go with him?"

Ellie blinked. In her mind, Tammy was just one of many women Carl had been unfaithful with. It'd never occurred to her they might still be together. "I don't know."

"Well, who would know?" Sean asked.

"Marty, I guess."

"Call him, then. Here, use my cell." As he handed her his cell phone, he raised the volume to high so he could eavesdrop.

With trembling fingers, she pressed the eleven numbers that connected her to the past she'd run from months before. The number, which she had used to call night after night in futile attempts to get Carl to come home, would be forever etched in her mind.

Sean could hear the phone ringing on the other end.

"Turley's," said a male voice.

"Marty?"

"Yeah, who's this?" came the terse reply.

"It's Ellie Stuart again. I still need to find Carl. I was wondering if Tammy went with him when he went to Savannah?"

"Hell, I don't know. I don't keep track of all the waitresses."

"Well, does Faye know?"

"Hold on. Hey, Faye!" Marty's voice grew muffled as he presumably clapped a hand over the receiver. Sean gazed into Ellie's gray-blue eyes, reading every mixed emotion washing through her.

Marty spoke up. "Yeah, Faye says she left with Carl, and she's got a forwarding address. You got somethin' to write with?"

Sean shot to his feet to rummage in a kitchen drawer. He waved for Ellie to relay Marty's words so he could write them down. Printing out the Savannah, Georgia, address, he felt a tingle of excitement climb from his fingers to his scalp.

"Thanks, Marty," said Ellie, severing the call. She looked at Sean with grim determination. "I guess I have an address."

"And heading to Savannah on Interstate Ninety-five would take you straight through North Carolina, where the car was dumped," Sean pointed out with growing excitement. "Ellie, I think we're on to something. We should tell the FBI."

Hope and skepticism warred in her eyes. "But why would Carl want the responsibility of three boys now when he never wanted it before? It makes no sense."

"Maybe it was Tammy's idea," Sean suggested.

"Why would any woman want someone else's kids?" she argued again.

"I don't know," he said, glancing down at the address.

The phone in Ellie's hands gave a sudden buzz, and she held it out to him to answer.

"Chief Harlan."

"Chief, this is Hannah Lindstrom with the FBI."

He lowered the volume. "Yes, ma'am. Thank you for calling."

"No problem. I've spoken to the special agent in charge of the investigation, and he says he definitely wants to talk to you, but he's still at Jones Lake State Park where the car was found. He won't make it to Virginia Beach until tomorrow."

"What if we went to him?" Sean asked. She had to know as well as he did that the longer the boys were gone, the less chance they had of finding them.

"I'll ask him that and get right back to you."

"She's going to get back to us," Sean said, clipping his phone to his waistband.

Ellie pushed slowly to her feet. "I need to shower and dress."

Glancing at her long, creamy-looking thighs, Sean jerked his gaze up and reminded himself firmly that she was still off limits. He'd exorcised his lust; it was over—kaput. "Everything you need is in my bathroom," he told her, oh so tempted to hold her up and soap her down while the water sluiced over her. He felt an immediate physical response to the private fantasy. Obviously, his three days with Tiffany hadn't done a lick of good.

His cell buzzed a moment later. "Harlan," he answered.

"It's Hannah again." A baby shrieked in the background, reminding Sean that Luther had a baby boy, almost Colton's age. "I spoke to Butler, and he says he's fine with you driving down to talk to him. It would expedite matters."

"Great. Where's he staying?"

"At the Best Western just outside of the state park. And here's his number. He wants you to call when you get close."

Programming Butler's number into his cell phone, Sean thanked Hannah and hung up. It was true that the odds of finding the boys decreased over time. But the real reason he wanted to get out of Dodge was to avoid the local police, who seemed to be out gunning for him.

Chapter Five

✦

Circling the dimly lit parking lot of the Best Western motel, Sean parked his GTO in front of room 143. "This is it," he said. "You ready?"

"Yes." Avoiding his pitying look, Ellie pushed open her door and started struggling out. She was more than ready to talk to someone who might actually go looking for her boys, rather than wasting more time by questioning her again.

Sean came around to help her. Even in her misery and preoccupation, she was conscious of his firm, steady grip as he led her to Butler's motel room.

"Thank you," she whispered, so grateful to him for standing by her at this time that she wanted to weep.

"Don't thank me, Ellie," he gruffly replied. He gave a swift hard knock on Butler's door.

It popped open, and there stood a man in his forties, with an average build, thinning hair, and bland, unremarkable features. He sent them both a penetrating look before nodding and stepping back. "Thanks for coming," he said in a voice as nondescript as his appearance. "Step in. Have a seat."

Sitting tensely on the end of the queen-sized bed, Ellie stared at him, hungry for news. The agent sat at the desk, his laptop within reaching distance, and slipped on a pair of reading glasses. "I've spoken to Sergeant Peyton of the Virginia Beach Police," he admitted, flicking an uneasy look at Sean, who'd remained standing. "He relayed to me your recollection of the abduction, Mrs. Stuart," he added, nodding at her with sympathy. "Let me first say that I'm very sorry you had to experience that."

"What have you found here?" Ellie prompted through the lump in her throat.

"We have only a few leads," Butler admitted. "Unfortunately, the lake water in the car erased any fingerprints or DNA that might have been helpful in identifying the abductors. The phone has blood on it, though, and as soon as the results of the DNA tests come back, we'll know whose it is."

Ellie shuddered at the impersonal remark, and Sean put a hand on her shoulder, a gesture Butler followed over the top of his glasses.

"We found a second set of tire tracks close to where the car went in," the agent added. "The forensic team has taken a cast of them to see what kind of vehicle we're talking about."

"It was a van," Ellie told him. "A white van, with two doors in the back and no windows on the sides."

"Yes," he replied, consulting some notes scribbled on a notepad. "Sergeant Peyton already gave me that description." He tapped a key on his laptop, rousing the monitor. "The team also found a boy's shoe, which we've bagged and sent to the lab." He swiveled the laptop so that Ellie could see a picture of it. "Does this look familiar, Mrs. Stuart?"

Ellie gasped. The blood drained from her head to her heart. "That's Caleb's shoe," she whispered, feeling light-headed. "We just bought them at Payless. He liked the red stripe on the sides. What . . . what do you think happened to him? Why did it fall off?"

Sean abruptly sat next to her, putting a comforting arm around her.

"He might have been trying to run away," Butler guessed, his gaze over the rim of his glasses both watchful and sympathetic. "The area was trampled, suggesting a tussle."

"Oh, God," Ellie cried, pressing a hand to her mouth as nausea roiled up.

"Caleb's tough," Sean insisted in her ear. "He was putting up resistance. That's a good sign, Ellie."

It was only a good sign if he was still alive—if they were *all* still alive. But to voice those fears would be to give credence to the unthinkable.

"Listen," said Sean, pulling Carl's address out of his back pocket and extending it to the agent. "We managed to track down Ellie's ex. I think you should pay him a visit."

Butler took the paper and frowned down at it. He laid it aside. "We'll certainly look into it," he promised, dividing a narrow-eyed look between them. "How long have you two known each other?" he inquired.

Ellie stiffened at the renewed suggestion that she and Sean were lovers. "I've known Chief Harlan since last summer," Ellie answered, "when I came out east from

Mississippi. He leases one of his houses to me." Sean had removed his arm from around her shoulders.

"Then you're his tenant," said Butler with a dubious gleam in his eyes. "And you're a Navy SEAL," he added, taking in Sean's musculature with a quick, assessing look.

"Yes, sir."

"And where were you the night the boys were kidnapped?" the agent asked Sean.

Ellie gasped with affront. "Sean had nothing to do with my boys being taken!"

"Perhaps *Sean* would like to answer the question," Butler suggested gently.

As Ellie blushed at the reprimand, Sean answered tersely, "I was out of town with a friend."

"I'll need a name and a contact number," Butler added mildly.

With a grimly set jaw and jerky movements, Sean opened his phone, accessed his address book, found the entry he was looking for, and handed his cell wordlessly to the agent.

Butler looked down at it, then up at Sean.

An unspoken message seemed to pass between them. Without a word, Butler jotted down the information onto his notepad in writing too small for Ellie to read. She was left to wonder if Sean's friend was also a SEAL, a private person whose identity was best protected. An agent of the FBI would understand that, though her curiosity twitched.

"Can I reach you both at this number?" Butler asked, exiting the address book and querying Sean's cell to discover his number.

"That's fine," Sean agreed, watching him. Butler handed the phone back, and Sean put it away, asking, "When are you planning to question Ellie's ex?"

"Soon," promised the agent, sitting back in his chair. "Why don't you two rent rooms here for the night? We may have more questions for you in the morning."

"We'll think about it," Sean replied, pushing to his feet. "Right now I think we'll catch a bite to eat. Thanks for talking to us," he added, extending a hand.

The man grimaced at the force of Sean's handshake. "Good night, Mrs. Stuart," he added, sending her a compassionate nod. "We'll have the results of the DNA tests by morning," he promised.

Having hoped for something more tangible, Ellie headed mutely to the door. They'd driven all this way just to identify Caleb's shoe. Shouldn't they have found more clues than that?

As she and Sean stepped into the fresh night air, he drew her wordlessly toward his car, unlocked it, and held the door. She dropped inside, disappointment taking her to the verge of a breakdown. Sean slipped behind the wheel and sat for a moment, his profile grimly thoughtful. "Something's not right," he announced.

She choked out a sound that was half sob, half hysteria. Without her boys, nothing would ever be right again.

"The man isn't the least bit suspicious of Carl. I don't understand that," Sean puzzled.

"That's because I convinced Peyton that Carl didn't do it," Ellie managed to reply. She wanted to hide behind her hands and sob with disappointment.

"You don't know that for sure," Sean retorted.

She hugged herself hard, gritting her teeth to keep

them from chattering. When would this horrendous trembling stop?

"He sounded more suspicious of me than of Carl," Sean reflected, making her snatch her head up.

"What?"

"Every time I touched you, he took note, like he wanted to justify his suspicions."

Ellie shook her head. "He's paid to think of everything, Sean, that's all. You have an alibi, right?"

"Right," he muttered, lost in dark thoughts.

Curiosity nearly made her ask who he'd been with, only it was none of her business. He was just her landlord, at most a friend.

"I think we should go to Savannah and look for Carl ourselves."

His suggestion dragged her up from her well of misery. "Do what?" she asked.

"Savannah's less than four hours south of here," he added, his blue eyes burning through the gloom as he regarded her.

Ellie frowned at him, puzzled by his insistence. "But you don't have Carl's address anymore. You just gave it to Butler."

"I looked it up on MapQuest while you were in the shower. I've got the directions right here," he said, pointing to his head.

Ellie considered the suggestion. "I don't know," she answered nervously. Butler had sounded far more helpful than Sergeant Peyton; she trusted him to do his job. "Maybe we should just let the FBI handle it."

"Handle what, Ellie? Butler isn't planning to do anything about Carl."

She gripped herself harder, hating the helpless shudders that radiated from her spine to every extremity of her body.

"If we find Carl and question him, would you know if he was lying?" Sean wanted to know.

Her lips curved toward a cynical smile. "He has a tick in his cheek that gives him away every time," she admitted. "I'd know."

"Okay, then," Sean persisted. "Let's go talk to him."

"But what will the authorities think of us, just up and leaving?" she argued.

"We'll be back in Virginia in no time. Come on, Ellie," he urged restlessly. "I'm not going to sit on my ass while they frame you or me—or both of us."

The authorities wouldn't do that, would they? Recalling Peyton's threats that morning, she wasn't so sure. Besides, if the law spent all its effort trying to prove Ellie and Sean's guilt, then who was out looking for her boys?

Doing something—anything—was better than waiting. "Okay," she agreed, and her trembling subsided. "But if we go," she added, "I'm driving for a while."

Sean just looked at her. "No one drives this car but me," he replied.

Ellie reached deep for composure. "Either I drive," she insisted carefully, "or I'm not going." This had to look like her idea. She didn't want Sean getting into trouble if they were stopped.

Sean shook his head.

Tears stabbed at the backs of Ellie's eyes. "Do you know how it feels," she added, revealing the pressure that was building up in her, taking her to the edge of sanity, "to have your whole world turned inside out and upside down?"

His gaze filled with sorrowful compassion as it rested on her.

"Like you have no control over anything anymore?" she added hoarsely.

"Yeah," he admitted roughly. "Yeah, I know how that feels." He reached for her hand unexpectedly, giving it a soft, reassuring squeeze. "You can drive," he relented. "Just promise to take it easy."

As their palms brushed and fingers twined, a dart of sexual awareness penetrated Ellie's misery. Startled, she drew her hand from his and pushed out of the car to trade places.

Slipping behind the wheel seconds later, she was conscious of Sean's protective gaze as she adjusted the seat and mirrors. Starting the engine, she found reverse and backed them fluidly out of the parking spot. She hadn't grown up in the sticks without learning how to drive.

Leaving the Best Western motel and the last known location of her boys, Ellie tried to brace herself for what was bound to be a futile encounter with Carl.

Driving to Savannah was the one and only variable in this hellish equation she had any control over.

He was known to the Elite Centurions as the Culprit. His advanced position in the FBI made it feasible to manipulate the evidence, to make anyone culpable of any given crime. In this case, the Elite had chosen a Navy SEAL to take the fall.

This circumstance gave the Culprit brief pause before

generating his to-do list. What if Chief Petty Officer Sean Harlan were to one day discover the Culprit's part in engineering his guilt? It might be an unpleasant thing to be on the receiving end of a SEAL's revenge.

But then again, as an esteemed special agent in charge in the FBI, revered and respected by Centurions and non-Centurions alike, he was above reproach. The likelihood of any nightmarish ramifications was negligible. With a dismissive grunt, the Culprit put the point of his pencil to paper and wrote his list:

Alter the evidence. This was a simple task. The SEAL's white Chevy truck, parked on the side of his house, had left tire imprints in the sandy dirt there. Tonight, under the cover of darkness, he'd make a second cast to replace the one found at Jones Lake State Park.

Locate a murder weapon. This, too, was laughably easy. Any Navy SEAL worth his salt had weapons hidden in his house—ideally, a knife of some sort with his fingerprints already on it.

Implicate the weapon. Piece of cake. Samples of the boys' DNA had been lifted from Ellie Stuart's home three days before. Preserved in a special solution in the lab, it was a matter of smearing the swabs onto the knife and—presto—the blade had obviously been used to commit the crime. Or if the weapon had been recently cleaned, as if blood had been washed from it, that would look highly incriminating, also.

Discover the motive. The Culprit bounced the rubber end of his pencil off the desk and thought.

This would have to be a good one—a motive that would cinch Harlan's guilt in the eyes of the jury and impel them to recommend the death penalty. A brilliant scenario came to mind, except the Culprit would require the assistance of a computer expert, which could be done if only the man was also a Centurion. This bore looking into.

Reviewing his list, he jotted down his final task:

Eliminate all alibis. Sean Harlan had just one, a woman by the name of Tiffany Hughes. A smirk lifted one side of the Culprit's thin lips. Having her killed would cost him next to nothing. Hired killers practically vied for the chance to snuff a woman versus a man. The key was to find one smart enough not to leave his DNA behind.

Honestly, this business of manipulating evidence to implicate the unwitting was scarcely a challenge anymore. It was practically child's play to a man as savvy and powerful as he was.

Ellie's competence had lulled Sean into falling asleep. With his soft snores playing backdrop to the country music on the radio, Ellie thought about the last time she'd driven like this, ten months ago, on her flight from Mississippi to Virginia. At the time, she'd been scared, but at least her sons had been with her. God, how she missed the noise, the chaos and confusion that combined to make her life a crazy form of paradise!

All she'd ever wanted was a better life for them than what she'd had. She ought to have protected them more fiercely. She ought to have realized that those men had intended them harm.

She'd failed them.

The ache in her chest became excruciating as she approached their destination. On the other side of the glinting Savannah River, the historic city slept in the predawn darkness. To the east, plumes of smoke smudged the sky where the sun would soon be rising. The sulfuric odor of a paper mill permeated the car. Suddenly the world seemed so corrupted by filth. Tears blurred Ellie's vision faster than she could blink them away.

What if the boys were gone for good?

The awful thought bathed her in a clammy sweat. Then everything she was, everything she strived to be, meant nothing.

She felt suddenly disoriented, dizzy. The precipitous, rain-slick surface of the bridge flew beneath her tires. The bridge rail flashed by, alarmingly close. A concrete barrier was all that separated her from oncoming vehicles. She made a fearful sound as she jerked the steering wheel to keep from colliding with it.

Sean startled awake. He took one look at Ellie's face, noted their position at the height of the bridge, and bolted upright. "Whoa, there," he rasped, reaching out to put a steadying hand on the wheel. "Easy now, honey; you're going too fast."

The shock of seeing her speed so high made her snatch her foot off the gas. She transferred pressure to the brake pedal, her knees as wobbly as gelatin, making the simple task difficult.

Over her gasping breaths, she was conscious of Sean giving encouragement, of his deft hand on the wheel between her slippery palms.

"Let's pull off for a while, huh?" he suggested as they eased down off the bridge. "Right over here." He indicated the parking lot of an empty welcome center.

Ellie hated herself. No matter how hard things got, she'd always buckled down, kept her composure. As the car rolled to a stop, she thrust the door open and staggered out to clear her head.

With her hands on her knees, she drew deep breaths of balmy air to keep from throwing up. The smell of river water mingled with the odor of distant factories.

Pride forced her to stand upright. "I'm sorry 'bout that," she choked out as Sean approached.

"Don't." He reached for her, his grip on her upper arms nearly all that kept her standing. Ellie's gaze fell to his hard, handsome face, his mouth, and suddenly she wished, more than anything, that he would infuse her with his certainty and his strength. She'd never needed a man's touch more than she did right now.

He must have read her mind.

With a sudden step forward, he lowered his head, put his warm lips against hers, and left them there, giving her all the time in the world to pull away. Of course, she didn't. She closed her eyes and leaned into him, savoring the intimate touch.

Her panic eased. As warm, fuzzy feelings rose up within her, her trembling subsided, allowing her tense muscles to relax at last.

"Better now?" he asked, transitioning his kiss to a hug.

She wished she could stay in the safe circle of his arms forever. But then she'd never find her boys. "Better," she murmured, gathering her strength to pull back. They hadn't come all this way for her to have a breakdown. "Let's go find Carl," she reminded him.

Intermittent gas lamps cast a romantic glow on the facades of the quaint mismatched buildings in Savannah's historic district. Each building, with its own unique shape and history, faced a grassy square sheltered by immense live oaks dripping with Spanish moss.

Ellie had trouble envisioning Carl here.

Sean turned down Abercorn Street, traveled several blocks, then slowed before a run-down Victorian. The only light in its darkened windows was a neon sign that read VACANCY. Carl, apparently, rented a room.

Sean cut the motor. "Let's talk about this," he said, leaning over Ellie's knees to open the glove compartment. "How about I talk to Carl first?"

"No," Ellie argued, her mouth going dry as he pulled out a holster and a wicked-looking handgun.

After checking the chamber for rounds, he flicked it shut again.

"I'll talk to Carl," she insisted, reaching for the door.

With a grim set to his mouth, he leaned forward to strap the holster around his waist. Then he got out, tucking the gun out of sight as he joined her. "I'll wait right here for you," he said, shutting her door.

Traffic hummed several blocks over, but this particular square was quiet. Her heart thumping unevenly, Ellie climbed creaking steps to the main entrance. She dreaded waking all the house's occupants to talk to just one.

No one answered her tentative knock.

"Knock again," Sean called, "harder."

She knocked hard enough to bruise her knuckles, and light leapt on in one of the upstairs windows. Someone thumped loudly down the stairs. "What do you want?" demanded a woman.

Recognizing Tammy's husky voice, Ellie announced herself. "I'm looking for Carl," she admitted.

The door swung open, and there stood Tammy, her voluptuous figure encased in a silky bathrobe. She'd neglected to remove her heavy makeup. "Ellie, what're you doin' here?" she asked, gaping at Ellie, who blinked against the light.

"Looking for Carl," she repeated. "Is he here?"

"That bum?" Tammy scoffed. "I threw his lazy butt outta here months ago," she boasted. Her gaze went past Ellie to where Sean stood waiting. "Who is that?" she purred.

"A policeman," Ellie lied. "Carl's in trouble. I need to know where he went."

"Hell, I don't know where he went," Tammy said convincingly. "He's probably living on the streets," she added with a careless gesture. "God knows he can't keep a job. So, what did he do that got him in trouble?" she asked with a smirk.

Ellie weighed the point of telling her. "Someone kidnapped my boys," she admitted stiffly.

"And you think it was Carl?" Tammy's laughter was incredulous. "What would Carl want with them?" But then she realized Ellie's plight, and her eyes widened. "Oh, honey," she exclaimed, instantly remorseful. "I am so sorry. You must be sick to death!"

Desolation made Ellie weave on her feet. The steps creaked as Sean shot up them to join the women. "Ma'am," he said to Tammy, who perked right up, "you wouldn't happen to have a picture of Carl lying around, would you?"

"Oh, Lord, no." But then she caught herself. "Now, wait just a minute. I do have his box of trophies and such that he left behind. It's full of old pictures. Why don't y'all come up?" She opened the door wide to admit them.

Tammy had let them take the box.

An hour later, Sean and Ellie sat in a patch of morning sunlight on the floor of their room at the Holiday Inn Express and sorted through it.

Ellie remembered Carl's I-LOVE-ME box only too well. It was filled with his memorabilia, most of which was more than ten years old, relics of his glory days as the all-star high school quarterback.

"I guess he was pretty good," Sean concluded, setting the trophies to one side to access the photos underneath.

"Guess he was," Ellie agreed, repulsed by the scent of stale cologne emanating from the cardboard. Carl used to pour the stuff on himself before going out at night.

Every familiar item reminded her of a time in her life she'd rather forget. There were plaques, certificates, newspaper clippings, and letters from potential colleges. What was not in the box was a single suggestion of Carl's romance with a high school sophomore, a girl who'd naively worshiped him.

But there were dozens of photos of Carl, some in frames, looking young and athletic, his hair sun-bleached, a big smile on his face.

He'd had dreams for himself. Big dreams. The future welcomed him with promises of a full-ride scholarship to Mississippi State, screaming fans, and a shot at the NFL.

She, little Eleanor McKenzie, had ruined all that by getting pregnant. And Carl's grandparents, who'd helped his single mother raise him, had firmly insisted he do right by her or else face being cut out of their family business. In the end, that business had gone under, anyway. And not a single day of Ellie's eleven-year marriage had gone by without Carl reminding her that she'd destroyed his life.

Why would a man that resentful of the past want to be stuck with three little reminders?

"There aren't even pictures of the boys in here," Ellie exclaimed, tossing down the photos in disgust. The dust rising from the box made her nose itch. "He didn't take them," she stated unequivocally.

"We don't know that, Ellie," Sean insisted, picking up the stack of photos she'd tossed down.

At her continued silence, he glanced up at her, his gaze locking on her awful expression. "We don't know what's going through his mind right now," he stated. "All we know is that he's hard up, right? If he's living on the streets, he'll do anything for money."

"He isn't *capable* of organizing a kidnapping like that," Ellie replied through her teeth. Certainty grew like a weed, choking out any lingering doubts. "He didn't do it, Sean. He couldn't have!" Her voice had risen to a note of crisis. Her heart felt like it was going to burst with grief. They'd come all this way for nothing. She couldn't bear this anymore. She couldn't.

Shoving the box from her, she rolled away to lie, limp and exhausted, on the carpeted floor. If Carl hadn't taken her boys, then that left just one other possibility: They'd been stolen by pedophiles who would rape and murder them, if they hadn't already. Raising her hands to her head, Ellie fisted handfuls of her thick hair and pulled. Making her scalp hurt helped alleviate the agony in her chest.

"Ellie, don't," Sean pleaded. She heard him move the box aside, felt him straddle her hips and grasp her wrists. He put pressure on points that rendered her hands immediately useless. "Listen to me, sweetheart," he coaxed, pinning her hands to the floor. "I still think we're on to something," he said, his blue eyes calming, filled with resolve. "Carl's circumstances have changed. We don't know what they are or whether they motivated him to steal his kids, but there may have been a trigger somewhere."

Though she was utterly skeptical, the certainty in his eyes was an elixir that she drank like a woman dying of thirst. With his thighs straddling her hips, his weight on her pelvis, the desire to be kissed by him again rose up in her sharply.

"We've got pictures now, Ellie," he continued, unaware of her desperate yearning. "Today we're going to hit up every homeless shelter in Savannah and ask who might have seen Carl. You ready?"

"Sure," she whispered. But she was nearly comatose from their long night of driving. Making queries at homeless shelters was bound to result in disappointment. Carl didn't have the boys. Someone else did—someone who was purely evil.

Tears pooled at the corners of her eyes, spilling over her lashes.

"Now, what would Caleb say if he saw you crying?" Sean scolded, seeing them. "He'd say, 'Mama, stop wastin' water and get busy findin' us.' "

Sean's imitation of Caleb's Mississippi drawl summoned a watery laugh out of Ellie.

"That's better," he added. "Don't quit on me now, Ellie. Come on. Get your butt off the floor and throw some water on your face. Let's go." Rising fluidly to his feet, he hauled her up after him, giving her a not-so-gentle push toward the bathroom door.

No sooner had Ellie closed the door behind her than Sean's cell phone vibrated. He walked to the window to keep Ellie from overhearing him. "Chief Harlan," he answered.

"This is Special Agent Butler," said the careful voice on the other end. "Where are you?"

"We drove down to Savannah last night," Sean admitted. If Butler considered him a suspect, he probably knew exactly where they were. Sean had purchased the room with his credit card.

"Trying to do my job, Mr. Harlan?" he questioned with just a hint of irritation.

"Figured we'd save you the trouble," Sean replied.

"Have you found Mr. Stuart yet?"

"Not yet," Sean admitted.

"In that case, why don't you head home?" Butler advised him. "It doesn't look good for the two of you to take off together," he added darkly.

"I don't think I like your insinuations, sir," Sean countered coldly. "Have you checked out my alibi yet?"

"We're working on that. Miss Hughes is out of town."

"I gave you a cell phone number," Sean said suspiciously.

"I'm sure she'll be calling us back as soon as she checks her voice mail."

"So, until then I'm considered a suspect?" Sean pressed.

"Person of interest, Mr. Harlan," Butler corrected him smoothly.

"What have you heard about the DNA?" Sean demanded.

"That was my reason for calling," the man replied. "The DNA from the bloodstains matches the swab lifted from Caleb Stuart's toothbrush."

Sean sank weakly into the chair by the window. *Shit*. Of Ellie's three boys, Caleb reminded him most of himself—the rebel, the fighter.

"I'm sorry to have to tell you that," added the agent as Sean kept quiet.

"At least we know," Sean muttered.

Butler sighed. "Look, I'll give you forty-eight hours down there," he relented, proving he couldn't be too suspicious of Sean. "After that, you need to return to your homes or risk being slapped with a grand jury subpoena and an obstruction warrant."

"Forty-eight hours," Sean agreed. Battles had been won and lost in less time.

"If you find Mr. Stuart, make sure you contact me before approaching him," the agent cautioned. "Let us do our job."

"I wish you would," Sean retorted. "You should've been down here days ago."

"We have procedures, Mr. Harlan," the agent defended himself.

"Right, well, I don't. That's why I'm here doing everything I can to bring those boys home," Sean explained, putting an abrupt end to the call.

Almost immediately, his cell phone buzzed again. This time it was Reno.

"I have news about the DNA," said his lawyer, the

same man who'd strongly cautioned Sean against going to Savannah last night.

"I already know," Sean answered. "It was Caleb's blood. The FBI special agent just called."

"Does he know where you are yet?"

"He said he'd give us two days down here."

"Then you'd better be back by Tuesday," Reno grimly warned. "Oh, there's something else you might want to know. One of Ellie's neighbors told the police that a van had parked in front of his property two nights in a row prior to the kidnapping. He didn't get plates or anything, but it sounds like the same van Ellie's boys were put into, and that takes some of the suspicion off of Ellie."

"Good," said Sean, only the news really wasn't good at all. Between Caleb's blood and a white van sighted days in advance of the kidnapping, all signs pointed to a well-planned, well-executed abduction. And according to Ellie, Carl couldn't have tied his own shoelaces without making knots. "Thanks, Reno," he murmured.

"I'll be in touch," the lawyer promised. "Oh, by the way, that Wavy News Ten lady wants to get a hold of you."

Sean puzzled for a moment, then figured out exactly whom Reno meant—Vinny's fiancée, Ophelia. If she was hitting up Reno for his number, that meant Vinny was holding out on her. Good for him. "I'm saving the media card for later," Sean replied. It had occurred to him that Ophelia could actually be useful if he could talk her into taking Ellie's side.

Hearing Ellie turn the water off at the sink, Sean put a quick end to the call. Given Ellie's faltering hopes, this wasn't the time for her to learn everything Reno had told him.

The boys had been missing for almost four days now. He didn't have to be a cop to know the odds of finding them alive and unharmed were diminishing rapidly.

Chapter Six

✦

Dale Robbins, a graduate of the Centurion Boys' Home in Savannah and special agent with the Cybercrimes Division of the FBI, took a call at his cubicle that sent his adrenaline pumping.

"Is this Dale Robbins?"

"Yes."

"What song does the mockingbird sing?"

It was the question he'd been told to expect at any time in his life, without ever knowing first the day or the hour.

For a panicked second, Dale couldn't remember the reply. But then it came to him, and he stammered out the pass phrase.

"The Consul has need of your services," said the caller cryptically.

Dale trembled as an image of the Consul sprang to mind. Stern and imposing, the man's oil portrait hung in Dale's meeting hall in a suburb of Washington, D.C. "Of course," he replied, eager to serve the brotherhood in any way.

"He requires you to discover whether Eleanor McKenzie Stuart, or Ellie Stuart, has a registered e-mail account with any of the free service providers—Hotmail, Yahoo!, Juno, and so forth."

"No problem," said Dale, relieved that the task was one he could readily perform.

"I will call again in twenty-four hours," warned the caller before hanging up.

With trembling fingers, Dale Robbins jotted *Eleanor McKenzie Stuart* on the back of a gum wrapper. He cast surreptitious glances at his colleagues, busy working at their cubicles; seeing that no one was watching him, he began his search through Telnet.

By four o'clock that afternoon, Ellie had hit a wall. She and Sean had toured two of the city's three homeless shelters, canvassing hundreds of individuals, dispersing and collecting photos of Carl. The hopelessness and apathy, the smell of unwashed bodies, and the repeated negative responses were like spikes being driven deep into her heart.

With the sun still high in the sky and plenty of time to visit the third and last shelter, an exhausted Ellie dropped into the passenger seat of Sean's car and closed her eyes. The throb of the engine lulled her instantly to sleep.

"Hey." Sean shook her gently awake ten minutes later. "We're at the hotel. You want to walk or should I carry you in?"

"What . . . why are we here?" she murmured sleepily, recognizing the hotel's parking garage.

"You need to rest, Ellie. We'll go back out tonight."

"No, there's another shelter," she insisted, but her eyelids felt sticky, and her heart cracked with grief at the like-lihood that no one would recognize Carl's photo there, either.

Her boys would be lost to her forever.

"We'll get there, Ellie," Sean comforted with a squeeze of her hand. "Trust me, right now, you need to sleep." Pushing out of the car, he collected her on the other side and led her, nearly catatonic, to their room on the fourth floor.

Trust me, he'd said. For the first time in her life, she wanted to do just that—put her faith in another human being, something she'd done only once before, when she'd trusted Carl to love and honor her forever.

"Wake me up in a couple hours," she begged, her speech slurred as she crawled, fully clothed, onto one of the two double beds and flopped back to sleep.

Two hours later, Sean didn't have the heart to wake her. Growing restless but loath to leave her, he watched the news on TV, scowling at the thirty-second segment allot-ted to the case of Ellie's missing boys. It was just enough time for them to identify the blood smeared on the cell phone as Caleb's and to mention that his shoe had been found in the woods nearby, suggesting he'd put up a struggle. Was that all the boys were worth now, just thirty fucking seconds?

Sean leapt off the bed and started prowling. By 9:30, he couldn't stand to be inactive any longer. Their forty-eight-hour grace period was dwindling rapidly. Instead of waking Ellie, he scribbled her a note, saying he'd be at one of the bars just up the street. *Call when you wake up*, he added, jotting down his cell phone number.

He stuck his gun in the holster at the small of his back, slipped one of Carl's photos into his back pocket, his wallet with the keycard in the other, and quietly left the room.

The jazz music pouring out of Isaac's corner bar drew him to its open doors two blocks from the hotel. A pungent bouquet of grilled grouper, perfume, and cigarette smoke greeted him as he sauntered into the dark, cozy pub.

He sat a moment at the crowded bar, noting that the clientele ranged from yuppies to local watermen. As a pretty blonde started crooning lyrics on the microphone, he drained his Diet Coke, pulled out Carl's picture, and started making his rounds.

But no one recognized Carl. "Are you a cop?" several people asked him.

"No, just looking for an old friend."

Making his way toward the tables at the rear, he sidled up to two guys who looked prison-rough. Both were in their midforties, dressed in navy-blue coveralls, suggesting they'd come straight from a laboring job. One was small and wiry with a narrow black mustache that reminded Sean of Hitler. The other was fat and greasy with a crude, jailhouse tattoo on the knuckles of his left hand.

Sean knew trouble when he saw it. He even knew when the words *escape* and *evade* were apropos. He just couldn't resist dipping a toe in to test the waters. "Hi," he said, and the men eyed him with sullen disbelief, like, *Where the fuck do you get off talking to us?*

"I'm looking for a friend," said Sean, sliding the photo between them. "You seen him anywhere?"

"No," said the small man without even glancing down. But his partner's curiosity got the better of him. He angled his thick head to look, and recognition flashed across his face before he managed to conceal it. He looked up at Sean with his mouth hanging open but didn't say anything.

An awkward silence fell over the table.

"Maybe you need more time," Sean suggested. "I'll go use the head," he added, intentionally leaving the photo on the table as he backed away. He ducked into the two-stall restroom and waited, his blood thrumming with anticipation. Wouldn't it beat all if these guys could point him in Carl's direction?

Of course, they might need a little coercion first. He checked his gun, then tucked it out of sight. With a breath of resolve, he left the restroom.

Only the men were gone.

Crap. They'd even taken the photo with them.

Sean headed briskly for the door.

"Where you goin', policeman?" purred a brunette who'd flirted with him earlier.

He pretended not to hear her. The thugs couldn't have gotten that far, plus the street was a better place to question them.

Pausing on the front stoop, Sean looked around. Young people thronged the sidewalk to his right. Instinct told him the men would have headed toward the waterfront, so he struck out in that direction. The dark alley on his left drew his watchful gaze, but it was too late. A brief whistling preceded the arc of a two-by-four as it made stunning impact with the side of his head.

Sean staggered but managed to stay on his feet. Two women to his right screamed and scattered. Other pedestrians gave wide berth while eyeing Sean with interest. Bent double, with his ears ringing and fighting to focus on the cobblestones under his feet, Sean felt rough hands grab him and drag him into the alleyway.

He was shoved against a stone wall and held there by the fat man's forearm, his Glock pinned uselessly between the wall and the small of his back.

A beefy fist plowed into one side of his face, snapping his head back.

Goddamn, that hurt!

"Who are you?" The smaller man stood off to one side, glaring up at Sean's swelling profile.

"Friend of Carl's," Sean gritted, waiting for just the right moment to turn the tables on them. "We went to high school together."

"Oh, yeah? Hit him again, Grimes."

Sean ducked, and the fat man's fist hit the wall. He howled, whirling away to nurse his bruised knuckles. Sean whipped his Glock out and leveled it at Little Hitler. "Your turn," he said, calmly releasing the safety. "Tell me where Carl is."

"Fuck you," said the little man with genuine bravado.

"That's not the way it works," said Sean, bearing down on him. With his free hand, he grasped the little man by his coveralls, swung him around, and pinned him to his chest, nudging the barrel of his Glock against his temple. "This is how it works," he added in his deadliest murmur. "Grimes here tells me where to find Carl or I shoot your brains out and drop your body in the gutter."

At the threat, the fat man ceased his howling. He swung

a panicked look between the two of them. But then a smile of triumph split his broad face. "Cops are comin'," he announced with glee.

Sure enough, a siren chirped nearby. Blue light strafed the faces of the adjacent buildings, and Sean cursed. How'd the cops get here so fast? "Tell me where Carl is," he insisted, gouging Little Hitler's temple harder.

"Don't tell him shit," the little man warned his companion. "He ain't gonna shoot me. Not with the cops this close."

He was right, damn it. Not that Sean had planned on killing him in the first place, but the authorities couldn't know that. Furthermore, he didn't have a concealed-carry permit for the state of Georgia.

With a mutter of annoyance, Sean looked around. The far end of the alley was blocked by a Dumpster and a privacy fence—no deterrent to Sean, who could clamber over just about anything.

Thrusting Little Hitler at his fat companion, he turned and bolted up the alley, putting his gun away as he went.

"Hey, where you goin'?" the fat man shouted. The smaller man gave chase, but Sean easily outstripped him. Hitting the steel Dumpster at full speed, he did a pull-up on its lip and clambered on top. With a glance back at the gaping thugs, he leapt over the privacy fence and landed on the next street over.

Brushing his hands off, Sean eased casually out of the shadows to join the knot of people cruising toward him. He circled the block with them back to Drayton Street. Glancing up the street at Isaac's, he saw two squad cars parked with their noses in the alleyway. Police officers now interrogated Little Hitler and his fat companion, Grimes.

Huh. Who'd have thought guys like them would have stuck around? Sean mused. Maybe they had friends in the force.

Crossing the street to head back to the Holiday Inn Express, Sean cursed his bad luck. He'd come so close to discovering Carl's location.

Unlocking the door with scarcely a sound, he realized that Ellie was already awake. The light flooding in from the hallway showed her sitting up in bed, her back to the headboard, hugging a pillow.

A vision of her holding Colton hit him like a punch in the gut. "You're up," he said, closing the door and flicking on the bathroom light. "I thought you would call me."

"What happened to your face?" she asked in a dull, scratchy voice.

He touched his swelling cheekbone with his fingertips. "I came across some guys who recognized Carl's photo," he announced, laying his gun, his wallet, and his cell phone on the bureau.

Ellie's gaze had snagged on the gun as if she were just realizing he was a warrior—not a regular guy. In this particular mission, he was her warrior. He watched her swallow uncomfortably before asking, incredulously, "And they hit you?"

"Yeah, well, first they denied knowing him," Sean replied. "Then they lured me out of the pub and hit me with a two-by-four. What they didn't do was tell me where Carl is," he added irritably. "I might have gotten answers if the police hadn't shown up."

"Did you tell the police what happened?"

"No," he said, turning toward the bathroom to keep from explaining his reasons. Cops who chatted with ex-cons made him uneasy. "I'll call Butler in the morning."

Five minutes later, he came out smelling of soap, wearing just his boxers. Ellie was still in her ragged nightgown, her back to the headboard, clutching the pillow.

It hurt to look at her, to have nothing more encouraging to say. "I need to sleep some, Ellie," he said, snapping off the bathroom light behind him, "but you can turn on the TV if you want."

She said nothing until he'd crossed to the second bed and pulled the covers down.

"What did those men look like?" she asked with the faintest thread of hope in her voice.

"One was big and fat and went by the name Grimes. The other was small with a mustache." He'd seen the composite sketches of the kidnappers. Only Grimes bore some resemblance to one of the sketches, but it was too much to assume that just because he was fat, he was one of the kidnappers.

Given Ellie's relapse into silence, she realized that, too.

He sat down, wriggled under the covers, punched his pillow up, and closed his eyes.

A second later, he opened them to look at her. Ellie still sat there, staring into darkness.

He couldn't stand seeing her like this. "Ellie," he insisted, "Carl is somewhere in this city. Those men recognized him, and for some reason, they're protecting him. Maybe tomorrow we'll discover why. And if we can't, then Butler will."

She didn't acknowledge his encouragement, didn't break down and weep. Hell, she barely even breathed.

With a sigh, Sean kicked off the covers, rolled out of bed, and stepped to hers. "Move over," he told her.

That finally got her attention. Her pale face tipped up at him. "Why?" she asked.

"Because sometimes the only way to get through a bad time is to hold on to the guy next to you."

Her light gray eyes seemed to cut the gloom as she assessed him. "Would you make love to me?" she whispered unexpectedly.

Sean's skin seemed to shrink. His only intention had been to console her in her desolation, but the invitation set his imagination on fire. Blood rushed to his groin. His heart started pounding.

Make love to Ellie? The woman who'd tormented his dreams since his return from overseas? The sexy mama who'd driven him into the arms of another woman in the hopes of dissipating his lust?

He wanted nothing more.

Only, not like this. Not when, for Ellie, making love was second only to suicide. What she needed was morphine or valium—not sex.

"Sweetheart," he growled, tamping down his disappointment, "making love isn't going to make this any easier."

It might even make things worse. For one thing, Sean had sworn to Butler that they weren't lovers. And it'd make him a liar if he took her up on her offer.

Silence greeted his reply. Ellie moved stiffly over, stuffed the pillow under her head, and dropped into a prone position.

Sean sighed. Now what? She'd made room for him, but on the heels of her mind-blowing invitation, how was he supposed to sleep beside her without lying there all worked up?

"You coming in or not?" she said shortly, obviously humiliated.

With the voice of reason cautioning him strongly, Sean eased between the sheets, doing his utmost not to touch her, not to succumb to the urge to scoop her up and shelter her from one more ounce of pain or disillusionment, because he couldn't trust himself to stop there. But then she stuck her icy feet under his and wriggled closer, and he could tell she wasn't just cold; she was trembling.

"Damn, woman, you're freezing."

"S-sorry," she whispered.

He suffered a sudden, irrational desire to heat her blood to boiling. "Maybe this isn't a good idea," he muttered, starting to extricate himself.

"Don't." She looped a strong arm around his waist and clung to him like a life raft. "Please don't go."

As if he could, with her athletic body pressed up against him, her thigh thrown over his, holding him securely against her. His heart started pounding. Desire swamped him, leaving him fully aroused and wide awake. He sure as hell wasn't going to sleep a wink like this.

He tried one last time to reason with her. "Ellie," he said in a gruff voice, "we told the authorities we weren't lovers."

"They don't believe us, anyway," she replied.

"What happened to not needing a man in your bed, thinkin' he's all that and a bag of chips?"

"This isn't my bed."

The answer dragged a chuckle out of him. Okay. The message was pretty clear. This was just a one-time deal, something that she, in her desperation, needed that he could give her.

This might also be his one and only chance.

With his mind made up, his conscience quieted, he turned and swept her onto her back, kissing her thoroughly.

Her kiss was everything he'd dreamed it would be—slick, hot, wet, deep, and delectable. Beneath the firm mounds of her breasts, he could feel her heart thudding, assuring him that she was just as enthusiastic as he was.

Dragging his mouth from her lips, down the satiny length of her neck, he sought her nipples with single-minded anticipation. They'd teased him for months, peeking coyly through her thin cotton clothing. With a groan, he sucked the succulent nubs deep into his mouth, then rolled them with his tongue, delighting in their taste and their firm, fruity texture.

Ellie moaned. She seemed to explode in his arms, writhing beneath him, raking his back with her nails. He broke into a sweat anticipating the pleasures to come. But then she started wriggling out from under him. Apparently she'd changed her mind.

With sharp regret, he let her go, only to find himself thrust onto his back, paralyzed now, because she was stripping off that pathetic, ratty nightgown and—*holy hell*. He'd imagined a hundred times over what she looked like naked, only reality couldn't top this, not with a suggestion of moonlight gilding her breasts, her long wavy hair tumbling in disarray around her shoulders, her eyes glazed with passion.

He could come just looking at her.

She slithered out of her panties, and suddenly she was climbing on top of him, her shapely hips and thighs locking him into place, keeping him tongue-tied.

As she lowered her head to kiss him, he splayed his hands on her trim hips, loving the baby-soft texture of her skin, the taut firmness of her buttocks. He squeezed them with relish, giving rise to a moan that affected him like lightning. Her scent tormented him. He wanted to taste her first, but he could feel her preparing to take him inside.

"Slow down, honey," he begged. He wanted to savor this, make it last forever.

She, on the other hand, wanted to jump straight into the storm.

With a flip and a twist, Sean evaded her assault, reversing their positions. Now Ellie lay flat on her back, spread-eagled beneath him, which put her squarely at his mercy.

Oh, yeah. He liked this much better for now.

With a groan of frustration, Ellie lifted her hips in silent invitation. "Please," she begged. She needed him to overwhelm her *now,* to distract her from the agony in her heart and give her reason to draw her next breath.

Only Sean didn't heed her pleas. Instead, he lowered his mouth to her belly, nuzzled her thighs, and put his lips to the aching emptiness between her thighs.

Sensations, pure and sweet, overrode her disappointment. She'd never been pleasured like this, but there was no question Sean knew what he was doing. Delight licked over her, circling outward like rings following a disturbance on the surface of a pond. Her heart raced. Pleasure stormed the myriad pathways of her nerves and tingled on her skin, bathing her in cool sweat, while deep within, she melted into something pliable, an object for Sean to reshape at will.

His murmured words flashed erotic images across the screen of her mind. Added to his exquisite assault, the effect was just too devastating. Pleasure overflowed its banks, drowning her in sweet oblivion. For all of ten seconds, she forgot, in the all-consuming power of her release, that her boys had been stolen away.

As the memory impaled her anew, Sean covered her with his larger, more powerful body. She had scarcely caught her breath when he kissed her, putting the taste of abandon on her lips. In the same motion, he filled her, thick and determined, encroaching her being with ever-deepening penetration.

"Yes!" she cried, reveling in his usurpation. *Help me to forget*.

The shudder that wracked him followed by his low-throated growl told her he, too, was spellbound. They strained together, driven to get closer, and closer still, until they clung together in a fierce embrace, deeply joined.

"Damn, I knew it would be like this," Sean rasped, sounding shaken. He began to move with slow, deep thrusts that swept her into a world of primal rhythms and animal instinct. With greedy hands, she raked his hot skin, reveling in his citruslike scent, in the power of the muscles that clenched and rippled and prolonged her escape from despair into ecstasy.

He began murmuring promises of what he was going to do and how many times he would do it. She came a second time, immediately, her convulsions drenching them both, lending slick, wet sounds to the melody of their creaking bed.

Then he praised her for her responsiveness, words she'd never imagined being directed at herself. Words that made her feel valued, cherished.

Two hours and five earth-shattering orgasms later, Ellie's bones felt elastic, her muscles weary, her body sated. She lay across Sean's chest, scarcely conscious. The crushing pain in her heart had dwindled to a throbbing ache. She told herself she would move in just a minute, once she caught her breath, once her heart resumed a steady beat.

And that was her final thought.

Roused by the jangling of the private line, Owen Dulay came up on one elbow and glanced quizzically at the bedside clock. It was just past midnight. Tossing back the covers, he waded through moonlight to the adjoining office to snatch up the phone at his desk. "What is it?" he snapped.

"What song does the mockingbird sing?" asked the voice of his most loyal servant.

Tempering his impatience, Owen gave the expected reply. "You'd better have good reason for waking me up at this hour, Bates," he warned.

"Yes, sir. To get right to it, there's a stranger in town looking for your man Carl."

Carl? Owen stiffened at the unpleasant news. "Did he say what he wants?"

"He said he went to school with Carl, but I'm not buying it. They don't talk the same."

"I don't pay you to speculate, Bates. What's this stranger look like?"

"Like a fucking mercenary, if you'll pardon my language, sir. He's bald and built like a brick wall, but quick on his feet."

Owen searched his memory. Only one player in this intricate scheme fit Bates's description, but he was the fall guy, not some third-party investigator. "Await my orders," Owen decided. "Let me find out who this man is."

"Yes, sir." Bates hung up, sounding disappointed.

Drawing upon his faultless memory, Owen tapped out the number to the Culprit, an ally he'd relied upon numerous times to assuage suspicion.

The Culprit answered groggily.

"Are you aware that the boyfriend is making inquiries down here?" Owen demanded, bypassing the cipher phrase. Surely the Culprit recognized his voice by now.

"Why, has he caused any trouble?" came the enigmatic reply.

"Not exactly. He's asking questions of my employees. I fail to understand why he's down here."

"Not to worry," the Culprit insisted smoothly. "At the time of his trial, it'll appear that he and his girlfriend were taking a vacation, unencumbered by children. Also, I find it simpler to accomplish certain tasks when he's not around. I promise you, Consul, a warrant for his arrest is impending."

Mollified by the man's efficiency, Owen muttered a brief warning. "If the SEAL becomes a problem, I'll take care of him myself."

"Oh, he won't," the Culprit assured him. "He'll be back in Virginia Beach, behind bars, within a week."

* * *

Ellie was awakened by hazy sunlight blazing around the edges of the drapes. She jerked to a sitting position, realizing in the same instant that she was naked and tender in places she hadn't been in a long time. Memories of the previous night had her searching the room for Sean.

To her relief, he wasn't around.

Oh, my God. She fell back into the pillow, assaulted by memories that warmed her from the inside out and put butterflies in her belly.

And now what?

A tight, anxious feeling built within her chest. Ellie threw back the covers and rose on jittery legs. She just wouldn't think about it. She was crossing the room when she saw the white note stuck to the door—with chewing gum.

I do believe, Sean wrote in his ridiculously messy handwriting, *you've been hiding your light under a bushel. Back by 11AM. Sean.*

Ellie swung a glance at the digital clock. She had half an hour to shower and dress. As for his teasing remark, she was best off ignoring it. Sean was a hedonist, a ladies' man. If she didn't nail that fact like a shield across her heart, then she had no one to blame but herself.

Locking herself in the bathroom, she sought to steam the scalding memories of her five orgasms out of her mind.

It wasn't until she turned the water off and reached for a towel that the realization hit her: She'd fallen asleep before Sean had enjoyed a single one.

Chapter Seven

♦

Balancing a cardboard tray topped with steaming mochaccinos in one hand and clutching a plastic sack and a bag of muffins in the other, Sean rapped on the hotel door in lieu of using the key card. He had no idea what to expect from Ellie after last night. Hell, she never did what he expected, anyway.

"Thanks," he said when she popped the door open. "My hands are full."

As he crossed to the bureau, he noticed she looked rested for a change, recharged. Good thing, since they had less than twenty-four hours to find Carl. As promised, he'd called Butler this morning to relate last night's incident. Butler had reiterated that they were not to approach Carl in person if they found him. The experts would handle it.

Passing Ellie the bag of muffins, Sean tossed the plastic sack onto the bed. "I hope you like lemon poppy seed. Careful with your mochaccino. It's hot."

"Thank you," she murmured, pulling a muffin from the bag. She ate it where she stood, eyeing the plastic sack with shy curiosity and avoiding his regard.

So much for a quick romp in the sack this morning, Sean mused, giving up the hope with a shrug. He carried the remaining muffin and cup over to the armchair. "Why don't you sit down?" he suggested, indicating the foot of the bed.

"I'm okay." She tore off a little piece of muffin and stuck it in her mouth.

He regarded her thoughtfully. "You know, you really don't have to beat yourself up for last night," he told her. "I could've just said no."

Her gray gaze swivelled toward him briefly. With a suggestion of a blush, she went back to feeding herself mouse-sized bites. Obviously, she still had no appetite.

Sean tried again. "Sometimes when life really sucks, you need to do something to make it better, you know?"

Her gaze snapped up at him again. "So, that was you takin' pity on me," she concluded, her accent sneaking out. A riot of color streaked up both cheeks, and her eyes flashed.

Sean just laughed. He'd never seen that one coming, but, damn, she was cute when she was mad. "No, sweetheart, it wasn't a pity fuck, if that's what you're asking."

Her entire face turned red. "Don't use that word!" she objected, turning away to snatch her mochaccino off the bureau.

Sean grinned. She'd liked that kind of talk last night.

"What are you grinning about?" she demanded, working herself up into a full lather. "The way I remember it, you didn't even . . . you never even got to . . ." She floundered for the right euphemism.

"Come?" he offered helpfully. "Ejaculate?"

"Finish!" she retorted, hiding her face behind a swig of coffee. Sean chuckled as she startled and gasped, fanning her mouth.

"Told you it was hot," he drawled. "And the main reason I didn't finish is because I didn't have a condom *at the time*." He glanced meaningfully at the sack on the bed. He had plenty now, though.

Surprise, chagrin, and then real concern chased across her features. She slowly put her coffee down, turning wordlessly away to collect an article of clothing on the floor.

"You won't get pregnant," he comforted. "If you do, we'll cross that bridge when we get to it. And if you're worried about STDs, the military checks us all the time, and I just came up clean."

Her face had gone permanently pink. "What they ought to do is teach you how to pick up after yourself," she retorted, flinging his T-shirt at him. "You're messy!"

"When I'm distracted," he agreed, fascinated by her complexity. "Maybe you'll stay awake long enough next time for me to finish," he added, pressing his luck.

She threw him her most prickly look. Only now that he knew what lay under Ellie's pincushion, that look made him hornier than ever.

"Well, are we going or what?" she demanded on a desperate note.

Reading the banked desolation in her eyes, Sean kicked himself for forgetting, even for an instant, about her boys. Today they would visit the third and last shelter in Savannah. If no one knew Carl there, it was over. There'd be nothing left to do but trust the FBI to find him and return to Virginia to face the fallout.

* * *

Wherever he went, Drake carried his backpack, with his cell phone and listening devices tucked into a hidden compartment. The hot May sun left the pack sticking to his back as he hurried to the shelter for lunch. He could see the sandstone building on the corner up ahead, its carved griffin statues guarding the gate that led to a mulched enclosure and the shelter's double doors.

All morning long, Drake had sat in Wallace Square, two blocks west, staring at the pigeons pecking at his feet, listening to a man in a Civil War cap play his saxophone, and mulling over his options. There weren't many left.

Yes, living at the shelter had gotten him one foot into the world of the Centurions, but in order to find evidence incriminating its leader, he would first have to slog his way through the ranks, and that took time—lots and lots of time—which the Undercover Division was unwilling to invest.

They urged him to find informants, to befriend men close to Dulay, like his shifty-eyed gardener, Carl Stuart, who accompanied him to weekly meetings. The man had been promoted to the rank of Princeps Prior in a remarkably short period of time. Drake couldn't fathom why Dulay was so invested in him.

So maybe Carl Stuart would make a good informant. Drake would rather, however, befriend Dulay's daughter, but she'd avoided him since their conversation a week ago. He could only assume his supposed drug addiction and immaturity had dissuaded her from getting to know him more personally. Then again, her soul-numbing obligations to both her father and her ailing mother were enough to keep anyone troubled and preoccupied.

Regardless, Drake had been warned by the special agent in charge—his father—that time was running out. Unless he made substantive progress in a week's time, he'd be pulled from this assignment and given another one, the setting of which would likely be an urban high school, where Drake would be sent to ferret out drug dealers and gang leaders. The opportunity to expose the Centurion machine for what it was would be lost, at least to him.

The rumble of a powerful motor dragged Drake's gaze from the sidewalk. He watched a black '69 Pontiac GTO glide into a parking space ahead of him. The engine died, and a muscular man with a shaved head rounded the vehicle to fetch his companion.

Drake's stride faltered. This was no ordinary man. Every muscle in his hewn body screamed of highly skilled military training. Did this soldier boy work for Owen Dulay?

The woman was nothing unusual, as far as Drake could tell. Young and pretty, her pained expression bespoke of a personal hardship.

He timed his steps so he would overtake the pair. "Dude, nice car," he commented.

The man gave him a cursory inspection. "Thanks."

"You, uh, you lookin' for someone?" Drake asked, jerking his head at the shelter.

Blue eyes skewered him. "What makes you say that?"

"Well, you're not homeless if you're driving that thing," Drake pointed out.

Soldier boy pulled a photo from his back pocket. "Have you seen this man?" he asked, handing it to Drake.

Drake was startled to recognize Carl Stuart. "I'm not sure," he hedged, playing his cards close.

"You're not sure," soldier boy repeated dubiously.

"Nope," said Drake, handing back the photo with a shrug. "I've seen a lot of guys come and go," he added apologetically.

"Uh-huh," said the bald man, sounding unconvinced.

"You might want to talk to Miss Dulay, though," Drake suggested. "She kind of runs the place."

"Thanks." Drawing his companion with him, soldier boy headed for the gate.

Drake pretended to admire the car a minute longer. He was dying to hear Skyler's response to the couple's inquiry. Would she admit to knowing Carl Stuart, or would she protect her father's privacy?

In just a minute or so, he'd wander in and find out.

Standing at the head of the soup line, Skyler took immediate note of the couple's entrance. Grizzled heads came up to ogle the newcomers, especially the woman, since women were sent to the Magdalene Project for shelter. Not that this well-kempt woman looked homeless. Neither did the man, who carried himself with the kind of self-assurance the men at the shelter lacked.

"Mary, would you take over?" Handing her ladle to the nearest volunteer, Skyler rounded the table to assuage her curiosity. Heavens, the young woman looked just like that poor mother in the news whose children were kidnapped.

"Welcome to the Centurion's Shelter," she greeted them warmly. "Can I help you?"

"Are you Skyler?" asked the bald man, who was handsome with twinkling blue eyes that put her at ease.

"Yes."

"Sean Harlan," he introduced himself. "And this is Ellie."

Skyler blinked. Then she was the young mother in the news! What could have brought her to Savannah?

"We're looking for someone," the bald man explained, handing her a photo. "His name's Carl Stuart. Any chance you recognize him?"

Skyler's breath caught as she recognized her father's pet project. "He sure doesn't look like this anymore," she couldn't help but comment.

"You know him?" the woman exclaimed, her gray eyes flying wide. The man put a steadying hand on her arm.

"He works for my father," Skyler admitted.

"Is there somewhere we could talk in private?" asked Sean.

His request heightened Skyler's curiosity. "Of course. There's a meeting room on the second floor. Why don't you follow me?"

Leading them to the paneled, windowless chamber where the Centurions held their weekly meetings, Skyler admitted the pair and shut the door. "Have a seat," she invited. There were dozens of chairs available, all facing the oil-on-canvas portrait of her father. Behind the paneled walls lay secret compartments filled with relics and curiosities, enticement to remain in the brotherhood, to lure the seeker to the next great secret. But Sean and Ellie couldn't possibly know all that. Skyler only knew from overhearing snippets of conversation throughout her childhood.

"Was Carl one of the homeless here?" Sean inquired, declining her invitation to sit. Ellie sat tensely on the edge of a stool.

"No. My father hired him ten months ago to tend our garden," Skyler admitted, "though I've heard he's going to be my father's chauffeur now."

"Carl couldn't keep weeds alive," Ellie remarked bitterly.

"Carl is Ellie's ex-husband," Sean explained.

"Really?" The wholesome-looking woman didn't seem at all like Carl's type. "I've seen you on the news," Skyler admitted, earning a startled, desolate stare from the woman. "I'm so sorry about your sons."

"Thank you," Ellie murmured.

"Does Carl know about the kidnapping?" asked Sean.

"I don't know." Putting two and two together, she asked, aghast, "You think he had something to do with it?"

"What do you think?" Sean countered.

The thought of Carl wanting to care for three children was inconceivable. "Um, I don't think so," Skyler answered as tactfully as possible. "I certainly haven't seen any young boys with him."

Ellie's shoulders slumped. She looked down at the floor.

"I'm so sorry," Skyler added, wishing she could do something to ease the woman's heartache.

"Could you arrange for Ellie to ask him herself?" Sean asked, shocking her with his request.

Daunted by the prospect of sneaking behind her father's back, Skyler hesitated. "I don't know. My father's a very private man."

"Please," said Sean. His blue eyes enjoined her cooperation.

Glancing at Ellie, Skyler's compassion won out over fear. "Okay," she agreed. "Carl lives in our carriage house. Perhaps you could meet him in the garden on the side of the house. I could unlock the gate so you could get in. You would have to be terribly discreet, though," she cautioned. "If my father catches you trespassing, he'll have you arrested."

Sean didn't look at all intimidated. "Can we do it tonight?" he asked, putting added pressure on her. "We're due back in Virginia tomorrow."

Skyler paced to the podium to think, her heartbeat quickening. Lately, her father had taken to leaving the house after supper and not coming home until ten or so. But the sun set late in the evenings. "What about nine o'clock tonight?" she decided. "The house is just off Abercorn on East Jones Street, number twelve. It's a big brick Federal home with a garden on the left. If the gate's unlocked, that means it'll be safe to enter. Keep to the shadows and out of sight of the windows. Carl should come out within fifteen minutes."

"You're sure he'll come?" Sean asked.

"Oh, yes," said Skyler, meeting Ellie's bitter gaze very briefly.

"Tonight at nine," Sean agreed, extending a hand. "Thank you."

"You're welcome," she murmured as his hand engulfed hers. "Please, if you're caught, don't tell anyone that I helped you," she added as an afterthought.

"No worries," he replied. "Ellie, you ready?"

Ellie pushed to her feet. "Thank you," she added, sending Skyler a grateful grimace.

"I hope you find them," Skyler called, trailing them to the door.

Sean had pulled it open. Halfway out the door, he hesitated and frowned at somebody retreating down the hall. "Who's that kid?" he asked shortly.

Skyler leaned out in time to see Drake dart around the corner. "Oh, that's Drake. He's a runaway teen," she informed the man.

With a thoughtful grunt, Sean reached for Ellie's hand. He drew her down the stairs and out the shelter's front doors.

Skyler watched them go, wondering at their relationship. Her stomach churned with mixed excitement and dread. The thought of luring Carl to the garden left her faintly nauseated. Still, if it helped poor Ellie locate her missing children, the ick factor would be well worth enduring.

"Everything okay?"

The voice in her ear made her gasp and whirl. "Drake, you startled me!"

"Sorry." He grinned apologetically, his eyes alert as they rested on her flushed face. His proximity had the same effect as it always did, whether they spoke or not. Her heart felt lighter, her senses sharper. She was aware of everything about him, from the appealing curve of his lower lip to his clean scent. He was one of the few men who showered every day. He owned maybe three different outfits, which he washed and rotated regularly.

"Can we talk?" he asked her unexpectedly. "In private?" He nodded toward the meeting room.

"Oh, I don't know if that's a good idea," she demurred, her mouth going dry at the thought of being alone with him.

"Look, I couldn't help overhearing you in here with that couple," he admitted.

Skyler gasped. "You were eavesdropping?"

"I was checking up on you," he insisted. "That guy looked kind of dangerous."

Flattered by his concern but worried that he might now reveal their plans, Skyler firmed her mouth and marched into the meeting room, closing the door behind him. "Drake, you can't tell anyone what you heard," she insisted, struggling for an authoritative tone.

He regarded her at length through lush, dark eyelashes. "How are you going to lure Carl into the garden?" he finally asked.

Her heart tripped over itself at the jealous-sounding question. "That's none of your concern," she retorted. Nonetheless, heat flooded her cheeks, betraying her.

His mouth twisted into a bitter smile. "Yeah, that's what I thought," he muttered. "Tell you what, how 'bout you help me get Carl's job, and I'll forget what I heard here."

His ultimatum confounded her. He wasn't the easygoing wanderer she thought he was.

"You need a gardener, right?" he pressed. "Carl's going to be the chauffeur."

"Right," she agreed, marveling that he'd heard so much through doors hewn out of chestnut.

He spread out his hands and shrugged. "So, I need a job," he reminded her. "Then I can leave this place."

And live with the servants on the third floor of my

house, Skyler thought, shocked that her blood heated at the prospect. Of course, she was supposed to marry Ashton at the end of the month. Even if there was time for an affair with an eighteen-year-old, what good could it accomplish? Not that she was even considering such a thing. Still, as the thought took hold, desire clawed at her insides, exhilarating and insistent.

"I'll see what I can do," she promised him shakily. "Just . . . please, stay out of this business with Carl."

"I will," he agreed, flashing a boyish grin that left her weak in the knees.

She wished that he would back her against the door and kiss her until all thoughts of her impending marriage to a man twice her age just melted away.

Obviously, she was losing her mind. Drake was the last guy on earth she ought to be attracted to. Groping for the latch, she hauled the door open and fled through it, before temptation—and the will to live free—got the better of her.

Cybercrimes Special Agent Dale Robbins nailed the pass phrase immediately this time. Of course, he'd been expecting a call.

"Do you have an answer for me?" asked the dry, uninflected voice.

"Yes, I do," said Dale with a nervous glance over his shoulder. "Ellie Stuart opened an e-mail account with EarthLink on September fifteenth of last year," he murmured, "using a PC belonging to the library at Tidewater Community College."

"Excellent," said the stranger. "I want you to take possession of that address."

"Uh, I'll need a supervisor's clearance to do that."

"It's sitting in your box in the mailroom."

A shiver of awe coursed through Dale's spine. Who was this man that he could pull strings with the ease of a puppet master?

"Once you have administrator rights to the account, you will transpose the messages coming into your Inbox . . . now. Take a look at them."

Dale's computer chimed to signify the arrival of new mail. With shaking fingers, he opened the anonymous message to find three attachments. Each was a letter allegedly written by Ellie Stuart, addressed to a Sean Harlan with a military e-mail extension, each dated a couple of months ago.

"I want this correspondence to appear authentic. Can you make the dates work?" asked the voice.

Dale broke into a light sweat. "I can alter the sent date at the client server, but the stamp on the receiving server will reflect the actual time received."

For a tense moment, the voice remained silent. "That'll have to do. Print the e-mails before you send them. Place the hard copies in an envelope and mail them in-house to Special Agent Greg Butler, CID."

Butler was a criminal investigator with limited powers—he couldn't be the owner of the voice.

"Yes, sir," he replied, honored to be part of a society so well networked yet still so secretive. "He'll have hard copies by tomorrow morning," he promised quietly.

Without a word of thanks, the caller hung up.

*　　*　　*

Within the walled garden steeped in shadows, Ellie waited. Sean had positioned her behind a broad azalea bush beside the wrought-iron gate. Peering through leafy branches, she could make out the brightly lit fountain in the center of the enclosure. The scent of ivy and honeysuckle hung in the humid air. Over the gurgling of the fountain and the chirping of crickets, she could hear the faint thud of her own heart as it rocked her subtly, to and fro. Her upper lip tasted of salt as she licked it nervously.

What if Carl had taken her boys? What would she say to him?

The sound of a stem breaking under someone's heel made Ellie freeze. That had to be Sean. He'd promised to remain nearby, yet no matter how carefully she sought his silhouette in the dense foliage all around her, she couldn't see him. Still, his presence was a comfort. Knowing he would protect her from physical harm was a luxury she'd never before known.

"Miss Dulay?" Carl's singsongy voice cut across the garden, silencing the cricket symphony. "Are you here?"

Ellie's skin crawled at the familiar-sounding lilt. Peering through leafy branches, she watched Carl tiptoe toward the fountain where the light at its center briefly illumined him. He'd grown soft around the middle since she'd seen him last. Life was treating him well, but well enough to raise three boys?

"Show yourself, pretty bumblebee," he crooned, moving past the fountain toward the shadows in which she hid.

She waited, as Sean had suggested, for Carl to duck under the branches of a blooming crape myrtle before stepping from her hiding place. Repugnance rose up, and her nervousness subsided as she stepped onto the path in plain sight. "Hello, Carl," she announced herself.

He froze. Even with the shadows obscuring his features, she noted his gaping mouth and the whites of his eyes. "Ellie! Wh-what're you doin' here?" he croaked, taking a step back. He looked around guiltily, as if still expecting Skyler to show up.

"What do you think, Carl?" she countered on a steely note. "I'm here for my boys. Tell me where they are—*now*."

He bobbed his head in a gesture of indignation, reminding her of a nervous chicken. "How would I know? I didn't take 'em."

"How do you know someone took them?" Ellie demanded, jumping on his slip of the tongue like a dog on a bone.

"It was on the news, so what?" He shrugged. "I don't know nothin' about it." He took another step back.

Though wary of being seen from the windows, her suspicions were unexpectedly roused. She pursued him, desperate to see his face more clearly. Hope pounded through her. She hadn't thought Carl would know about the kidnappings. Surely, as a parent to the missing boys, he would have come forward to aid in the effort to find them. "You knew?" she hissed, forcing him farther back, driving him toward the light. "And you've done nothing to try and help me find them?" Disgust and contempt mingled with suspicion, making her want to claw his eyes out. She poked him in the chest instead.

"Ouch," he yelped, and backed out of arm's reach, his face to the light at last.

"If I find out you had anything to do with this," Ellie

warned, eyeing him for the smallest sign of suspicion, "so help me God, Carl, I will kill you." With a ragged breath, she reined herself in to keep Sean from having to interfere.

"I ain't lyin', woman," Carl insisted with disgust. "Why would I kidnap our boys? You know I can't look after 'em."

His assertion abruptly cooled her fury. There was nothing in his expression now but self-righteous resentment.

"I can't believe you came all the way down here to accuse me," he added. "Would've thought you knew me better'n that," he added, flicking his stringy hair from his eyes in a familiar gesture.

But the muscle in his cheek didn't twitch. Not once.

"You swear you didn't take them or pay someone to do it?" she demanded. Her voice quavered as hope tumbled toward despair.

"Hell, no," he insisted. "I barely make enough money to feed myself."

She studied him long and hard, waiting desperately for the telltale sign that he was lying. It never came. "Well, then," she answered, made hoarse with the urge to weep, "I guess I'm wasting my time here."

"I guess you are," he countered with a smirk.

Was that mockery lacing his voice?

Too overwrought to analyze such subtleties, Ellie whirled and walked blindly to the gate. Through eyes that ached with unshed tears, she glanced back to see Carl stalking toward the house, muttering. A wisp of his sentence reached her ears: "That bitch." She couldn't say whether he meant her or Skyler, whom he'd probably just realized had tricked him.

Swinging the gate open, Ellie stepped onto the quiet, tree-shrouded sidewalk and waited, hugging herself to maintain composure, fighting the desire to crumple where she stood.

Seconds later, Sean dropped from the top of the garden wall and landed almost silently beside her. Closing the short distance between them, he swallowed her briefly in his embrace, then pulled her across the street to his parked car.

"You did good, Ellie. Really good," he praised gruffly. "Here, get in." He put her into the driver's seat, rousing her from her self-absorption. "I want you to start the car up," he added, unexpectedly pressing the keys into her hand. "Drive once around the block—slowly. Then come back and pick me up."

"What?" she cried, confused by his odd instructions. "Where are you going?" But he had already closed the door and melted into the darkness.

"Whatever," Ellie breathed, struggling to focus through her despair. Carl hadn't kidnapped her boys. She'd already known that. And still she felt as if she'd come up against a wall so broad and high that she would never get around it. Functioning purely on autopilot, she started the car and eased into the street to do Sean's bidding, too heartsick to ponder what he might be up to.

Drake waited for the rumble of Sean Harlan's GTO to fade before daring to release the breath he'd been holding. Since accidentally stepping on a stalk that snapped under his shoe, he'd been sweating bullets, thinking Mr. Harlan, who was a freaking Navy SEAL, was going to realize he was in the garden with them and rat him out.

But now that the couple had left, Drake was free to leave his hiding place, a narrow aperture behind a trellis woven by climbing roses. It was the kind of space a large man wouldn't think to hide in, which was why he'd chosen it six weeks ago, when he'd started watching Dulay's mansion.

Tonight he hadn't been tracking Dulay's movements. He'd hidden in the garden to make sure Skyler didn't get caught up in a drama that didn't concern her—a kidnapping involving the sons of Owen Dulay's gardener. It was curious that an event attracting such media interest had washed right up on Owen Dulay's doorstep, and still Dulay tolerated Carl living and working for him. The man's answers to Ellie's questions suggested his innocence, but to Drake they also raised an interesting possibility.

Could Owen Dulay have masterminded the kidnappings? If so, why?

With a grimace, Drake eased from his hiding place, managing to escape with just a few extra scratches. The thorns were well worth the trouble when they kept even a Navy SEAL from suspecting his presence.

With the garden now deserted, Drake threaded his way through the shrubs and flowerbeds and low-hanging branches toward the gate. The gate was unlocked; he didn't need to climb it, not tonight. The well-oiled hinges scarcely made a sound as he swung it inward, peeked out onto empty sidewalk, and emerged unseen, closing the gate behind him.

With a soft whistle, he turned in the direction of the shelter. Too late, he realized he wasn't alone after all.

Sean Harlan stepped from behind the trunk of a live oak with his weapon drawn and his eyes flashing.

"We meet again," he said in a menacing voice that suggested he wasn't surprised. Grabbing Drake's arm, he nudged the barrel of his handgun under Drake's shoulder blade and suggested coldly, "How 'bout we go for a drive?"

Just then, the black GTO cruised around the corner with Ellie at the wheel. Drake shook his head in self-recrimination. *Idiot!* He should've known better than to test the instincts of a sniper. Now, either he admitted to being an undercover investigator—which could blow the lid off his entire investigation—or he kept his mouth shut and dealt with whatever punishment a Navy SEAL could dish out.

Somehow, the first option sounded slightly more appealing.

Chapter Eight

At the light tap at the door, Christopher jerked his face out of the book he was reading and eyed his visitor with mixed feelings. Mr. Dulay, Consul of the Centurion School for Boys, had taken to visiting him at night, just before bedtime, when Caleb was already asleep.

Five days ago, the silver-haired gentleman had met them as they were ushered from the van into this building of marble and stone. "Your mother is dead," he'd informed them gently. "You will remain here until your father can be found. I advise you to embrace your new circumstances."

He'd gone to shake their hands, and Caleb had bitten him.

They'd been here for almost a week now. To Chris, it seemed a lifetime. To Caleb, who'd been fed only bread and water as punishment for three days, it must have seemed like eternity.

The door opened a crack, and Mr. Dulay peered in, his dark eyes going first to Caleb, asleep in his bed, and then to Chris. He smiled with approval at the book in Chris's lap.

Chris wanted to detest the man the way Caleb did, only the Consul was kind to him. He brought him stuff to look at—curious artifacts, like a bronze spearhead that once belonged to Julius Caesar and the shrunken head of a Nigerian captive. Speaking of far-off places and powerful leaders in history, he carried Chris's imagination through the locked doors, beyond the stone walls that confined him. Best of all, he brought him books that helped him to forget, for intervals at a time, how very much he missed his mother.

"Good evening, Mr. Stuart," the man said now, approaching his bed.

"Hello," said Chris, setting his book aside.

"How do you like it?" asked the Consul, hitching a trouser leg to ease onto the foot of Chris's bed. "I see you're halfway done."

Chris was a slow, thorough reader, but the comment sounded like a compliment. "Yes, sir," he said. "I like how the grandfather goes searching for his grandson."

Mr. Dulay gave a nod of satisfaction. "Family is important, don't you think?"

Reminded of his mother, Chris's voice grew clogged with longing. "I want to go home," he dared to whisper.

Impatience flashed briefly in Mr. Dulay's eyes, but he spoke in a voice that was kind and patient. "I've told you, Christopher, your home is here now."

Chris's heart constricted with pain. He flinched with surprise when Mr. Dulay reached out unexpectedly, laying a hand on the top of his head. The man seemed truly dismayed to see him so sad. "I have good news tonight," he announced, eyeing him closely. "Your father has been found."

An indistinct image of a bitter, unpredictable man came to Chris's mind.

"Aren't you pleased?" Mr. Dulay queried with a quizzical smile.

Chris didn't want to say the wrong thing. He knew what Caleb would say, though: *He ain't my dad.* Mr. Sean had been more of a father to them before he went away.

"I'll bring him here shortly," Mr. Dulay added. "Then you may see him for yourself."

Chris gave a tiny nod of acknowledgment.

"Now, let's see here." The gentleman reached into the pocket of his lightweight blazer. "What have I got for you tonight?" With a sphinxlike smile, he withdrew a magnifying glass and handed it over. "You'll need this," he predicted, "to examine some very old documents I'll be bringing with me in the future. Keep it from your brother," he added, glancing at Caleb, who was snoring loudly.

"Thank you," Chris murmured.

"I will leave you to your reading now," Mr. Dulay decided, pushing to his feet. "Until tomorrow," he promised on his way to the door. "I'll be later than usual. I have a meeting to attend first. Good night, my boy," he called from the door.

"Good night."

As the door shut, Chris looked over at his brother. "I know you're awake," he said.

Caleb stopped snoring. His blue eyes snapped open.

"Did you hear?" Chris asked him.

"Yep," said Caleb, pushing up on one elbow. "He's

lyin' again," he predicted. He also refused to believe that their mother was dead.

"I don't know," said Chris, glancing down at his book. "He's weird. I keep thinkin' he knows something he's not telling us."

Caleb rolled out of bed. "Lemme see that magnifier," he demanded, taking it out of Chris's hands. "Maybe we could use it to send a distress signal."

"Stop lookin' for ways to escape," Chris scolded him. "You know it's not going to work."

"Why not?" Caleb demanded.

An odd chill tickled Chris's scalp. "Mr. Dulay would find us, no matter what," he finally answered, meeting Caleb's fiery gaze. He knew it was true, though he couldn't explain exactly why. He just knew Mr. Dulay would track them down, like the grandfather in the story he was reading.

He wanted them for something. He especially wanted Chris.

Sean shoved the little Peeping Tom face-first onto the hood of his car, frisked him down, and found a switch-blade inside his right sock but no other weapons. With Ellie's eyes shining like twin moons at him through the windshield, he opened the passenger door, flipped the seat forward, and pushed his captive into the backseat. Keeping his gun trained on him, he dropped into the front seat and said in his calmest voice, "Keep driving, Ellie."

"Where did he come from?" she squeaked, clearly realizing this was an aberration. "Why are you pointing your gun at him?"

"Calm down, sweetheart. I'm just going to ask Drake some questions while you drive around town, nice and slowlike."

"I suggest you head for a different street," the kid piped up, sounding grim but not at all intimidated. "Dulay will be home any minute."

Sean propped his left shoulder against the back of his seat and stared at him hard. "You're not a homeless kid, are you?" he demanded.

For a second, it wasn't clear whether Drake was going to answer him. "I'm an undercover special agent with the FBI," he announced unexpectedly.

Sean shared a startled look with Ellie. *FBI?* The kid didn't look old enough to be out of school, let alone be working for the bureau.

"You got any proof of that?" Sean asked.

"Not with me."

"Then why would I believe you?"

"Well, for starters, I could tell you who *you* are."

Sean's scalp tightened. He didn't like being at a disadvantage. "Go ahead."

"You're Navy SEAL Chief Petty Officer Sean Harlan, stationed with Team Twelve in Virginia Beach, person of interest in the abduction of Ellie Stuart's three sons."

Ellie made an incredulous sound. Sean placed a reassuring hand on her knee. "I didn't kidnap Ellie's boys," he told Drake angrily.

"Obviously," the man replied, snatching the wind from his sails. "You wouldn't be here looking for them if you did."

"Okay, so why the fuck are you following us? Did Butler send you?"

"I don't know who Butler is. And I wasn't following you today, per se. I'm investigating Owen Dulay, Skyler's father, Consul of the Centurions."

Sean laughed. "The what?"

"The Centurions. They run the shelter."

"Yeah, I got that part."

"They're a secret society made up entirely of men. At the end of the Civil War, plantation owners banded together to recoup their losses. They started into money laundering, racketeering, and mob-related activities, all of which they hide, very successfully, behind their civic charities."

"Okay," said Sean slowly. "So, what's that got to do with us?"

"I'm not sure," Drake admitted. "I overheard Carl tell Ellie he had nothing to do with the kidnapping."

"He didn't," Ellie interjected on a strained note.

"Right," Drake replied. "*He* might not have kidnapped your boys, but his employer has every resource to make three boys disappear."

"Skyler's father? Why would he do that for Carl?"

"I don't know," admitted the young agent gravely. "I'm not saying he did. It's just that Centurions have this book—it's like their bible that tells them how to lead an upright life and all that. But the main emphasis is on leaving a legacy to your sons—daughters don't count. Now, Carl's already a Princeps Prior. That's pretty high up in their internal hierarchy, but without sons to carry on his legacy, his status is meaningless."

Ellie gave a bitter laugh as she drove them around a lamp-lit square. "So suddenly Carl's children are his legacy," she mocked, "when a year ago he sat there drunk as a skunk, demanding to know if they were his in the first place!"

"Easy, Ellie," Sean advised, assessing their location with a quick sweep of his eyes. "There's a cop right there. Watch your speed, hon." He glanced back at Drake. "You're saying Dulay might have helped Carl secure his legacy."

"Maybe," Drake conceded.

"Why would he break the law for his gardener?"

"I'm not sure. All I know is that he and Carl attend the meetings together every Wednesday night at the homeless shelter. Carl even sits on his right side. Dulay obviously looks out for him, and no one really knows why."

A shiver of excitement sped Sean's pulse, but Ellie's hard profile told him she wasn't buying it. "We need you to look into this for us," Sean entreated, holding Drake's dark, intelligent gaze. "Please. Ellie and I have to head back tomorrow. If Dulay is responsible for the kidnapping, and he's that well connected . . ." He cut himself off, hating to think what it might mean. "Just keep an eye out, would you?"

"As long as you don't blow my cover," Drake insisted. "Don't tell anyone who I really am," he demanded, seeming to forget that Sean still held a gun on him. "Not Skyler, not Carl, not even this Butler you mentioned, whom I assume is FBI. I promise I'll keep my eyes and ears open. If I overhear anything suspicious, I'll alert the right authorities."

Sean considered the offer. He wished Drake could do more than that, but the man had his own agenda. "Agreed," he said, jamming his Glock back into its holster. "Sorry for the mix-up."

"No big deal."

He extended Drake a handshake and found the man's firm grip to his liking.

"You should drop me off here," Drake suggested, peering outside. "Don't want any of my homeless buddies seeing me in this car."

"Go ahead and pull over," Sean instructed Ellie. He got out to set Drake free, catching him by the arm as he shot out of the back. "You catch this son of a bitch," he told him sternly.

"I fully intend to," Drake said with a glitter in his eyes.

Letting him go, Sean ducked into the passenger seat and watched him cross the street. As he loped toward the sidewalk, Drake took on a subtle slouch and a hoodlum's cocky stride. *Damn, he's good,* Sean mused.

Turning his attention to Ellie, he found her gripping the wheel with white-knuckled hands, staring straight ahead but not looking at anything. "You want me to drive, hon?" he asked her gently.

They were five blocks from the hotel.

She moved a hand automatically to the stick shift. Without answering, she pulled the car into traffic, heading back toward their hotel.

"I take it you don't buy Drake's theory."

She took a stiff right turn. "I don't know what to think anymore," she answered hopelessly.

Sensitive to her distress and the real reason for it—tomorrow they were heading home without her sons—Sean pulled his cell phone from the glove box. Locating Butler's number, he placed a call to the FBI agent.

"Mr. Harlan." The man sounded agitated. "It's about time for you to head back to Virginia."

Sean ignored that. "You told me to call if I found Carl Stuart," he reminded him.

A subtle pause ensued. "Why do I get the feeling you approached him when I told you not to?"

Sean ignored the rhetorical question and got right to the point. "He works for a man named Owen Dulay; maybe you've heard of him."

"Can't say that I have." A pencil drawer opened and closed. Butler was evidently working late tonight.

"He's the leader of a group called the Centurions."

"I have heard of that," the man conceded.

"Are you familiar with the importance they place on having male heirs?"

"No. What are you saying?"

"Carl's a Centurion. He has a motive for wanting his sons back. They're his legacy. I'm also suggesting that his employer has the means to help him pull off a well-executed abduction."

"And why would Mr. Dulay—that's the name you said, right? Why would he commit a crime to help his employee?" Butler asked dubiously.

Sean hesitated. "I don't know."

"Well." Butler sounded bemused at best. "That's an interesting theory you've put together, Mr. Harlan," he admitted a little dryly. "Tell you what, I'll run it by my supervisor and call you back. If you don't hear from me, remember that I expect you in Virginia Beach by morning."

"We'll be there," Sean replied, ending the call. He

glanced at his watch. They'd have to drive all fucking night.

Swinging into the hotel's parking garage, Ellie found a spot close to the elevator. As they headed wordlessly to their room, defeat sat like a cinder block on Sean's shoulders. He'd let Ellie down. Her silent despair was heartbreaking. He knew the last thing in the world she wanted to do was go home to an empty house.

"We need to pack," he told her gently. "Then we'll sleep a couple of hours before we head back."

She went wordlessly into the bathroom and shut the door.

Crossing to the window, Sean nudged aside the drapes to gaze down on the street, still bustling even at this hour. Turning Drake's suggestion over in his mind, he sought to fit the Centurion conspiracy with what he knew of the kidnapping and what he'd seen firsthand in this Southern town.

If Owen Dulay *had* helped Carl abduct his kids, then who were the thugs at Isaac's bar? Friends of Carl's? Maybe they were fellow Centurions, followers of Owen Dulay. One was clearly an ex-convict, given that tattoo on his left knuckle. Why would a man like that want to talk to the police on the heels of an altercation? Ex-cons were usually skittish of police. It made no sense.

Ellie emerged quietly from the bathroom. She crossed to the bed, lay down stiffly on the mattress, and closed her eyes. Lying there so pale and pained in the lamplight, she looked just like a wounded soldier. He'd seen enough of them to know.

"Come on, Ellie," he cajoled, hating the defeat written on her face. "It's not like we didn't find out anything tonight. We know Carl's a Centurion and his employer has the resources to help him. That's something, right?"

She cracked a lackluster gaze at him. "Why would a man like that help Carl get his *legacy* back?" she asked, spitting out the word like a curse.

"I don't know. To make Carl indebted to him?"

"For what?" Ellie cut him off impatiently. "Carl doesn't even *want* the boys. He told me that straight to my face, and I know he wasn't lying. Besides, a rich man like Dulay doesn't need gratitude. He can pay people to do his bidding."

True, Sean conceded to himself, but her pessimism still annoyed him. "You could at least be open to the possibility," he argued. "There's something strange about this place. What about those guys who wanted to jump me last night? Who were they protecting? Just Carl? I don't think so."

Ellie didn't answer. She'd gone back to looking like she wished she could die.

"So, that's it for you," he taunted, approaching the bed to glare down at her. "You'd rather just assume some faceless pedophiles took your kids?"

Her eyes snapped open and her fists clenched. "They weren't faceless, damn you!" she raged, stiff as a board. "Don't you think I see those men every time I close my eyes? And when I do, I think, 'Why didn't I stop them from taking my boys away from me?'" She raised both her fists and shook them at herself.

He wasn't immune to her self-blame, but the fire flashing in her eyes and the color surging to her cheeks sparked his own frustrations. He was a man of action, used to getting results, hitting his mark every time, only in this case, when there was no clear target, he had failed. "Poor Ellie," he lashed back, giving as good as he got. "She's the only person in the world who's ever had her heart broken."

With a gasp of outrage, she jackknifed to a sitting position. "How dare you!" she shouted.

"Oh, I dare," he assured her. "You're the one who's giving up on your boys."

Growling with fury, she snatched up the closest object within reach—the guest information binder—and hurled it at him, striking him hard on the shoulder.

"Ow!" He jumped back, rubbing the tender spot.

"How dare you mock me!" Ellie shouted, leaping out of the bed. She went nose-to-nose with him, shoving him with both hands as she added, "You don't have children!" Tears sparkled in her eyes as she added hoarsely, "You have no idea how I feel!"

"Is that right?" Sean countered, feeling his own temper simmer. He grabbed her wrists to keep her from shoving him again and locked them behind her back, which brought their hips flush. A spark of lust sizzled up his spine as she continued to struggle. "Then you know all about Patrick," he added before he completely lost his train of thought.

She opened her mouth to rail at him again, only to blink in confusion. "Who?" Her suddenly husky voice told him she was just as aware of the sudden friction between them as he was.

"Patrick," Sean repeated. Releasing one of her wrists, he pulled his wallet from his pocket and flipped it open to his younger brother's last high school picture.

With a telltale pulse still fluttering at the base of her neck, Ellie examined the photo of a youth who obviously resembled Sean but had a headfull of strawberry-blond curls, freckles, and a smile that was pure sunshine.

"Your brother?" she guessed, raising wide, wet eyes at him.

"Yeah," he rasped, feeling grief rise up in him. Grief was like a tide that waxed and waned but never went away. "Patrick and I were Irish twins, eleven months apart. We did everything together. When he was fourteen, he was diagnosed with leukemia."

Ellie made a sound of dismay.

"Back then, kids didn't have the kind of odds they have today," he continued. "He fought hard. He lost all his hair, lost a bunch of weight. I shaved my head so he wouldn't be the only bald kid in school. But three years later, he had nothing left to fight with, and he died. So don't try to tell me about loss. At least we're still in the game here, Ellie."

She stared at him, aghast, her gray eyes filled with apology. "I'm so sorry," she murmured in a strangled voice, clutching his shoulders, clearly uncertain how to comfort him. Tears pooled just above her lower lashes.

Ah, shit. Sean tossed his wallet aside and put his arms around her. "Oh, Ellie, I didn't tell you that to make you feel worse," he admitted gruffly. At least she'd forgotten her anger long enough to let him hold her. Damn, but she felt good in his arms.

She hid her face in his T-shirt, her chest heaving with deep, racking sobs that tore at Sean's heartstrings.

He'd wondered when it would come to this. It was a miracle she'd kept it together this long.

And now all he could do was hold her. Hold her and hope to God the Centurions were behind the kidnapping and the FBI would find them and get them back. The Ellie he'd admired and desired would never be the same without them. The loss of her sons was the only thing bad enough to break her indomitable spirit.

With a sniff, she lifted a tear-streaked face from his shoulder and demanded, unexpectedly, "Make love to me."

Feeling her pebble-hard nipples abrade his chest, his body responded powerfully. She lifted her mouth to his and kissed him, like she needed his kisses to breathe. The floor seemed to tilt and then spin as a ferocious tide of longing roared through Sean, warming him from his toes to the tips of his ears.

Suddenly, without warning, Ellie slipped through his embrace and dropped to her knees. He watched in disbelief as she sought to release his belt with trembling fingers. Then the snap on his jeans. Oh, Jesus, she wasn't going to go down on him just like that . . .

Wow. Apparently she was.

He watched in anticipation as she parted his fly, reached in and drew him, now fully aroused, toward her seeking mouth. He sure wasn't one to turn down a blow job but . . . "Ellie, you don't have to do this."

She opted not to hear him. He closed his eyes as she pulled him deep into her warm, wet mouth, rubbing her tongue along the underside, her lips applying suction.

Oh, yeah. Oh, honey.

His fingers slid into her hair. He couldn't believe that Ellie was being so uninhibited—his proper, prickly Ellie Stuart. He opened his eyes to confirm that reality.

The lamp put gold streaks in her light brown hair. Her stormy-gray eyes rose up at him, and the unguarded longing in them punched him right in the gut.

He stepped back out of reach. For some reason, he felt more vulnerable than usual. Or maybe it was just Ellie's emotional fragility scaring him. Either way, he wanted to turn out the lights. "Come on, Ellie. Let's go to the bed."

She stood up, blocking his trajectory to the lamp, and started unbuttoning her pink blouse, then wriggling out of her jeans. He forgot about turning off the light and stared.

Never had plain cotton undergarments, no doubt purchased at a discount store, looked so fucking sexy.

Reaching around her for the latch on the bra, he freed her magnificent breasts and groaned. Holding them like mounds of buried treasure, he raised her nipples to his mouth and suckled ardently. She arched to him, crying out in soft encouragement as she clutched his head in her hands.

She was so damn responsive, he was dying to see her face when she came. Intending to spill her across the surface of the bed, he tripped her intentionally, only to wind up sprawled on top of her. She'd grabbed him on the way down with a grip that was surprisingly strong.

He had to laugh. No woman had ever managed that before.

"Ellie," he muttered, kissing her neck with deep appreciation. Delving under the elastic of her panties, he found her slick and hot and ready for penetration. With impatience, he dragged the cotton barrier down her hips, put his mouth where his hand had been, and buried his face.

Over the plane of her clenching belly, he watched her as she rocked her hips and moaned. He wallowed in her lushness, saturating himself in her sweetness, her scent. He couldn't say who enjoyed it more—she or he.

A fine sheen of perspiration shone on the underside of her breasts, and he throbbed with enchantment. She was beautiful.

Then he felt her convulse, heard her cry out with such abandon that he almost spilled himself prematurely. As she sighed and went limp, he lunged for the drawer, pulling out a condom and ripping it open with his teeth.

"Smart man," she breathed, watching him through her lashes. "You have no idea how fertile I am."

He sheathed himself ineptly, his hands actually trembling. "Yeah, I'm starting to get that," he said thickly.

She held out her arms to him, and he dove into her, forgetting the light yet again as he drove himself with a groan into her sweet gripping warmth.

This was sex for sanity's sake, he reminded himself, closing his eyes, aware that she was now watching him. The circumstances were desperate. That had to be the reason for these over-the-top sensations.

But not for a second did he think there wouldn't be a price to pay. He'd violated his personal code by sleeping with a single mother, not once but two nights in a row. He would have to pay the piper one day— at least he hoped he would. Because then it would mean that the boys had been found.

He sought to slow the tempo, to give Ellie the reprieve he'd given her last night. But within ten minutes, they lay in a sweaty embrace, their breath still gusting with the ferocity of their mutual climax. Their gazes collided briefly.

Holy shit, Sean thought, his heart still jumping in his chest. *Holy, holy shit. I might never get enough of this.*

His cell phone rang, saving him from having to digest

that disturbing realization. He jumped out of bed and found his phone clipped to his jeans, lying on the floor. "Harlan," he answered breathlessly.

His gaze slid involuntarily to the naked woman sprawled on the bed.

"Butler here. Listen, I ran your conspiracy theory by my supervisor, and he thinks there might be something to it."

"Really?"

Ellie came up on her elbows to regard Sean. His gaze slid to her breasts, and his cock twitched with renewed interest.

"Instead of driving back tonight, why don't you stay put? As soon as I wrap things up here, I'll drive down there and join up with you. Where are you staying?"

Sean hesitated. Maybe it was just the sniper in him, but announcing his location always made him feel like a sitting duck. "We're, uh, we're at the Hyatt," he lied, naming the huge hotel across the street. Of course, if Butler really wanted to find him, he could just trace his credit card.

"The Hyatt," Butler repeated, the scratching of his pen audible through the phone. "I should be down there the day after tomorrow."

"So we're not going to get subpoenaed for staying down here," Sean clarified.

"No, no. I've cleared this with the right people. Let me work on this more, and I'll call you back," he added, ending the call.

Sean looked at Ellie and shrugged. "We're staying," he said.

"Oh," she answered. Then, to his intense gratification,

she held her arms out to him, wordlessly inviting him to be her refuge, her port in the storm.

Hours later, with her head pillowed on Sean's shoulder, Ellie stared into the darkness, listening to the even cadence of his soft snores.

Deep within her being, she was conscious of the fragile shell that held her heart together. She shied away from giving it a name, from facing the possibility that it might one day crack open, causing all the pieces to come tumbling out.

She would only acknowledge this: that her connection with Sean, intensely physical and deeply gratifying, was the only thing keeping her sane right now.

Chapter Nine

✦

"Look, Mama," said Skyler, bending over her mother's shoulder as Matilda Dulay stared sightlessly out the window of her room at Hospice House. "This is your garden journal. Do you remember writing all this?"

Flipping through the pages, Skyler managed to capture her mother's attention with the noise she made. Her mother's deep blue eyes lowered to focus on her own dainty scrawl, and a frown creased her brow as she regarded the drawing of irises made by her own hand ten years ago.

"My garden," she murmured, and Skyler's heart leapt.

"Yes, Mama," she cried, dropping to her knees so she could see the light of recognition in her mother's eyes. "You wrote about every plant and shrub and tree. You loved your garden, didn't you, Mama?"

"Where . . . where did you get this?" Matilda asked, placing a veined hand on the open page.

"You gave it to me," she reminded her mother. "Along with the key to your heart." She held her special pendant up for her mother to see. "Remember?"

The expression on Matilda's once-lovely face was

nothing at all like the look of blank apathy she'd worn with increasing frequency over the years. To Skyler's delight, her mother seemed to be having a lucid moment.

"The key," Matilda murmured, reaching out to rub it between her thumb and forefinger. "Skyler, this is the key to your future."

The sound of her name on her mother's lips brought tears of joy flooding into Skyler's eyes. "Oh, Mama, you remember me today!" she cried, throwing her arms around her mother's frail shoulders. Joy morphed into relief followed by bottomless sorrow that, all too soon, her mother would forget her again. As her mother stroked her hair, murmuring, "There, there," Skyler wept.

Then, realizing she was wasting precious seconds, she dashed the tears from her cheeks to remind her mother, "Not my future, Mama. It's the key to your heart, remember? You gave it to me when I turned sixteen."

A look of alarm crossed Matilda's face. "How old are you now?"

"Twenty-three," Skyler reminded her gently.

Matilda reached for her daughter's left hand, seizing it in a surprisingly firm grasp to examine the gaudy diamond solitaire. "Who are you going to marry?" she demanded with real fear.

Confused by her mother's horror, Skyler sought to soothe her. "It's Ashton Jameson, Mama. You remember Daddy's friend, don't you?" It came as such a relief to share her burden with her mother and know that she was being heard.

"*No.*" A pallor bleached Matilda's face, and she gripped her hand harder. "No, Skyler. You have to save yourself. You cannot end up like me."

"It's okay," Skyler reassured her, frightened by her mother's distress. Pinpricks of alarm stabbed her arms and legs. "I'll be fine."

"Listen to me," Matilda commanded, her quavering voice the first sign that her brief lucidity was beginning to fade. "Use the key," she repeated anxiously.

"I don't understand, Mama," Skyler whispered, certain her brain synapses were starting to misfire. The key was nothing but a pendant. It didn't go to anything.

"Father Joseph knows," her mother added, confirming Skyler's sad conclusions. Father Joseph was a priest at the Cathedral of St. John the Baptist, a long-time friend of her mother's. He made a point to drop by the Hospice House on a regular basis.

"Did he come visit you today?" Skyler asked over the lump of disappointment swelling in her throat.

Her mother didn't answer. Lapsing into a long stare, her gaze strayed past Skyler's shoulder toward the window again.

A tap sounded on the privacy window. Carl, who guided the pompous silver Bentley up the interstate toward a rendezvous point halfway between Savannah and Charleston, spent a flustered moment searching the dashboard display for the switch that lowered the partition between the front and rear seats.

Sweating in his new chauffeur's uniform, he braced himself for a negative comment on his less-than-solid driving skills. Hell, he hadn't even owned, let alone driven, a car this past year, and definitely not a luxury car like this one. He was lucky he still had a license. "Sir?" He craned his neck to see Dulay in the rearview mirror.

The man had just put away his cell phone. His dark eyes snapped with anger as if he'd received some bad news. "Have you been approached by anyone about your sons, Carl?" he demanded peremptorily.

Carl turned hot, then cold. Swallowing a sudden knot in his throat, he wondered how his employer could have discovered so quickly what had happened last night. How much should he say? Or was there any point to hiding the truth when the old man seemed to know everything?

"Y-yes, sir," he admitted, a river of sweat now trickling between his shoulder blades. "My ex-wife tracked me down," he confessed, making no mention of Skyler tricking him. "She asked me if I had anything to do with her boys bein' taken."

"How would your ex-wife know where you are?" Dulay demanded coldly.

"I . . . I don't know, sir," Carl stammered. "Last time I saw her was near a year ago." He'd been drinking at Turley's Show Bar when Ellie had marched right in with all of her brats, demanding money to feed them.

"Bates," Dulay muttered to himself.

"What's that, sir?"

"Never mind. What did you tell her?"

"Nothing." Carl's denial came out on a squeak. "Honest, sir. I . . . I don't know a thing about them."

Dulay's faint smile relieved him immensely. "You just keep singing that tune, Carl," he encouraged. "If you're approached again, by anyone, your answer remains the same. Understood?"

"Yes, sir," Carl breathed. Was that it? Dulay must not

have realized Skyler's involvement, nor was Carl stupid enough to betray her and implicate himself in the process.

"Once the fuss dies down, you may visit your sons," Mr. Dulay added, implying that the boys were, in fact, in his possession, while not telling Carl exactly where. "Until then, I wouldn't want you to have to lie."

"No, sir." That suited Carl just fine. He wasn't in any hurry to see them, anyway. Not that he could envision Ellie ever allowing the fuss to die down. She'd be on a crusade for life, a thorn in Carl's side for years to come. "About my ex-wife, sir," he hedged, wondering how to warn Dulay of her persistence.

"Let your ex-wife be my concern," his employer cut in smoothly, shaking out his newspaper.

"Yes, sir." It sounded like Dulay planned to get rid of Ellie once and for all. He wondered, with only a pinch of regret and a much larger dose of relief, if she was going to spend her life in jail for a crime she'd never dream of committing.

"I'm going out for a while," Sean announced as Ellie ventured from the bathroom, showered and dressed in one of her plain button-up blouses and faded jeans. "Why don't you order some room service and watch TV till I get back?" he suggested.

She drew up short, pinning him with an astute gray gaze. "And what would you be doing that I couldn't go with you?" she demanded.

He prudently skirted the question. "Just trust me, Ellie.

You'll be safer in here than you would with me out on the streets."

"Why, what are you planning?"

"A party," he answered grimly, "with Grimes and company."

Her eyes widened with concern. "What if they hurt you again?" she asked, humbling him unintentionally.

"They won't," he insisted. "This time I'll be ready for them. You, on the other hand, might get hurt—or worse, used as leverage against me. You can't come with me, Ellie. I don't know what's going to happen."

Her mouth pursed into a stubborn knot. "Whose sons were taken?" she demanded. "Yours or mine?"

"Come on, Ellie. You know those boys are like sons to me," he muttered uncomfortably.

"Oh, don't give me that crap. They're my boys, and I'm going to be with you when you find them." She snatched up her card key and stuck it with intent into her back pocket.

Sean blocked her trajectory toward the door. "Look," he said, trying persuasion. "All I'm going to do is parade myself around town in the hopes of drawing out these guys, who obviously know something. Things could get ugly after that."

"I can handle it," she retorted firmly.

"No," he repeated.

She took a threatening step in his direction. It made him lean back, surprised. There weren't many men willing to go nose-to-nose with him, but Ellie was right up in his face, her face flushed pink. "I have been dragged by a car because of these fucking assholes," she said, making his ribs tickle at her use of profanity. "They took my boys from me. Now, what do you think they can do that's worse than that?" she growled.

Visions of carnage flashed through his mind. In his line of work, he'd seen unspeakable things men had done to women. "You'd be surprised," he muttered grimly.

"Then keep me safe," she ordered with simple faith that rocked him. Since when had he earned that kind of trust from her?

"That's what I'm trying to do now, by not letting you come," he pointed out.

"If you leave without me, I'll just head out on my own," she threatened with an obstinate glitter in her eyes.

She was maddening. He wanted to both throttle her and throw his arms around her to shield her from life. "Damn it!" he swore, wishing it didn't have to come to this, and they could just lock themselves in their room and have sex all day. Not only did her tagging along add risk to a potentially dicey situation, but she also distracted the hell out of him. "This is not a good idea," he informed her, conceding defeat. "If you want to come with me, we're going to establish some ground rules."

"Okay," she agreed, instantly amenable.

"First," he said with a meaningful glare, "if we run into our guys, my priority will be to put you somewhere safe. Once I put you there, you stay there. No heroics. No coming to my rescue. I'm good at what I do, and I don't need your help doing it."

Her eyes got a little wider as she presumably pictured him at work.

"Second, if we get separated for any reason, you take public transportation and you get your ass back to this hotel. Then," he said, fishing his wallet from his pocket and thrusting Reno's card at her, "you call Reno." He'd apprised Reno earlier this morning of his suspicions regarding the Centurions' involvement in the kidnapping. Reno had been dubious at first, then thoughtful as Sean supplied his reasons for suspecting them.

"Why not call the police?" Ellie asked, puzzled.

"Because I suspect that half of the police here are Centurions," Sean said shortly.

That gave her pause. She looked at Reno's card and stuck it in her pocket with her card key. "Okay, what else?"

He heaved a sigh as he searched himself. "I guess that's enough for now. Just listen to my directions and follow them, no questions asked. Got it?"

"Yes, sir," she quipped.

"I'm not an officer," he countered, pulling her into a fierce embrace. "And I sure as hell ain't a gentleman," he murmured, nuzzling her neck and squeezing her firm bottom, marveling that his body responded immediately to her scent. "Come on," he growled, shepherding her toward the door. "We won't find the boys any faster by foolin' around."

Their first stop was the open-air shops overlooking Savannah River's bustling port. Recalling the coveralls Grimes and his partner had been wearing the other night at the bar, Sean figured they were dock workers. Most of the boats were loaded and unloaded farther upriver, but if he sat right out in the open at a table by the coffee kiosk, wearing a bright yellow T-shirt, his bald head reflecting the sunlight, he just might be seen. Putting Ellie's back to the kiosk, with the umbrella stand in front of her, he made certain she wasn't so exposed.

With his senses set to high, he counted eighteen clangs of a ship's bell and watched an enormous tanker ship, piled with crates, glide by, most likely en route to the South Seas. A family of tourists from New York City—he could tell by their speech and mannerisms—fawned over the purses and T-shirts for sale in the open stalls.

Raking the faces of people ambling along the ballast-paved street, he saw no sign of Grimes or Little Hitler. His sixth sense told him they weren't here. This place had too much of a family atmosphere.

Sean tossed back his coffee. "Let's take a walk," he suggested, surging to his feet.

Ellie rose immediately, without question. He could tell she was trying to follow his guidelines without fault. For some reason, that made him smile. It couldn't be easy for her.

Cruising past the shops in the renovated warehouses on River Street, they ascended the cobbled hill to Bay Street and pressed into the heart of town on Drayton.

Isaac's had just opened its doors for business. This morning, the pub looked like just another friendly establishment. Its windows sparkled; its tiled floor had been freshly mopped. He felt no qualms about leading Ellie inside.

Four businessmen held an impromptu meeting at one of the tables. One loner sat at the bar's far end, drowning his miseries in morning beer, but otherwise the pub stood empty. The same barkeep who'd been working the other night glanced up at them and went back to hanging goblets on a rack.

"What can I get you?" he asked as Sean gestured for Ellie to join him on the bar stools.

He ordered two iced teas, waited for the crusty older man to slide their glasses over the smooth wooden counter, and then asked, "You remember me from the other night?"

Ellie cautiously stirred her tea.

"Yeah, sure," said the barkeep.

"Remember the guys sitting at the table in the back?"

"Nope," he said.

"Two tough-looking guys," Sean elaborated. "One was wiry with a black mustache; the other was a big, greasy-looking guy with a tattoo on his knuckle. I think his name is Grimes."

Ellie frowned into her tea.

The bartender's flat expressionless eyes told Sean he wouldn't admit to anything. "Sorry, I don't remember." Sticking a toothpick in his mouth, he turned his back on them.

"Of course not," Sean muttered, wondering at the wisdom of reaching over the counter and swinging the man around. He looked like the type to carry a weapon, though, and Ellie was liable to end up getting hurt.

"How about you let them know I'm looking for them?" Sean suggested, slapping a five-dollar bill on the counter. "Come on, hon," he said, urging a quiet Ellie to get up and leave her untouched drink.

As they stepped into the sunshine, Sean cut a look through the window and met the barkeep's narrow-eyed glare. It wouldn't be long before those goons came looking for him, so long as he stayed out in the open. The problem was, that put Ellie squarely in the middle of a fight.

With her hand in Sean's but her thoughts turned inward, Ellie scarcely noticed where Sean was leading her. Something he had said to the barkeep had her thinking of the night her boys were taken and the awful moment the door handle of her car had slipped from her grasp.

She remembered fixing her gaze on the dark mark on the man's left hand, fighting with every ounce of strength to keep it in sight. "Sean!" she cried as her certainty grew, goose bumps sprouting on her skin.

"What?" he asked with a tolerant, sidelong glance.

"That tattoo you mentioned," she began, cautioning herself not to be too hopeful. "Was it, like, right here, on the man's left hand?" She touched the knuckle on her index finger.

Sean stopped abruptly in his tracks. "How'd you know that?"

"Oh, my Lord." She reached for him as the blood seemed to drain from her head. Shock and hope struck her simultaneously, leaving her nearly speechless. "I saw it," she breathed.

Sean turned her to face him. "What do you mean? When?"

"The fat man who dragged me from my car. He had a tattoo right there."

"Are you sure? I've seen the composites. He didn't look like either one of them."

"That's because I never got a good look at his face. All I knew was that he was fat with small eyes. The other guy was strong and burly with acne scars. I got a good look at him."

"Then who's the little guy with the mustache?" Sean inquired.

"I don't know. Maybe he drove the van." It had been pointed out to her later that a third person had to have driven the van.

Sean scrubbed his eyes with frustration. "Why wasn't the tattoo included in the kidnapper's description?" He was clearly irked that he'd been face-to-face with one of the kidnappers and hadn't realized it.

"Until you mentioned a tattoo just now, I thought it was just a stamp like you get at a bar."

"Could you draw it?" he asked.

"I don't know. It was just black lettering of some kind, maybe numbers."

"That's what I saw, too," said Sean, glancing up the street. He patted his pockets. "We need a pen and paper. And I want to look at those composites again."

Peering across the street, Ellie spied a sign that read OLA-WYETH PUBLIC LIBRARY hanging on a building wedged between two shops. "Over there," she said.

Grabbing her hand, he pulled her deftly through moving traffic and to the woodsy-green double doors.

Bells jangled as he swung it open for her. They stepped into a room crammed with shelves and overflowing with books of a bygone era. Dust motes sparkled in the sunlight that sneaked through the blinds in the windows up front, but the rear of the library remained dismally shadowed. A single computer hummed quietly in the corner.

"Can I help you?" An elderly black lady stepped

abruptly from between two racks of books. Her wrinkled face made her look a thousand years old.

"Morning, ma'am," said Sean with a winning smile. "Do you mind if we borrow that computer there?"

Ellie noted the pens and scraps of paper next to it.

"Not at all," said the old woman, beckoning them warmly. "Just don't ask me how it works." She shuffled over to the desk and jotted down the password. "My name's Edith. If you need me for anything, just give me a shout. If it's history you're after, I can lead you straight to a book or journal, but I don't know a thing about the Internet."

"We'll be fine, thank you," Sean promised, pulling up a seat for Ellie so they could sit side by side. He nodded at the pencil and paper. "Draw what you remember," he requested. "I'm going to look up those composites."

Biting her lip in concentration, Ellie drew the general outline of the fat man's tattoo. It had squared-off edges reminiscent of block lettering or numbering, but nothing specific came to mind. Glancing up, she saw that Sean had gone straight to the FBI's official home page and had navigated to a page entitled "Kidnapped/Missing Persons."

As the photographs of Christopher, Caleb, and Colton popped onto the screen, Ellie drew a pained breath. God, how she missed them! Sean groped for her hand and clicked on Christopher's name, taking them to a description of the abduction and the composite sketches of the suspects.

"That one," said Ellie, nodding at the fat man. She glanced at Sean's furrowed brow. "Is it him?"

"I think so," he said with confidence. "The chin's the same. That's about it, though."

"I never got a good look at his face."

"That's okay. You saw his tattoo. Let me see that." He took her rendering of the tattoo, spun it upside down, and smiled grimly. Grabbing the pencil, he began amending it to fit his own recollections. "What about this?" he asked.

As she regarded the drawing, tears of hope flooded her eyes. "That's it."

"We've found the sons of bitches, Ellie," he whispered hoarsely. "This means the boys are probably here!"

With a cry of relief, she threw her arms around his neck. "Thank you!" she cried, giving him all the credit for hounding down the bastards.

He pulled back, catching her face in his hands. "Listen, hon," he urged. "We have to be discreet about this. What if Drake was right? What if Dulay did mastermind the kidnapping?"

Ellie swallowed hard as she searched Sean's worried gaze. Drake had made the Centurions sound so menacing, so well organized, so above the law.

"It's okay," Sean assured her, snatching his cell phone off his hip. "We'll call Butler. We'll get the FBI on it."

As Sean placed a call to Butler, Ellie eyed the composites in a new light. What if the kidnappers were Centurions? What hope did she have that the FBI could get her boys back when it took an undercover investigation to prove their leader's crimes?

"He's not answering," Sean told her with the phone to his ear.

Reading the words "ALSO WANTED FOR QUESTIONING," Ellie scrolled to the bottom of the Web page.

Seeing a photo of herself and of Sean, she gave a strangled cry.

He glanced up and nearly dropped his cell phone. "Holy shit," he exclaimed. At the same moment, Butler's voice mail beeped loudly enough for Ellie to overhear. "Sir, this is Sean Harlan," he rapped out. "The kidnappers are here in Savannah. I've run into at least one of them personally. And I'll bet you my trident they're Centurions, working for Owen Dulay. Maybe you could get down here before tomorrow. And while you're at it, you can take that fucking announcement off the Web site about me and Ellie being wanted for questioning. Call me back," he added angrily.

They both looked up as Edith shuffled down the aisle toward them. "You there," she called, wagging a finger at them, her old voice quavering. "What are you doing?"

Sean came politely to his feet. "Ma'am?"

"What are you doing in here, mentioning that name?"

He blushed at the reprimand. "Which name, ma'am?"

"The Centurions," she whispered with fright.

"Do you know about them?"

"Hush!" she cried, holding out both hands to ward off further words. "Did anyone come in while I was in the back?" she asked.

"No ma'am," Sean assured her.

"Then wait," cautioned the woman as she scurried to the window to snap the blinds fully closed. Bolting the front doors, she flipped a sign over, advertising the library as closed, and circled back to them, her mouth pinched in dread.

Ellie and Sean shared a mystified look.

Edith leaned close, smelling of rosewater, to whisper

in their ears, "One must never mention the Centurions in public. People who do so have a way of ending up dead."

"Sorry," said Sean, darting a bemused look at Ellie.

In the gloomy room, the woman's sunken eyes seemed to have disappeared in her face. "Now," she added, "what is it you were saying about them? Something about a kidnapping?"

Sean nodded at Ellie.

"We think they kidnapped my sons," Ellie admitted, a small part of her still incredulous.

Edith hissed in a breath. "Poor child," she exclaimed, sinking into Sean's empty seat to clasp Ellie with soft, dry hands.

"You're not surprised?" said Sean.

The old woman's face screwed up into a bitter mask. "My father was a Centurion," she admitted darkly. "He was killed for falling in love with a woman who wasn't his wife, a black woman, my mother. Such a crime was unforgivable."

A cold shudder moved up Ellie's spine. How had her boys fallen into the clutches of such a narrow-minded society?

"Is there something you can tell us," Sean prompted, "that would maybe help us find Ellie's sons?"

Edith pressed a gnarled hand to her mouth, as if to stem the flood of secrets she had harbored for decades. But then she removed it. "What can they do to me now?" she reasoned, chuckling at her dark humor. "All my life, I've lived in fear that they would come for us, too, to kill us as they did my father. I'm eighty-eight years old," she reflected with bitter irony. "I've kept quiet for too many years."

"Please," Ellie pleaded, desperate for some insight, some understanding, anything that might be useful in recovering her boys.

"Wait here," the woman decided, pushing painstakingly to her feet. She hobbled toward the back of the library.

Sitting in the seat she'd vacated, Sean gave Ellie a much-needed hug. With her ear to his chest, she could hear his heart pumping hard and swift. Were they really this close yet still this far from finding them?

As Edith returned, Sean released Ellie and she looked up to see Edith extending to them something wrapped in newspaper. "Only a sworn Centurion can own one of these," she divulged, peeling back the paper to show them the slim leather volume inside. "This was my father's. He lived and breathed its instructions and philosophies, but it couldn't keep him from falling in love with Mama. It's the only thing I have left of him. Take it but beware. There are Centurions everywhere—not just in the South. Their network is complex and far-reaching. Keep it hidden," she added, wrapping it up again. "If you're seen on the streets with it, you may soon find yourself in a heap of trouble."

"We won't forget your kindness," Ellie promised.

"I'd rather you did forget it," said Edith honestly. "Be careful," she added, touching Ellie's arm. "And good luck."

To Ellie's sensitive ears, she didn't sound too hopeful of their success.

With the Centurion handbook tucked under his arm, Sean led Ellie back into the blinding sunshine.

* * *

Feeling that time was running out on him, Drake trod the uneven sidewalk, passing the Colonial Park Cemetery and the Cathedral of St. John the Baptist with its massive double spires.

Skyler's absence at the soup line today had left him feeling uneasy. Aside from the Sundays she took off regularly, this was the first day since his arrival at the shelter that she hadn't come to tend the homeless. He left shortly after lunch to look for her, his feet carrying him along the familiar route down Abercorn toward Dulay's mansion on Jones Street.

Time was running out for Skyler also. Wasn't she due to marry at the end of the month?

The sight of a cream-colored Lexus turning the corner up ahead made his heart leap. He was both relieved and pleased to see Skyler at the wheel. Pulling her car along the curb, she lowered the passenger window to greet him. "Hi, Drake."

"Hey," he called back, heading toward her with a grin. Stooping to look through the window, the first thing he noted was her casual attire. Wearing shorts and a T-shirt, she looked young and carefree, the way she was supposed to look. He had to drag his gaze up from her golden toned thighs. "We missed you today," he scolded.

"Sorry. I went to visit my mother, but my father's out of town, so I'm playing hooky from the soup line," she admitted with an unrepentant little smile and a glitter in her eyes.

"Really?" The announcement both intrigued and worried him.

"I'm glad I ran into you," she added, reaching under

her seat. "I wanted to give you this." She handed him a notebook.

"What is it?" He peeked inside, frowning at the sketches of flowers and delicately penned notes.

"My mother's garden journal. I figured you should brush up on your landscaping skills before your interview tomorrow."

He looked at her sharply. "What interview?"

"My father agreed to interview you for the gardening position," she announced rather smugly.

"Oh, man!" he exclaimed, unable to contain his excitement.

"Don't get your hopes up. He doesn't know you very well," she warned.

"This is awesome!" he insisted, taking another peek at the notebook. Every shrub, every flower was named and described in detail. He actually had a shot at getting the job now. She might have just saved his ass without knowing it.

"Mama loved her garden," Skyler reflected, sorrow creeping into her voice. "When she realized she was getting Alzheimer's, she wrote everything down so that someone else could care for it the way she did."

Drake ran a finger over the drawing of an iris. "Thank you," he said sincerely. "I promise to give it right back. What time's the interview?"

"Tomorrow at eleven. Do you know where we live?"

"Yeah," he admitted with a sheepish smile.

"Okay." She sent him a curious look. "Just announce yourself at the front door, and Jakes, the butler, will let you in."

"Will you be there?"

Her mouth drooped abruptly, and she looked away. "No. I've got a fitting in the morning."

He suffered a familiar, overwhelming urge to kiss that frown away. "Where are you headed now?" he asked.

She drew a deep breath and let it out. "Oh, I don't know. The beach?"

He nodded approvingly. "Good. You could use some time to yourself."

She flicked a shy, contemplative glance at him but didn't answer.

"You still going to marry that guy?" he blurted, feeling as tactless as an eighteen-year-old. It maddened him that she was going through such misery.

"I don't know." She shrugged, unable to look at him. "I guess so," she murmured.

According to FBI analysts, the Charleston millionaire Ashton Jameson was fifty years old. Picturing Skyler under his heaving body made Drake want to puke.

"You could cancel," he suggested, trying to keep his tone light. "I mean, hey, we're in the twenty-first century. Arranged marriages aren't hip anymore."

Skyler gnawed at her lower lip. "I have to go," she said, glancing in the rearview mirror.

"Wait." He put his hand firmly on the car door, keeping her there. Her wide blue gaze traveled from his knuckles to his mouth to his eyes. Desire seemed to leap out and grab hold of his throat.

"Let me come with you," he heard himself beg. Then he waited for her answer, the air stripped from his lungs.

"Drake," she whispered, a trace of longing evident in her fearful tone.

"Your dad's out of town, right? He'll never know," he

persisted. He couldn't believe he was soliciting himself so boldly. But an opportunity like this would never come again.

She assessed the area with a fearful sweep of her eyes. "Get in, quick!" she decided unexpectedly.

In a flash, he leapt into the car, tamping down his guilt as Skyler swung into traffic, driving them swiftly toward the Islands Expressway. Yes, he was taking advantage of her misery, but he was desperate to get her to himself. She might know nothing of her father's crimes. The only way to know for certain was to ask her.

Tiffany Hughes balanced her rolling suitcase on one hip as she stuck her key into the lock of her condo door. The damn thing didn't want to go in. With a mutter of annoyance, she tried again, unlocking the door this time, and reached in to flick on a light.

She'd been swinging golf sticks for four days, then staying up late partying with the champions last night. She was sore. She was tired. She wanted nothing more than a hot shower and a long night's rest.

Locking the door behind her, she dragged her suitcase down the tiled hallway to the master suite. She left it right inside the door to unpack tomorrow, stripped in the adjoining bathroom, then got in the shower. Standing under a hot stream, she reveled in the glide of warm water over her aching muscles, her tight scalp.

With the lyrics of a drinking song playing over and over in her head, she stepped from the shower and toweled dry. The open door showed a bedroom standing in darkness. How 'bout that? She'd been so beat, she hadn't even turned on the light.

With a shrug, she turned to the sink to brush her teeth. As she dragged a comb through her damp, dark hair, she softly sang a line from the ditty in her head.

The sight of a middle-aged man stepping out of the shadows changed her song to a startled scream. She whirled, thrusting the comb out to ward him off.

He hushed her with a finger to his mouth. Seeing the latex gloves on his hands, she dragged in a breath to scream again, only he lunged at her. Rough and powerful hands closed over her mouth and nose, closing off her airways. He pulled her by the head into the darkened bedroom.

"We have a potential problem," the Culprit admitted to Owen Dulay.

Coming on the heels of nine rounds of golf with his buddy Ashton Jameson, the news cast a shadow over Owen's sunny mood. "What now?" he growled, jamming his golf club into the bag on the back of the cart and stalking to a distance where his cell-phone conversation could not be overheard.

"The Navy SEAL is putting the pieces together," the Culprit explained. "He identified Grimes as one of the kidnappers, and he insists the Centurions were responsible for the kidnapping. As of yet, he's only mentioned this to the FBI investigator, but if he takes his suspicions beyond the circle, it could spark an inquiry."

"Damn it," Owen swore, reining in his annoyance with a deep breath. "You should never have allowed him to come down here."

"Evidently." The Culprit smirked. "Who knew your man Grimes would be so careless as to show his face in public."

"Enough," Owen cut him off. "I'll have the SEAL brought in. He won't get the chance to talk."

"Are you certain your people can handle him?"

"Don't deign to condescend to me," Owen thundered quietly, turning his back on Ashton's curious scrutiny. "You forget to whom you pledged your service."

"And you forget," countered the Culprit with a dark smile in his voice, "who protects you."

Owen simmered with private rage. "Then do your job," he charged harshly. "With the Navy SEAL out of the way, it shouldn't be all that difficult."

"Consider it done," said the Culprit with disdain.

Stabbing the END button with his thumb, Owen willed his blood pressure to subside. He paid the Culprit phenomenal sums to cover his trail; still, here he was, having to step in and handle matters himself.

Perhaps it was time to cultivate a new ally at the bureau. Power, unchecked, had gone to the Culprit's head. It was time he was reminded who was really in charge.

With a superior smirk, the Culprit slipped his private phone into the lining of his jacket. He leaned back into his creaking leather seat and gazed with relish at the file marked TOP SECRET lying open before him.

The file had been one of many included in a briefing packet from the Undercover Division. While skimming its contents, the Culprit had stumbled onto something that had his blood thrumming with possibility.

The Undercover Division had placed an investigator within Dulay's sphere of operation. It was just a matter of time before they had sufficient evidence to arrest the Centurion.

The Culprit, thanks to the steps he'd taken to remain anonymous, stood in no danger of being implicated in the process. Nor was he sufficiently loyal to warn Dulay of the FBI's scrutiny. The man had condescended to him one too many times.

The Elite, direct descendants of the original one hundred, would reel. Dulay's arrest would be a crippling blow to their unity. It would leave them terrified of government persecution. With just the right timing, the Culprit would approach each one, offering them protection. They would turn to him in gratitude. They would look to him for leadership!

He could feel the power rising up within him.

With a cold, grim smile, he signed the briefing packet, signifying that he'd reviewed it. Owen Dulay was on his way out. There was a new sheriff in town.

Chapter Ten

The sky was a spectrum of violet, indigo, and cobalt melting into black on the elusive horizon. Drake had strolled along the beach next to Skyler for miles, just listening to her voice, admiring the dainty imprints of her feet in the sand, the way her gold ringlets swung about her slender neck. Enchanted, he let her talk, his personal agenda forgotten.

This afternoon, this evening, was for Skyler, who, given the memories and personal musings tumbling from her lips, had craved a listening ear for some time.

Her voice grew husky when she talked of special times with her mother. He realized her childhood had been much like his own. His father, busy and aloof, was a man he'd feared; his mother, friendly and concerned, had been his ally. The same had been true for Skyler, who confessed to wanting to emulate her mother's gracious spirit. "She was so beautiful," she sighed, "inside and out."

So are you, Drake thought, wishing this evening would last forever.

"I know she's still with me, but . . ." She wiped the tear

streaking down her cheek, catching the last suggestion of sunlight. "I miss her so much."

It was not the time to ask if Matilda had kept daily memoirs as well as a garden journal. Skyler needed comforting. He reached for her hand. Startled, she glanced at him with wide eyes but kept her hand nestled in his.

Their fingers folded harmoniously together. Drake's breath shortened; desire tugged at him.

If he wasn't careful, he'd spill out his heart to her and jeopardize everything. He kept his questions focused on Skyler, careful not to mention the parallels in their lives. "Did your mother know your father planned to marry you to Ashton Jameson?"

She came to a startled stop. "You remember his name?" she asked with amazement.

"Yeah, of course." He played it off. "He's the luckiest guy on earth. How could I forget it?"

She looked down and away from him. "You think so?" she asked him sadly.

He pulled her around to face him. "I know so. Skyler, you're incredible. You're beautiful, kind, intelligent— "

"You don't know me," she protested, tugging her hand free to hug herself in misery.

"I do," he insisted.

"No. You want to know why I'm marrying Ashton?" she asked him unexpectedly.

"Why?"

"Because I killed someone."

"What?" He thought he must have heard her wrong.

"It's true." She nodded, her voice fraying with shame. "When I was a freshman in college, I got drunk one night and tried to drive home. Suddenly this man stepped in front of my car, and I hit him. I got out to look, and I realized I'd killed him," she breathed in recollected horror.

Oh, honey. "What did you do?" he asked, picturing her distress.

"I called my father, who called the police," she said with a helpless shrug. "Only, they never arrested me. They said the man was homeless, anyway; no one would miss him. I never even went to court; my father made it all disappear. For the rest of my life, I will owe him for that."

Fucking bastard. "You don't owe him shit," Drake growled.

She shook her head, dismissing his objection as irrelevant. "See, I'm not wonderful. And I won't blame you if you hate me now," she added, the tears in her eyes sparkling in the dark.

"Hate you?" With a groan of self-discovery, Drake realized he was actually perilously close to falling in love with her. "I could never hate you, Skyler." It saddened him that she was still punishing herself. "That's why you work at the shelter," he realized out loud. "You're trying to make up for what you did."

Her face crumpled suddenly, and with an exclamation of dismay, he put his arms around her, delighting in the feel of her smaller frame pressed close to his. They fit perfectly together. The urge to protect her, to whisk her away from her evil father, had him adding gruffly in her ear, "Your father's been blackmailing you, hasn't he? He's fed on your guilt and shame to make you do what he wants. Am I right?"

She nodded, hiccupping back a sob.

"Listen to me," he added, catching her wet face between his hands. "You don't have to marry Jameson. There's got to be another way."

"What way?" she demanded helplessly. "I'm not as brave as you, Drake. I can't just run away. Who would look after my mother?"

The need to tell her who he really was, to promise her shelter under witness protection, trembled on the tip of his tongue. Only, he couldn't be sure whether Skyler's fear of her father outweighed her desire to be free of him. "I don't know," he answered gruffly. "But I'll find out."

She hugged him with what was clearly gratitude. "You're so kind," she breathed, giving him a searching look. "I never knew a man could be so kind."

He knew the exact moment she recollected that he was just an eighteen-year-old runaway with a history of drug abuse. Pulling away from him stiffly, she shook her head, as if to tell herself it wasn't right for her to like him this way. "We'd better head back," she suggested with an awkward smile.

He wished bitterly that he could tell her everything. But it was too soon. "Yeah," he agreed, turning with a grimace toward her car.

To his gratification, she caught his arm up in a friendly manner, a compromise to the hand-holding they had done before.

Perhaps one day soon, he could tell her everything. Right now his priority was to get the gardening position at Dulay's mansion. A job like that would give him access to Dulay's files, allow him to put a tracer on his vehicle, to bug his office, even splice into his private phone line. He couldn't let his impulse to rescue Skyler stand in the way.

*   *   *

" 'The Centurion symbol is that of the griffin, part lion, part eagle,' " Sean read from the handbook as Ellie lay next to him on her stomach, following along. " 'The lion, which represents Centurion strength, forms its base. The eagle's head and wings, a symbol of our nation, sits atop the lion's shoulders, signifying the glorious day when government is ruled by Centurion might.' "

Ellie gave a snort of disbelief.

"It says here, 'Centurions may identify each other by wearing a signet ring stamped with the symbol of the griffin,' " Sean added.

A memory pierced Ellie's consciousness. "Peyton," she breathed, a chill sweeping over her.

"What?" Sean prompted.

"Sergeant Peyton," she repeated. "He had a ring like that."

"Are you sure?"

"Yes, it caught my eye more than once. Oh, Sean," she cried, grasping his muscled forearm to steady herself, her heart beating unevenly. Until that moment, she hadn't fully believed that the Centurions had masterminded the kidnapping. "No wonder Peyton wanted to frame me."

"Who else is a Centurion?" Sean muttered darkly.

Every muscle in Ellie's body tensed. "What if there are Centurions working for the FBI?" she whispered, thinking of their photos and the WANTED message on the FBI Web site.

Sean's cell phone vibrated, preventing him from answering. He glanced at it and grimaced. "Butler's finally calling back," he announced.

Ellie released him with trepidation. Surely Butler

wasn't a Centurion, not when he'd expressed sincere sympathy for her loss. He'd even given them permission to snoop around the city of Savannah looking for Carl.

"Harlan," Sean answered. "It's about time you called back."

"You're not at the Hyatt," Butler accused, ignoring Sean's jibe.

So, the man had finally traced his credit card. "Are you worried?" he needled. "You think we're headed for the Mexican border?"

Butler sighed. "No, Mr. Harlan. I'm concerned for your safety. I've been reading up on these Centurions," he added gravely.

"Well, that makes two of us. Are we both still wanted for questioning or do you believe me now?"

"Look, I'm not responsible for the Web site," Butler retorted. "I apologize if it offends your sensibilities."

Fuck you. Being wanted by the FBI offended his honor, his integrity, everything that went into being a Navy SEAL. "Are you going to arrest Grimes or not?" he countered.

"I'm waiting for warrants."

"Are you aware that Centurions hold meetings every Wednesday evening at the homeless shelter?" Sean inquired.

"No. How'd you find that out?" asked Butler, scratching himself a note.

"I asked around," he lied. In fact, Drake had mentioned it during their little tête-à-tête last night. "It occurred to me that if you get down here tomorrow, maybe you could arrest Grimes, assuming he attends the meeting."

"This is a complex investigation, Mr. Harlan. If we

arrest just one man, it'll tip off the others. We wouldn't want the boys being moved to a new location because we acted too rashly. I'm sure you can appreciate that."

"Yes, sir," Sean muttered, tamping down his impatience.

"I'll be down there tomorrow at noon. We'll talk specifics then. Now, where would be a good place to meet?"

With the hopes of still drawing Grimes and his buddies out into the open, Sean picked a public location. "City Market," he decided, naming the bustling art center four blocks from the waterfront. Butler didn't seem like the type to make a public spectacle. If he wanted to arrest Sean, he'd do it later, not that Sean expected it to come to that.

"City Market at one P.M., then," Butler agreed. "I take it you enjoy playing cat and mouse, Chief," he observed dryly.

"I'm not the one playing games," Sean pointed out. "Take my picture off the Web site, and you'll find me more amenable."

"I'll see what I can do. How's Mrs. Stuart holding up?" asked the agent.

Sean glanced at Ellie, who watched him with a worried crease on her brow. "She's all right," Sean answered, admiration creeping into his voice. "She's anxious for you to nab the bad guys and find her boys," he added meaningfully.

"Tell her I'm doing my best," said Butler. To Sean's keen ears, he sounded stressed and regretful.

"I'll tell her," he promised. "See you tomorrow." Ending the call, he laid the phone on the bureau.

"What'd he say?" Ellie asked, eyeing him hopefully.

"He says he's gonna come down here and kick some Centurion ass," Sean lied, hoping to boost her spirits.

Her grateful semismile told him she could see straight through him. Only with Ellie did he feel that transparent.

The need to hold her and be held in turn had him crawling back onto the bed. He shoved the blasted handbook off the bed, sending it tumbling to the floor, and gathered her in his embrace.

Heaving a long sigh, she laid her head on his chest and closed her eyes.

That's better, thought Sean. But he couldn't shake the uneasy feeling in his gut that things were going to get a lot worse before they got better.

Braiding her hair an hour later in preparation for bed, Ellie regarded her pale, drawn face in the mirror and pondered the likelihood that the boys were here, in Savannah, perhaps dreaming of their mother as they slept.

Passages from the Centurion handbook wafted through her mind, stirring up feelings of disquiet. The secret society had been founded nearly a hundred and fifty years ago. Could it have grown so large that agencies within the government were now controlled by them? If Sergeant Peyton was a Centurion, didn't it stand to follow that there were also lawyers and doctors and lawmakers who owned signet rings and met in halls across the country, preaching sovereignty through unity?

How had Carl, who was lazy and not the least bit politically minded, become part of such an ambitious group? And why would Centurions be willing to break the law for one paltry member, to risk FBI investigation, simply to return Carl's legacy to him? It made no sense.

Clearly there were pieces to this puzzle still missing.

Laying her brush on the marble counter, Ellie heaved a weary sigh. Unanswered questions would probably keep her wide awake the rest of the night.

In the middle of the night, Skyler awoke with a start, her heart thudding. Moonlight pierced the chiffon canopy draped over her bed. Kicking off the sticky sheets, she padded across the carpet to the window that offered a view of the dark, deserted street.

Memories of the evening before filled her with bittersweet longing. Before that precious escape, she had never fully realized how much she stood to lose by marrying Ashton. Not once had she felt desire when holding Ashton's hand. She took no delight in his company, had never stood in awe of his kindness. Yet, a runaway teen had inspired all of those feelings, and having felt such strong attraction, how could she deprive herself of feeling that way ever again?

It was like asking herself to die an emotional death.

With her forehead against the window's cool glass, Skyler fingered the pendant hanging from her neck. Closing her eyes, she recalled the dream that had awakened her. She had dreamed she'd found a box beneath her bed, and the key hanging from her neck had opened it. Inside the box lay a ribbon of paper with a familiar but meaningless message: *Father Joseph knows how much I love you.*

Father Joseph again.

With a small shake of her head, Skyler assured herself

that the dream meant nothing. It was just her mind attempting to connect her mother's disjointed messages, seeking meaning where there was none. Surely that remark about Father Joseph had nothing to do with the key.

And yet, the dream had seemed so real. What if the key did, in fact, open a box?

Goose bumps played chase over Skyler's bare arms. *This is the key to your future,* her mother had said. She hadn't called it the key to her heart. What if the discrepancy had been intended? Or were the words just ramblings of a mind ravaged by disease?

Rubbing the notches of a key worn smooth by age, Skyler determined she would visit Father Joseph tomorrow. It couldn't hurt to go to confession or to seek his counsel. Unlike many religious leaders in Savannah, he was not a Centurion. She need not fear that he'd report her rebellious thoughts to her father.

But would he think it sinful that she would rather run away with an eighteen-year-old than marry a fifty-year-old man?

Owen Dulay reminded Drake of a raptor, complete with a beaklike nose, talons tucked out of sight, and eyes that saw everything. Having heard many a speech delivered by Dulay on Wednesday evenings, Drake knew what the Consul respected: hardworking, closemouthed individuals determined to pull themselves up by their bootstraps.

Drake portrayed himself as exactly that, a young man eager to climb the ranks of the secret society, to pledge allegiance to the Centurion agenda, and to perform whatever ungrateful task he might be called on to do.

"I'm a philanthropic man," Dulay remarked, eyeing Drake across the acre of polished cherrywood that was his desk. "I take pleasure in enriching the lives of those less fortunate, a fellow Centurion, such as yourself."

"Thank you, sir," Drake answered, fighting to keep his incredulity from showing. It was believed the man owned a sweatshop in Vietnam where children were forced to work twelve-hour days for paltry pay, and he had the audacity to call himself philanthropic? "Does this mean I have the job?"

"Not so fast," Dulay cautioned, lifting a lean, manicured finger. "First, we'll take a look at the garden. I'd like to get a feel for your experience."

Thanks to his photographic memory, Drake didn't suffer a moment's worry. "Sure thing," he replied.

Thirty minutes later, Dulay's handshake sealed the hiring process. Drake would show up 6:00 A.M. sharp tomorrow to begin his gardening duties. He would be allotted one of the three bedrooms reserved for staff on the third floor. He promised to keep off the streets and remain in good standing with the brotherhood. The forcefulness of Dulay's grip left his knuckles aching as he headed out the wrought-iron gate.

He couldn't wait to get on his cell phone and call his father with the news. The investigation wasn't over yet. Thanks to Skyler, he'd gotten the big break he was hoping for.

"Let's take a carriage into City Market," Sean suggested, tugging Ellie out of the hotel lobby into the early afternoon heat. He drew her straight toward the horse-drawn buggy waiting at the curb.

Ellie roused from her introspection to send him a searching look. "I thought we were just going to meet the FBI agent."

He had to shake his head at her insightfulness. "You know me too well," he admitted sheepishly.

"You're hoping the kidnappers are watching us, and they'll follow us to City Market."

"Where Butler will be waiting," he admitted.

"Okay." She cast the carriage a considering frown. "Although it makes us a pretty big target if they want to just get rid of us."

"That's why you're sitting behind the driver," he replied, approaching the man to pay him for a ride.

Ellie eyed the seat in question. Sheltered on three sides by the body of the carriage and sitting beneath an awning that provided shade, she'd be far safer than Sean, who no doubt intended to sit out in the open.

A shiver of apprehension rippled through her as Sean helped her climb into the box. Sure enough, he sat opposite her, putting himself in the exposed position, his blue eyes in constant motion. The reminder of his extensive training calmed her nervous jitters. She settled back onto the leather seat, resolved to enjoy her first carriage ride ever.

Sean had a hunch Ellie'd never been in a horse-drawn buggy before. As the two jet-black mares clip-clopped up Bull Street, turning onto Broughton to travel under branches dripping with Spanish moss, it was hard to keep his gaze from straying to the look of novelty on Ellie's face.

The vibration of his cell phone took his gaze briefly off his environment. The caller ID read PRIVATE. With a frown, he answered, aware of Ellie's penetrating look.

"Sean, this is Hannah."

"Yes, ma'am." Surprised to hear from her, he raised the volume to drown out the rumble of the carriage, wondering why she sounded tense.

"Are you aware that Butler's on his way down?"

"Yes, ma'am. We're meeting him downtown at thirteen hundred." He glanced at his watch. It was only 12:30.

"Sean, I'm hearing things that are pretty disturbing to me," Hannah said unexpectedly.

"Like what?" he asked, keeping his tone light for Ellie's sake, sweeping the faces of pedestrians and drivers for the slightest indication of malintent.

"Like the rumor that the casts made from the tracks at Jones Lake State Park match the tread on your truck tires," she replied.

Sean fought to keep his incredulity from showing. "So what? It's probably a common brand of tire."

"So Butler was granted a warrant to search your vehicle, and that search turned up a Gerber blade that had trace DNA of all three boys on it."

His ears started humming. *What the fuck?* "That's impossible," he said, keeping his voice modulated, hiding his sudden deep concern. Ellie was staring at him hard, but she couldn't possibly hear what Hannah was saying to him.

"Did you ever show the boys your knife at any time?" Hannah queried.

"Negative," he replied unequivocally. "I would never have done that." A cold, uncomfortable feeling settled over him, exactly how a sniper felt upon realizing he'd just been spotted. "Hold on," he said to Hannah. "Ellie, duck down," he ordered. As she slunk lower, the color draining from her face, Sean raked the immediate area for a cause, only nothing unusual caught his eye. "You can sit up," he told her.

"Sean, are you there?" asked Hannah.

"Yes, ma'am."

"Do you have someone who can vouch for your where-abouts on Thursday the thirteenth, the night the boys went missing?"

The question actually relieved his anxiety. With Tiffany as his alibi, he had nothing to worry about—well, almost nothing. "I do, actually." He glanced at Ellie uneasily. "Do you need that information now, or . . ." He dreaded having to mention it in front of Ellie, though it was getting to the point where he'd better tell her before she heard it from the wrong source. He sure as hell didn't want her knowing the FBI had so-called evidence against him.

"Just make sure Butler has that information," Hannah advised him. "I know you had nothing to do with the boys' kidnapping, Sean. I'm just concerned by what I'm hearing, that's all."

"Well, I appreciate you giving me a heads-up," he countered, fighting to keep his tone light, disappointed that they were approaching City Market without any sign of being followed.

"No problem. Good luck with Butler. If you're not stricken as a suspect soon, I want you to call me."

"Yes, ma'am," Sean promised. If Butler truly suspected

him of involvement, why would he be going along with Sean's conspiracy theory? Surely the man had spoken to Tiffany Hughes by now.

Hiding his uneasiness behind a grimace, he put his phone away. Ellie's gray gaze remained fixed on his face. "What's going on?" she demanded as their carriage slowed to a stop.

"Just stupid stuff," he insisted. "I'm sure we'll clear it up once Butler gets here." He reached for her hand, helping her to descend. "You see him anywhere?"

Ellie shaded her eyes as she scanned the pedestrian promenade lined with hibiscus planters. "Not yet."

He wondered if now was the best time to tell her about Tiffany—but how? Surely Ellie would rather know he'd been with another woman that night than suffer the least suspicion that he'd been involved with the kidnapping.

Jesus, what sick fucker had come up with that idea? And how the hell had his knife ended up in his truck covered in the boys' DNA?

Reeling at the implications of Hannah's phone call—his career could be doomed if he was arrested—Sean lapsed into silence. He led Ellie to the center of the promenade. Whimsical shops and restaurants offered an array of local wares and Southern fare. He gave the area a 360-degree inspection. No sign of Butler yet. No sign of Grimes and Little Hitler, or even the ugly guy with acne scars.

The late-summer weather had attracted a bevy of tourists. Maybe that was why he felt like he was being watched. People tended to stare at bald, buff guys as if they were inherently dangerous. "We're early," he said, glancing again at his watch.

"You want to sit and wait?" Ellie asked, nodding at a bench in the shade.

Sean wanted to pace. "No. Why don't we window-shop?"

She gave a careless shrug, letting him lead her to one side of the promenade. The smell of grilled seafood poured through the open doors of a restaurant. The glaring sun made Sean sweat as he fretted over how to broach the subject of Tiffany Hughes. He couldn't understand why Ellie's opinion of him mattered so much when she was just one more woman in a line of many.

He felt distinctly off balance, like a rug was being yanked out from under his feet. The displays behind the windows of ceramic art and beaded jewelry blurred indistinctly as he cut constant glances over his shoulder.

Ellie shifted closer, offering him a light and comforting touch. Just then, a familiar silhouette darted through Sean's peripheral vision. He whipped his head around in time to see Little Hitler disappear into a jewelry shop.

Adrenaline jumped into Sean's bloodstream. Son of a bitch, how'd that man get so close without Sean seeing him?

With sweat beading his brow, he hustled Ellie into the next shop over, Savannah's Candy Kitchen. The scent of pralines, fudge, and saltwater taffy sweetened the air-conditioned environment. She cast him a questioning look as he all but dragged her into the back of the store, into a separate room where custard stood in a multicolored display. "Here, buy yourself some custard," he said, pushing the change from their carriage ride into her hand, "and stay here at one of these back tables."

Ellie blanched. "Who did you see?" she demanded.

"Grimes's companion, the little guy. He's following us. I need to grab him. Then we wait for Butler."

"What do I do?" she asked, looking eager to help.

He broke into a cold sweat just thinking of her getting in the way. "Stay here," he grated firmly. "Don't leave this shop until I come and get you. If you're approached by anyone, start screaming. Do *not* let them take you anywhere."

His heavy-handed tone had her regarding him oddly.

"I'm sorry," he apologized, giving her lips a quick kiss.

"Be careful!" she called as he wheeled away.

Stalking back to the adjoining room, Sean noted an exit out the back and slipped through it. If he moved fast enough, he could sneak up on Little Hitler when the man went in the front door after them.

Rounding the building, Sean snuck a peek around the corner. Sure enough, there stood his quarry, peering through the panes of the candy shop door, about to pull it open. Despite the summery heat, he wore a jacket and was reaching into it.

"Hey!" Sean called, one hand on his own weapon, holstered at the small of his back. "You lookin' for me, pal?" he demanded.

The suspect glanced at him, smirked, and whirled away. To Sean's confusion, he took off running, scattering pedestrians as he cut a diagonal path toward Congress Street.

"Shit!" Sean swore, undecided on whether or not to go after him. It could just be a ploy to lure Sean from Ellie so that his partner could go after her.

On the other hand, he couldn't afford to let the kidnapper get away, not with Butler due to show up any minute. The man had to know where Ellie's boys were, or at least where he'd helped deliver them. That fact more than any other determined his decision.

Chapter Eleven

His mind made up, Sean dashed after Little Hitler. Skirting crowds of milling tourists and hibiscus planters, he managed to close the gap between them. But then the man darted around the corner at the Signature Arts Gallery, disappearing from sight.

Loath to lose him, Sean burst into a sprint. Rounding the corner at full speed, he plowed into an old man walking his Chihuahua. The man gave a strangled cry as Sean threw his arms around him. Twisting through the air to keep them from hitting the sidewalk, they crashed into the building's brick wall. With a yip and a growl, the dog sank his teeth into Sean's heel.

"Sir, are you okay?" Sean asked, setting the man on his feet as he attempted to shake the dog loose. *Ouch!*

"I . . . I don't know," said the man, quite obviously shaken.

"I'm so sorry," Sean apologized, glancing up the street in time to see the wiry man jump into a Buick and take off. The driver might have been the third kidnapper, the scar-faced one. He thought he saw Grimes in the back seat. *Son of a bitch,* Sean inwardly raged. At least they weren't stalking Ellie while his back was turned, but damn it, they'd gotten away.

"You sure you're not hurt?" he asked the geriatric.

Speaking of hurt, the dog would not let go.

"I don't think so," the man relented, straightening his jacket, patting himself down. At last he noticed his growling mutt. "Cisco, let go," he commanded, and the dog released him.

"I'm really sorry," Sean repeated.

"Sir, do you have a complaint against this man?" chimed in a stranger.

Sean had seen the blue uniforms out of the corner of his eye when he'd first started giving chase. *Aw, hell,* he thought.

Setting his jaw, he turned and slowly faced the two police officers now standing behind him, both in a defensive stance, one with a hand already on the butt of his semiautomatic. *Double hell,* Sean thought. He raked the faces of spectators gathering, praying for Butler to step forward and shoo the cops away, only he didn't.

Then, instead of answering the policeman's question, the old man ducked his head and shuffled to one side, dragging Cisco with him. *What the fuck?*

"Sir, let me see some ID," the older cop demanded of Sean, his eyes hard and focused as they zeroed in on him.

Sean expected them to protest the old man's leaving, but they let him go, a circumstance that raised an immediate red flag.

He wordlessly handed the officer his military ID, keeping his sudden consternation to himself, his mouth shut.

He heard Ellie's approach before he saw her. *Go back,* he willed, sending her a psychic message to turn and walk away. Of course, she didn't.

"What's going on?" she asked, sidling up to him, a cup of lemon custard in her hand.

"I told you to stay put," he growled, letting his frustration show.

"But I saw the police head this way," she protested. "I figured they were arresting the kidnapper."

"He got away," Sean admitted shortly.

The officers were eyeing Ellie in a way that raised Sean's hackles. Every instinct told him both men already knew who they were.

"Ellie Stuart?" asked the older officer, confirming Sean's intuition.

She paled, flicking a wide-eyed look at Sean and said, "Yes?"

"And Sean Harlan," he said, reading Sean's name off his ID. "You're both wanted for questioning by the FBI," the man announced in a dry, emotionless voice. "Sir, I have to ask you to step aside, turn around, and put your hands against the wall."

With a shake of his head, Sean did as he was told, kicking himself for what he knew was bound to happen. They'd search him and find his gun, and wouldn't that be a lovely start to this clusterfuck?

"Ma'am, you, too," the officer barked, causing Sean to turn his head and glare at him. The cup of custard fell from her hand, hitting the sidewalk and splattering.

"It's all right, hon," Sean soothed as she turned and splayed her hands against the wall beside him, her breathing fast and shallow. All around them, people were murmuring and taking notice. Ellie had turned as pale as a sheet. He wanted to reassure her that once Butler showed up, everything would be all right. Where was the son of a bitch?

"Are they arresting us?" she whispered.

"Just do what they say," Sean advised.

"Quiet," barked the older cop as he stepped close to pat them down. "No talking."

Sean suffered a rough, thorough search, cursing inwardly as the officer probed his pockets, taking his wallet, his cell phone, his car keys, and finally, noting the holster at the small of his back, confiscating his Glock.

"You got a license to carry a concealed weapon, sir?" asked the man, letting it dangle dramatically from his finger as the crowd gasped and drew back.

Sean ground his molars together. "Only in the state of Virginia," he conceded.

"Well, seein' as how Georgia doesn't have reciprocity with Virginia, that would make it illegal to carry one here, wouldn't it?" the officer pointed out.

Sean didn't answer. He glared at the second cop, who was frisking Ellie. "Take it easy," he gritted, offended by the sight of another man's hands on her body, especially hands that were rough and uncaring.

"There's no call to treat us like criminals," Ellie insisted. "All we're doing is trying to find the men who took my boys—"

"Ma'am, why don't you save it for the FBI?" the cop cut her off coldly.

"We're supposed to be meeting Special Agent Butler of the FBI right now," Sean grated. "One P.M. in City Market."

Ignoring him, the officer snapped handcuffs on Sean's wrists, setting them intentionally tight. He did the same to Ellie. Pulling them both around, he ordered them to march toward City Market's far end, where a squad car sat parked at the curb. Sean searched the area futilely for any sign of Butler.

Cuffed and humiliated, Ellie walked with her back straight, her chin in the air.

"Hey, that's the lady we saw on the news," came a distinct comment from the crowd. "I bet you she killed her kids."

"Easy, Ellie," Sean advised, seeing her eyes flash, her head turn. His own ears burned with fury at the unfeeling remark. He sent the kid who said it a steely-eyed glare.

Butler, if he was anywhere about, did not step forward.

As Sean and Ellie were stuffed into the backseat of the cruiser, Sean murmured reassurances he didn't fully believe. Hannah's concerns were evidently warranted. Somewhere along the line, the disturbingly false evidence had convinced Butler not to show up after all.

A cold, uneasy feeling settled in Sean's stomach. He'd broken the law by carrying his gun out of state. Being in the Navy, that meant the Uniform Code of Military Justice was also going to get involved, which wouldn't look good on his record. Lieutenant Commander Montgomery's admonishment to keep personal ties from interfering with professional obligations had just been blown to hell and back.

*   *   *

Ellie's stomach hurt. Wedged in a cage of Lexan glass in the rear of a squad car, she tried to get comfortable on the slippery plastic seat, but with her hands cuffed behind her, that was impossible.

"I'm scared," she admitted as the policemen got into the front of the cruiser. They pulled out into traffic, spectators gaping after them.

Sean's sidelong glance was both comforting and regretful. "It'll be all right, Ellie. Don't forget, we've got good people on our side."

"How could anyone think I killed my own children?" she cried, the boy's accusation stinging her like salt poured into an open wound.

"Just stay calm, hon," he reasoned, grimacing as he adjusted his shoulders.

"What happened?" she asked. One minute she'd been paying for her custard, peering out into the main room for signs of the kidnappers, when she saw Sean go running past the store. A minute after that, two uniformed officers had followed him. She'd thought for sure they were coming to Sean's rescue, at the behest of Butler.

"Some old man and his little dog stepped in my way. The kidnapper jumped into a car and took off."

He looked so suddenly grim and thoughtful that Ellie knew a terrible thought had just occurred to him.

"What?" she prompted, but he merely gritted his teeth and shook his head.

Fear encased her heart in ice. What wasn't Sean telling her? It had to be something unspeakable.

His blue gaze slid her way, and catching the fearful look on her face, he summoned a smile and even leaned over to put a sweet, swift kiss on her cheek. "I'm sorry, hon," he rasped. "This should never have happened. Especially not to you."

Touched by his apology, she drew a shaky breath. "I don't know if I can stand to be questioned again," she admitted, dreading the hours to come.

"I'll be with you this time," he comforted.

Tears of relief mingled with tears of uncertainty. She slid closer to him, taking comfort from his solid presence.

They fell silent as the cruiser took them through town, right past the homeless shelter with the twin griffins grinning down at them from atop their pillars at the gate.

"Ellie, I've gotta tell you something," Sean suddenly admitted.

She sensed his reluctance immediately. His news couldn't be good. "Tell me what?"

"It's about where I was when the boys were taken, why Solomon couldn't get a hold of me," he added roughly.

Ellie drew a deep breath and held it. She'd wondered about his unwillingness to talk about that night.

"I took a short leave to unwind for a couple of days. I tend to ignore my phone when I do that. I don't watch the news or listen to the radio, either."

She slowly exhaled. That didn't sound so bad. "Where'd you go?" she asked, picturing him fishing or camping, generally relaxing.

He stared straight ahead, avoiding her gaze. "I went to stay with a friend. A woman," he added flatly. "I've known her for a long time."

It took a full second to process just what he was telling her, but when she did, she pulled away, just then realizing how much she'd come to rely on him.

So, while she'd been fighting with every ounce of strength to keep two strangers from abducting her boys, Sean had been getting off with some woman he'd apparently known for years. . . . Sean had a lover?

She couldn't speak. The thought of Sean doing with another woman what they'd done together for the past few nights stripped the air from her lungs. Unbidden, illicit images flashed in her mind, feeding her disillusionment, her sense of betrayal.

"Look, I'm sorry," he muttered, his blue eyes convincingly regretful. "We weren't . . . we hadn't . . . it was just . . . Hell, forget it; it doesn't matter. I just wish you didn't have to find out. At least not like this."

"It's not your fault," she insisted shortly. "You don't have to explain yourself."

It was her fault. She should never have slept with him in the first place—not even to fill the yawning emptiness within her. She'd forbidden herself to rely on a man for anything, and that included her sanity. This was what she got for letting her guard down. She deserved a bitter dose of reality.

Refusing to reveal the pain pressuring her chest, Ellie focused on the scratches in the Lexan glass in front of her. In the grand scheme of things, Sean's sleeping with another woman counted for little compared to her fears that her boys might never come home—or that she might find herself in jail for a crime she hadn't committed. She'd gladly give him to the first woman who'd take him if it meant she could have her boys back. She'd do well to remember that.

As the squad car pulled into a parking lot behind an older brick institution, Ellie focused on the difficulties ahead of her. She swallowed against the dryness in her throat.

Now the nightmare would begin all over again.

As they were pulled from opposite sides of the car and herded toward a back door, she cast a harried glance at Sean. Half a dozen squad cars assured her they'd arrived at a station of sorts, but it seemed too small to be the sheriff's office.

Manhandled up a set of steps to the second story, they were thrust into a quiet hallway and led to a closed office door. One of the officers gave a knock.

"Come," said a nondescript voice.

The door swung open on a nondescript office space. A man in a Navy blue suit rose from the laptop he'd been typing on and turned to greet them. With a gasp, Ellie recognized Special Agent Butler.

"Thank you, Officers," he said to the police. "I'll take her from here," he added.

"What the hell is going on?" Sean interrupted. "You said you'd meet us down in City Market."

Butler sent Sean a shrug that was chillingly apathetic. "Change in plans," he said simply. With a flick of his fingers, he gestured for the officers to take him out.

Only Sean wouldn't budge. "I am not leaving Ellie," he insisted. "You are not going to question her and intimidate her without me here."

"I'm sure she appreciates your loyalty, Mr. Harlan," Butler drolly replied. "But it really would be better for her to dissociate from you."

"Look, if you're talking about the so-called evidence against me, Hannah Lindstrom told me all about it," Sean snapped. "It's bullshit. There's no way I was involved in the kidnapping. You have to know that. I gave you my alibi's number."

"Your alibi hasn't returned my call, Mr. Harlan," the agent answered with forced patience. "You're under arrest for carrying a concealed weapon without a permit. That's it, for now. I won't discuss impending charges for abduction and murder."

"What!" Ellie gasped, regarding the agent in disbelief. "We told you, the Centurions kidnapped my sons so their father would have his legacy. You said you believed us!"

Regarding her with grim sympathy, Butler gestured again for the officers to take Sean out. "Take him to Central Booking."

"You're making the biggest fucking mistake of your life, Butler," Sean gritted, resisting long enough to add intensely, "Don't say a word to him, Ellie. Call Reno Silverman. He'll know what to do."

"Wait!" Ellie cried, her knees wobbling with fright. "I don't understand what's happening." But it was too late. Sean was gone, and the door thumped shut, leaving her alone with a man she'd thought was an ally. How could he have done this to them?

"Have a seat, Mrs. Stuart," he said in a distinctly warmer voice.

"I don't want to sit," Ellie snarled, suspicious of the benign expression now on his face. "I have nothing to say to you. How dare you turn the tables on us! You should be ashamed of yourself for accusing Sean of harming my sons. He's done nothing but go far out of his way to help me!"

Butler took a long, measuring look at her. With a sigh and a shake of his head, he said regretfully, "Perhaps I should make you aware of the evidence against him, Mrs. Stuart. The tire tracks of the second vehicle at Jones Lake State Park match the tread on Mr. Harlan's truck tires. When we searched his truck, we found a knife with trace DNA of your children all over it."

The room seemed to slowly turn. "You mean blood?" she whispered. Her own blood rushed from her head, leaving her dizzy. She sank into the chair Butler had indicated earlier.

He shrugged. "The knife had been wiped down, so trace DNA was all that was left."

For one brief second, Ellie allowed herself to consider the possibility of Sean's guilt. Her thoughts returned to the conversation they'd had the night he'd wrestled open her electric panel. *Look, it isn't you,* he'd said. *I just don't date women with kids.*

No. Impossible. The Sean she'd come to know and cherish might be a womanizer, but he most certainly wasn't a murderer. She knew him well enough now to be certain of that.

"You're lying," Ellie accused, her voice fraying as she attacked him verbally. "Sean wouldn't harm a hair on my boys' heads. He adores them!"

"The same way you adore them?" Butler asked, regarding her closely.

The question rendered her speechless for a moment. "I'm their mother. Of course I would love them more. But he's . . . he's been like an uncle to them."

Stepping toward his desk, the agent plucked up a small pile of papers and held them under her nose. "Perhaps you've forgotten these e-mails you sent to Mr. Harlan while he was stationed in Afghanistan."

She didn't intend to say another word, not when Sean had warned her to keep quiet, but the agent made no sense. "I never wrote him any e-mails," she retorted. "I don't even own a computer."

"You have access to computers at your college library," he reminded her mildly. "You created an e-mail account with EarthLink on August twenty-seventh of last year," he added.

"For my English class," she agreed, thinking back to the previous semester. "My professor wanted us to e-mail our essays rather than hand them in."

Butler nodded patiently. "These were among the e-mails in your Sent box. "Perhaps if you read them, you'll remember."

Baffled, knowing full well she'd never sent Scan any e-mails, Ellie glanced down to read.

Dear Sean,
    There are just weeks left now till your return, and not a day has gone by that I haven't dreamed of our future together.

"I never wrote these words!" she exclaimed with certainty.

Butler appeared perplexed. "Perhaps you've just forgotten. Read the next e-mail," he invited, shuffling the pages.

With great reluctance, she looked at the second e-mail. The words leaping off the page turned her cold with their implication.

If only I didn't have three mouths to feed. I work all night and day, and there's never enough to go around. Sometimes I just don't want to be a mother anymore. It's just too hard to do it alone. Life would be so good if it were just the two of us.

"No!" Ellie stated loudly, shooting to her feet in outrage. "I never wrote these e-mails, and you know it!" With a violent twist of her shoulder, she knocked the pages from his hand and into the air, where they rocked gently to the floor in the now-silent room.

Too late, she realized she hadn't taken Sean's advice, and now this man had her twisted into knots. With a supreme effort, Ellie dragged in several calming breaths, clamped her jaw shut, and sat back down, her heart thumping heavily.

Butler seemed deeply troubled by her assertion of innocence. Picking up the papers one by one, he laid them back on his desk, then stroked his chin and paced the room. "I don't know if you've considered this, Mrs. Stuart," he said gravely. "But perhaps your SEAL friend is making sure that you go down with him. I hope you won't let that happen," he added with grave sincerity. "We can clear any suspicion regarding your participation in this crime with a simple test, a polygraph, which, if you pass, will eliminate you as a suspect once and for all. Then I can focus all my attention on who really made your boys disappear."

Tears of helpless confusion swarmed Ellie's eyes, blurring her vision. Her muddled thoughts were no clearer.

How could Butler be so certain Sean had murdered her sons? She'd relied on Sean for the roof over their heads, for her sanity. She'd trusted him alone with her boys too many times to count. Could she have been so blinded by his appeal that she'd failed to see the monster within him?

No, it couldn't be. She knew Sean—every inch of his powerful and sexy body, his humorous and caring soul. And yet, he was a sniper for his SEAL team. Killing was his job, and she knew by the respect Solomon gave him that he was good at it, remorseless and deadly accurate.

What if her judgment had failed her as it had eleven years ago when she'd thought Carl was the man of her dreams?

Squeezing her eyes shut, shaking her head in helpless confusion, Ellie was certain of only one thing: her innocence. And here Mr. Butler was offering her the opportunity to prove it, immediately, without a lawyer's fee. He couldn't make the polygraph test show that she was guilty, so what was the harm? "I'll take it," she agreed on a choked whisper.

Butler had kept respectfully quiet while she made up her mind. "Let me uncuff you, Mrs. Stuart," he offered gently. "And then I'll call your lawyer for you."

Alone in the back of the cruiser, supposedly on his way to jail, Sean shook off the remaining effects of having been hit with a Taser. No sooner had he stooped to get in the car than one of the cops had pegged him in the small of his back. Fifty thousand volts of electricity had seared Sean's spine and convulsed his muscles. *Sons of bitches!* he'd thought as they'd closed the door on him, chuckling at his helplessness.

With the top of his head and his extremities still tingling, Sean pulled himself up into a sitting position and glared at the scumbags now escorting him to jail. *That was so unfucking necessary,* he thought, simmering with fury. He sure as hell planned to pay them back one day. As soon as they got to jail, he'd call Reno, whom Ellie ought to have gotten hold of by now. Reno would have this crazy misunderstanding sorted out by the end of the day.

In the meantime, poor Ellie.

Sean had promised he'd be with her this time as she was being questioned. But, no, they'd had to cart him off to jail on concealed weapons charges, while implying he was guilty of murdering her sons.

Christ, he hoped Ellie didn't believe them.

Fighting a sudden headache and blinking against the bright sun, Sean peered outside the windows. The cruiser had turned east, onto the Islands Expressway on-ramp. Was this the way to jail?

Recalling the events leading up to this moment, Sean realized that every step had to have been orchestrated: first the kidnappers had lured Sean into a trap. Even the old man had played a part. They were probably all Centurions, members of the brotherhood.

Butler, too? Surely the FBI was thorough in screening their agents, weeding out those with affiliations to secret organizations, especially ones with ties to the mob. If Butler wasn't one of them, he'd realize his mistake the minute Tiffany returned his call. What was taking her so long? One sentence from her and Butler would see there was no way Sean could have been at Jones Lake State Park the night the boys were abducted. Aside from being fined for carrying his gun out of state, he'd be off the hook despite the odd circumstance about his knife and the boys' DNA.

With a deep, calming breath, he closed his eyes and relaxed his shoulders, hoping to alleviate the discomfort now wicking up his arms. Goddamn, the cuffs were tight!

Opening his eyes again, he caught sight of water, winking behind a screen of marsh grass to his left. Other than an occasional building, there wasn't much else on this stretch of highway bearing them toward the ocean. The county jail was a ways out of town, apparently.

Ten minutes later, the cruiser exited the expressway. Sean watched alertly as they turned onto a two-lane road that crossed a low-lying area surrounded by marsh. The instinct for danger had him sitting up straighter.

Hold on, now. It didn't make sense to build a jail near water, especially not in a hurricane-ridden state like Georgia. Imagine evacuating hundreds of dangerous inmates every time a hurricane swept toward shore.

Glancing at the officers up front, Sean tried to guess their intentions. The cruiser turned onto a gravel drive leading to an old marina consisting of a rusting boathouse and several listing piers. An old fishing vessel bobbed at one pier, manned by two fishermen who seemed to be waiting for them.

Sean couldn't think of a single viable reason for the cops to bring him here. His heart started thumping. Adrenaline spilled into his bloodstream.

Leaving him locked in the cruiser, the officers walked to the pier to confer with the fishermen. Then with expressions of malicious anticipation, they headed back to collect him, confirming Sean's suspicions.

He tensed for action. The second his door swung open, he exploded out of it, frustrating their attempt to grab him.

"Halt!" the men yelled as Sean sprinted toward the safety of the sand dunes, running in a zigzag pattern in case they decided to shoot.

Which they did. Bullets pelted the sandy ground at his feet, lending him speed. A third bullet whizzed by his shoulder, prompting him to break left. He had just reached a mound of sand, intending to throw himself over it when—*bam*—he got tagged on the side of the head, hard enough to send him reeling.

Darkness closed in on all sides.

Chapter Twelve

✦

Owen Dulay reached eagerly for the ringing phone. He'd been expecting this call from the Culprit since Bates advised him earlier that the mission was accomplished. The Navy SEAL had fallen for the ploy, and both he and Ellie Stuart were now in police custody. Provided they hadn't convinced anyone else of Centurion involvement, they'd no longer be a source of concern.

"What song does the mockingbird sing?"

The Culprit's voice held a chilling note that put Dulay immediately on edge. What made the man sound so arrogant?

Countering with the expected reply, he asked, "What do you have for me?"

"The Navy SEAL has been silenced. He's no longer a threat."

"Excellent. Has the press been informed that he eluded officers on his way to jail?"

"Of course. That was an ingenious solution." The Culprit's praise surprised Owen. Perhaps the man recognized his superior intellect after all. "Not only will the public be convinced of his guilt, but it also saves us the necessity of going to trial and risking outside scrutiny."

"Where are we with the woman?" Owen asked, eager to sink the final nail in Ellie Stuart's coffin.

"Her polygraph results were inconclusive."

"What does that mean?"

"It means we'd have to amass more evidence than we presently have if we hope to convict her."

"But you can do that," Owen insisted. "You've done so in the past."

"I would say there's no need to convict her," the Culprit smoothly replied.

"How so?" Owen demanded, glancing through his study window where his new gardener pruned the climbing roses.

"Only in a courtroom does she pose a threat to us."

"Explain," Owen demanded.

"She's a white-trash girl from Mississippi," said the Culprit with contempt. "What's she going to do without her boyfriend to help? She has no money. She'll get nowhere appealing to state or federal law enforcement, who will, at the very least, consider her guilty of convincing her lover to kill her sons. On the other hand, if she's brought to trial and given a court-appointed attorney, she'd have the chance to defend herself, to imply Centurion involvement. And though she might not be able to prove it, someone somewhere might believe her. I say we're better off releasing her. Who's to say some accident won't befall her later," he added meaningfully.

Owen had to admit, the Culprit might be right. Why tempt fate in a trial when the woman could be quietly killed at a later time?

"Be sure to advise the media of her release, then," he instructed. "Let them know the results of her polygraph were inconclusive. That ought to convict her in the public eye."

"Indeed," the Culprit agreed, his tone now condescending.

With a shudder of dislike, Owen dropped the receiver into its cradle, severing the call. Resolved to replace the man in the not-so-distant future, he rose from his leatherback chair to open the cabinet that housed his media center. He programmed his computer to record the evening news, then retreated to his bedchamber. It was time to dress for an evening function at city hall. He had more important things to do than fret over the likes of Ellie Stuart.

"Thank you for your cooperation, Mrs. Stuart. You are free to go."

The sweat on Ellie's palms dried abruptly. "I'm sorry?" she asked, confused, suspicious that Butler was simply toying with her. An hour ago, he'd been shaking his head at the algorithmic charts on his laptop, leaving her to think that she had miserably failed the polygraph administered by a bespectacled examiner.

"The results were inconclusive," he stated with a magnanimous shrug. "You will not be arrested at this time. There's no need to call your lawyer after all."

Returning to the door he'd just reentered seconds ago after leaving to confer with his boss, he gestured for Ellie to leave.

Cautious relief washed through her, draining the strength from her limbs as she pushed to her feet. "What about Sean?" she asked, balking at the thought of being released alone.

"Ah, well, that's a different story," said Butler, his hand on the doorknob. "I'm afraid there's been an incident with Mr. Harlan," he admitted with a troubled look.

"Incident?" Ellie drew up short. Her cheeks turned cold.

"En route to jail, Mr. Harlan escaped his police escorts," Butler solemnly announced. "Needless to say, there is now a tremendous effort under way to recapture him."

Ellie just looked at him. "Why would he do that?" she demanded, not believing him. Sean had been understandably frustrated when they carted him away, but his advice to her earlier had been to cooperate. He'd been certain that the testimony of his alibi would resolve the issue of his guilt.

"The evidence against him is overwhelming, Mrs. Stuart," Butler gently explained. "I cannot stress this enough: If he tries to get in touch with you, you must contact me right away. I would hate to see you drawn into this any more than you already have been."

The thought of Sean contacting her filled Ellie with mixed hope and fear. On the one hand, Butler had planted tiny seeds of doubt in the soil of her mind. On the other hand, without Sean, she had no idea what to do next in the quest to get her boys back.

Keeping her thoughts to herself, she firmed her lips and brushed past him as he pulled open the door.

"Good luck, Mrs. Stuart," he called with what sounded like sincere concern.

Shaking her head, Ellie stumbled blindly down the hall

toward the stairs. How could he be so certain of Sean's guilt when every bone in her body screamed that he was innocent? Her footsteps echoed loudly in the stairwell as she fled down the steps toward the exit. By the time she burst through the door, the lens of confusion had fallen from her eyes. She exited the building with indignant certainty.

There was no way on earth Sean had murdered her three sons, just as there was no way she'd written those awful e-mails. He'd been framed—they'd both been framed. Yet for some strange reason, the law was letting her go.

Or was it the Centurions who were letting her go?

Was there any difference?

Edith's warning echoed in her mind, chasing a chill down Ellie's spine. *There are Centurions everywhere— not just in the South. Their network is complex and far-reaching.* And wasn't that the truth. She'd just witnessed firsthand how manipulative and convincing they could be.

Reeling with fright, stricken with vulnerability, Ellie tottered down the stoop into the sultry heat of early evening. A mockingbird twittered with incongruous joy in the limbs of a magnolia tree.

Now what? She had nothing on her person to aid her circumstances—no money, no car keys, no cell phone. The police had confiscated all of Sean's goods.

Feeling in her back pocket, she found the card key to her hotel room, along with Reno's card, both overlooked earlier by the officer who'd frisked her. Thank God she had somewhere to go, someone to call, but the hotel wasn't blocks away. She'd have to walk miles to get there.

As she stepped onto the sidewalk determining which

direction to take, a group of well-dressed individuals standing at the corner caught sight of her. "There she is!" cried one of them, and suddenly Ellie realized the media had caught wind of her release and were looking for a statement.

"Ma'am, can we ask you some questions?" called a heavily made-up woman trotting up the sidewalk to confront her, a mike in her hands and a cameraman on her heels.

Ellie drew back warily. She was tempted to turn tail and flee, only what message would that send to the Centurions? Ellie Stuart was no coward, and now that she'd realized the measures they'd taken to cover up their crimes, she was more determined than ever to find her boys.

She held her ground, planting her heels and raising her chin to meet the cameras thrust in her face as the reporters thronged around her.

"Miz Stuart, we understand your boyfriend was arrested today on charges of carrying a concealed weapon. Were you with him when he was arrested?"

Unable to deny that Sean was her boyfriend, Ellie cleared her throat to give her voice more strength. "Yes. Yes, I was."

"Are you aware that he has eluded the police and that there's a statewide manhunt for him?"

"That's what the police say," Ellie countered.

The journalist faltered at Ellie's unexpected retort, and another one, a man, cut in, thrusting his mike toward her. "Is it true that you failed a polygraph concerning the whereabouts of your boys, Miz Stuart?"

"Failed?" Ellie took affront to the word. "The results were inconclusive."

"Isn't that the same thing?"

"No, it isn't. I wouldn't have been released if I'd failed the test," she pointed out.

"Do you believe Mr. Harlan killed your sons, Miz Stuart?" asked the woman, elbowing her competitor out of the way.

"Sean Harlan would never have killed my sons," Ellie retorted definitively. "And my sons aren't dead. They were brought to Savannah by Centurions so that my ex-husband could secure his legacy." Righteous anger propelled the words from her mouth.

"The Centurions are a charitable organization," commented one incredulous journalist. "Are you accusing them of kidnapping your sons?" The others looked intrigued.

With the fatalistic certainty that she was risking her own life, Ellie answered, "Yes." Then, frightened by the implications of her open challenge, she pushed past them, calling over her shoulder, "I'm done talking."

"Wait, Miz Stuart! Tell us more about your suspicions."

But Ellie kept walking. Striding briskly down the sidewalk, she was conscious of the cameras filming her retreat. How pathetic she must look, a lone woman without so much as a purse to carry, wearing blue jeans and a faded pink blouse, with pumps that were worn from waiting tables, the braid in her hair loose and unraveling.

Who was she to take on the Centurions?

But that's exactly what she'd done.

Fright lent her speed as she hurried under boughs dripping with Spanish moss, following her nose toward the riverfront in order to better gather her bearings.

With a nervous glance over her shoulder, she realized the reporters were following her in their vans. She veered off the sidewalk, cutting through narrow alleys and cramped backyards, only to have a fence force her onto the road again.

What was to prevent the Centurions from sending a hit man now to take her out? With a dry mouth, she realized that was probably exactly what they'd intended all along, only they'd be smart to wait until the media speculation died down, lest viewing audiences put two and two together.

The sun began to sink behind the rooftops, affording her shadows to hide in. The news vans that had been stalking her fell away, discouraged by her evasiveness, by the dwindling sunlight, and by the increased traffic in the historic district.

As she drew closer to the hotel, a longing for Sean rose up in her sharply. What had happened to him? She was certain he hadn't tried to escape the police. It was far more likely that they'd done something awful to him, something to ensure he'd never threaten the Centurions again. They'd made him disappear, right along with her boys.

They'd gotten rid of him.

The certainty impaled her with its finality, drawing her to a sudden standstill across from city hall. She covered her mouth with her hand, trying desperately to slow her ragged panting. The sound of children playing on the steps of the looming structure reminded her of her sons.

For their sake, she had to keep her wits about her. Fighting her panic, Ellie dragged in a breath of resolve.

Either she thought her way through this, methodically

and cerebrally, or she returned home alone, defeated, just the way the Centurions wanted her to.

Over my dead body, she thought, squaring her shoulders.

Straight ahead, the light from the Holiday Inn Express blinked on, urging her forward. Once safe within her room, she'd find a way to contact Reno at last.

Reno would know what to do.

"Now *that* is a story," Ophelia Price declared, turning from the monitor where they'd just watched Ellie Stuart implicate the Centurions of Savannah of kidnapping her sons. "I want to go down there and cover it."

"There are plenty of reporters already covering the abduction," refuted her boss, Reba, a hard-driving news woman with decades of experience in field reporting. "The story's been overdone if you ask me."

"Not from the angle that I want to take," insisted Ophelia, tossing her copper curls over her shoulder as she argued her point. "What if Ellie Stuart is telling the truth? Everyone's been assuming that she had her boyfriend kill the kids. My fiancé, who is close friends with the boyfriend, swears Sean Harlan didn't do it. So, maybe the ex-husband took them? Why hasn't the focus been on him? And what about the Centurions? How much does the average American even know about them, anyway?"

"Oh, I've heard of them," admitted Reba, propping red acrylic nails on her bony hips. "I even tried getting an insider's story to do an exposé, but that was years ago. I never did get anywhere with that," she admitted bitterly.

"Well, maybe it's time the media tried again. What if

Ellie Stuart is right, and the Centurions are actually behind her sons' abduction? Just think how exciting it would be to get her side of the story, do a little probing and see what we come up with. Please, Reba? I can sense something huge here."

Reba pursed thin lips and tapped a toe. "All right, Lia," she conceded. "Find Ellie Stuart and set up the interview. Take Reggie with you. I'll get you out on a flight in the morning."

"Make it an early one," Ophelia pleaded. "I don't want someone else picking this up before I do."

"You'd better guarantee me that Ellie Stuart will talk to you," Reba warned.

"Oh, she will," said Ophelia, picturing how Ellie had looked on tape, defiant but utterly alone. "I've met her boyfriend, remember?" And she was going to use that ploy to win Ellie's trust.

But first she'd have to convince Vinny that this was all for Sean Harlan's benefit, and that would not be easy. Not after that *talk* they'd had earlier in the week, at which time he'd made her swear on his rosary that she'd drop the Ellie Stuart case completely.

Grabbing her briefcase, she hurried for the exit. Traffic would be hell in Virginia Beach on a Friday night, and she had a lot of work ahead of her to prepare for this trip.

She hoped she wouldn't regret this. Vinny was usually super supportive when it came to her career. This time, though, he'd been adamant that she stay well away from a story that could ruin the name of a Navy SEAL, a fellow teammate, and a good friend.

She got that. She really did. And even though it was probably going to drive a huge wedge between them, she was going to ignore Vinny's wishes this time. Because the way she looked at it, both Ellie and Sean were going to need her help getting out of this mess.

Regaining consciousness in a cramped space, Sean's first terrorizing thought was that he'd been shot in Afghanistan and put in a coffin to be shipped home. But then he remembered that he wasn't overseas anymore. Memories of Ellie, her lost boys, and his subsequent encounter with Savannah police had him wondering where the hell he was now.

His wrists were still cuffed behind his back. He lay with his numb arms trapped beneath him on a sloped wooden surface, in what appeared to be a container of sorts. The smell of salt water and brine and the bobbing of the container all suggested he was on a boat.

That old fishing boat that had been moored at the marina.

He tried shifting his position and discovered his feet were also bound. Peering through the murky shadows, he saw that they were bound with rope. The end of the rope was connected to—he shifted, touching it with his running shoes—an anchor.

A big, thick, fifty-pound anchor.

Oh, crap. Lifting his head to see it better, Sean groaned at the pain that drove deep into his right temple. Gingerly, he lay back down. They'd shot him, he recalled. The bullet must have just grazed the side of his head, leaving a burning gash above his ear. One more inch to the left and he'd be dead right now.

Holy crap.

Perhaps thinking him dead already, they—the cops or the fishermen or both—had stuffed him in this hold with the anchor, obviously intending to place his body on the ocean floor.

That was one way of keeping Sean from being found.

The thought of such a fate awaiting him bathed him in a clammy sweat. Oh, hell no. It wasn't that he was afraid to die, not in the field of battle, anyway, where death would be a noble sacrifice, done in the name of his country. But drowning at the hands of some scumbag he'd never laid eyes on? No way in hell.

He couldn't let that happen.

Gritting his teeth against the pain in his head, Sean began to squirm. Priority number one was to get the handcuffs off. He couldn't even feel his fingers anymore.

Rolling onto his left side, he spied a spool of what looked like wire, shoved into the corner of the little hold, giving off a dull gleam. Wriggling toward it and craning his neck to reach it, Sean managed to bite the end that poked out. Stiff with rust, it'd probably been used to mend broken crab pots. He turned his head to pull on it, then let go and bit it again. Within seconds, he'd freed a length long enough to grab with his hands, provided he rolled the other way.

Houdini might have relished this.

Sean hated it. He rolled over. His arms, revived by the blood pushing its way into collapsed capillaries, burned as if on fire, reminding him of the time he'd been attacked by thousands of red ants while lying in hiding just outside a village in Ramadi.

Only this was worse.

Ignoring as best he could the fiery pain that seared his

arms and shot deep into his fingertips, Sean worked the end of the wire into the lock of the cuffs that kept him helpless.

Sweat drenched him, matting his shorts and T-shirt to his body as he fought to concentrate. With every beat of his heart, a hammer seemed to slam into the side of his head. Nausea and dizziness welled up, forcing him to pause in his labors, to breathe, in and out, all the while aware that the waves on which the boat rode were getting higher. And that meant just one thing: They were moving into deeper water.

With a quiet click, the handcuffs suddenly gave way.

Yes! As they clattered to the bottom of the hold, Sean shook his arms out, swallowing a moan of agony mixed with relief. He bent to investigate the situation with his feet, only to curse at his discovery. His ankles were bound separately and knotted multiple times by someone who tied knots for a living.

But provided he had enough time, he was certain he could free himself.

Following many minutes of frustration while gritting his teeth against his pounding headache, Sean managed to loosen the rope's grip around his right ankle, perhaps enough to free it if he kicked his shoe off. The other remained firmly trapped.

He set to work loosening it also, his head pounding so ferociously, he was forced to stop to still his pounding heart and breathe deeply.

The sudden cessation of the boat's engines made his pulse rocket right back into overdrive. He bent to work on the ropes more frantically.

But it was too late. Hearing voices approach, he lay

prostrate, pulled his arms beneath him, and grabbed the handcuffs. Cool, fresh air rushed in as the hatch was lifted. Slitting his eyes, Sean made out two burly, bearded men bending over him, backdropped by a night sky.

"He's still out," declared one rough voice. "You get the anchor. I'll get him."

Praying the rope wouldn't tighten up as they moved him, Sean suffered bumps and bruises as he was heaved from the enclosure and dragged toward the side of the boat. He fought to keep the tension out of his body, praying neither man noticed that he now clutched, rather than wore, the handcuffs.

As the man dragging him fought to lift him over the ship's railing, Sean peeked at his environs through his lashes. Starlight bounced off sloshing water. The beacon of a lighthouse told him in which direction the shore lay. He had one hell of a swim ahead of him, and that was a best-case scenario.

"On the count of three," growled the man, who'd managed to prop Sean in a modified sitting position. He shifted his hold, positioning to shove him backward off the railing.

Poised to somersault over the bow rake into the water, Sean drew a slow, deep breath as the man began to count, "One. Two. Three!"

Propelled backward into thin air, Sean's feet swung up and over his head. With a mighty splash, both he and the anchor struck the warm water simultaneously. For two brief seconds, Sean remained near the surface, where he quickly shucked his shoes. But then the slack rope went taut, and he was yanked straight down.

Fast.

Wriggling his right foot free, he kicked instinctively toward the surface.

Of course, that got him nowhere. It also sapped his strength.

Ceasing his struggles, he bent to claw at the rope still looped around his left leg. Down he sank into the darkness. Recollections of a training exercise in BUDs, Basic Underwater Demolition training, flashed through his head. His instructors had disconnected his breathing tubes and tied them into knots. It had been his job to fend off his attackers and unravel his breathing tubes, both at the same time.

He pretended this was training all over again. But the pressure in his ears increased as he sank deeper, deeper, making little headway on the coils that gripped his left ankle. Overhead, he detected the whir of the boat's propellers as it moved leisurely away.

The air in Sean's lungs dwindled. But as long as he pretended this was just a training exercise, he made progress, slipping each loop of the rope over his heel, one at a time. Then, with just a few loops remaining, he whirled like a dervish and freed himself, striking out for the surface.

He never let himself think he wouldn't make it. Failure was not an option. Ever.

With his lungs convulsing and burning, he felt the pressure of the deep subside. To avoid the bends, he forced himself not to rise too quickly. Then, with his last ounce of strength, he burst from his watery prison to gasp in air—sweet, glorious, beautiful air that he swore he'd never take for granted again.

Flipping onto his back, he floated on the swells of the Atlantic as the pounding in his head mushroomed into pain so debilitating that it threatened to rob him of consciousness. Fighting to keep his awareness, he floated lifelessly on the swells. He hadn't come this far to black out now and drown.

Slitting his eyes, he stared up into a sky bedecked with stars and considered how close he'd come to dying. It wouldn't be so bad to be with Patrick again, but Ellie, whom he'd left in police custody, needed him now more than ever. The law was in cahoots with the Centurions. And the Centurions were trying to frame him for murder.

If ever there was a time to die, this was not it.

And so, with a deep breath of resolve, Sean craned his neck to eye the lights twinkling on the distant shore. Summoning his energy reserve, he rolled into a modified combat swimmer's stroke, one that kept his thudding head as stabilized as possible, and scissor-kicked in that direction.

Chapter Thirteen

Vinny held the phone to his ear with a hand that had a distinct tremor in it. A Navy SEAL corpsman's hands were not supposed to tremble, but the emotions whipping through him weren't your basic run-of-the-mill, scared shitless type of feelings that he suffered on dangerous missions. The confusion, anger, and disillusionment were new for him.

He was calling Commander Montgomery to tell him the bad news, that Chief Harlan had been arrested in Savannah, Georgia, for illegal possession of a concealed weapon. That in itself wasn't so bad, but adding that Sean had supposedly fled the police and was now considered a dangerous fugitive was definitely worse.

The CO didn't immediately buy it. "Are you sure this is our Sean Harlan?" he asked. Because it was utterly out of character for Sean to do something as stupid as run from the law, even when the stakes were fairly high. But, then again, according to Lia, the stakes were probably higher than anyone realized.

"Yes, sir, I'm sure," Vinny replied. "It's all over the

local news down there. I just got online and watched a broadcast. He was with that woman, Ellie Stuart, down in Savannah looking for her boys when the police picked him up."

"I know where he was," interrupted the CO. "I signed his leave chit." He sounded awfully grim. "Thanks for letting me know," he bit out. "I'll look into it."

"Sir, there's more," Vinny said, glancing down the hallway toward his bedroom, where Lia was packing her suitcase. "My fiancée swears that Sean's been framed by a group of men called the Centurions. She thinks that they were the ones who kidnapped Ellie Stuart's kids, and now they're making it look like Sean did it."

The commander's silence didn't reassure him any. "I'll call Hannah Lindstrom," decided the CO. "Maybe she knows what the hell is going on."

His duty done, Vinny put the receiver down. He took one last look at the news article he'd found online—NAVY SEAL WANTED IN CONNECTION WITH BOYS' ABDUCTION—and pushed back the desk chair.

He did not want Lia involved in this, not even when she swore she was going to Savannah to be Ellie Stuart's advocate. Not when Sean had made it perfectly clear that Ophelia was bottom on his list of people he respected.

Drawing up short at their open door, Vinny watched Lia zip her brightly colored suits into a garment bag. As she glanced his way, he caught that stubborn gleam in her turquoise eyes. That look told him plainly she was going, anyway, despite his clearly stated wishes.

Hurt put pressure on his chest. She'd never *not* taken his wishes into consideration before. "So you're leaving, anyway," he accused, jamming his hands into the pockets of his BDUs.

With a sigh, she turned and faced him. "I told you, Vinny, this story is big. I can't just sit by and wait for some other journalist to jump on it. Besides, Sean's your friend. Don't you want me defending him?"

"You're just going to take on these Centurions—whoever the hell they are—alone? Think about it, Lia. In order to have had Sean arrested, they had to have paid off the police. If they can make Sean disappear, they sure as hell can make you disappear."

"Wrong," she countered, her beautiful face glowing with the self-assurance she used to lack. "They won't dare come after me, because if they do, it'll be obvious that they're behind the kidnapping. Now, if you'll excuse me, I'm going to take a shower and get to bed. I have to get up at four in the morning to catch a plane."

"You were going to go with or without my permission," Vinny accused.

Lia's eyebrows shot up. "Oh, I need your permission now to do my job?" she retorted hotly.

"When it takes you away from me, yes. When it puts you in danger, yes," he countered, his Italian temper coming to an equally quick boil.

"Well, I'm sorry," Lia said as she attacked the buttons on her blouse. "Right now, my career comes first."

Her words felt like cold water dousing him from head to foot. "Over me," he said, his heart contracting painfully. He sent her a pleading look, longing for her to withdraw her statement.

She hesitated, her blouse halfway undone. But then,

averting her gaze, she turned wordlessly away, went into the bathroom, and shut and locked the door.

Awash with sorrow, Vinny sagged against the door-frame. So, they'd come to their first big hurdle, and it had tripped them both flat. How were they going to get through the rest of their lives, especially when they were both so young with so much living ahead of them? Sure, Lia deserved to become the next Diane Sawyer, but at the expense of their relationship?

He took one last look at the locked door, then turned and headed blindly down the hall. He needed to talk to Senior Chief about what had happened to Sean. If Lia thought she was going to fly down South to expose the biggest cover-up of the century, maybe Vinny and Solomon ought to get on board with that and see how two Navy SEALs could help their brother.

If he wasn't already beyond help.

Sean roused to semiconsciousness. Was he dreaming, or was this real? A crab scuttled across his field of vision, its tiny claws making scrabbling sounds on the damp sand. The roar of the ocean told him he was sprawled on the beach. He could feel sand lodged in every crevice of his body, but this wasn't Basic Underwater Demolition training or even Hell Week.

This was worse. He tried to get up, but his limbs were so cold, so weak, they wouldn't cooperate. And when he lifted his head to look around, pain knifed through his skull.

Through a haze of windblown sand, he thought he saw

a figure jogging toward him. *Friend or foe?* he wondered, regarding her with helpless suspicion.

In the pale pink light of dawn, he saw that she wore her dark hair in a ponytail, workout sweats, and sneakers. As she hurried toward him, he rolled gingerly onto his side—the best he could do—to greet her.

"Do you need help, sir?" she called, huffing up to him. "You've got a nasty gash on your head," she observed, exhaling warm, minty breath on his face as she sank to one knee beside him. He noticed she was pretty but not especially young.

"Concussion," he guessed. It hurt just to talk.

"You could use sutures," she commented, eyeing the wound more closely. Her swift appraisal took in his stockinged feet, his soaked and sandy clothing, and the marks on his wrists. "When I saw you, I thought maybe you were dead," she added.

He had nothing to say to that. He felt about as close to dead a man could get.

With a sudden inhalation, she pulled away from him. "You're the man on the news," she exclaimed with consternation. "The Navy SEAL."

Sean grimaced. *Great.* He really needed this—to be turned in to the cops by some helpful citizen. "You believe everything the media tells you, ma'am?" he gritted. Slitting his eyes, he watched the thoughts ebb and flow on her intelligent-looking face.

"No," she said at last, definitively.

"Good, 'cause I'm not a bad guy, and I need help. 'Course, you could always just leave me here."

He knew the second she made up her mind. "I'll help," she decided. "Do you think you can walk?"

He groaned at the thought. "Maybe."

"You'll have to," she said. "I can't drive my car out on the beach."

In the maze of shadowed corridors beneath the Cathedral of St. John the Baptist, Skyler finally located Father Joseph's office. The old priest had retired years ago, but he still volunteered his time as a counselor, which was why she discovered him in front of his bookshelf, scanning reference material.

At her knock, he turned to greet her. Regarding her through thick spectacles, he obviously didn't recognize her immediately, but as he waved her into the office, his face lit up with pleasure. "Why, Skyler," he said, "what a lovely surprise."

They'd crossed paths from time to time at Hospice House, but since the priest's retirement, she'd ceased to see him at Mass. "It's been a while," she admitted.

"How's your mother?" he asked gravely, taking her hand.

Skyler swallowed down her grief. "She had a lucid moment recently," she said with a forced smile. "That's why I'm here, actually. It was something that she said."

The priest darted a look at the door. "Please," he said, urging her toward the chairs. "Take a seat."

As he closed the door to afford them privacy, she eased into one of the chairs arranged in a circle. Father Joseph was well known for his work with families in crisis. The irony of that did not escape her as he took a seat across from her and pinned her with his sharp eyes. "Poor Skyler," he said, "you've endured much sorrow for such a young woman. How can I be of help?" he asked.

"I don't know if you can," she tentatively began. "My mother gave this to me when I was ten," she explained, pulling the key out from under her sweater. At his sudden stillness, the flash of recognition on his face, her heart beat faster. "It goes to something, doesn't it? She said you knew."

The priest touched a hand to his chin. His eyes glazed with worry. "You've heard of Pandora's box, have you not?" he warily replied.

"Of course. When it was opened, it released all the evils of mankind," Skyler answered with a shiver of apprehension. "Why?"

Instead of answering, he got up, crossed to the shelves she'd found him standing at, bent to open the cabinet beneath, and rummaged within it. At last, he pulled out a medium-sized metal box, and brought it to her.

"When your mother gave me this," whispered the priest as he kneeled to put the box down, "she called it Pandora's box. She said it was never to be opened by any hand but hers."

"But she gave me the key," Skyler reasoned, both curious and frightened to discover its contents.

"Then use it," the priest offered with a shrug, "if that's what you feel your mother wants."

Skyler slipped the key from her neck and inserted it in the box with shaking fingers. The lock released with a click. With her heart in her throat, she lifted the lid, half expecting demons to come shrieking out. Instead, she found herself regarding half a dozen journals, not unlike her mother's garden journal.

Slanting a look of surprise at the priest, Skyler lifted out the one on top and riffled through it, noting the date: 1998, just ten years ago. She began to read.

Owen's guest tonight was a Russian embezzler by the name of Semion Mogilevich. I believe he's wanted by the FBI. He ate his dinner with a knife. Then he and Owen retreated to the study where I overheard Owen offer use of his shipping port at the harbor where, of course, no one dares to regulate the goods that come and go.

Skyler closed the journal hastily and reached for another. The year was 1992. *Owen has been selling all our shares in AT&T stock, tipped off by a friend on the board of directors that it is about to plummet.*

The humming in Skyler's ears was the sound of her blood racing. It came as no surprise to read that her father was neck-deep in smuggling and insider trading. She'd long suspected charities like the homeless shelter and Hospice House were used to cloak more nefarious deeds. These journals proved it.

And suddenly Skyler knew why her mother had wanted her to have them. *This is the key to your future,* she'd said.

It was the key to freedom!

As the priest moved discreetly toward his desk, she skimmed the other journals, overwhelmed by the detailed testimony her mother had compiled, by the sheer amount of damning information at her disposal. No wonder Matilda had hidden these journals in a box and given them to the priest to protect. Her husband would have killed her if he knew. . . .

That thought brought Skyler to sobering reality. Suppose she turned this evidence over to the FBI—what was to prevent her father from enacting some kind of punishment, either toward her ill mother or toward her, if he discovered she'd betrayed him?

The realization turned her hot, then cold.

Would the diaries of an old lady with Alzheimer's really be enough to bring down one of the most powerful men in the nation?

Slowly, thoughtfully, she put the journals back in the box and locked it. As she dropped the key once again around her neck, the priest looked over at her inquiringly.

"Father, would you keep this box a little longer for me?" she asked, rising shakily to her feet.

He approached her with grave concern. "Of course, my child. Is there anything else I can do for you?" he asked.

"Yes, Father. Please pray for me," she begged. Feeling the weight of the world on her shoulders, she quietly turned and left the room.

A brisk knock on the hotel-room door startled Ellie from her sleep. She jerked to one elbow, her heart jumping from her chest in fear that the Centurions had tracked her down.

Sunshine blazed around the window drapes, telling her she'd slept at last, having paced the lonely room all night, fretting, plotting, and weeping.

Without Sean, and even with Reno's promise that he'd

be down the next day, the loss of her boys seemed insurmountable. Reno wasn't like Sean, who took on the enemy directly. He was a lawyer, forced to play within a set of rules, rules that Centurions had manipulated successfully for decades. How could Reno really help?

The knock came again. "Ellie, are you in there?" called a woman.

Ellie didn't recognize the voice. She remained in bed, curled into the warm blanket, too wary to answer.

"My name's Ophelia," called the voice. "I'm a friend of Sean's."

Ellie's stomach dropped. *A friend of Sean's?* Just how many female friends did he have?

"My fiancé works with Sean at Dam Neck. His name's Vinny. Sean might have mentioned him."

Vinny. Yes, Ellie knew that name. The realization had her kicking out of her cocoon and crossing to the door. She set the chain first, then cautiously cracked it open. The woman outside jumped back. "Oh, you're here," she exclaimed with relief. "I'm Ophelia," she repeated, taking in Ellie's rumpled clothing, the dark circles under her eyes. "You must be so upset," she said with seeming sympathy. "I'm hoping I can help you."

Ellie looked her over. Ophelia was perhaps a year or two younger than she was, dressed in a violet suit that enhanced both her figure and her copper-colored curls. "How?" she asked frankly in a voice that sounded like sandpaper.

The woman winced self-consciously. "I'm a reporter," she admitted, putting her hand on the door before Ellie could even consider closing it. "But I'm also a friend. I heard what you said to those reporters yesterday and I *believe* you. I want to get *your* story. I want to expose the Centurions and find out their reason for taking your boys."

Ellie put a hand to her aching eyes and rubbed them. Her brain was still groggy with exhaustion.

"Tell you what," said Ophelia, sensitive to her state. "I'll run down to the lobby and get some coffee while you think about it. Fair enough?" She was already retreating down the hall, copper curls swinging between her shoulder blades as she glanced back and waved.

Ellie quietly shut the door and stood there. *My story,* she thought, mulling over the offer.

Would it make any difference for a journalist to run a sympathy piece on her plight? It might persuade people who'd unjustly condemned her to rethink their assumptions. It might get the public interested in just how powerful and how ruthless the Centurions were. And if there was even a glimmer of a chance it could expose the whereabouts of her boys, then, yes, she'd do it.

Stumbling into the bathroom, she flicked on the light and groaned at her reflection. Lord have mercy, if she was going to have to be on camera, she'd better do something about the way she looked.

Drake's initial task as Owen Dulay's gardener was to prune the trees and bushes Carl had let grow too large. Having tamed the riotous vegetation and bagged the clippings, a task that took until midafternoon, Drake returned the garden shears to the locker just inside the carriage house. There, he intercepted Owen Dulay in the process of leaving his home.

"Spenser's Law Office, please, Carl," he told his chauffeur as the man rushed forward to open the rear door. "It's on Whitaker street."

"Yes, sir." Closing the door behind his employer, Carl threw Drake a superior smirk and jumped into the driver's seat. The automatic garage door rumbled open, revealing the street at the back of the house, and Carl drove out into a cloud-covered afternoon without remembering to first don his seat belt.

With a shake of his head, Drake shucked the gloves he'd worn, placed them alongside the shears, and closed the locker. He wondered if Carl even knew that Spenser was Dulay's formidable attorney, a man who, for years, had routed the FBI's attempts to subpoena information from Dulay, defending Dulay's privacy with the ferocity of a pit bull.

As the garage doors rumbled shut, Drake turned and hurried into the house via the kitchen entrance. Only when Dulay was absent did he dare place a call to headquarters, updating his father on Dulay's movements. Although, HQ should already be tracking him, thanks to the tracer Drake had secured to the Bentley's undercarriage.

With a nod at the cook and the housekeeper, Drake passed straight through the bustling kitchen and into the foyer toward the servant's staircase at the back of the house. He'd been given a small room on the third floor adjacent to the rooms of the other servants. Only Carl got accommodations like the apartment on the second floor of the carriage house.

As he reached the narrow opening, the door at the front of the house eased open, and in stepped Skyler, looking flustered and breathless. Perhaps hoping to avoid intercepting her father's departure, she had parked out front. Her gaze went straight down the length of the foyer, pinning him where he stood.

"Hey," said Drake, feeling like he'd been caught trespassing.

"Hi," breathed Skyler, putting her back against the door. He wondered at her flushed cheeks, the wild look in her eyes. "Are you okay?" he asked.

"I don't know," she admitted.

The odd reply prompted him to approach her. She stood as if transfixed, unmoving. With every step in her direction, the tension between them thickened and crackled. He hesitated, wondering if it was just in his own mind.

But then she pushed abruptly from the door to rush at him. Going tiptoe, she kissed him desperately and passionately.

Shocked by her boldness, Drake still managed to respond like a warm-blooded male. Hooking an arm around her waist, he kissed her back. Her mouth was warm and luscious. Within seconds, he was lost in the moment.

Skyler released him and grabbed his hand. "Come upstairs with me," she whispered urgently.

He could no more turn her down than he could stop his heart from beating. He didn't know what had brought about this sudden spontaneity, but it struck an equally impulsive chord within him. As they raced up the stairs together, he spared a glance back to assure himself no one was watching.

"Skyler, what are you doing?" he asked with laughing disbelief as she pushed him into her room and locked the door.

"Shhh," she answered, her eyes wide and fixed on his, her finger to her lips as she slowly approached him.

Her bedroom was a sea of cream brocade, gold gauze, and tassels. Her canopy bed loomed invitingly near. He yearned to feel her soft and naked and lying under him.

Pausing directly in front of him, she stripped her light-weight sweater off over her head, making further questions unnecessary. It was pretty damn clear what she was doing.

The sweater dropped silently to the floor, leaving her in a white lace bra that lifted her modest breasts enticingly. She looked so pretty he wanted to weep. "Why are you doing this?" he asked.

"Because I can," she insisted, that wild defiance back in her eyes. Releasing the zipper that secured her skirt at her waist, she slipped it over her slim hips. Drake's mouth went dry.

She wore matching panties and high heels. With a whispered exclamation, he reached for her, pulling her to him with all the hunger of a full-grown male. She melted into his embrace, a perfect fit.

"Skyler," he murmured against her ear, "I've wanted to do this for so long," he admitted. Cradling her face in his hands, he savored the vision of her sweet, plump lips, and then he kissed her.

Her ardent response narrowed his awareness to her alone. The way she trembled, the way she breathed, the way she smelled, a beautiful womanly scent that made his heart pound, was all he could take in. Their mouths merged in a desperate but futile quest to get closer.

Drake offered up one last appeal to sanity. "What if your father finds out?" he asked, gasping for breath.

"I don't care anymore," she declared. "All I care about is this minute. Right now. With you."

Need clawed at him, overruling all his reasons why jeopardizing his position in Dulay's household was a bad idea. By then, her hands had found their way beneath his T-shirt, tormenting him with the decadence of her touch. He stopped kissing her long enough to tear it over his head, to unbuckle his belt and shuck out of his jeans and socks. Naked, trembling with the force of his need, he reached for her again, scooped her up like a bride, and carried her to the thronelike bed.

He laid her on her back and stood there, admiring her. Sunlight shining through the chiffon curtains bathed her in a golden shimmer. With a groan of adulation, he bowed his head over the flat plane of her belly, inhaling the subtle scent of her perfume, mixed with the essence of woman.

"Skyler," he groaned as she sank fingers into his dark curls. "Please tell me you won't marry some old man."

"Don't talk about it," she begged him. "It's not going to happen. I just have to find a way—" She cut herself off. "Please, just give me what you can."

Drunk with desire, he heard himself answer, "You don't even know what I can give you. I can save you, Skyler." Immediately, he kicked himself for revealing that much.

Fortunately, she mistook his assertion for youthful confidence. Coiling her limbs around his, she pulled him closer. "Save me," she breathed, tipping her hips toward his so that his erection rode the damp panel between her thighs.

Drake pledged himself to ensuring Skyler would never forget this moment. Unlatching her bra, he whispered words of reverence as he suckled her taut, pink nipples.

She raked his back with her nails. She writhed and sighed. He trailed nips and licks down her torso and outlined her lace panties with his tongue until she begged for him to take them off. And even then, he did so slowly, kissing her exposed skin inch by inch, lathing her lush, swollen sex.

She gave a sob that had him glancing up in concern. He found her weeping.

"Skyler?" He swiftly covered her, cradling her wet face in his hands. "We don't have to do this," he reluctantly reminded her.

She shook her head in denial. "No, no, I want to," she insisted. "I just thought . . ." She broke off with a sob.

"Thought what?" he prompted.

"I thought once would be enough," she admitted, crystal droplets sliding from the corners of her eyes.

Her honesty robbed him of platitudes. Once would never be enough. The realization shook him deeply. It changed everything—his agenda, his future, *her* future. He had to save her now. He couldn't let her give herself to Jameson.

"I have to tell you something," he heard himself admit.

"What?" she whispered, inviting him with glistening eyes to speak the truth.

"I'm not who you think I am," he said in a rush. But then caution reined him in. The chances were too great that telling her would impact his investigation. He didn't want to disappoint his father or the Bureau, not when they'd invested so much time and effort, not when they were so close to exposing Dulay.

"It's okay," she whispered, confusing him with her reassurance, stroking the side of his face. "You don't have to justify what you've done and where you've been. You're a good, kind man, and one day you'll make a woman very happy."

Her praise was as unsettling as the admiration shining in her eyes. *Damn it!* Hiding his face against her cheek, he kissed the salty wetness of her tears, sought the slick center of her womanhood, and pushed gently inside her. With a sound between a sob and a gasp, she raised her hips in welcome.

In the next instant, he was lost in the incredibly sweet grip of her flesh. Beneath heavy eyelids, he watched the reflection of his bliss in her eyes, in her face, felt it in the undulations of her body. She was, like him, a willing prisoner to her enthrallment.

Slipping a hand between them, he sped her toward release, kissing her deeply to muffle her impassioned cry. As her pleasure poured into him, he surrendered his control, leaving a ribbon of ejaculate on her thigh as he hastily withdrew.

A loud rapping at the door startled them both from their sensual lethargy. "Miss Skyler," called the familiar voice of the housekeeper. "Mr. Jameson's on the phone."

The suffering look that crossed Skyler's face made Drake's stomach cramp. "Tell him I'll call him right back, Betsy. I'm changing," she called shakily.

"Yes, Miss Skyler." Betsy departed, hopefully none the wiser.

"You'd better not keep him waiting," Drake said. Rolling from the bed, he snatched up his T-shirt and used it to wipe the moisture from her thigh while Skyler looked on. He was almost grateful to Jameson for sparing him from the tender moments after. How could he share his feelings for her when he hadn't even told her who he was?

She, on the other hand, had been achingly honest with him. But would she feel the same when he told her of his intent: to put her father behind bars where he belonged. Would she still care for him then?

With guilt urging him to escape, he stepped into his boxers and jeans and picked up his shoes and socks, not slowing to put them on. "I should go," he muttered, sparing her a quick kiss.

"Drake," she called as he turned away.

He looked back reluctantly. She looked so lovely lying there that his heart clutched with regret. "Yes, Skyler?"

"I hope you don't feel like I used you."

"No." He ground out that single word, unlocked the door, and hurled himself into the hall, so ashamed that she'd taken his feelings into consideration that his ears burned.

Chapter Fourteen

♦

"Ellie Stuart, thank you for sharing your story," said
Ophelia. "I'm sure I'm not the only one who hopes your
sons will be quickly found."

"Thank you," Ellie murmured, relieved that the interview was over.

The cameraman ticked three seconds off his fingers as
Ophelia gazed intently into the lens.

And then it was really over. Ellie released a long sigh
and felt her tension ease.

"I think that went well," Ophelia pronounced brightly.
"You couldn't have sounded more sincere. Public opinion
is going to shift a hundred and eighty degrees. How do
you feel?" she asked Ellie.

Ellie searched herself. "Better," she realized. The
reporter's timely arrival had alleviated her frightening
solitude and given her a means of fighting for her boys.
"Sorry for crying like a baby," she apologized. She'd
been appalled when her tears had turned into full-blown
sobbing as she relayed the painful details of the last

moments of the abduction and her feelings of terror, fear, and helplessness.

"Are you kidding?" Ophelia retorted. "That was perfect. Believe me, you don't want to come off looking unemotional. Then the public would never believe someone else took them, let alone the Centurions of Savannah. You did great," she reassured her, offering her a swift hug as she stood from one of the two chairs they'd placed before the hotel room's curtained window. "The only thing I can't understand is why the Centurions abducted your sons in the first place. If we could just prove they had a motive."

Ellie frowned. "I've been thinking a lot about that," she admitted, having returned to the question again and again. "I've tried putting myself in Carl's shoes, trying to understand why he wanted his sons back when he couldn't have cared less about them a year ago."

"And?" Ophelia prompted, her eyes bright with curiosity.

"Well, the most important thing to a Centurion is having a male heir to leave his legacy to. Now Carl has three," Ellie pointed out.

"That doesn't explain why the Centurions would break the law for him or enact an elaborate cover-up to hide their involvement. And from what you've told me, it sounds like stealing the boys was their idea in the first place."

"Right. Also, why is Owen Dulay, leader of the Centurions, so taken with Carl?" Ellie wondered out loud. "The man is rich and powerful, and yet he chooses a deadbeat like Carl to nurture and protect?"

"Maybe Carl's like the son he never had."

The women shared a long, thoughtful look.

"If Dulay doesn't have a son," said Ellie, articulating their common realization, "who's he going to leave his legacy to? Carl?" It was not only inconceivable; it was laughable.

Ophelia narrowed her jewel-like eyes. "Let's reason this out," she proposed. "Owen Dulay earned a masters in business from Rhodes University, and his tax returns from the last three years put him in the top two percent nationally for gross earnings. Where did Carl attend college?"

"He didn't. He was offered scholarships to play football, but he married me instead," Ellie admitted stiffly.

"Football?" Ophelia mused. "Owen Dulay played college ball."

Ellie got up to fetch Carl's I-LOVE-ME box, which she'd wedged between the bed and the wall. "If you want to know more about Carl," she explained, heaving it onto the bed, "it's all here." She gestured for Ophelia to help herself.

"Carl's birth certificate," Ophelia noted after a moment. She pulled it out and scanned it. "There's no father's name?"

Ellie looked to where she was pointing. "No, Carl never had a daddy," she recalled. "His mama lived with her parents. She never did marry."

Ophelia laid the certificate aside and pulled out Carl's photographs. "Oh, my gosh, I can't believe I'm saying this, but he looks just like a younger Owen Dulay. I did tons of research on him before I came here. I knew there had to be a connection somewhere!"

The observation stopped Ellie's heartbeat for a full second. "No way," she breathed.

"Why not? Isn't Dulay old enough to be Carl's father?"

"I guess so," Ellie relented, peering at the photograph, "but it just seems so far-fetched." The similarity wasn't apparent to her, but then again, she'd never seen an early photograph of Dulay, only the oil-on-canvas portrait at the homeless shelter. "He has a grown daughter named Skyler," she added.

"The one who volunteers at the homeless shelter," Ophelia recalled. "We need to talk to her," she added, placing the photos alongside the birth certificate.

Ellie glanced at the clock. "She's probably there right now."

"And that's where the Centurions hold their weekly meetings, right?"

"Right," said Ellie.

"Okay, then," said Ophelia, tugging down her purple jacket. "Let's see what Skyler has to say about the possibility of Carl being her father's illegitimate son."

"I'm going with you," Ellie declared, swinging a look between the reporter and the cameraman.

Ophelia gave her a candid inspection. "You'll have to disguise yourself first," she replied. "After all those news reports last night, you'll be recognized anywhere you go in this town. Also, you'll need to stay somewhere else," she added. "I had no trouble finding you here. It wouldn't take the Centurions any time at all to find you and silence you."

"Like they've done with Sean," Ellie murmured, pressing a fist to her roiling abdomen.

"Oh, honey, I'm sorry," Ophelia apologized. "Sometimes I just say things without thinking." She offered Ellie a comforting hug. "You can stay with me," she offered magnanimously. "And changing your appearance won't cost a dime. All you need is my hair straightener, a little makeup, and some clothes. You'll look like an entirely different woman." Which, obviously, would be an improvement, in the reporter's opinion.

"But what about Sean?" Ellie asked, glancing at his duffel bag, which she'd carefully repacked last night, pausing to smell his clothes, savoring his scent, worrying for his safety—despite the fact that the last time they'd spoken, he'd shaken her with the truth of his alibi. But, then again, the possibility that he'd been killed for helping her find her boys went a long way toward easing her illogical jealousy. "How will he find me?" she asked, refusing to consider that he might already be dead.

"The first thing he'll do when he resurfaces is check in with his command," Ophelia replied with certainty. "I'll make sure Vinny relays the message that you're staying with me at the East Bay Inn. Or you can stay here and take your chances," she added with a shrug.

It wasn't the threat of reprisal that made up Ellie's mind. More than anything, she wanted to follow Ophelia, to be there if there was any news about Sean, to learn if the preposterous idea that Owen Dulay was Carl's father could actually be true. "I'm going with you," she decided.

"Excellent," said Ophelia. "Hurry up and pack. We'll check you out now and let the Centurions think you left town."

Sean found himself in a semidark and unfamiliar bedroom, with a clock beside the bed that read 5:23—in the morning or evening?

The sky beyond the heavy curtains was still light. He kicked off the covers and looked down. The unfamiliar boxers on his otherwise naked body had him looking around in confusion.

Then he recognized the room from a previous surfacing to consciousness. Oh, yes, his rescuer had brought him in here after her last attempt to wake him up. Before that, he'd lain half-slumped on her couch, wrapped up in a blanket. She'd annoyed the hell out of him by repeatedly tapping his cheek, talking to him, ordering him to keep his eyes open.

Having been trained to obey orders, he'd complied as best he could. He'd wanted to be coherent, to get on the phone and call for help. But between the concussion and his exhaustion, his body had refused to cooperate. Sleep was what he'd needed. The woman must've finally seen that.

Sitting up slowly, Sean felt a dull thudding in his head, but nothing compared to the excruciating headache he'd suffered earlier. He touched his temple tentatively and realized the wound had been bandaged.

Cautiously, Sean swung his feet to the carpeted floor. Thank God, his dizziness was gone.

The sound of a refrigerator closing drew him out of the bedroom and into the living area, which had a soaring ceiling and glass windows that offered a breathtaking view of the Atlantic Ocean. His gaze went straight to the woman working at the stove with her back to him.

"Hi," he said, and she jumped, whirling in surprise.

"You're up," she exclaimed, her gaze sliding briefly over him. "How's the head?" she asked a little breathlessly.

Sean was used to women gawking at him. Only Ellie

pretended not to stare. Mascara now enhanced the intelligence behind the woman's light brown eyes.

"Better," he said. "Thanks for letting me crash in your bed," he added.

"You didn't give me much choice," she retorted dryly.

"Whose"—he indicated his hips—"boxers am I wearing?"

"My ex's," she confessed. "Come on in here. I bet you're thirsty."

As he stepped into the arena of granite-covered counters, she poured him a tall glass of orange juice. "Thanks." He drained it in four long swallows.

"You're welcome, Sean," she said, startling him by calling him by name. Of course, she said she'd seen him on the news. "I'm Maggie," she added, offering him a handshake.

"Thank you, Maggie," he repeated.

Pulling a flashlight out of a drawer, she clicked it on. "Look at me," she ordered, touching the side of his face with cool fingers as she flashed it in his eyes. "Your right pupil is still dilated," she reported, putting it away. She returned to the stove to stir the meat and vegetables.

"Are you a doctor?" Sean asked, looking around the room for a telephone. He spied a cell phone charging on the kitchen counter.

"Yes, actually, but not that kind of doctor. I'm a forensic anthropologist."

He wondered if she'd thought about calling the police.

"There are clothes hanging in the bedroom closet," she announced, her gaze glancing off his chest. "Once you're dressed, you can use my cell phone if you like."

Obviously, she'd caught him eyeing her phone. With a grimace, Sean retreated to the bedroom.

Five minutes later, he ventured out again in a short-sleeved tropical shirt that barely met in the front and Bermuda shorts that showed off his farmer's tan.

Maggie bit her lip as if to keep from smiling. "Here you go," she said, handing him the cell phone and gesturing toward the living room.

"Can you tell me where I am?" he asked.

"Tybee Island," she said with a pitying look. She jotted her address onto notepaper and handed it to him.

"Thanks." Taking the phone and the note to a recliner in the far corner, Sean watched Maggie with one eye as he punched in the number to Spec Ops with the other. It was Friday evening. The only person there at this time would be the duty officer.

Vinny DeInnocentis answered the call. Sean wanted to lunge through the phone and kiss him on both cheeks. "Yo, bro," he said, leaving it to Vinny to guess who he was.

"Harley! Shit, is it you?" Vinny asked with great relief.

"It's me," Sean confirmed as Maggie measured out soy sauce and poured it in a bowl.

"What the hell is going on?" Vinny asked. "We heard you were arrested in Savannah and that you eluded the police on the way to jail."

"Not exactly," drawled Sean. "They just did their best to kill me."

"Yeah, they were bought off by the Centurions," said Vinny.

Sean sat forward. "How do you know that?" he asked intently.

"Ophelia saw Ellie Stuart on the news. Ellie accused the Centurions of kidnapping her boys for her ex-husband."

Ellie, on the news? Christ, what was she thinking, openly challenging the Centurions like that? "I need your help, Vinny," he said. "I don't have my cell phone, my ID, nothing."

"You got it. Senior Chief and I were gonna take a military hop tomorrow morning and come looking for you. Where are you?"

As Sean relayed the address, Maggie whisked her sauce in a ceramic bowl.

"We'll be out to get you tomorrow," Vinny promised. "The CO gave us three days off. He's shitting bricks over this. You want me to call him?"

"Yeah, give him this number. Also, I need to talk to Lieutenant Lindstrom's wife, Hannah."

"I think he's already been talking to her."

"Tell them to call me, whoever wants to talk to me first."

"You got it, Chief."

Ending the call, Sean sat for a moment, thinking. For Ellie to speak with reporters, she had to be out of police custody, back at the hotel.

He called information for the number, got the front desk to connect him to room 317, and listened to the phone ring and ring until the message service picked up. What if the wrong person learned that he was still alive? The less Ellie knew, the safer they both were. With reluctance but wanting desperately to reassure her, he hung up.

Reno, he thought, thinking hard to remember his lawyer's number. It'd be safer for Reno to get in touch with Ellie. Plus, Sean truly needed him now that he was considered a fugitive.

"Hello?" Reno answered.

"Hey, buddy, this is Sean."

The sound of a bed creaking told him Reno had just jumped to his feet. "Where are you?" the lawyer asked with gunfire urgency. Apparently he'd already heard of Sean's circumstances.

"I'm safe," Sean replied. "Have you talked to Ellie?" he asked, craving reassurance of her safety.

"I did last night," the lawyer answered. "She called from the hotel room, distraught, of course. She said the police didn't charge her but that they'd arrested you, that you'd evaded police on the way to jail and were wanted as a fugitive. I thought I'd better fly down and see what the hell was going on."

"I'm being framed," Sean said shortly. "That's what's going on."

"Sean, I just came from a meeting with Butler," Reno announced unexpectedly.

"I hope you didn't believe a fucking word he said," Sean defended himself. "I sure as hell didn't kill those kids. Why would I be down here helping Ellie look for them?"

"I know you didn't. Anyone who knows you would realize a charge like that is ludicrous."

"Then where did this so-called evidence come from?" Sean demanded. "Supposedly they found a Gerber blade with the boys' DNA on it in my truck," he whispered, not wanting Maggie to overhear. "That's bullshit. I would never have let those boys play with my knife. Butler's trying to frame me," he insisted.

"I'm not so sure it's Butler," Reno countered. "We spoke at length yesterday. He admits that after speaking to Ellie, he began having second thoughts. But your subsequent disappearance made you look guilty all over again."

"I didn't disappear," Sean insisted, his temple throbbing. "The officers who were supposed to drive me to jail took me to a marina out in the middle of nowhere. When I realized what they were up to, I tried to run and they shot me. I woke up on a fishing vessel with a concussion and a fifty-pound anchor tied to my feet!"

"Jesus," muttered Reno. "Hold on. I need to write that down." A scribbling sound followed as the lawyer jotted himself a note. "Okay, listen. I need to try to straighten this out. As your attorney, I'm supposed to urge you to surrender to the authorities—"

"I'm through with trusting the authorities around here. Just find Ellie for me, will you? Let her know that I'm all right." He hoped to God she hadn't been convinced by Butler's lies.

"I will," Reno promised. "Sean, I have to admit that there might be something to your Centurion conspiracy. Everything points to a massive cover-up, with someone in a position of authority pulling strings. If that's going to be our defense, then we need a motive. Carl's being a member isn't enough. Why would the secret society go to such lengths to help him?"

"I don't know," Sean admitted. "I only know that Centurion privileges are passed from father to son."

"Be careful, whatever you do," Reno pleaded. "The more time I have to work on this the better."

"Will do," promised Sean. "Oh, my alibi," he recalled. "Maybe you could get a hold of Tiffany Hughes on Lakeview Drive in Greenbriar. Butler said she never called him back, and given all that's going on, I'm worried something happened to her."

"I'll look her up now," Reno promised. "If I can't get a hold of her, I'll have a friend swing by and pay her a call."

"Thanks, buddy." The phone beeped in Sean's ear. He glanced at the incoming number. "Listen, I have to go," he said to Reno. "Hannah Lindstrom's calling."

"Take care, Sean. Stay in touch."

"Bye." He pressed the TALK button. "Yes, ma'am. Thanks for calling."

"No problem," Hannah tensely replied. "Bring me up to date."

He spent the next five minutes telling Hannah what he'd just told Reno and what Reno had told him. "Look, I don't know how Butler came up with the evidence he has, but I don't trust him. I think he's been bought off by Centurions, or he is one himself," Sean added.

Hannah kept notably quiet for a moment. "You need to keep that allegation to yourself for now, Sean," she warned him. "Let me see who assigned him to the case."

"There's something else you should know. The FBI has an undercover agent already scrutinizing the Centurions' leader, Owen Dulay." He spent a moment telling her about Drake Donovan. While Sean had sworn not to reveal Drake's cover, the dire straits in which he found himself made it necessary. "Maybe his division can shed some insight."

"I'll look into it," Hannah promised. "Can I call you back at this number?"

"I guess," said Sean. He glanced at Maggie, who was ladling food onto two plates.

As Sean brought communications to a close, Maggie waved him over. "Take a break and eat," she invited. "You'll feel better if you get some food in you."

The smell of beef simmered in garlic sauce compelled him to join her at the glass-top table. His hand trembled weakly as he forked up a bite of savory meat and vegetables. "It's good," he murmured, nodding his appreciation, aware that Maggie was studying him intently.

"Sounds like you've been through hell," she stated, proving she'd been listening to his calls.

He shrugged and kept quiet.

"I've never heard of the Centurions," she admitted, reaching for her iced tea.

"They're originally from the South," Sean explained, "but now they're everywhere."

"And I'm from upstate New York," she said. "Where are you from?"

"Missouri."

She regarded him as if he were a puzzle that needed solving. "What's a boy from the boot heel doing in the Navy SEALs?"

He shrugged again. "Beating back terrorists."

She smiled a little at his patented answer. "I'm sure it's not that simple," she wagered.

"Probably not," he agreed.

Her interest in him was faintly disturbing. Not that

women hadn't been interested before, but it was his body they wanted to know better, not his history. He was relieved when the cell phone jangled. "Excuse me," he said, snatching it up and leaving the kitchen area to seek some privacy.

"I guess you won't be coming in to work on Monday, Chief," Commander Montgomery needled in lieu of a greeting.

"No, sir," Sean agreed, wincing. The CO sounded good and ticked.

"I suppose being AWOL is better than being dead," the man relented with a trace of irony.

Sean swallowed hard. Would the commander really report him AWOL? "Sir, there are extenuating circumstances—"

"It's okay, Sean," the CO cut him off. "I'm just razzing you. For some reason, I get a kick out of it."

Yeah, I wonder why, Sean wanted to retort. Couldn't have anything to do with carrying a grudge, could it?

"We'll just adjust the date on your leave chit," the CO offered.

"Thank you, sir."

"I've been in touch with Hannah. She promises to keep me posted on what's happening. I've heard of the Centurions before, by the way," he added. "I used to work for a captain who wore a signet ring with a griffin on it. Kimball was a strange man. Always seemed to have some agenda other than that of the mission."

"Yes, sir," Sean agreed, grateful for his commander's implied support. Without it, he'd be facing serious charges under the UCMJ.

"You've got a week to get yourself out of trouble," the man warned, now sounding stern again.

"Thank you, sir," Sean told him fervently. He hoped a week would be enough. If not, life as he'd known it would never be the same.

Ending the call as abruptly as he'd started it, he was left with no choice but to sit across from Maggie and finish his meal.

"More?" she asked when he scraped his plate clean.

"No, thanks," he said. His stomach wasn't up to being overfilled. "Listen, I don't want to outwear my welcome. Thanks for saving my life, but I can stay somewhere else if I make you uncomfortable."

She sat back and stared at him in amazement. "First of all," she retorted, "it would take more than a concussion to kill you, so I didn't save your life. Second, you're in no condition to go anywhere. Besides, your friends will be picking you up here in the morning."

He wondered for a second if she had ulterior motives, like getting him to have sex with her. It wouldn't be the first time a woman had attempted coercion, to which he usually submitted. He allowed himself to consider what it might be like to be with Maggie. She was divorced. He was single. They would be alone all night together.

Immediately, he thought of Ellie, and his worry resurfaced, chasing off the temptation.

"Is she your girlfriend?" Maggie asked, seeming to read his mind. "This Ellie Stuart? She's been on TV an awful lot."

Ellie, his girlfriend? He didn't have girlfriends; he had sex partners. Ellie just happened to be the best one yet. "She's innocent," he asserted, sidestepping the question.

"I know that," Maggie replied. "I knew the first time I saw her face on the news. Same with you."

"I guess you can read people pretty well," Sean commented.

Maggie shrugged. "I guess I can," she agreed.

He couldn't resist flirting with her just a little. "So, what do you see when you read me?" he asked, meeting her gaze directly.

She sat back, contemplating him. "I see a confident and highly trained warrior who probably knows over a hundred ways to kill the enemy but would never hurt a friend."

The comment hit a spot in his heart that made him feel especially vulnerable.

"I see a man who probably puts himself on the edge of danger to keep from thinking about something in his past," she added.

Immediately, he thought of Patrick. The vulnerable feeling grew, along with a sudden, inexplicable urge to cry.

"That's enough," he decided gruffly. "Sorry," he apologized for his harsh tone. "I've got a lot on my mind right now."

"That's understandable, given the trauma your brain's been through," said Maggie matter-of-factly. "I'm going to take a walk on the beach," she added. "Why don't you get some rest? You can leave in the morning when your buddies come." Leaving the dishes in the sink, she departed through the sliding glass doors and disappeared.

Sean crossed to the window to keep an eye on her. The big house had cast its shadow over the beach. As she waded across the sand toward a turbulent-looking ocean, her dark curls whipped in the breeze. He thought of Ellie and quickly redialed Reno's number. "Were you able to get in touch with Ellie?" he asked.

Reno hesitated and then said quickly, "Sean, Ellie checked out of the hotel room this afternoon."

The announcement made Sean's full stomach cramp. His head started to pound again.

"I had to impersonate a police officer to get that information," Reno added. "I don't know anything else."

"Shit," Sean swore. "Where would she have gone? What about my car? Is it still there?"

"I asked that question. The hotel had it towed."

Double shit. Where would Ellie have gone, alone in a strange city with no money and no friends to speak of?

"She has my number, Sean," Reno reassured him. "I'm sure she'll get in touch with me eventually."

"Yeah." If she hadn't been hauled off by some Centurion on a mission to silence her. After what they'd done to him, he could only assume the worst. "Thanks, Reno," he rasped, hanging up.

He stood there a moment, staring at the cell phone, planning to call Solomon next. He just needed a second to pull himself together. The possibility that Ellie was in serious, serious trouble unraveled his thoughts, making it hard to think. All he could do was *feel*. And he hadn't felt this scared, this helpless, since Patrick started dying.

Chapter Fifteen

✦

Consumed in private thoughts, Skyler didn't even glance at the individuals ambling up the walkway as she stepped through the shelter door and headed for the gate. It was supper time, when homeless men trickled in, searching for a hot meal. The light-skinned African American man approaching her looked no different. But then he stepped to one side, revealing two women in his wake. As Skyler spared them a curious glance, one of them spoke to her.

"Excuse me," she said brightly. A gust of wind ruffled her copper-colored hair. "Are you Skyler Dulay?"

"Yes," said Skyler, taking in her professional attire and her youthful age with curiosity.

"I'm Ophelia Pricc, a field reporter with a Virginia-based news station." She held out a hand for Skyler to shake. "And this is my cameraman, Reggie." The blond woman in sunglasses who hung back at a distance did not get introduced. "Could I ask you a few short questions about the Centurions' civic charities? I understand your father, Owen Dulay, is responsible for the shelter's operation."

"Yes, that's right," said Skyler unenthusiastically. She didn't have the will or the energy to tout her father's philanthropic endeavors, especially when she knew they were just a farce.

"Owen Dulay is Consul of the Centurions, is he not?"

"Yes, that's his title," Skyler said shortly.

"And the Centurions meet here at this shelter once a week; is that right?"

"Yes," Skyler answered.

"Have you heard the recent allegations made against them?" asked the reporter unexpectedly.

Skyler regarded her more closely. The shrewd look in the young woman's eyes shook her from her own disturbing questions of how and when to submit her mother's journal to the FBI. She realized the cameraman had hoisted a box on his shoulder and was filming her answers.

"No, I haven't," Skyler admitted, feeling suddenly cornered. "What allegations?"

"That the abduction of Ellie Stuart's sons was in fact perpetrated by the Centurions. What's your response to that, Miss Dulay?"

Skyler took a backward step while swiftly trying to deter further questions. "The Centurions are an organization committed to improving the lives of men," she carefully replied, certain her father would hear of this interview if not watch it firsthand. "Abduction doesn't fit into their mission."

"Membership into the upper hierarchy is inherited, is it not?" the reported continued, undaunted.

Skyler sensed her zeroing in on something more specific. "It is," she admitted.

"But you won't inherit your father's position as Consul because you're a woman," pointed out the reporter.

"That's correct," said Skyler stiffly.

"Does your father have a male heir, Miss Dulay?"

"No," said Skyler, determined to extricate herself before she said something her father would take umbrage to and make her escape plans more difficult.

"What about Carl Stuart?" suggested the woman. "The father of the three missing boys."

Carl? Was she out of her mind? "Carl is my father's chauffeur," Skyler retorted, tempering her mockery.

"Your father seems tremendously taken with Carl Stuart. Is it possible that he's chosen Carl to be his heir?"

The walkway under Skyler's feet seemed to tilt. As she steadied herself, her gaze flew to the woman wearing sunglasses on this overcast evening, and suddenly she knew exactly who she was.

"Miss Dulay?" prompted the reporter.

"Turn off the camera," Skyler hissed, taking a step toward Reggie. "Turn it off," she insisted, "or I'll reveal who's with you." Obviously, they wished to keep Ellie's identity a secret or they wouldn't have changed her appearance so drastically.

With a grimace, Ophelia Price signaled for her reporter to quit filming, and Reggie took the camera off his shoulder, clutching it in front of him.

For a long moment, the trio eyed each other warily. Skyler's heart beat fast and irregularly as she decided what to do about them. Perhaps she could use them to her benefit, to strengthen her own resolve. "Do you have a car?" she asked, glancing around to make sure they weren't being watched.

"We're parked on Reynolds Square," answered the reporter eagerly, "in a Chevy Caprice."

"Then follow me." With a nod and a final glance at Ellie, Skyler headed toward her reserved parking spot on Broughton. Once in her car, she eased into rush-hour traffic and drove automatically toward the Islands Expressway, to the beach where she and Drake had talked.

The suggestion that her father intended to make Carl his heir encased her heart in ice.

Would her father really do that? Leave his legacy to a shiftless, leering loser simply because he had no male heir? He had a daughter who'd done nothing but try to please him, yet all she got in return for her faithfulness was a husband thirty years her senior, another Centurion telling her what to do.

It was time she faced down the fact that her father had little, if any, love for her. Time to take control of her own life, once and for all.

Standing on a lonely strip of beach fifteen minutes later, buffeted by a breeze that promised inclement weather, Skyler compared the two photographs the newswoman had handed her. One was of Carl, the other a computer printout of her father playing football for Baylor.

Lightning sparked far out over the ocean where dark clouds surged over choppy waters. She looked up at the trio awaiting her reaction.

"You're telling me you think Carl's my half brother," Skyler concluded, pushing the words through a tight throat. The thought made her skin crawl.

"Your hesitation is perfectly understandable," Ophelia Price assured her. "Carl isn't somebody anyone would want to claim as kin, but the resemblance is undeniable, and my sources tell me that Carl's mother attended Baylor University at the same time that your father was there."

Skyler shook her head, wanting desperately to deny it.

"What I think and what I've convinced Ellie of," the reporter continued, "is that your father abducted Carl's sons—*his grandsons*—in the hopes that one of them will be a more fitting heir than Carl." She shrugged, planting the seed gently.

Skyler handed back the photographs. Glancing at Ellie, whose complexion remained waxen despite her makeup, Skyler considered the enormity of the woman's burden. The capable Navy SEAL who'd championed her was gone, supposedly having fled police on the way to jail. The woman must feel so helpless, so alone—just like she did. "Tell you what I'll do," Skyler decided. "If I find any proof to support your theory, I'll let you know. Tell me where I can reach you."

"We're all staying at the East Bay Inn," said the newswoman, handing her a business card. "But please don't tell anyone. After what happened to Sean, we're concerned for Ellie's welfare."

"I understand," Skyler promised. Was her father really capable of making people disappear? Of being so calculatingly ruthless? Yes. The knowledge galvanized her as nothing else had ever done.

"Thank you for your time and willingness to listen, Miss Dulay," the newswoman offered, looking deep into Skyler's eyes, seeming to understand that she was as much a victim to her father's schemes as she was a witness. "We won't make your statements public," she reassured her. "And I really do want you to call me for anything, okay?"

With a nod of acknowledgment, Skyler sent Ellie an empathetic nod before slogging across the soft sand, shoes in hand, toward her car.

Dropping onto the cold leather seat, she shut the door and just sat there, watching beachcombers race to their cars as fat raindrops splattered her windshield and distorted her view.

Too stunned to drive, she replayed the reporter's allegations. If Carl was her father's son, born out of wedlock, that certainly explained the time and energy her father had expended on Carl, who by anyone else's standards was beyond improvement. It also gave her father a motive for wanting to abduct Carl's sons. With grandsons to inherit, his legacy could continue in Centurion fashion for another seventy-five years, at least.

But, dear Lord, he'd ripped three little boys from their mother's arms just to suit his needs! He might even have pulled far-reaching strings to make a Navy SEAL disappear.

His cruel, blatant manipulations were almost impossible for her to comprehend—almost. Hadn't she found out at age eighteen just how effortlessly he could manipulate an entire hit-and-run case, making it disappear into thin air? She had paid the price of overwhelming guilt, and that poor man's family had never known the truth.

It was time to put a stop to her father's machinations, but a lifetime of fear made her palms sweat, her heart pound. Once she opened her own Pandora's box, how would she protect her mother from her father's wrath? How would she protect herself?

*   *   *

Scrutinizing Carl across the table, Skyler watched him lick the last drop of mint sorbet from his spoon. This wasn't the first night he'd been invited to eat supper with her and her father, but with her suspicions firmly planted, the physical attributes he shared with her father were suddenly all too obvious. They had the same angular jaw, the same long, bony fingers.

"Are you finished?"

She swung a guilty gaze at her father and realized he was speaking to Carl, who wiped a drop of sorbet off his chin with the back of his hand and nodded. He pushed back his chair, looking ill at ease in a collared shirt that once belonged to his employer.

"Where are you going?" Skyler inquired as both men stood. It was pouring rain outside. Thunder rumbled ominously. Lightning cast an eerie greenish glow behind the dark clouds.

Her father sent her a quelling glare. "To a meeting," he answered shortly.

But not a Centurion's meeting, she noted, for it wasn't Wednesday. Could he be taking Carl to visit his sons? Was that why Carl was dressed for some special occasion?

Averting her gaze, she stuck a spoon in her own sorbet and pretended disinterest.

They left her to finish her dessert alone. Over the drumming rain, she listened for the telltale rumble of the garage doors opening and closing, signaling their departure. The grandfather clock in her father's study chimed eight times as she rose cautiously to her feet. She could hear the servants conversing in the kitchen where they shared their meals, even Drake, who ate with them.

With no one to waylay her, Skyler slipped across the

marble foyer and entered her father's study. She stood a moment with her back to the closed door, allowing her eyes to adjust to the gloom.

Violet shadows quilted the cherry woodwork. Where in this lair of shelves and files and locked drawers might she find tangible evidence of Carl's parentage?

Slipping into the desk chair, she imagined briefly how it felt to be master of an empire—how intoxicating, how corrosive to the human soul. Carefully, she slid the top drawer open, feeling past the bills and sundry papers for the box that held the key she'd seen her father put away— the key that accessed his files.

Finding it, she clutched the key in her damp palm as she crossed to the standing file cabinet. She inserted the key into the lock, releasing all four drawers with a click. Pulling open the first one, she sought the files beginning with *C,* for Carl.

Lightning lit up the room for a scant second, allowing her to see that there were only investment reports for Construction Contractors, a company her father owned, filed under *C.*

Opening the second drawer, she fingered the tabs until she came to *S,* this time for *Stuart.* A file marked *Spenser and Weis Attorneys at Law* was the last folder filed under *S.* Sliding a hand behind it, she felt an envelope and withdrew it. But with no more lightning forthcoming, she moved to the nearest window to catch the glow from the lit water fountain.

D. Stuart, Manachie, Mississippi, read the return address. The letter had been sent to her father.

Withdrawing scented stationery, Skyler angled it to read the faint scrawl, her heart scarcely beating.

Dearest Owen,

I know you never expected to hear from me again, but life deals unexpected cards, as I've grown to realize. When you spurned me twenty-eight years ago, you never knew I was carrying your child, a son, whom I named Carl, after my father. Since you'd chosen your path, I felt it my right to keep my secret. I also determined not to tell Carl who his father was, only that he was conceived in love, though in the end, you married another. Now, as I find myself losing a battle with breast cancer, I wonder if I was wrong never to tell Carl what a great man you've become. He is a son I take little pride in acknowledging, a lazy and dissolute man who shirks his obligations—exactly the opposite of yourself. I think it ironic that you are, perhaps, the only soul on earth who can redeem him. That is why I've decided to inform you of his existence. Whether you choose to act on that knowledge or not is up to you. I've made peace with my past. It's only right to allow you to do the same, in your way.

Sincerely,
Darlene Stuart

Skyler released the breath she was holding, trembling at her discovery. The proof had been here all along, like a malignant cancer, just waiting in those files to be discovered. If ever she needed a sign that she was about to do the right thing, this was it!

Folding the letter with shaking hands, she slipped the envelope into the pocket of her denim skirt. She was about to leave her father's office when a shadow moved through the line of light shining under the door. The door handle jiggled.

With a gasp, Skyler ducked behind a settee, fearing she had just been caught. The door opened and closed, quickly and quietly, and the lights remained extinguished. She sensed she was no longer alone, but who would stand still and silent like that?

A chill swept over her. But then she detected soft footfalls as the intruder crossed the room to the file cabinet. Too late, she remembered she had left it ajar. With a faint click, a beam of light shot across the floor, tracking toward her. She cringed, certain of discovery.

But then the beam changed direction. At the whisper of a file drawer opening, she dared to peek around the arm of the settee. To her disbelief, she recognized Drake. He stood holding a penlight between his teeth and a wandlike object that emitted a blue glow in his right hand. As she watched him, he drew the wand across the contents of the file in his left hand.

Disbelief morphed into incredulity, followed by realization and outrage. He had lied to her! About everything.

He wasn't a runaway teen—in hindsight it was obvious. She doubted he was eighteen years old, and without her mother's journal, he probably hadn't known a daisy from a jonquil!

But then, who was he? Uncertainty kept her paralyzed several minutes longer. She had given herself to him in trust, believing his interest in her stemmed from a mutual attraction and friendship, when all along he had been using her as a pawn to gain access to her father's house, to her father's files.

Outrage overcame fear. She surged to her feet, startling

him into dropping the penlight. "Just what do you think you're doing?" she demanded in a low, quavering voice.

"Skyler!" he exclaimed, putting the file away hastily. "What are you doing here?"

"What am *I* doing here?" she retorted, stalking toward him. "I don't think that's really the question, do you, Drake? Or is that even your name?" she demanded, furious with him. "How dare you use me to get to my father!" she accused, stopping before him with her fists clenched.

"Shhh!" he hushed her, bending to snatch up the penlight, switching it off. "Skyler, please." He sounded agitated. "We can't be caught. Come up to my room, and I'll explain."

"Explain what? That my father's a crook? That you used me to get to him—for what reasons I have yet to figure out and probably don't even want to know?" Her voice was rising to a louder pitch with every word.

She gave a startled gasp as he took a sudden step forward, caught the back of her head in one hand, and silenced her by kissing her soundly.

"That's an apology," he explained gruffly when he finally raised his head. "I've wanted to tell you the truth for as long as I've known you," he added convincingly. "I just didn't know whether family loyalty would force you to give me away."

"Who are you?" she asked, befuddled. His voice, his scent, the taste of his kiss were all so familiar, and yet he was still a stranger.

"I'm an undercover agent with the FBI," he murmured in her ear. "Your father's been under investigation for years."

She shook her head in confusion, fright, and, oddly, relief. "Then you're not eighteen," she determined, clutching his strong arms with newfound respect. "You're an FBI agent?" she whispered cautiously.

"Undercover," he added, his white teeth flashing in the dark.

"Prove it," she retorted. She'd had the wool pulled over her eyes for too long to ever trust again so easily.

With a sigh, Drake reached into the backpack sitting at his feet. Withdrawing a slim black phone, he pushed a series of numbers, then held it to her ear. "You have two saved messages. Message one: 'Drake, it looks like we have an in-house security breach,'" growled a man's voice. 'Somehow, someone in the organization now knows what you're up to, and they've asked for a personal favor. Supposedly our suspect is responsible for the abduction of three boys. They want you to keep your ear to the ground. I'll expect your call tonight as usual.'"

"Your father?" Skyler asked, daunted by the commanding voice on the other end as Drake put the phone away.

"Yeah," he admitted with a helpless shrug. "I guess that part about running away from him was just a fantasy."

Skyler's head spun. So much had happened so quickly. First she'd learned that Carl was her half brother and that her father had kidnapped three boys, and now she learned Drake was with the FBI. Life as she'd known it would never be the same. She could feel the chains of obligation that shackled her to her father falling away. "Drake," she breathed, certain he could hear her heart pounding with the promise of freedom. "You don't need to search my father's files anymore." She gripped his arms to keep the room from spinning. "My mother wrote everything down in journals. *Everything*. If I give them to you, will you protect me?"

Skyler's confession cast a net of disquiet over Drake's excitement. "How many journals?" he asked, relieved that she'd apparently forgiven him for his deceit. "What's in them?"

"There are ten altogether, going from 1988 to 1998, when my mother's memory started to fade. There are names, events, places. Everything he did both publicly and privately. You won't believe the details, Drake. Mogilevich—does that name sound familiar?"

The Russian embezzler. He'd been sought by the FBI for years. "Yes," he admitted hoarsely.

"My father had him over as a guest. He offered him use of his shipping port."

"Skyler," Drake grated, pulling her into his embrace and holding her firmly, now willing her to be silent. Stark sorrow compressed his heart, overshadowing the excitement of stumbling into such a boon. This was the big break the FBI needed to bring Owen Dulay to heel. Only, the price Skyler would have to pay to submit such evidence was too high.

She was still explaining. "My pendant. It opens a box at the Cathedral of St. John the Baptist. Father Joseph has been protecting it all this time."

"Skyler, listen," he whispered, casting a nervous glance at the door. He could hear the servants moving about in other parts of the house. "If you give me those journals, you have to start your life over again under witness protection."

Her sudden stillness told him she hadn't realized what her contribution would cost. "But you could protect me," she asserted, her eyes shining with faith visible even in the darkness. "Me and my mother."

Beyond her words, he heard a message of hope for a future between them, and his heart contracted with real regret. "No, love," he whispered, hearing her gasp at his endearment. "Regardless of how I might try, I couldn't keep you safe. You and your mother would go to a new location, undisclosed even to me. You'd start your life over again."

"Then I would never see you again," she realized with a catch in her voice.

"Not for a long time," he agreed. "It'll take months before your father is convicted—years, probably, for your testimony to be forgotten. Even then, your father and his associates will never forget. You'll be viewed as a traitor to all Centurions, and for that, they'll try to make an example of you by killing you and your mother."

Skyler shuddered in his arms. With a frightened sob, she fell against his chest. Drake held her firmly, letting her make her own decision. The feelings that had sprouted so naturally between them should not be a determining factor, and yet he couldn't help but wish for what could never be.

"I have to do it," she whispered, sounding terrified but equally resolved. She lifted her head to explain her reasons. "I can't let him get away with the things he's done. I have to stop being a coward and do this for myself—and for my mother."

"You're sure?" he asked, his eyes burning with love and admiration.

Paper rustled in her hand as she drew a letter from her pocket. "About that kidnapping rumor you were told to listen for"—she thrust an envelope into his hands—"this letter proves Carl Stuart is my father's heir. Those boys are his grandchildren. I'm almost certain he took them."

Toward the crack of dawn, Ophelia's cell phone rang. Ellie bolted upright next to her, jarring Ophelia awake when she would've just let the phone keep ringing.

"It's my cell," Ophelia croaked, groping for it as she cracked an eye to read the clock—4:30 A.M. Only Vinny and his SEAL buddies were awake at this ungodly hour. "What?" she whimpered, answering his call.

"Why didn't you return my call?" Vinny demanded in lieu of a greeting.

"Maybe I didn't want to talk to you," she mumbled.

"Well, did you get my message?"

"No, what message?"

"Sean's alive," he announced, sounding wide awake and breathing hard as he hurried somewhere. "Solomon and I are about to take a hop to Hunter Army Airfield. Then we're going to pick up Sean. He wants to know if you found Ellie."

"Of course I found her," Ophelia retorted, rubbing grit from her eye.

"You did? Awesome. Keep her safe till we get there. Where are you?"

"It's called the East Bay Inn on East Bay Street," Lia mumbled.

"Terrific. We'll be there around ten hundred or so."

" 'Kay."

"Go back to sleep, beautiful."

"Fly safe," she murmured, ending the call. Her heavy head sank back into the pillow.

"What'd he say?" came Ellie's anxious whisper.

It took Lia a moment to remember. "Oh, he said Sean's alive. He and Solomon are going to get him now."

"He's alive!" Ellie cried. "Oh, thank you, Lord!"

Lia suffered an effusive hug that she was too tired to reciprocate.

"Is he hurt? Is he okay?"

"I don't think so. Vinny didn't say."

Ophelia thought she heard Ellie shed some quiet tears. Poor thing, if she stayed with Sean—which would make her Sean's first serious girlfriend—she'd ride this same emotional roller coaster over and over again.

A SEAL was never safe until he was home in his woman's arms.

Chapter Sixteen

✦

"How did you end up way the hell out here?" Solomon groused, leaning out of the driver's window of a black sedan, no doubt borrowed from the motor pool at Hunter Army Airfield.

"I swam," Sean retorted, standing up on the stoop where he'd sat waiting. Wearing a straw hat that covered his bandaged head and complemented the tropical shirt, he looked like a tourist on vacation, which was Maggie's idea.

He turned to her now, extending a hand of gratitude. "Thank you again," he repeated, eager to get going. At her wistful smile, he pulled her into a swift embrace.

"Good luck," she called as he leapt off the stoop. "I'll be watching the news. Don't disappoint me," she warned as he loped across the wet sand in her front yard. The storm had moved northward, leaving behind a beach setting as pristine as if it had been power washed.

"Sit up front," Vinny offered, giving up his seat to move to the back.

"Thanks," said Sean, clapping him on the back. "Hey,"

he said to Solomon as he ducked into the passenger seat. "Thanks for coming to save my ass." He sent Maggie a final wave.

"No problem." Morning sunlight glanced off the car's hood as Solomon backed them briskly into the street and tore off in the direction of town. He cast Sean a keen sidelong look. "Aside from the clothes, you look pretty good," he observed.

Sean showed him the bandage under his hat. "Bullet came this close," he admitted matter-of-factly. He glanced over the seat at Vinny. "What's up?"

"My fiancée is already down here covering the kidnapping," Vinny said quickly.

"Shit," Sean retorted irritably. "I told you to tell her to back off."

"I did, okay?" Vinny defended himself. "But she's like a pit bull when it comes to getting to the truth. Plus, she's dying to prove these Centurions kidnapped the kids."

Sean simmered for a moment. "Maybe we can use the media to our advantage," he relented.

"Aye," said Solomon with an approving nod.

"You want to hear some good news?" Vinny asked.

"Yes." There'd been a real scarcity of good news lately.

"Lia found Ellie," Vinny added. "They're both staying at the East Bay Inn. I told her we'd meet them at ten o'clock."

Sean hadn't been able to sleep a wink last night, worrying that the Centurions had done her in. Without warning, he lunged over the backseat and kissed Vinny soundly on the lips. "Thank you!" he exclaimed.

"Ugh!" Vinny protested, wiping his mouth with the

back of his hand. "Jesus, Harley. You know I hate it when
you do that."

Solomon chuckled.

Sean sat back and drew a deep, cleansing breath. The
prospect of seeing Ellie again, alive and kicking, made
him want to stick his head out the window and release
a rebel yell. He'd never come so close to dying for a
woman. He'd never spent so much time worrying about
a woman, period.

That had to be why his heart was pumping with exul-
tation. It wasn't because he was falling in love. Hell, no.
Not with a woman who'd sooner take him down a peg
than put him on a pedestal. How crazy would he have to
be to take her on for any time at all . . . or even forever?

Maggie's cell phone, which she'd insisted on giving
him, gave a sudden ring. Sean snatched it up, recognizing
Reno's number. "Ellie's been found," he said by way of
greeting.

"Thank God," said Reno. "Where is she?"

"Staying with Vinny's fiancée, who wants to do some
kind of *60 Minutes* exposé on the Centurions."

"I'm glad she's safe," Reno replied, sounding awfully
grim. "Sean, I have some bad news, I'm afraid."

How could anything be worse than what Reno had
shared with him yesterday? "What is it?"

"It's about your alibi, Tiffany, and the reason she didn't
return Butler's call."

His stomach cramped with dread. "Go ahead."

"She was shot in the head three nights ago and left for
dead."

A cold spot formed on Sean's scalp under the straw hat.

Left for dead. "Is she still alive, then?" he asked, stunned and shocked.

"Barely. She's in a coma," Reno answered. "In ICU. Her father wants to talk to you."

Sean felt sick to his stomach. He had to open the window to catch a breath of balmy air and clear his head. Solomon was speeding them past the same marshy area where the cops had shot him and foisted him off on the fishermen.

"I'll call him as soon as I have some answers," he promised hoarsely. Bathed in a clammy sweat, he couldn't get his brain to think. "I need to call Hannah," he decided. "Butler's the only person who had Tiffany's contact information," he added irately. "Now, fucking tell me he's not working for the Centurions."

"Don't be so hasty, Sean. You'd be leveling some serious charges at the man. I'll try to find out who he shared that information with."

"How long will you be down here? You want to meet up?"

"Actually, I need to get home this afternoon. My oldest is giving a piano recital."

More than anything, Sean admired how Reno put his kids first, but this was pretty damn crucial.

"I can fly back down tomorrow or any day after that if you need me," Reno promised. "Frequent-flyer miles," he added. "In the meantime, you know it's my sworn duty to tell you to turn yourself in to the authorities, right?"

"Yeah, I know, Reno. I get you. I'll be careful." Careful plotting to get every last Centurion who'd made Ellie, her boys, and now Tiffany suffer. Sean had no intention of remaining in hiding while the Centurions celebrated their victory over him.

With a click, Reno was gone.

Still swimming in shock, Sean silently dialed Hannah's number. He envisioned Tiffany in ICU with tubes coming out of her, attached to life support. "Damn it!" he snarled as the car got quiet enough to make the ringing audible to all.

"Sean, I'm glad you called," Hannah greeted him.

"Yeah, well, you won't be," he retorted, telling her what had happened to his only alibi. "Butler was the only person I gave her contact information to. He tried to fucking kill her so he could frame me."

"I understand that you're upset," Hannah said quietly. "I promise I'm looking into that assertion. Butler doesn't work alone, Sean. He reports to two division chiefs, forensics and investigations. Listen, I wanted you to know that I contacted the undercover division," she added, "and you're right. Drake Donovan is currently working in Dulay's household. His father, who is the special agent-in-charge of the Undercover Division, has promised to alert him to the alleged kidnappings. He wanted you to know that the tracer was put on Dulay's car two days ago. Apparently he's been visiting the Centurion's home for boys."

Sean's spirits rallied from despair. "Are you serious? The Centurions run a home for boys?"

"That's right."

"I bet that's where Ellie's boys are," Sean exclaimed, feeling immeasurably better.

"I'm submitting a request for a search warrant," Hannah answered. "It'll take at least twenty-four hours for me to hear back on that. In the meantime, I'm flying down to Savannah to put together a SWAT team."

"Whatever you do, don't let the local police know that," Sean begged. "I sure as hell don't want Dulay moving those boys if that's where they are."

"I realize that," Hannah drawled.

"Sorry. I don't mean to tell you how to do your job."

"And I'm not going to try telling you how to do yours," Hannah answered cryptically.

She seemed to be saying that if the SEALs intended to scope out the boys' home, that was their prerogative. "Yes, ma'am," Sean agreed.

"Keep in touch, Sean, and I'll do likewise."

Ending the call, Sean rubbed his gritty eyelids and spared his silent companions a sober look. Shit, he'd never meant for that to happen to Tiffany.

And, holy God, if it'd happened to Ellie, there was no telling what he might do. He turned his head in time to see a sign that read SAVANNAH 9 MILES. "Can't this cheap piece of shit motor-pool car go any faster?" he roared.

Solomon gunned the motor, bouncing Sean's neck off the headrest and pushing the hat down over his ears.

"Look what Skyler just gave me!" Ophelia cried as she returned from the lobby. The announcement prompted Ellie to turn off the hair iron at the antique vanity. Her unruly hair wasn't going to get any straighter today. She barely recognized herself already in Ophelia's turquoise blouse and matching jacquard skirt.

Crossing the Victorian carpet, Ophelia waved papers

in front of her that looked like photocopies of a letter. "Recognize the return address?" she asked.

Ellie frowned down at the photocopy of the front of an envelope. "Darlene Stuart," she exclaimed, recognizing the name and the address. "That was Carl's mama. She did know Owen Dulay!" she gasped, noting who the letter was sent to.

"Oh, she knew him," Ophelia agreed, waggling her eyebrows dramatically, "and I do mean in the biblical sense. I told you Carl was his son."

"But Darlene was such a kind, churchgoing woman," Ellie protested.

"Read the next page," Ophelia invited, brimming with excitement. "Oh, this is good," she exclaimed, rubbing her hands in ecstasy. "This will put Owen Dulay right where we want him."

Ellie barely heard what else Ophelia had to say. Skimming the letter, she realized that Darlene had once loved Dulay, whom she must have known when he was a younger, kinder man. Her plea to him to make Carl a better man must have led him to lure Carl to Georgia. But finding Carl to be a waste of flesh, he'd looked beyond his son to his grandsons, whom he'd gathered to him like so many lost sheep, raising them to be seemingly upright Centurion men.

No! she thought, shooting to her feet. *They are my sons to raise as I see fit. You cannot have them.*

But for the time being, Dulay did have him. The question was, where?

A knock at the door had both women whirling to face it. They'd been expecting the men to arrive any moment, but it could just as well be Centurion hit men looking for Ellie.

"Who is it?" Ophelia called, tiptoeing closer.

"Yo, Adrian. It's me," said a voice in a perfect imitation of Rocky Balboa.

"Vinny," Ophelia exclaimed, throwing the door wide.

Three hulking men filled the doorway. Ellie's gaze flew straight to the man wearing a straw hat and a tropical shirt. His blue eyes burned across the space between them. "Sean!" she whispered, clapping a hand to her mouth, so happy to see him alive she nearly burst into tears.

He crossed the room in four long strides, pulled the hand from her mouth, crushed his lips to hers, and banded his arms around her, pulling her to him. With her toes scarcely touching the floor, Ellie could have stayed in his arms all day. The room got awfully quiet.

Just as abruptly, he let her go. "Why didn't you tell Reno where you went?" he scolded, his expression awfully grim, his complexion unusually pale.

"I lost his card when I had to pack everything. Maybe it fell into Carl's box."

"Don't worry about it. I'm just glad you're okay," he added, stroking her hair. "What's with the new look?"

"It's so the Centurions don't recognize me." She gestured to his tropical getup. "Where'd you get these clothes?" she asked.

"From the person who found me on the beach," he said quickly.

"The beach?" Lifting the hat off his head, she gasped at the bandage taped along one side. "Sean, what happened?" The wound explained his pallor, as did the implication that he'd washed up on shore like a ship-wrecked sailor.

"It's a long story. I'll fill you in later," he promised.

"The police tried to kill you, didn't they?" She trembled as she envisioned it.

"Something like that," he answered. "I have something good to tell you," he added, his gravity lightening.

"What?" she asked, sensing something big.

Sean glanced at the others. "We might know where the boys are," he announced with a gleam in his eyes.

Her legs wobbled. "What?" she cried. "Where?"

"According to Hannah, who spoke to the undercover division that Drake works for, Owen Dulay has visited the Centurion Boys' Home. It might be a long shot, but there's a possibility they might be there."

A rash of goose bumps rippled over her. "Where is it? Let's go get them!" she cried.

"Slow down, sweetheart. The FBI's working on a warrant to search the building. We can't just go in and look for them. But my buddies and I are going to check the place out," he promised.

"I'm going with you," she declared, turning to look for her shoes, a pair of Ophelia's pointy-toed high heels.

"I have a better idea," Ophelia interjected, her eyes sparkling with conjecture. "Why don't I go to this boys' home and tell the people running it that I want to adopt a baby? They'll have to give me a tour, right? I'll wear my brooch with the hidden camera—"

"We're not here to do a story," Vinny countered, cutting her off.

"Just listen. My camera will show you what the building looks like inside. Maybe I'll even get to film the boys. You plan on sneaking in later, right?"

The men did not deny that possibility.

Vinny glanced helplessly at Sean and Solomon.

"The idea has merit," Solomon conceded with a shrug.

"Fine," Vinny allowed, "but you're not going in alone," he said to Ophelia. "You need a husband."

She cocked her head to consider him. "In that case, Senior Chief can be my husband, because you're way too young to be a father."

Vinny's dark eyebrows shot together. "You just had to point that out, didn't you? How long are we going to be mad at each other?"

"I'm not mad," Ophelia insisted. "I'm just stating facts."

"Enough," Solomon cut in with authority. "I'll go into the building with her."

Vinny shut his mouth against a ready retort.

"Hold on a sec," said Ophelia, turning to rummage in her luggage. "Let me have Reggie make sure this thing even works."

As they waited, Sean pulled Ellie against him for another long hug. With her ear plastered to his chest, she could hear his heart beating fast and hard. The tension in his body told her something was troubling him. She clutched him back, holding him as hard as she sensed he needed to be held. Her heart swelled with intense affection, and suddenly she knew. *She loved him.*

God help her, she loved this man to pieces.

When had it happened? she wondered. Was it way back when he'd changed Colton's diaper? Was it when she realized that he was acting as her warrior, willing to take on anyone or anything on her behalf? Either way, she was in too deep now to back out.

"I missed you," he said gruffly in her ear.

Ellie's eyes stung at how close those words came to what she was dying to hear, at how far short they fell. "I missed you, too," she whispered. She couldn't possibly tell him how she really felt. Nothing was more guaranteed to send him running than a confession of love. She knew him well enough to know that.

"Okay, I'm ready," Ophelia declared, returning from Reggie's room next door with the brooch clipped to her collar. "Let's go find these boys."

The possibility of being reunited with her sons pulled Ellie out of Sean's arms. This whirlwind experience wasn't about falling in love with Sean. It was about getting her boys back and taking on the most frightening entity she'd ever encountered—Owen Dulay and his Centurion followers.

The Centurion Boys' Home gave Ellie the creeps.

The three-story stone structure looked as if it might have served as a prison back during the War of Northern Aggression. A wall of the same dark stone flanked either side of the building, turning to enclose a yard at the back. Not a single tree cast shade on the flat, green lawn out front. Ellie suspected the Spartan appearance carried over into the interior as well.

As Vinny parked the black sedan along the curb on the far corner of the expansive grounds, Solomon and Ophelia continued past them in the Chevy Caprice, turning in to forge the long, gravel driveway. While they would make inquiries inside the building, Sean and Vinny planned to acquaint themselves with the grounds. Without the cover of night to cloak their movements, they were forced to keep to the tree line set a good fifty feet from the wall.

"Let's wait five minutes and see if they get in," Sean advised, keeping them in their seats.

They watched as Solomon and Ophelia got out of their car. Ophelia clutched her "older husband's" arm as they strolled up the stone steps to knock at the double doors. They waited for what seemed an eternity before they were admitted.

Watching them, Ellie chafed to join them. Imagining her sons behind the cold gray walls made her want to leap from the car, tear up to the building, and pound on the doors.

"Sean, I want to go with you and Vinny," she begged, sitting abruptly forward. "Please. I won't get in the way."

With a sigh, he twisted in the seat to reason with her "Sweetheart, you're wearing high heels," he pointed out.

"So? I'll take them off."

"And go barefoot in those clothes?"

Ellie seized his muscled arm. "I can feel the boys here," she insisted, straining to see through the distant, glinting windows, hoping for a glimpse of their faces.

"I understand," he said patiently. "But we gotta do this right. We're here to look around, not be seen."

"But I want to know what you're seeing," she tried again.

"Here. Vinny, give her your cell phone. I'll call her on mine."

"I thought the police confiscated your phone," she said

as Vinny surrendered his cell phone wordlessly. "Thank you."

"I've got another one," Sean replied, patting his shirt pocket.

"They're in," said Vinny.

Ellie looked back at the building. Sure enough, Solomon and Ophelia had been welcomed inside.

"Time to go," Sean declared, opening his door. "If someone asks you what you're doing parked on the street, tell 'em your husband went in the woods to take a leak."

Rolling her eyes, Ellie kicked off Ophelia's high heels and slouched in the seat to avoid being seen. Vinny and Sean darted into the woods and, within seconds, disappeared behind a screen of foliage.

"My husband," Ellie murmured, feeling out the words on her tongue. For a brief moment, she gave her mind liberty to conjure what having Sean for a husband might look like. As she pictured him fathering her boys into adulthood, teasing blushes from her for the next fifty years, a sharp, deep longing made her heart bleed.

What were the odds that Sean would ever want to settle down, especially with her? Ellie Stuart wasn't anything special. He probably thought of their intimacy here in Savannah as just a temporary madness. Not even Carl, a one-time all-state quarterback, had loved her enough to stay faithful. Sean, with his laughing blue eyes and easy smile, could have any woman he wanted. He wouldn't ever choose a small-town Mississippi girl to be his one and only.

She'd get nothing but heartache thinking about happily ever after.

Chapter Seventeen

✦

"I'm afraid we don't have any babies," said the kind-faced, gray-haired matron who'd introduced herself as Myrtle Banks. "Our youngest available child is four. His parents died in a terrible fire. It took every member of his family, including two older siblings."

"Oh, that's awful," Ophelia replied, feeling for the child despite their purposeful agenda. "But I thought I heard a baby crying when we came in."

The woman sent her a blank look. "Oh, that baby," she said, looking away quickly. "No, no, he's been reunited with his father. He's not available for adoption."

"Would that father be Carl Stuart?" Ophelia asked, and the senior chief's biceps flexed with surprise beneath her palm. Leaning on the man was like hovering next to a ticking bomb.

Miss Banks appeared flustered, which was exactly Ophelia's intent. "How do you know Mr. Stuart?" she asked.

"Well, he's Mr. Dulay's chauffeur," Lia replied, implying that Carl had driven her about in Mr. Dulay's car.

"Oh, I see," said the woman thoughtfully. "Yes, I believe he's the father," she admitted.

Lia squeezed Solomon's biceps to convey her excitement. The boys *were* here! "Could you show us around a bit?" she requested, waving a hand to encompass the central flight of stairs and the dark and dreary hallways on either side. The building smelled of Lysol overlying the dreary odor of an aging institution.

"Of course," said the woman, having concluded that Ophelia was a family friend and should therefore be accorded every courtesy. "The boys are in their classrooms now, so we can't do more than take a peek," she warned.

"That's fine," said Ophelia. "I wasn't aware that they were educated here instead of at a public school."

"Oh, yes," said the woman, trudging ponderously up the steps before them. "They receive a rigorous classical education far superior to that of the public schools."

Ophelia and Solomon shared a knowing look, both of them realizing that the "classical education" Myrtle touted was actually a thorough form of brainwashing.

"How long have you been here, ma'am?" Solomon surprised Ophelia by speaking up suddenly.

"Thirty years," Myrtle answered proudly. "I came here shortly after Mr. Dulay's father founded the home. Here's the first Mr. Dulay's portrait," she added, pausing to indicate an oil painting hanging at the top of the stairs. The cold gray eyes of the home's founder implied he'd been a forceful, powerful man. Like father, like son.

Only, in the case of Carl Stuart, that proved not to be the case.

As they headed toward the east wing, the sound of children's voices behind closed doors became audible.

"This is our upper elementary classroom here," said Myrtle, allowing them to peer through the glass inset. "These boys are all eight to twelve years of age."

"How did they end up here?" Ophelia asked, fiddling with her brooch to capture images of studious boys bent over their desks.

"Oh, many of their parents are too poor to look after them. They leave them here knowing their sons will have a brighter future."

As minions of the Centurion empire, Ophelia thought, concealing her disgust. No doubt the Boys' Home had churned out doctors, lawyers, police officers, and even government officials, all of whom pledged allegiance to Owen Dulay.

"And farther down the hall, we have two classrooms for younger children," continued Myrtle, oblivious to Ophelia's private thoughts.

These rooms were much noisier, with children out of their seats and milling around. One boy sat in the corner, his face to the wall. Ophelia felt Solomon tense as his gaze alighted on the blond head. "That boy there," he said, calling Myrtle's attention to him. "Is he in trouble?"

The boy under discussion turned his head to one side, and Ophelia stifled her gasp. Solomon had just found Caleb Stuart—or at least a boy who looked just like him. Solomon, she recalled, knew the Stuart boys well. In fact, for several years, Ellie had raised Solomon's son, Silas, along with her own three boys.

"Oh, that one," said Myrtle with a sad shake of her head. "He's a troubled boy. It may take him a while to settle in with the others. But don't worry. His teacher will get through to him eventually."

Beneath his black mustache, Solomon's lips thinned.

Suddenly, the boy under discussion glanced their way. Solomon stepped abruptly out of his line of sight, pulling Ophelia behind him. "Let's not be the cause for further disruption," he murmured.

Sure enough, the sound of running feet preceded that of the doorknob jiggling. A little face jumped up to peer out the window.

The teacher's voice cracked like a whip through the murmur of voices. "Mr. Stuart, return to your chair this instant!"

Ophelia overheard a struggle as the teacher presumably dragged Caleb from the door. Solomon all but hauled her toward the stairwell with the vision of Caleb's hopeful blue eyes plucking at her heartstrings.

"What else is on this wing?" Ophelia asked, recalling her purpose for being here. Having seen Caleb with her own two eyes, she was more determined than ever to spring the boys free.

"The staff live there," Myrtle indicated, heading down the stairs.

"Where do the children sleep?"

"With me, on the third floor," she answered impatiently.

"Could we take a look upstairs?" Ophelia pressed, pushing her luck.

"I assure you the living conditions are excellent," she answered, continuing doggedly downward. "If you'll excuse me, I'm expected in the cafeteria at this time."

Ophelia and Solomon shared a look. With Ophelia's persistence Myrtle had realized they weren't friends of Owen Dulay but were probably members of some social or health services organization. And now she was quietly but firmly sending them on their way.

Convinced the woman's heart was in the right place, Ophelia reached into her bag for a printout of the FBI Web site for missing persons. Caleb's, Christopher's, and Colton's pictures were circled in red.

"Thank you," said the senior chief tersely as Myrtle hauled open the heavy front door.

As it groaned on its hinges, Ophelia thrust the paper at her.

"What's this?" the woman asked, frowning down in perplexity.

"These children were kidnapped, Mrs. Banks," said Ophelia, ignoring the senior chief's glare of outrage that she'd just revealed the purpose behind their visit. "They were ripped away from their mother and brought here against their will."

"That's a lie," Myrtle protested, her sallow complexion paling. "I was told their mother was dead."

"She is very much alive," Ophelia countered. "Those children belong with her."

As Myrtle gaped at Ophelia in mixed denial and shock, Solomon tugged the paper from her hand. "Don't pay her any attention," he assured the woman, holding the page behind his back. "She's too nosy for her own good."

"Oh, for God's sake," Lia snapped. "Don't you watch the news?" she demanded of Myrtle. "Haven't you seen the boys' photos and the pictures of their poor, heart-broken mother?"

"I don't watch television," Myrtle answered. "It's for-bidden here."

"Enough," Solomon growled, propelling Lia forcefully out the door and down the steps.

With her appeal made, Lia allowed him to lead her away. Yes, she may have just blown the SEALs' chances of sneaking in tonight and stealing the boys back, but why go to the trouble if Myrtle could be convinced to do the right thing?

"I can't believe you just did that," Solomon snarled, dragging her to their vehicle.

"Trust me," Lia retorted. "That woman had her own suspicions. She just needed a little proof, that's all."

As he yanked open the driver's door for her, he crushed the FBI printout in his free hand. "She served the Dulay family for over thirty years, remember?" he reminded her, his silvery eyes as cold as ice. "What makes you think she'll be disloyal now?"

Ellie's stomach churned with helpless agitation.

Time had crept by in painful increments. Growing hot, she'd cracked her door open. Next she'd unfastened the two top buttons on the turquoise blouse, loath to leave perspiration stains on an item that had to be dry-clean only. More than thirty minutes had elapsed, and still Sean hadn't called her as he'd promised. Only one car had passed her on the street, not even slowing down.

At last the phone in her hand gave a ring. Ellie snatched it open, praying the unfamiliar number belonged to Sean. "Hello?"

"Sweetheart. How's it going?"

Just the sound of his voice improved her mood drastically. "Nothing's happening," she admitted, letting her frustration show. "Only one car has driven by. What about you?"

"Well . . ." He hesitated, which wasn't encouraging. "The wall that wraps around the back is scalable, but I don't know how we'd get the boys out of the building, especially if they're up on the third floor."

Ellie's hopes for an imminent reunion took a nosedive. "So you're not going in tonight?" she concluded sadly.

"I wouldn't rule it out. We need to talk to Senior Chief. Have they left the building yet?"

"No, not yet. Oh, wait a minute. Here they come now."

Ophelia's rental flew toward the parked car, braking abruptly in the street. Wondering at the reason for her haste, Ellie jammed her feet back into her heels. As Solomon stepped out, his grim expression made Ellie's stomach knot. "Solomon looks mad," she relayed to Sean. Ophelia remained in her car, clutching the steering wheel firmly, an obstinate lift to her chin.

"We'll join up in just a minute," Sean promised, ending the call.

Shutting Vinny's phone, Ellie went to open the car door, but Solomon waved her back inside. He surprised her by joining her in the rear seat, stuffing his sturdy frame into the enclosure and heaving a sigh.

"What is it?" Ellie demanded, fearing the worst. "What did you see?"

For a moment, he just looked at her, his light-colored eyes reflecting mixed compassion and concern. "I saw Caleb," he said simply.

A gasp of wonder swelled Ellie's chest, then dissolved immediately into sobs of relief. She hid her face in her hands, fighting to get a grip on herself as Solomon looped an arm around her and pulled her ear to his chest.

"He's safe," he crooned. "He hasn't been harmed."

Ellie sensed a qualifier coming. "But you're still concerned about him," she guessed, searching his face through her teary vision.

"He's angry," Solomon conceded. "According to the matron who runs the place, they've had difficulty breaking his spirit."

"Oh, no," Ellie breathed, realizing that Caleb had been punished, probably severely.

"He's tough," Solomon reassured her. "He'll adjust fine when you get him back."

"What about Christopher?" she asked, now worried for her other boys. "And Colton?"

"I didn't see them," Solomon admitted. "We heard a baby crying when we first stepped in. And Ophelia filmed a classroom of older children. We may yet see Chris when we replay the film."

"Okay," Ellie replied, clinging to the hope that they, too, were in the building. She was about to ask if they were going to sneak in that night when Sean and Vinny stepped from the woods. Vinny took one look at Ophelia's tense expression at the wheel of the second car and changed direction to join her.

Sean glanced curiously at Solomon in the backseat. He noted Ellie's tears. "What happened?" he asked, slipping into the driver's seat.

"They saw Caleb," Ellie relayed, tears flowing again as she envisioned him angry and defiant.

"Let's go back to the inn and talk," Solomon suggested,

and Sean started up the car, waving at Ophelia to precede them.

As Sean executed a U-turn in her wake, Solomon announced softly, "Vinny's fiancée might have blown it for us."

Sean looked back at them through the rearview mirror. "How?"

"She told the woman who runs the place that the Stuart boys had been kidnapped. She tried to leave her a printout from the FBI's Web site," he added with heavy mockery.

"Well, shit!" exclaimed Sean. "What's to keep that woman from calling Dulay?"

The fear that her boys would disappear again strangled Ellie's windpipe.

"Our ace reporter seems to think the woman'll do the right thing," Solomon bit out, understandably irate.

"Damn," Sean swore, glowering at the Chevy Caprice ahead of him. Following his gaze, Ellie could see Ophelia gesturing elaborately as she drove. Vinny gestured back.

"Looks like World War Three up there," Sean commented.

Solomon just shook his head.

Ellie found her voice. "What if Dulay moves them?" she asked fearfully.

"We're not going to let that happen," Solomon reassured her. "As soon as we have a plan, we'll go back and set a watch. No one's going to come or go without us knowing."

Clenching her hands tightly in her lap, Ellie tried to believe him. She would die if they came this far, endured this much, only to let her boys slip through their grasp in the final hours.

* * *

Arriving at the inn in the wake of the other couple, Ellie, Sean, and Solomon walked into a room crackling with tension. Ophelia stood stone-faced over Reggie, who kneeled by the desk to sync the camera in her brooch with her laptop's hard drive.

Vinny glowered out of the second-story window, which overlooked the old city exchange bell, his hands fisted at his sides. At their entrance, he sent them an apologetic grimace and said, "I'm sorry. Like I told you before, she's like a dog with a bone, and she refuses to give it up."

Ophelia glanced up with her eyes flashing. "Are you calling me a bitch?" she demanded.

"That is a word for a female dog," Vinny mumbled sullenly.

"Children," Solomon cut in with forceful disapproval. "This is not the time or the place for dissension. From now on, we work together," he added, slicing Ophelia a warning glare, "and the mission won't be compromised. What have we got?" he added, addressing the technical expert.

Reggie's finger was poised in readiness over the keyboard. "You might want to move closer to see," he suggested.

"Let Ellie sit in front," said Sean, waving the others back.

Ellie sank onto the Victorian chintz rug directly in front of the monitor. The others perched on the end of the bed or hovered to one side. Six spectators trained their eyes on the video clip, which started with a knock on the door.

A long wait was followed by a genteel but tentative greeting before the couple was invited inside. The camera panned down a dreary hallway, then up a daunting stair-well, and Ellie shuddered. Her boys would have night-mares for years to come.

Yet, listening to the matron's voice as she led the two-some to the second level, it was clear she believed in the home's mission of improving the outlook of young boys' futures.

As she announced their arrival at an upper-elementary classroom, the camera lens gave a jerk, and suddenly Ellie could see a dozen or more heads bent over desks. Desperately, she searched the closely cropped heads for a familiar face. "Can you stop the film?" she asked.

Reggie hit PAUSE, freezing the action; however, viewed from behind and wearing identical clothing, the boys all looked the same. Tears of frustration stung Ellie's eyes. "I can't see Chris," she admitted.

Reggie tapped a key and the video continued. The matron introduced Ophelia and Solomon to a room of younger boys. The camera leapt again, then centered on a boy sitting on a stool in the corner. Ellie gave a cry as she recognized Caleb in his signature stance of mutiny. The sight was so heartbreakingly familiar that tears flooded her eyes.

The air shifted, and in the next instant, Sean was kneel-ing behind her, putting his arms around her. "We'll get them back, Ellie. It won't be long," he promised.

"Why can't we get them now?" she demanded, tipping her head back to send him a pleading look. "It's not right for them to have to stay there. Look what they're doing to him!"

"Sweetheart, we can't just blaze inside like a SWAT

team could and pull them out. We don't have the legal right."

"Of course, if we're not seen . . ." Solomon insinuated.

"Then go in tonight," she proposed, cutting her anxious gaze to the other two SEALs. "Please, get them out of there!"

The three men shared a long, thoughtful look.

"To scale that building, we'd need climbing gear—ropes, pulleys, and clips," Sean reflected. "And even then we'd have trouble lowering the children from the third story, where that woman just said they sleep," he added, nodding at the video, "down to the wall, then twelve more feet to the ground."

"We're better off inserting through the front door," Solomon added, tossing out a new idea. "We could cut their phone lines, disable their alarm, and try sneaking in once we're confident that everyone's asleep."

They shared uncomfortable glances.

"Why can't you do that?" Ellie asked.

"We probably could," Sean answered cautiously. "Normally, we study the environment first so we know what kinds of patterns to expect. We won't know if someone stays up all night keeping watch. If some kid gets up at night to use the bathroom. Whatever."

"It's risky," Vinny agreed.

"Chances are high that we'll be seen. A million things could go wrong. Colton could start crying when we go to take him out of bed," Sean added with a shrug.

"And we can't use weapons or tear gas," Solomon decreed, "not with children in the area. If we're compromised by adults, we'll just have to dissuade them in other ways."

"I say we do it. Tonight," Sean added.

"I agree," said Vinny. "The sooner the better."

Solomon glanced at his watch. "Seven hours till nightfall. Until then, I want us posting watch at the home in case Dulay gets suspicious"—he flicked an irritated glance at Ophelia—"and decides to relocate them. Vinny and I will cover the watch," he said to Sean. "You stay with the women here so that someone doesn't recognize you."

"Hooyah," said Sean with a crooked smile.

"Ma'am," Solomon added, directing an icy glare at Ophelia, "this story doesn't go to press until the children have been recovered."

"Of course not," she retorted, meeting his stare without flinching.

Vinny swung an uneasy look between them.

Solomon nodded. "Let's dress and move out," he said to Vinny. The men had secured a room of their own on the third floor. "Sean, have one of the women drop you off at the home at o'dark hundred. I'll leave some clothes for you to wear," he added, throwing a final mocking look at Sean's flowered shirt.

"Roger, Senior," Sean called, warming Ellie with a look that promised intimacy just as soon as he could get her alone.

Spying his big brother in his customary spot on the hot, packed-dirt playground, Caleb sprinted toward him, his heart so filled with excitement it felt like it would explode. "Chris!" he shouted, wresting his brother's gaze from the dirt on his shoes. All Chris ever did was sit on that swing and stare.

"Chris!" he repeated, coming to a gasping halt in front of him.

Chris looked up with empty eyes. "What?"

Making sure no kids were close enough to overhear, Caleb whispered, "I saw Solomon!"

Chris's expression didn't change. "No, you didn't."

"Yes, I did!" Caleb retorted, flushing with anger. "I saw him out in the hallway while I was sittin' in the classroom. He was with a woman."

"Jordan?"

"No, some other lady with curly hair."

"Then it wasn't Solomon," Christopher reasoned. "He'd never leave Jordan to find us here."

In his fury, Caleb punched his brother right in the jaw. "I'm tellin' you, I saw him!" he roared.

"Boys!" cried Mr. Spellman, Chris's teacher, who stood watch over their recess.

Caleb was immediately sorry, not just because Mr. Spellman was striding over to speak to them but also because Chris looked at him the same way Mama used to look at him, with disappointment in his gray eyes. "Sorry," he muttered, scuffing his heels and hanging his head.

"What is going on here?" demanded the teacher.

"Nothing, sir," said Christopher, slipping respectfully off the swing. "He just apologized."

The teacher swung a suspicious gaze between the two. "Both of you go play, and no more hitting."

Christopher grabbed Caleb's hand and pulled him to the far side of a large metal jungle gym. "You're gonna get in trouble again," he warned his brother with real concern. "Stop making up stuff."

"I'm not! And I'm not gonna get in trouble, either, 'cause I won't be here after today."

Chris closed his eyes and heaved a sigh. "What are you planning?" he asked tiredly.

Caleb glanced at the two little boys scrambling over the jungle gym. He stood on tiptoe and whispered in Chris's ear, "I'm gonna start a fire."

"How?"

"With your magnifier," Caleb answered, patting his right pocket. "I already got a pile of kindling," he added, gesturing to the corner of the yard, where he'd stacked leaves and twigs, small bits of tinder that had blown over the wall. "Once the fire gets goin', all the teachers will be over here tryin' to put it out, and I'll run for the cafeteria door. They unlock it every day at lunch for the delivery truck." He peered up at Chris, desperately seeking his approval. "And when I get out," he continued, "I'm gonna find Solomon, and we'll come back for you 'n' Colty."

Chris just looked away. "It won't work," he said, crushing Caleb's confidence.

"It will!" Caleb shouted, tempted to shove him. "Just watch!" he challenged, sprinting to the pile of kindling he'd collected. Dropping to his knees in the sparse grass, he whipped out the magnifying glass, angled it to catch the sun's full radiance, and waited.

It was good and hot today. Perspiration trickled from his hairline as he held the lens in place. Glancing over his shoulder, he realized Christopher had walked away.

Chapter Eighteen

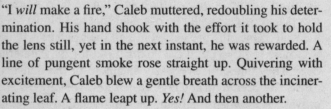

"I *will* make a fire," Caleb muttered, redoubling his determination. His hand shook with the effort it took to hold the lens still, yet in the next instant, he was rewarded. A line of pungent smoke rose straight up. Quivering with excitement, Caleb blew a gentle breath across the incinerating leaf. A flame leapt up. *Yes!* And then another.

He sat back, watching in amazement as the fire slowly spread. Flames danced from leaf to leaf. The little fire grew taller and hotter.

With a grim smile of triumph, he shot to his feet and ran from the fire to avoid being blamed for it. He trotted up to Mr. Spellman and said, "Can I go in and use the bathroom?"

"You can wait. Recess is almost over."

"Okay." He went and hovered by the door, jiggling up and down, looking like he had his mind on just one thing—peeing. Seeing Christopher again on the swing, he stuck his tongue out at him and then grinned. Chris glanced toward the back of the yard, caught sight of the fire, and jumped from the swing. "Mr. Spellman, it's a fire!" he shouted.

Caleb knew that was his cue. As Mr. Spellman rushed toward the little inferno, Caleb darted through the cracked door. He could hear shouts and exclamations behind him. Mr. Spellman was calling for a bucket of water.

Caleb ran straight into Mrs. Banks, who'd run from the kitchen to the cafeteria at the sound of alarm. "It's a fire," he exclaimed. "Mr. Spellman wants water in a bucket!"

"Oh, dear," she cried, disappearing right back into the kitchen to fetch the requested item.

Caleb shot toward the door on the far side of the yellow-tiled cafeteria. Sure enough, the lock on the chain hung open, just waiting for the food deliveryman.

As he sprinted toward freedom, his heart pounded in his chest and blood thrummed in his ears. He hit the door at full speed. It flew open, startling the black man about to open it from the outside.

"Whoa, there!" he exclaimed as Caleb crashed into him and whirled away, only to trip on the corner of a box-laden dolly. "Hold on!" exclaimed the man, catching Caleb by his collar. "Where do you think you're going?"

"Let go of me!" Caleb bellowed, fighting the man's grip with every ounce of his strength. He kicked and hit and flailed to no avail. The deliveryman was way bigger and stronger. He just swung Caleb under one of his burly arms, left his dolly right there on the walkway, and marched the boy who was bawling with frustration back into the building.

*   *   *

With a deep sigh, Ellie nestled more comfortably against Sean's chest. They'd stolen up to the bedroom Solomon and Vinny had changed in. The sheets of the antique four-poster bed now lay twisted around them, damp and smelling of sex. In a short while, Ellie would have to call housekeeping for a fresh set, but for now, she and Sean were free until dark. The mellow strip of sunlight that fell across the floor let them know their time was dwindling.

Sean mocked himself. "Forty-eight hours away from you and I couldn't wait to rip your clothes off."

Is it all about sex for him? Ellie wondered, masking a little pinch of hurt as she gazed across his chest at a silk lampshade.

Shifting his weight suddenly, he flipped her onto her back and gazed down at her. "No comment?" he queried.

"You haven't told me your story yet," she pointed out, anxious to hear where he'd been and what was weighing so heavily on his mind, robbing him of his ready smile.

"Oh, yeah," he replied, scrubbing a hand over his eyes. "Okay," he said with resolve. "Ready to hear this?"

She wasn't sure she was.

As he recounted the Savannah police's betrayal, she shuddered to think how close the bullet that had left the gash on his head had come to killing him. An unaccustomed fear encased her heart in ice.

She remembered telling him, and believing it, that she didn't need a man in her life. That she'd be fine without him. He'd gone and made a liar out of her.

"And then I woke up on a boat, with my ankles coiled in anchor rope."

The harrowing story ended with a record-long night-time swim after which he awoke on the beach with a splitting headache. "When I saw a woman coming toward me, I tried to get up but I couldn't."

The woman, whose name was Maggie, had nursed him through his concussion. Ellie listened, carefully masking the jealousy that twisted her insides. Maggie had bandaged his wounds and put him in her bed. She'd even given him her ex-husband's clothes to wear and her cell phone.

"Nice woman," he said in conclusion. "Smart. She's a doctor of . . . forensic anthropology," he recalled.

Ellie swallowed. The realization that Sean had lied to her earlier sat like a cinder block on her chest. He'd said before that people—plural—had given him the clothes he was wearing, when in fact, Maggie had offered him her ex-husband's clothes. Maggie who owned a big house on the ocean and had a PhD.

Suddenly, it didn't matter that Sean had made Ellie feel like the only woman in the world when he'd made love to her. He could have any woman he wanted, including one with a seaside mansion and a doctorate. Why would he ever want Ellie, who could barely scrape up enough to pay the rent, who just started going to college, who had three boys who would need special help getting over the trauma they were still being subjected to?

Nothing had changed between them.

"I'm glad you're okay," she said with a weak smile.

"I'm all right," he agreed, but a shadow seemed to fall over his face. She felt a tension in him immediately.

"There's something else you're not telling me," she quietly accused.

He looked at her sharply. "You know me that well?" he asked.

She had to swallow the lump in her throat. "I guess so.

What is it?" she asked as the lines bracketing his mouth deepened. She could tell it was something awful. Her heart clutched with fear.

"It's Tiffany," he admitted gruffly. "The woman I was with—"

"I know her name," she cut him off, not wanting to hear the rest. "What about her?" Jealousy twisted her insides anew.

"Someone tried to kill her."

"What?" Ellie sat up abruptly. "Oh, Sean," she cried, instantly ashamed of her pettiness. "What happened?"

He stroked a hand up the length of her spine. "I think Butler plotted to have her murdered so I wouldn't have an alibi."

"Butler?" she replied, envisioning the bland-faced FBI agent as a cold-blooded murderer.

"Or maybe one of his superiors," Sean offered with a shrug. "It doesn't really matter, does it? Tiffany's in ICU in a coma. I ruined her whole fucking life."

"Sean," she breathed with dismay. "It's not your fault. It's mine," she attempted to convince him. Tears of remorse and pity for a woman whose only sin was to succumb to Sean's charms tracked down her cheeks.

"Don't cry, Ellie," Sean begged, pulling her head down on his shoulder. "It is my fault. If I hadn't been trying so hard to get you out of my mind, I never would've turned to her in the first place."

Ellie gave a sharp sniff and lifted her head. "What did you say?"

His blue gaze looked deeply into hers. "I said I only went to see her because I couldn't stop thinking of you."

"Oh," she answered, her dismal spirits lifting. She cautioned herself not to make too much of his confession. He wasn't saying he loved her, just that he'd wanted to have sex with her and couldn't. She'd pretty much sent him packing at the mere suggestion.

"I think I'd better catch some shut-eye while I can," Sean suggested, closing his eyes and rubbing them. "I didn't sleep much last night."

She hadn't slept well lately, either, not until Vinny's call letting her know that Sean was safe. "Okay," she agreed, wriggling in his arms to find a comfortable position.

With her head pillowed on Sean's shoulder, Ellie released a long, uncertain sigh. Sean's confession about Tiffany gave her hope that he loved her the way she'd come to realize she loved him. Immediately, she reined in her optimism. What difference did it make if he loved her or not? She was determined to forge her own path, to stand on her own two feet. She didn't need a man in her life to make her whole, regardless of how much she might love him.

"Mr. Dulay?"

"Yes, Myrtle," Owen replied, recognizing Mrs. Banks's distinctive voice, though it sounded more tentative over the phone than usual.

"We've had another incident, sir, with Caleb Stuart."

"Have you?" Owen asked, tempering his annoyance. "What now?"

"He started a fire in the school yard, then used the distraction to attempt an escape through the delivery entrance."

"I see," said Owen, who needed no more proof that Ellie

Stuart had left her genetic imprint on the second son. "I assume he was caught and is now being reprimanded?"

"Yes, sir. He's been locked in his room with bread and water for the next two days."

Myrtle sounded truly shaken by the attempted escape.

"Not to worry," Owen soothed her, pinching the bridge of his nose. "Soon his father will have the means to look after his own sons, and you won't have to do it for him."

"Yes, sir. About that, sir . . ."

"Go on," he urged, troubled by something in her tone.

"You told me their mother was dead," she blurted with obvious affront and confusion.

Owen's heart skipped a beat. "Who told you otherwise?" he inquired. While teachers at the Boys' Home were well aware of Christopher, Caleb, and Colton's history, they were all loyal Centurions, men who'd never dream to question the Consul's actions. Mrs. Banks had been told the boys' mother was dead. Since she'd banned the use of television at the home and watched little, if any, herself, he'd thought his secret safe.

"A woman," said Myrtle. "She dropped by this morning with her husband on the premise of looking for a baby to adopt."

"You let them in?"

"Well, she implied that she knew you, sir. I thought, perhaps, she might take pity on one of our younger tykes."

"Our boys have everything they need," Owen reprimanded. "Foisting them off on others isn't necessary."

"Yes, sir. In any event, she showed me a flyer that said the boys were missing."

"And you believe everything you read?" Owen countered with just the right mix of condescension and confidence. "You trust me, do you not, Mrs. Banks?"

"Of course, sir."

"Then when I explain to you that the Stuart boys were being raised in filth by a drug-abusing whore, wouldn't you wish better for them?"

"Well, yes, sir, but—"

"Their mother was compensated for her loss. I can't help it if she spent the money and has now changed her mind. It isn't easy to be the champion of children, Mrs. Banks. But I assure you that they'll be far better off with their father."

"Yes, sir," said Myrtle in halfhearted agreement.

"What did this couple look like?" He was forced to reveal his curiosity in exchange for information.

"The woman was young, with reddish curls. The man had a military bearing and a silver streak in his dark hair."

He searched his memory, unable to match her description to any key players. The word *military* made him wonder if the Navy SEAL, who was now allegedly dead, had friends. "I see. Well, good day, Mrs. Banks. We'll be visiting all three boys again this evening," he added with the slightest hint of warning in his voice that she had better take no action.

"Yes, sir. The boys will be expecting you," she reassured him.

Ending the call, Owen sat back in his desk chair and mulled over the disturbing conversation.

The cat was out of the bag, so to speak. Yet he didn't fear Myrtle's betrayal. It was the faceless strangers who had come knocking who troubled him.

Were they friends of the Navy SEAL? Of Ellie Stuart?

Had he been a fool for letting the Culprit convince him to release her?

The wisest course would be to take precautions. He would remove the boys tonight, stepping up his plans to install them with their father at his hunting lodge outside of town. Set in the marshes, surrounded by water, the house was miles from the nearest neighbor.

In time, he reassured himself, rumors of a kidnapping would die away. Christopher would grow into a fine young man, capable of running his grandfather's empire.

"What are you doing?" Ellie asked as Ophelia took the keys out of her car ignition and shoved them into the pocket of her slacks. When they had dropped Sean off minutes before, he had instructed them to return to the inn and sit tight.

Despite the gathering dusk, Ophelia's sardonic look was unmistakable. "Did you really plan on going back?" she asked Ellie. "Come on, Reggie. Grab the camera."

In the backseat, Reggie started gathering up their gear.

"Well, no," Ellie admitted, thinking they might drive around until it was fully dark and then come back. "But I think we should at least move the car somewhere less conspicuous, don't you?"

"You haven't done this kind of thing before, have you?" Ophelia surmised, flashing her a knowing grin. "If you park too far away and have to run for your vehicle, you might get caught."

"Oh," said Ellie, seeing the logic in that. "Well, can we at least park across the street and not call attention to the men in the woods?"

"Sure," said the reporter with a shrug. Jamming the key back into the ignition, Ophelia revved the engine and executed a tight U-turn, only to put them straight into the path of an oncoming vehicle.

"Watch out!" Ellie cried, blinded by headlights.

The vehicle swerved abruptly, dropped two tires onto the shoulder to pass them, then bumped back onto the road, avoiding a direct collision. The driver blared his horn indignantly.

"Phew!" Ophelia exclaimed in a shaky voice. "Sorry 'bout that."

"That was Carl!" Ellie realized, recognizing his silhouette even in the dying light. She twisted to watch as the taillights of a fancy silver car turned into the home's long gravel driveway. "And Owen Dulay," she added, noting the passenger in the rear seat. "Keep driving! God, I hope he doesn't come after us."

Ophelia kept her foot on the accelerator, taking them swiftly back toward town. Bats twirled above the dark limbs of live-oak trees. Up ahead, streetlights beckoned insects. The sound of a jazz band spilled out of a nearby local haunt.

"Are they following us?" Ellie asked, too fearful to look back. If anything happened to compromise her boys' rescue, she didn't know what she'd do.

"No," said Reggie. "I don't think they got a good look at us, either. I think it's safe to return, only not so close this time."

Ophelia circled a residential block, then headed back toward the outskirts of town.

"Should we tell the others Dulay is there?" Ellie asked.

"Believe me, they already know," Ophelia reassured her. "Our boys see everything. Hey, Reggie," she added, "how close to Dulay do we have to get to film a close-up of him coming out of the Boys' Home?"

"Pretty close," said Reggie nervously. "The night-vision lens limits our range to fifty meters."

"Don't worry," said Ophelia optimistically. "You know those ghillie suits I put in the trunk?"

Reggie groaned. "I thought those were for your husband."

"Nope. Those are for us. Trust me, no one will see us even if we have to get that close. We'll look like two lumps of grass."

"You just said our boys see everything," Ellie pointed out.

"Oh, sure, *they'll* see us," Ophelia admitted. "But they won't compromise their agenda by chasing us away."

Ellie regarded her shadowed profile with admiration. "Do you think Vinny will forgive you?" she asked quietly.

Ophelia didn't answer right away. She swung the car into a clearing of newly developed land, killed the engine, and sighed. "When Vinny realizes that I'm just doing my job the way he does his, then, yes, he'll forgive me," she replied with certainty. "It's not about me," she insisted. "It's about exposing the truth. There are too many men like Owen Dulay. My job is to bring them down, the way Vinny brings down terrorists."

"He loves you," Ellie reassured her.

Ophelia's eyes glimmered in the dark. "There was never any question of that," she answered, pushing her door open. "Maybe you should keep the keys," she added, handing them to Ellie. "Are you going to be okay waiting?"

"Sure," said Ellie, accepting the key ring with disappointment. Her lot, apparently, was to sit in a dark car as the hours crept by, honoring the phone silence Sean had requested, and wait.

Wait for him to spirit her boys out of the institution that had housed them for . . . was it just eight days since their kidnapping? It seemed like a lifetime ago that she'd been pulled from her Impala and thrown onto the pavement like a bag of trash.

Funny, she used to wonder how Sean could kill in the name of national security. But now, having been on the receiving end of Dulay's brutality, she understood the mentality behind dispatching terrorists. Because of that, she felt closer to Sean than ever—of one mind, one body, one spirit.

She wasn't supposed to have fallen in love with him.

That may well be her most costly mistake ever.

"Heads up," Sean warned his teammates. He spoke softly into the mouthpiece of his interteam radio, which Vinny had borrowed from Team 12's supply closet without the commander's knowledge. "A van just pulled into the driveway."

As Sean peered down through his Night Vision Goggles, the van parked alongside Owen Dulay's Bentley, and the driver jumped out, his face briefly illumined by the interior light. "I'll be damned," Sean breathed. It was the little bastard with the mustache, the one who'd gotten him arrested, accompanied by Grimes and the third kidnapper—a pock-faced, hulking creature. "Reinforcements have arrived, three in number. These guys were the kidnappers."

"Roger that, Chief," Vinny whispered. "Can you tell if they saw Ophelia and her sidekick out there?" For the past half hour, Sean and Vinny, who had a view of the expansive front lawn, had watched two bumps slither closer and closer. Light reflecting off a camera lens betrayed their exact location, at least to the SEALs, who were trained to notice.

"Negative," Sean reassured him. "They're heading straight for the side entrance, but it's locked. Now they're knocking." Standing less than twenty meters away from Sean's concealed location atop the wall, the three thugs shifted, scratched themselves, and spit as they waited. They had no idea that Sean, dressed in Solomon's black clothing, his head covered in a knit cap, and his face smeared in camo paint, was close enough to trounce them. "Senior Chief?" Sean whispered.

"Dulay just left his office," reported Solomon. From his position at the back of the building, Solomon had watched Dulay hold a brief discourse with Mrs. Banks, who nodded and left. Carl and the boys were presumably together in some other part of the building.

Sean's pulse quickened as Dulay cracked the service entrance. "He's letting them in," he whispered. "Cancel that. He's handing them a piece of paper. Looks like he's giving them directions. Holy shit, I think he's moving the boys out tonight."

"Wait it out," Solomon instructed. "Vinny, fall back to the vehicle in case they do move out. At my command, bring it to the corner of the property, no lights."

"Roger, Senior."

"What's happening now, Chief?" Solomon asked.

Sean watched the three thugs examine the paper Dulay had thrust at them. "They're returning to the van," Sean reported. "Looks like they're waiting for someone else to come out. Dulay went back into the building. Do you see him yet?"

"Negative. Office door is closed. Lights are out."

With a cicada buzzing noisily beside him, Sean kept his eyes peeled for movement. Moments later, the service entrance popped open again. This time it was Carl Stuart who appeared, dragging a resistant Caleb behind him. Sean's heart somersaulted with joy to see the boy. Christopher followed with reluctant obedience. He threw a look back at Dulay, who watched from the door.

Seeing the van waiting with its rear doors thrown open, Caleb balked. "No!" he shouted. "I ain't going with you!"

"Stop it!" insisted his father, yanking him firmly forward. "You're the one who wanted to leave, so quit your complaining." Grimes, who'd gotten into the back of the van, reached out to haul Caleb in after him.

"Recovery targets in direct sight," whispered Sean, his eyes stinging at the welcome sight of Ellie's boys. "They're leaving with Carl Stuart. Even the baby," he added as a young woman hurried to catch up with the others. A not-so-little Colton rode her hip. "Add one young female, unidentified. They're all getting in the van." The interior light lit Christopher's solemn face as Carl handed him up next. At the last second, Chris turned and waved farewell to Dulay, who returned the gesture and stepped back into the building, closing the door.

The woman, who was scarcely more than a teen, was

the last to climb aboard. Little Hitler shut them all inside, stifling the baby's sudden wail. Rounding toward the
driver's side, he slipped behind the wheel and fired up the
engine.

"They're moving out," Sean warned, tensing in anticipation of leaping off the wall to give chase.

"Vinny, state your location," Solomon requested.

Sean could tell Vinny was running. Yet somewhere out
near the street, he heard an engine turn over. Surely Vinny
hadn't reached the car that quickly.

"Coming up to the car now," Vinny huffed, confirming
Sean's guess.

"We'll meet you at the head of the driveway," advised
Solomon.

A terrible suspicion skewered Sean as he slid down
the wall and dropped into the grass. If that wasn't their
engine turning over, whose was it? As he raced along
one side of the driveway, chasing the van's taillights,
he could see Ophelia's rental car through his NGVs,
creeping out from behind a screen of trees with its lights
extinguished.

Ellie, no!

As the van turned left out of the driveway, Ophelia and
Reggie jumped to their feet in their ghillie suits and raced
to intercept their car, looking for all the world like Big-
foot and his mate.

"Damn," Sean muttered, realizing the reporting team
was leading the way in chasing the van. The fact that Ellie
was driving worried him even more. Presuming she'd
watched her boys get into the van, the only thing on her
mind right now would be getting them back.

She'd risk her life to do it.

Chapter Nineteen

✦

As the front tires of the Chevy Caprice bumped onto the pavement, Ellie accelerated, only to brake abruptly so that Reggie and Ophelia could leap into the car in their wild ponchos.

"Hurry!" cried Ophelia, sprawling into the passenger seat as Reggie dove into the rear. "Before they get away!"

Ellie peeled out, filling the car with the smell of burnt rubber as she shot forward, chasing the van's twin taillights, now some distance ahead of her. The worst-case scenario was happening right before her eyes—Dulay was relocating her boys, snatching them away again before she got the chance to see them rescued.

With her headlights off, she drove blind, scarcely able to make out the road ahead of her. Live oaks, palm trees, and vines flashed by on either side, creating a deadly barrier that hemmed her in.

"Careful," Ophelia warned. "Just stay far enough back that they don't see us." She was breathing hard, fumbling for her seat belt. In the backseat, Reggie shook off his ghillie suit and clung to his equipment.

"What about Sean and the others?" Ellie asked, her voice high and thin.

"They're right behind us," Ophelia reported.

They are? A glance in the mirror confirmed the woman's observation. The black sedan was creeping up behind them; its lights were also off, and it was trying to pass them on this straightaway.

Fearful of colliding, Ellie clutched the steering wheel harder. As the dark sedan overtook them, she glanced over just long enough to see Sean's camouflaged face at the window, but he was gone before she could read his thoughts.

Somewhere in the car, a cell phone vibrated. Ophelia pulled it out from under her ghillie suit and answered it. A muted but clearly angry voice barked orders on the other end. Ophelia listened for a moment before quietly hanging up. "They want us to fall back and turn our lights on," she translated, putting the phone away.

Ellie was certain Vinny had said more than that, and she could also appreciate the reason for his upset. They were speeding along a rural, tree-lined road at sixty miles an hour in nearly total darkness.

And as with the time she'd driven Sean's GTO over the bridge into Savannah, panic held Ellie in thrall. She could no more reduce her speed than she could slow her wildly beating heart. She kept the rental car right on the tail of the black sedan, peering through its windshield to the van far ahead of them.

I'm coming, boys! I'm coming. She willed them to feel her presence, wanting desperately to reassure them that they would soon be safe. She could not, would not, let them get away from her again.

"They're pulling into the gas station," Sean observed as the van swerved without warning into a Texaco, the only structure for miles in any direction, lit up by a Texaco star.

Solomon took his foot off the accelerator. They'd chased the van twenty miles out of town, first onto a quadruple-lane expressway where they'd been surrounded by other cars, then down this two-lane rural road with nothing around them but marshland, shanties, and this lonely Texaco station. So far, the kidnappers didn't appear to realize they were being followed. "What do you think?" he asked the others. "Should we take them now?"

Solomon and Vinny assessed the situation. No other motorists were pumping gas. A single clerk manned the counter inside. The odds looked good, but the potential for bullets being fired in such a volatile environment gave all three SEALs serious pause. "Let's do it," said Vinny, who tended to be impulsive.

"It's risky," Solomon pointed out. "We don't know if they're armed and stupid enough to start firing. Plus, the clerk inside is a wild card."

"So we catch them off guard," Sean suggested, eager to abate Ellie's panic. The Caprice had kept constant pace with them, falling back just far enough to turn on its lights. "We subdue them, flexicuff them, and lock them all back in the van," he argued. "Where are the cuffs?"

"Right here," said Vinny, doling them out from among the supplies he'd borrowed from Spec Ops.

Solomon put on his blinker to signal his entrance into the gas station. He'd made up his mind to do this. Sean glanced in the side mirror to find Ellie practically on their bumper. "Damn it, Ellie. Fall back," he muttered.

Solomon pulled the black sedan along the opposite side of the pumps. With the wide pump between them, the pock-faced kidnapper, who'd stepped out to pump gas, couldn't immediately see who'd pulled up next to him.

"Vinny, you grab the driver. I'll get this big guy. Sean, take the back. Jump out on three. One. Two. Three. Out!"

All three SEALs ejected at the same time with their weapons drawn. Solomon descended on the pock-faced thug, spinning him away from the pump before he could reach for the nozzle and spill gas all over the ground. Together they barreled into the side of the van, setting it rocking, alerting the occupants to trouble.

Hastening to the back of the van, Sean wrenched the handles, only to find the doors locked. He yanked harder, but the locks held fast.

Vinny, who'd rounded the van to drag out the driver, ran into worse trouble. As he dragged Little Hitler from his seat, the man snatched up a semiautomatic rifle, firing it pell-mell. Bullets spewed in all directions, ricocheting off the concrete, hitting the Plexiglas canopy overhead. It splintered, raining down fragments of plastic.

Sean hit the ground, his adrenaline spiking. If a single bullet punctured a gas line, they would all go up in an explosive ball of fire. With Solomon grappling to overcome the bigger man, it was up to Sean to neutralize the situation. Taking a bead on Little Hitler's shifting feet, visible to him under the belly of the van, he fired his borrowed weapon, hitting the perp directly in his right Achilles tendon.

"Aaaagh!" With a scream, the man dropped the AK-47, which Vinny promptly kicked out of reach before tackling the man to the ground.

Sean still had to get to Grimes, who was inside with the kids. He leapt to his feet, easing along the side of the van, fixing a wary eye on the mirror for any hint of defensive maneuvering. The second set of doors on the van's side were as tightly secured as the first.

Damn! A glance over his shoulder revealed that Ellie had parked a safe distance away, but she was out of the car, standing there with her hand over her heart. He waved her back into her vehicle. Ophelia and her cameraman had scurried behind a tree and were filming the takedown. And all this time, Grimes was inside coming up with a plan. *Double damn.*

With Vinny grinding Little Hitler's face into the oil-stained concrete, Sean climbed cautiously into the driver's seat, his gun at the ready. He'd hoped to find a third point of entry into the back of the van. There it was, a flimsy metal door between the seats. He wasn't surprised to find it bolted, but three swift, mighty kicks ripped it right off its hinges.

It clattered inward. The young woman screamed. Pulling his feet back, Sean dared a peek inside, sucking in a sharp breath at what the dome light revealed.

Grimes had a pale-faced Christopher locked in front of him and was holding a blade across his neck. "Get out!" he called up at Sean. "Get out or I'll slit his fuckin' throat."

Peering in again, Sean assessed the sea of faces staring

back at him—Chris, who appeared to be in shock; Carl, who looked like he'd been caught with his pants down; the whimpering teenaged girl; Colton with his thumb stuck in his mouth; and a tense, watchful Caleb. "Hey, fellas," he said to the boys, realizing they had yet to recognize him.

"Mr. Sean!" Caleb forgot his brother was a hostage. He launched himself off the bench seat and hurled himself at Sean, forcing Sean to swing his weapon away from him. *Jesus*. He could feel Caleb's heart pounding against his own. A fierce protective feeling overcame him as he pulled Caleb safely into the cab with him.

"I knew you'd come. I knew it!" Caleb grinned, clinging to him tightly.

"Get out!" thundered Grimes in the rear. "You got one kid. That's all you'll get. Now get out or I'll cut him. I swear it!"

"And then what?" Sean called back. "Both of your buddies are in our custody." Looking out the windshield, he could see Solomon and Vinny's heads bobbing as they flexicuffed the other kidnappers. "You don't have any van keys," he added, wrenching them out of the ignition and tossing them out the open door. "Where do you think you're gonna go?" he taunted.

In the lengthy silence that followed, Sean whispered to Caleb, "Run to your mama." He helped him out of the driver's side door, giving him a gentle push in Ellie's direction.

She was out of her car again. As Caleb sprinted in her direction, Sean watched her sink to her knees, opening her arms wide to him, her tears streaming down her cheeks. *One down*, he thought as Caleb rushed into her embrace. *Two to go.*

"Time's up, Grimes," he called, swiveling to deal with the situation in the van's rear. "Let Chris go," he added persuasively. "You know you're not going to slit his throat. I don't think Mr. Dulay'd be too happy about that, do you?"

The silence that followed prompted Sean to take another peek inside. Grimes's facial muscles had gone slack. His deep-set eyes were glazed with defeat. "Give me the boy," Sean urged, stretching out a hand to take him. "Come on. That way, no one gets hurt."

With a sudden shove, Grimes sent Chris flying into Sean's path. Sean caught him as he stumbled and swiftly traded places with him, putting him in the driver's seat. "Hey, big guy. You okay?" He tilted his chin up, noting Chris's slightly expanded pupils. His neck had been nicked, but he wasn't bleeding.

"I'm okay," Chris whispered.

Sean nodded. "Let me get Colton." Keeping a wary eye on Grimes, who still clung to his knife, looking cornered and unpredictable, he motioned to the young girl. "Miss, hand me the baby," he ordered calmly.

Blubbering and trembling, she barely had the strength to hold Colton in the air. Sean edged cautiously into the cargo area to take him. Colton pulled his thumb out of his mouth and kicked with sudden delight. "Dadda!"

Sean glanced at him in surprise, but with no time to savor the moment, he squatted down to pass Colton to Chris. "Go to your mother," he ordered firmly. "Quickly."

Sean listened as Chris slipped out of the van. He waited for the sound of his running feet to grow inaudible and envisioned Ellie's joy as she beheld her oldest and youngest heading toward her. "You, too, miss," he urged the girl gruffly. "Go inside the store and wait."

As she scrambled past him, frantic to escape, Sean planted himself in front of Grimes. "Surrender your weapon," he commanded.

The man slanted a dark, defiant look at him and clung stubbornly to his knife.

Without warning, Sean seized the rail overhead and delivered a swift, hard kick to the man's head. "That's for hitting me with a two-by-four," he explained, snatching the knife away as the man swayed to one side, then doubled over, grunting in pain.

"As for you," Sean added, leveling Carl with an icy glare. "I hope some murdering convict makes you his little bitch while you're in prison. You deserve no less for what you've done to Ellie and her boys."

"It wasn't my idea," Carl piped up suddenly. Up till then, he'd watched the proceedings passively. "Owen Dulay kidnapped my kids. I swear, I had nothin' to do with it."

"Shut up!" Grimes snarled, snatching his head up to send Carl a murderous glare.

"Put your hands on your head!" Sean barked at him, sensing sudden volatility in the air.

"Come on, man," Carl pleaded with Sean. "I never wanted those brats in the first place. It was all Mr. Dulay's idea. These guys are the ones who took 'em. I swear, I didn't even know about it."

"Shut the fuck up!" Grimes seethed, scarcely following Sean's orders to keep his hands up.

"I'll testify against them," Carl offered suddenly, mistaking Sean for a cop. "I'm innocent. I swear to you—"

With a move that Sean had predicted but hadn't had time to prevent, Grimes lunged at Carl, seized him in a headlock, and with a single, vicious jerk, snapped Carl's neck. Dropping his victim, he lunged toward the rear doors. In less than a second, he was shouldering his way out the back, moving with remarkable speed for such a heavyset man. He had jumped from the van before Carl's limp body even slipped to the grooved floor.

Sean stumbled over it as he gave pursuit. Grimes was halfway across the parking lot, thundering straight toward Ellie, who'd gotten her boys into the backseat and, seeing the kidnapper's approach, jumped behind the wheel with a look of horror. To Sean's amazement, she slammed the car into reverse and careened backward, driving like a demolition derby driver.

Grimes stood no chance of pulling Ellie out of another car and driving away. But in order to fire at him, Sean would have to shoot straight in Ellie's and the boys' direction. The thought of his bullet hitting any of them made his blood run cold, but he couldn't let the bastard get away. Aiming his weapon, he steadied his trembling hand and fired at the man's buttocks—a reassuringly ample target.

Crack! The bullet sent Grimes sprawling face-first onto the pavement. He rose up again, staggered, then fell, groaning in agony.

Sean leapt from the van and hastened over to him. "That was for Ellie," he muttered, dropping a knee to Grimes's spine in order to flexicuff him.

Seeing the kidnapper subdued, Ellie pulled the car closer. When Sean looked up at her, she was staring with relief into the open doors of the van at Carl's prostrate body, fully illumined by the dome light. He doubted she could tell whether Carl was dead or alive. Belated horror shuddered through him when he considered just how violent Grimes was—just how badly this rescue could've gone down.

Pulling the flexicuffs extra-tight on Grimes's fat wrists, Sean left him immobilized and jogged the short distance to where Ellie waited with her boys. At his approach, she pushed out of the car and launched herself into his arms, hugging him with ferocious gratitude. "Thank you!" she cried, too overwrought with joy to say more.

Emotion put a stranglehold on his vocal cords as he held her tight and gazed into the backseat at three little boys, all buckled in and holding each other in unity, their eyes enormous. A sense of belonging coiled around him, making him want to jump into the car and stay with them—forever.

But the wail of a siren made that fantasy impossible. "Go on, Ellie," he urged. "Take 'em back to the inn and wait for me. I'll be there as soon as I can. Go," he repeated, helping her back into the car, reaching through the window to strap her seat belt for her. With a wink at the boys in the backseat, he stepped back and thumped the roof of the car. "Go," he urged again.

With a brave, grateful smile, and reaching out to touch him one more time, she pulled away.

The sirens were still about three miles out but were closing in. Ellie would have to drive right past them, but hopefully they'd ignore her vehicle—as long as she kept her speed down. Feeling as if she were carrying off his heart, he watched her drive away.

The sirens grew louder. Dragging in a deep breath, Sean turned to deal with Grimes. Grabbing the man's bound wrists, he dragged him back to the van, where Solomon and Vinny were hoisting the other two inside, alongside Carl's body.

"I guess Carl won't be testifying to anything," Solomon observed, flicking Sean a look. "What happened?"

"Carl started blaming Dulay, and Grimes went ballistic," Sean retorted shortly. "Help me out, will you? This guy weighs like three hundred pounds."

It took all three men to lift a groaning Grimes into the rear of the van with the others.

"Clerk must've called nine-one-one," Vinny observed. "Let's get outta here."

Solomon handed him the keys to the motor-pool sedan. "Follow us with the news crew," he commanded. "I've got the key to the van."

As Sean and Solomon jumped into the van, Vinny waved Ophelia and Reggie out of hiding. Together, the two vehicles spun out of the gas station, bouncing through potholes and heading in the direction opposite that of the approaching police.

Over the muttered curses of the men in back, Sean listened to the sound of sirens fading. As the danger of being intercepted by Dulay's law enforcers dwindled, he pulled out his cell phone to notify Hannah of the recent chain of events.

"Special Agent Lindstrom," she rapped, clearly occupied with pressing matters.

"Ma'am, the boys have been reunited with their mother. We have the kidnappers and the body of Carl Stuart in our possession."

"Hold on, Sean. Say again?"

He repeated himself more slowly.

"That was fast," she drawled. "Change of plans, gentlemen," she called, clearly addressing others on her end. "The kids aren't coming after all."

"Where are you?" Sean asked, perplexed.

"On Skidaway Island, southeast of the city. We received a tip that Mr. Dulay was transferring the boys to his hunting cottage. I've been waiting with a SWAT team to intercept them here."

"You were tipped off? By whom? Mrs. Banks?" Sean guessed.

"That's between your party and mine," Hannah answered obliquely. In other words, Mrs. Banks's betrayal was being kept a secret to safeguard her from Dulay's reprisal.

"Yes, ma'am," Sean answered, using the side mirror to glance with admiration at Ophelia in the black sedan. "I guess our ace reporter called that one right," he said, earning a startled look from Solomon.

"Where are you now?" Hannah asked him.

"Headed in your direction," Sean continued. "You want to meet up so we can pass these fuckers off?"

"Find a secluded place to pull off," Hannah advised. "We're on our way."

Solomon found a dirt road hacked into the dense, vine-smothered forest. Pulling in, they bumped along a rutted track for several yards before killing the engine and waiting.

Filled with restless agitation, Sean stepped out and rounded the van. Leaning against the taillight, he watched Vinny pull up behind them as he called Hannah one more time to advise her of their location.

"We'll be there in ten minutes," Hannah promised.

"That went pretty well," Vinny commented, stepping out of the sedan to confer with him.

"Yep," Sean agreed, but his thoughts were on that moment when Ellie had thrown her arms around him in gratitude, and he'd looked into the car at her three beautiful little boys. He'd wanted so badly to drive off into the sunset with them. That was how it was supposed to be. Only, once again, Ellie was having to go it alone, just the way she'd been doing for years. It wasn't fair to her. She deserved so much more. The boys deserved more. Hell, even he deserved more, after all his efforts to find them.

Only with Patrick and his family had he felt a connection this powerful. It wasn't something he thought he'd ever feel for anyone else, let alone for Ellie and three rowdy boys. But he could no more deny his longing to be with them right now, witnessing their joyous reunion, than he could cut out his own heart. Shifting restless feet in the wet soil, he kept his gaze fixed down the dark road for the first indication of Hannah's approach.

It took more than an hour to transfer the suspects and the body of Carl Stuart to the FBI. Each SEAL was made to give a sworn statement. Ophelia had promised to provide the FBI with a copy of her footage and to sit on the exposé until all the warrants were served.

It was close to dawn by the time Sean returned to the East Bay Inn, nodding at the desk clerk while still wiping camouflage off his face. As he rode the elevator to the third-story room Solomon had since relinquished, his heart pounded with anticipation, not to mention fear that they hadn't made it back. Sliding his key in the door, he eased inside and stopped, heaving a sigh of relief.

The bathroom light had been left on, casting a muted glow over their sleeping figures. They lay nestled, all four of them in one bed, one against the other, so close that Ellie's embrace encompassed all of them.

Is there room for one more? Sean wondered.

Kicking off his shoes, he lay down on the far side next to Chris. Just lying there, listening to their blended breaths, he basked in the contentment that flooded him and thought of all that he and Ellie had been through to get to this moment.

He'd nearly died, for one thing. And despite the evidence Butler had shown to Ellie, she had loyally stuck by him. She'd given him her body, her deep and honest passion. That kind of bond didn't just happen with any woman. It had taken a woman like Ellie—strong, determined, and independent—to bring his heart out of hiding.

The shifting of the mattress roused Ellie from a deep, contented sleep. She stretched out her hand, then stilled with a smile to feel three warm little bodies tucked against her. Slitting her eyes to behold them, to assure herself that they were really here and she wasn't just dreaming, her gaze intercepted Sean's. For a perfect, undisturbed moment, they regarded each other. It felt so right just to open her eyes and see him there.

"Hey," he whispered, sending her that slow, heart-stopping smile that never failed to make her heart flutter.

"Hi," she whispered back.

His gaze slid to the blond heads between them, studying each boy one at a time, just as she had earlier, eyeing them for signs of abuse, just taking in the miracle of their presence. "They look good," he told her.

She smiled in agreement, but their mental and emotional welfare remained a concern. "We'll see," she said. Broader concerns nudged her contentment aside. "So what happened? Is everyone back?"

"Yep. We caught all three kidnappers and turned them over to the FBI," he said.

"What about Carl?"

He drew a deep breath, then let it out again. "Sweetheart, Carl is dead," he told her gently.

Having seen him splayed on the floor of the van, she had wondered about that. "How?" she asked, praying Sean hadn't killed him. How would the boys handle that?

"He started talking crap about the kidnapping, how it was all Dulay's idea and how he was innocent. Grimes just lunged at him and snapped his neck. It was over before I could stop him."

Ellie regarded her boys' sleeping profiles. How was she going to tell them?

"I'll tell them if you want me to," Sean offered.

"No, I'll do it," she replied with a brief smile of thanks.

"We need to get up soon and head out," he told her, speeding her pulse with his message. "Dulay's got too many contacts in this town to make it safe for us to stay. And Ophelia's going live with her broadcast as soon as the first wave of warrants is served."

"Where are we going? Back to Virginia?" She wanted nothing more than for her life to return to normal.

"Hannah wants us to stay close for a while," he replied, disappointing her. "My commander offered us his time-share over at Hilton Head. That's only half an hour from here. Right on the beach," he added. "The boys'll love it."

Picturing the days ahead, Ellie summoned the energy to roll from the bed. Sean caught her as she started to move. "Not yet," he added. "Just lie there. Let me look at you."

The words flooded her with both tenderness and regret. For the boys' sake, their affair was over. They couldn't continue being lovers, not when the boys' hearts were this vulnerable. Soon she would have to dig deep to assert her independence.

She'd been through the worst that life could throw at her and had still survived. Living without Sean's teasing laughter, his laid-back charm, his warm, stirring kisses couldn't be all that hard.

She would set him free—free to live the life he'd chosen, as a Navy SEAL, footloose and fancy-free.

Chapter Twenty

✦

"This way, Hurry," Skyler whispered to Drake. The corridors at the Hospice House stood silent at this time of the
morning. Unlike most facilities for the terminally ill, the
hallways were painted a sea-foam green and hung with
landscape portraits that cheered residents and visitors
alike. The night-shift nurse glanced up at them as they
hastened through the foyer and turned down the hall toward Matilda Dulay's private room.

"Is that woman going to try to stop us?" Drake asked,
glancing over his shoulder.

"I hope not," Skyler replied. "Visitors are welcome at
any time, but she's never seen me here this early."

They had stolen out of the Dulay mansion before dawn
this morning, creeping individually down the central
staircase, praying her father wouldn't overhear the creaking floorboards.

Slipping out the kitchen door and through the garden,
Skyler had paused one last time to look back at her childhood home. Regret mingled with sorrow, then with bit-
terness as she reflected that the privileges she'd grown

up with had most likely been acquired at the expense of other human beings. She could never continue living here knowing what her father was and what he'd done. By betraying him, she was forced to abandon everything familiar and dear to her. Yet what choice did she have if she wanted to live in peace with her conscience?

"Here we are," she whispered now, arriving at her mother's door. Her heart beat fast and thready. But defiance gave her courage.

Feeling her way into the dark room, she found the bathroom switch and turned it on. Her mother, dosed with medications to help her sleep, didn't stir. Drake crossed uncomfortably to the foot of her bed and gazed at her once-beautiful face. Skyler went to stand next to him, gratified when he pulled her close, savoring their last moments together.

A knock at the door startled them apart. "Miss Dulay?" called a voice. "Is everything okay in there?"

"Talk to her," Drake whispered. Tiptoeing into the bathroom, he motioned her toward the door.

Skyler cracked the door a scant inch or two. "Hi, Cathy," she said with a forced smile. "Everything's fine. Today's my birthday. We just wanted to leave my mother a surprise thank-you-for-giving-birth-to-me gift."

"I see," Cathy replied, sounding unconvinced. "Are you sure your father knows?"

"Of course," Skyler reassured her. "It was his idea." She closed the door firmly between them.

Then she joined Drake in the restroom in time to hear him say, "I'll surrender the witnesses in exactly thirty minutes. Don't keep me waiting."

Hearing his words, true reality hit her. Until that moment, a part of her still thought of Drake as the young man from the shelter. She felt her head swim and her knees grow weak. As her legs began to fold, Drake leapt forward, slowing her descent down the wall. She pushed him away. Now wasn't the time to get clingy. Who knew how long it would be before she would see him again—assuming witness protection even worked. Who was to say some Centurion didn't work for that branch of the FBI?

"Skyler, I know you're scared," Drake murmured as he crouched next to her. "I'm scared, too. But there's a team on the way. We're going to meet up on the other side of the Talmage Memorial Bridge."

She managed to nod, signaling her understanding.

"They'll have a doctor in the car," he added, in consideration of her mother.

"Thank you."

"Don't," he pleaded. "I'm the one who should thank you. I hate that you have to do this, Skyler. Whatever it takes, I will find you again," he swore, wresting her from her misery.

She found his dark eyes shimmering wetly. "But your safety will always be my priority," he added. "Until I'm a hundred percent sure you're not in danger of reprisal, until I'm sure some Centurion isn't going to track you down by following me, I'm going to keep my distance. Just promise you'll keep me in your heart, because I sure as hell will be keeping you in mine."

His words reminded her of the key she had given him yesterday, sending him with clear instructions and a note to Father Joseph asking him to give Drake access to the box. He'd returned grim and pale with the news that Skyler and her mother would have to disappear at once.

Warrants for her father's arrest would be issued within hours.

His cell phone beeped. He glanced at it, reading the text message. "Time to go," he said with a grimace. "Are you sure your mother's going to stay asleep when we wheel her out of here?"

"I don't know. I've never tried it. What do you think?"

"I think we do it, and we run like hell," he decided, giving her a quick little kiss and pulling her to her feet.

They had parked near the emergency exit, which would save them from having to pass the information desk—not that their departure would go unnoticed. Opening the emergency exit would set off an alarm, but Drake had assured her they'd be gone by the time security responded. "Okay," he said, looking braced for action. "Are you ready to shake things up a little?"

If it meant eventually seeing him again, loving him as a woman free to give her heart to the man of her choosing, then, yes. She was up for anything.

Owen Dulay hadn't slept well. The fact that his phone hadn't rung once with an update from Bates was deeply troubling. He rose several times in the night to place calls to his henchman and directly to the hunting cottage. Regardless of which number he dialed, no one picked up.

Something had gone amiss. And recalling Mrs. Banks's virtual accusations the day before, he had to wonder if the faithful housekeeper hadn't turned traitor on him.

In which case, his goose was cooked.

At the sound of the kitchen door softly closing toward the break of dawn, followed by the distant but distinctive purr of Skyler's Lexus, Owen threw back his quilt and hurried to the window overlooking Jones Street in time to see a car turn the corner and disappear.

With an indrawn breath, he reached for his robe and threw it on as he hurried from his bedroom to race up the stairs. Thrusting open Skyler's door, he found her bed beneath the ghostly canvas undisturbed. Skyler was privately defying him. She'd fled. But where? For how long? With whom?

A thread of suspicion, based solely on a look he'd intercepted between his daughter and the gardener, had Owen lunging toward the steps to the third floor.

He crashed through the gardener's door, his darkest suspicion confirmed. The young man was gone as well. They'd fled together, foolish, foolish children. Didn't she know by now he could nullify anything she chose to do?

With a sneer and a growl, he turned away, hastening back to his first-story bedroom to jump into his clothes. This was an annoyance he didn't need, not when his grandsons' current situation was unknown. Had they arrived safely at the hunting lodge or not?

Unable to stanch his fears and furious with his recalcitrant daughter, he determined to take matters into his own hands. The tramp would not get far in this town, not with the police on alert.

Marching to his study, he tapped out the number to the sheriff's office. "Mark," he bit out, recognizing the voice of the dispatcher, a former Boys' Home resident. "This is Owen Dulay. I want every patrol car in the city on the lookout for my daughter's cream-colored Lexus convertible, with personalized plates, SKYLER 2."

"Uh, yes, sir," Mark replied. "Do you want us to detain her or . . ."

"I want you to arrest the boy with her on whatever charges you like. As for Skyler, drop her off here at the house."

"Yes, sir. We'll get right on it."

"One more thing, Mark. Were there any accidents reported on the Diamond Causeway last night? Or on Skidaway Island?"

"I'll check for you, sir. Would you like me to call you back or—"

"I'll hold."

Tamping down his impatience, Owen crossed to his entertainment cabinet to turn on the television. The earliest morning news program didn't air until 6:00 A.M. It was barely five. Having missed the evening news several nights in a row, he played the tape he'd recorded before the last Centurion meeting. While Mark took his sweet time finding the answer to Owen's simple question, Owen thumped onto his settee with the phone to his ear and watched news that had taken place three days ago.

To his consternation, he got his first real look at Ellie Stuart. A strangely vulnerable feeling ambushed him as he noted the steely determination in her gray eyes and listened to her accuse the Centurions of kidnapping her sons. What had compelled him to agree with the Culprit to let her go?

Mark spoke up suddenly in his ear. "Sir, there were no accidents on the Diamond Causeway. But police were called to an incident at a Texaco station on Skidaway."

Owen broke into a cold sweat. "What kind of incident?" he asked.

"Let's see. According to the convenience-store clerk, three men held up the occupants of a van. Some children were transferred to a third vehicle. The men in the van were all incapacitated, and all three vehicles took off before our officers arrived on the scene."

Owen swallowed against his suddenly parched throat. He realized with a stab of real fright that the van with Carl and the boys had been intercepted. His grandsons had been snatched from his custody and whisked away.

By whom? How had he not seen this coming?

It had to be the same people Mrs. Banks had warned him of, the ones who'd visited the Boys' Home.

Pressing a palm to his clammy forehead, Owen wordlessly hung up. He stood for a moment, reeling with the ramifications of what Mark had told him. Of course, the report was unconfirmed at this point, but Owen's instincts had been telling him for hours now that his masterful abduction was backfiring, no thanks to the Culprit, who'd convinced him to let Ellie Stuart go.

Owen had to get out. He had to leave, now. There was only so much that his minions in law enforcement could do for him if he became a suspect in the boys' abduction. Even more troubling than facing honest federal agents was the prospect of losing credibility with the Centurion Elite, men like himself who would view his carelessness as a threat to the brotherhood.

Dropping the phone on his desk, he hurried to his bedroom to pack a suitcase. It was time to pull the plug.

"We're being followed," Drake realized as he watched the white patrol car turn the corner behind them.

Skyler, who'd left the driving to Drake in order to sit in the back beside her mother, craned her neck to see out the rear window. "Police!" she whispered. "They work for my father!"

"Maybe they're just following their usual route," Drake added hopefully. But blue lights began to flash, ruling out the possibility and signaling that the cruiser was now in silent pursuit.

"What do we do?" Skyler cried, glancing with worry at her mother. "If she wakes up now, she'll be frightened."

"We're almost at the bridge," Drake stated, confident in the training that had prepared him to expect even the best plans to go to shit. "The agents are waiting on just the other side. We're going to outrun him," he said, shooting her a reassuring glance in the rearview mirror.

"Okay," Skyler squeaked, putting a protective hand across her mother as Drake accelerated suddenly, speeding them out from under the enormous live oaks lining Oglethorpe Avenue toward the double suspension bridge arching into a violet sky over the Savannah River straight ahead.

Behind them, the cruiser's siren started to scream.

Ignoring it, Drake gunned the engine, and the Lexus roared up the steep grade of the bridge, high above the silver river. Too soon he was forced to slow down again. Cars blocked both lanes ahead of them. "Come on!" Drake muttered, tapping his horn. "Move out of the way."

A good citizen in a Cadillac figured it was his civic obligation to block Drake's escape and let the cruiser overtake them. It surged closer, its blue lights flashing into the interior of the Lexus.

Drake pushed a button on his phone and stuck in his

earpiece. "This is Special Agent Donovan," he clipped. "Are you in place? Over."

"That's a roger, Donovan," replied a man. "We're parked on a pull-off just fifty meters past the far side of the bridge. Jesus, is that you being chased?"

"Yes, it is. Get in a defensive position with your fire-arms drawn. I'm going to pull around you and in on the protected passenger side. Let's show this clown who's in charge here."

"Will do, sir."

Caught behind another slow-moving car, Drake was forced to decelerate. With a roar, the patrol car tapped the Lexus's bumper, causing the tires of their vehicle to skid on the dew-slick surface. "Son of a bitch!" Drake muttered.

In the backseat, Matilda Dulay startled awake. "What!" she cried, fighting the constraints of her seat belt in wide-eyed terror. "What's happening?"

Skyler sought to comfort her. "It's okay, Mama. Don't panic. Drake's bringing us somewhere safe."

But as the police car bumped them again, sending the back end of the Lexus skidding into the cement blockade, Matilda released her own seat belt and lunged at Drake, clawing at him from behind. "Stop the car!" she cried feebly.

"Mama, let go of him," Skyler ordered, wrestling her back into her seat, struggling to refasten her seat belt.

At last the car in front of Drake moved out of the way, and as the squad car came in for another hit, Drake punched the accelerator, sending them flying down the opposite side of the bridge toward the South Carolina border.

He could see his colleagues now, parked on the other side of the street, facing oncoming traffic. As per his instructions, they stood behind their doors, badges and firearms drawn.

"Hold on tight," Drake warned, slowing just enough to execute a hundred-and-eighty-degree skidding turn.

Skyler clung, pale-faced, to her seat. In the back, her mother screamed. The antilock-brake system protested; nonetheless, the tires slid in a perfect arc, allowing Drake to drive straight between the federal vehicle and the tall marsh grass. "Go out that side, Skyler," he said, reaching across the passenger seat to flip it forward. "I'll get your mother."

As Skyler shot out of the Lexus, the squad car flew past them, tires squealing as it skidded to a stop. It was backing up by the time Drake had jumped out of the driver's seat to help Matilda Dulay from the rear. "Come on, ma'am. You'll be safe, I promise."

To his great relief, Matilda allowed him to assist her.

"Federal agents, FBI!" shouted Drake's colleagues, holding out their badges and firearms with fully extended arms as the pursuing officer glared through his lowered window.

"What in God's name is goin' on?" demanded the deputy.

"Nothing that concerns you, Officer," retorted an agent. "Everything is under control here. Why don't you get on back across the river?"

"I want to arrest that man"—the officer pointed a finger at Drake—"for reckless driving."

"Not today, Deputy," insisted the federal agent. "Now get on out of here before I ask for your badge number."

With a glare and a sputter of protest, the deputy flicked off his lights and executed a sloppy U-turn. Drake angled Matilda into the rear seat of a government-owned vehicle, where Skyler fussed over her and helped her to don her seat belt, all the while crooning assurances that everything would be all right. A doctor, also seated in the rear, took Matilda's pulse.

At last Skyler looked up and met Drake's regretful gaze. As she reached for him, he held on to her, wanting desperately to extend this moment with her. Lifting her hand to his mouth, he turned it over and pressed a kiss into the soft center of her palm. "As soon I know it's safe," he rasped, his voice strangled, "I will find you again. I promise."

"I won't forget you, Drake," she swore, her own voice cracking. "I'll wait for you."

The agents, wearing identical blue suits that made them look like twins, slipped into the front. The driver sent a pointed look into his rearview mirror.

"Time to say good bye," Drake added, gazing one last time into Skyler's blue eyes. On impulse, because he couldn't bear the thought of her ever needing him and not being able to find him, he withdrew a pen from his pocket and hastily scribbled his cell number on her hand. "Only if it's life or death," he whispered.

With relief shining in her eyes, she nodded. "Until then," she replied.

As he closed the door and stepped from the car, the locks gave a click. In the next instant, the official-looking vehicle swung into the northbound lane and pulled away.

Drake watched it move along the flat, straight road, its taillights growing fainter as the sky brightened overhead.

Thanks to Skyler's defiance and to Ellie Stuart's determined quest, Owen Dulay's crimes had come to light. Within hours, a team of federal agents would arrest him and seize his assets. Ideally, this would mean the beginning of the end for the Centurions. Drake's undercover efforts had blossomed into an unmitigated success.

Yet he'd never felt more torn than he did now, nor more desolate, as he watched Skyler slip out of reach, beyond sight, sound, or touch for years—possibly forever.

"Here we are!" Ellie exclaimed, touched by the sight of her little rental house sitting so prettily under the shade of the towering oak trees.

"Yay!" cried Caleb, who'd squirmed restlessly throughout the eight-hour car ride from Hilton Head. With little room in the back of Sean's GTO for three boys, let alone for the car seat they'd bought at the outset of their journey, squabbles had broken out and tempers had flared. To keep patient, Ellie reminded herself that she could just as easily be returning home alone. As for Sean, the squabbling rolled from him like water off a duck's back. Keeping a steady pace on the interstate, he'd gotten them to their destination by late afternoon.

Ellie pushed out of the car first, eager to smell the familiar scent of home. The boys tumbled out after her, suntanned from their week at the beach, and raced each other to the door, eager to get to their room and reacquaint themselves with their toys. Ducking back into the car to free the baby, Ellie watched Sean fetch their belongings from the rear. The time was approaching rapidly for her to tell him good-bye.

Holding Colton's hand, she let him toddle up the walkway as Sean carried their bags to the door. She wondered what he was thinking, whether he was dying to just drop them off and get a moment to himself, or whether he felt obliged to stay until they'd settled back in. Given the wrecked state of her house when she'd left it more than two weeks back, settling back in could take a while.

She didn't want him feeling obligated. She didn't want him hanging around, period—not if he was going to abandon them later. *If.* There she went again, hoping for more than she had. She should be getting down on her knees, grateful just to have her boys back and forget about having Sean, too.

It wasn't like he was going to stop coming by to check on the state of the house and on the boys. She'd overheard him reassure Caleb several times over the past week that he'd see them all the time. Over bologna sandwiches on the beach, he'd also explained, in that oh-so-patient way he had with her kids, what he did for a living. He'd said he had to rescue people in faraway places, which meant traveling for long periods of time. But when he was gone, he promised to keep them in his thoughts and maybe they'd like to remember him at bedtime prayers.

His words had melted Ellie's heart, totally and completely. But they'd also reminded her that nothing had changed. He would still get calls at 2:00 A.M. to go "wheels up," as he called it, and she'd still have three boys to raise, a degree to earn, and a career to start.

Hadn't Sean told her on one of their long beach walks that SEALs made lousy husbands because of the stress they put on their families? He hadn't said as much, but she knew things would go back to exactly as they were, only he would never snuggle up in bed with them as they had in Hilton Head with Ellie on one side, Sean on the other, and all three boys in the middle. There would be no more lovemaking as far as Ellie was concerned—just as before, only now she'd know exactly what she was missing. She couldn't afford to weaken, to let her independence slip and risk relying on a man for her happiness.

Yes, she'd been given a second chance—a third chance, really—to get her life on track. Nothing about that had changed.

Yet, in other ways, things would never be the same again. Never again would she take her sons for granted. No matter how loud, grubby, or naughty they might get, she would imagine life without them and be grateful. Thanks to Ophelia's exposé, which had begun midweek last week, public opinion had shifted in Ellie's favor. She and the boys had been swamped by offers to appear on prime-time television talk shows. But Ellie, who relished her privacy far more than she craved the money, had turned them all down.

In Savannah, the city was in an uproar over the arrest of Owen Dulay, caught by FBI agents trying to steal aboard his private plane bound for Venezuela. A shakedown of Savannah's infrastructure had resulted in the arrest of the city mayor, the chief of police, and Dulay's personal accountant.

Within the FBI, however, the intensive investigation to discover how fabricated evidence had found its way into the lab was beginning to lose momentum. Special Agent Butler, who had voluntarily submitted to a polygraph test, had been cleared of all suspicion, as had his immediate supervisor. A cybercrimes analyst named Dale Robbins had confessed to generating the false e-mails, but he could not identify the FBI employee and fellow Centurion who'd requested his assistance in creating them. With high-level agents complaining that the internal investigation had the hallmarks of a witch hunt and with many threatening to resign, the prospect of finding and prosecuting any single individual looked unlikely.

"Here, I'll get the door," Ellie called as Caleb and Chris vied for space on the narrow stoop and Sean juggled three suitcases in two hands. Scooping up the baby with one arm, she groped in her purse for her keys with the other.

When Ellie thought of all the money Sean had spent on them, first for the cost of the hotel in Savannah, plus food, then clothing the boys had needed for a week at Hilton Head—including a new pair of sneakers for Caleb—her pride stung. If it took her months of living without air-conditioning and rationing food, she'd pay back every cent she owed him.

"Lord, I hope this house isn't as bad off as I remember," she remarked, wriggling the key into the lock. With a twist and a click, the door swung open and the boys tumbled inside, racing to see who could get to their bedroom first.

An inviting floral scent had Ellie stepping cautiously inside.

Not a trace of the destruction the police had wrought was still in evidence. Someone had put the room in order, picking up every spilled toy and righting every overturned piece of furniture. "Who on earth?" she cried, raising the blinds to bring the light flooding in. "Oh, my heavens!"

"Jordan and Solomon," Sean supplied, his little smile

now an open grin. "They wanted to do something nice for you." He put the bags down.

"They didn't!" Ellie exclaimed, peeking into the kitchen and finding its surfaces gleaming. "They shouldn't have," she protested, sending Sean a torn look. "How could you ask them to do that?"

"I didn't ask them, Ellie. They offered. You know, it won't kill you to let people help you sometimes," he added ruefully.

Reminded of all that she owed him, Ellie straightened her spine and marched back into the living room. "Well, maybe I don't like owing people. Maybe I like standing on my own two feet," she said, angling her chin into the air.

His smile faded and his eyes became watchful. "Why do I get the feeling you're trying to tell me something?" he asked warily.

Ellie drew a deep, resolved breath. "Sean, please don't take me wrong. I am so grateful for everything you've done," she began, her voice fraying with mixed emotion. "Lord knows I could never repay you for the kindness you've shown me and my boys, and I swear I will pay back every cent you spent to help me find them." She dragged in a breath, wary of the frown gathering on Sean's forehead. "It's just that . . ." She groped for the words. "When I came here, I didn't want a man in my life. Lord knows I'd been bit and cured of that. But then we . . ."

"Made love?" Sean supplied, obviously trying to follow her line of reasoning.

"Yes, that, too, but I let you take *care* of me, of us," she cried, letting him see how that distressed her. "And I'd sworn, when I left Mississippi, that as long as I have breath in my body, I'd never ever do that kind of thing again."

"Have sex?" he asked, still studying her as if she were some lunatic.

"Yes! No, I mean, I'd never be dependent on anyone again. You don't get this? I have to know I can make it on my own." She gestured with a hand, at the same time swallowing the lump in her throat.

For what seemed an eternity, Sean stared at her like she was a puzzle he would never figure out. She fought to look him in the eye without letting him see that her heart felt close to bursting.

"You're saying you want me to leave," he reiterated with a nod of understanding.

"You know it's time," she said, pushing the words through a tight throat.

"Even though I own this house," he added, causing her to gasp.

"You wouldn't make us leave, would you?" she asked.

He crossed his arms over his massive chest and shrugged. "Depends," he said equivocally.

"Depends on what?" she demanded, ignoring the baby, who'd tipped over an entire bucket of Lego pieces and started mucking in them.

"On whether you need more room," said Sean, confusing her with his reply. Bending over, he plucked Colton off the floor and squeezed a Lego piece out of his mouth by pinching his cheeks.

"Dadda!" said Colton, slapping Sean's neck.

"Why would I need more room?" Ellie asked, dismayed and touched by Colton's confusion.

"This house isn't big enough for the five of us," Sean

pointed out. Keeping Colton in his arms, he blew raspberries in the crook of his neck.

Ellie's mouth dropped open. "You can't be serious," she breathed. Maybe she had heard him wrong. Had he said *the five of us*?

"Why the hell can't I be serious?" he asked her mildly.

"Were you not listening to me?" she demanded, going rigid from head to toe, her throat equally tight. "First, I told you that I need to do this on my own. You can't just adopt us like some strays from the local shelter, Sean. Secondly, you are not the marrying kind; you told me that yourself just a couple weeks ago. And third, I'm not shacking up with you!" she added hotly.

He chuckled at her word usage. "I don't have any intention of shacking up with you," he replied. "And why do you think being married to me would hold you back? I'm not trying to steal your independence, Ellie. I just want to be around to cheer you on. I want the next fifty years of my life to be as good as this last week."

His slow smile coupled with his rebuttal turned her brains to mush. She lost all track of her argument.

"Now, I *was* gonna find you the perfect engagement ring and do this right," he groused, "but since you're all fired up and trying to kick me out of my own house, I suppose I'll have to do it now."

A giggle at the head of the hallway dragged Ellie's gaze toward her two older boys, who were down on their knees, peeking around the corner at them.

"Do what?" she asked, completely distracted and flustered.

Putting the baby down, Sean took a step in her direction, hooked an arm behind her back, and brought her hips flush with his. Desire shimmered in Ellie's womb, shortening her breath, further befuddling her thoughts. "Ask you to marry me, banana," he told her, gazing deep in her eyes.

She stared back at him, too stunned to reply. The walls of the room seemed to dance around them.

"This is where you're supposed to say yes," he prompted, starting to look a little worried.

"But . . ." Ellie tried to reason with him. "Why?" she asked faintly.

His expression turned suddenly serious. "The night we got the boys back, Ellie, I realized I am a part of this family. That's something my heart's been trying to tell me for a long time, only my head wouldn't listen. I don't want to marry you so I can take care of you. I like your independence. I need you to be strong and hold the family together whenever I have to leave. I need a woman who can pick up the pieces if—God forbid—something happens to me. So long as I can make life better for you, the way you do for me, then why not marry me, Ellie? I love you. I belong in this family," he added, including the boys with a nod.

"Say yes, Mama!" Caleb cried impatiently as he and his brother looked on.

"Yeah, Mama. You love him, too, don'tcha?" Chris chimed in.

Suddenly, what had seemed so complicated before was embarrassingly simple. "I do love him," she realized out loud, and all her fears and doubts fell quietly away.

Heat flared in Sean's eyes, and he grinned with tri- umph. "Say it to *me*," he commanded, pulling her into a rough embrace. "Come on. You're head over heels in love with me," he proclaimed with certainty. "Say it."

She slapped him playfully for his boastfulness. "I will not say it," she insisted, trying to squirm away.

"I'll make you say it," Sean threatened. "I'll tickle you till you say it."

"No!" Ellie cried, laughing as she struggled to free herself.

"Yep," insisted Sean, swiping her feet right out from underneath her. She couldn't get the better of him this time. In an instant, he had her pegged to the floor, squirming helplessly beneath him. "Come on, boys. Help me get her to talk."

With a squeal and a roar, they attacked, dropping to their knees to rub their knuckles over Ellie's ribs as she shrieked with helpless laughter. Even Colton joined in, straddling her free leg and using it as a hobby horse. "Stop! Stop!" she cried, gasping for breath between peals of laughter, tears streaking into her hairline. "Okay," she relented. "Okay, okay, I'll say it!"

The tickling ceased. The boys drew back with expectant, happy faces. Ellie focused her watering eyes on Sean in time to see him swallow hard. His artery pulsed in his neck as he regarded her as if his whole future hinged on this moment.

Sitting up, she reached for his hand and carried his callused palm to her cheek. Her heart flooded with feeling. "I'm not just crazy about you," she confessed, self-conscious enough to feel her face heat. "I'm over the moon in love with you," she admitted quickly. "And if you're crazy enough to take us on, then, yes, I'll even marry you. Why not?"

With a long exhalation, he released the breath he was holding. "Phew, I had to work for that one," he commented, wiping imaginary sweat from his brow.

"Oh, hush."

"But you always make it worth that little bit of effort," he added, his voice growing raspy as he leaned in to cover her lips with his.

"Ew!" exclaimed Caleb, crawling away and giving them a wide berth.

"Come on, let's go back to our room," Christopher suggested, snatching up the baby as Colton started crawling into his mother's lap. There wouldn't be room enough for him there in another few seconds.

Whispering with excitement, they retreated down the hall, leaving their mother lost in Sean's all-consuming kiss.

Epilogue

◆

At the sound of approaching footsteps, Owen Dulay looked up, his heart faltering as he recognized Ashton Jameson being escorted by a prison guard to Owen's private cell. The door scraped open, and Ashton edged inside, keeping his back to the light, his face in shadow.

Owen had been expecting this visit. He rolled from his cot to greet him. Even in humble captivity, a Centurion was expected to display gentility. "Ashton," he called, waving him deeper. "Come in."

As Ashton took an obliging step forward, his sunken eyes touched disdainfully upon the orange coveralls Owen was forced to wear. "I can't stay long," he began, ignoring Owen's outstretched hand.

The snub was intentional. Owen lowered his hand at the sobering realization that he'd get no help from the brotherhood now. Days of loyalty were over. As his trial approached, no doubt they feared he would betray them with a plea bargain. Surely Ashton knew him better than that.

"I came to give you this," said his longtime friend in a

pained voice. Taking a vial from his pocket, he set it on Owen's humble sink.

For a long moment, with his blood running cold, Owen regarded the brownish vial. He knew what it contained. His death would be violent but swift. "Have you seen my daughter?" he inquired, dragging his gaze upward.

"No," said Ashton with contempt. "It is rumored that she will testify against you."

Owen grunted his acknowledgment. His daughter's betrayal did not surprise him. She was, after all, the spitting image of her mother. "There won't be a trial," he answered softly, with resignation.

Ashton nodded his approval, looking vastly relieved. "Well, then." He groped for further words, but there was only one. "Good-bye."

"Good-bye, Ashton," Owen replied.

He waited for his fellow Centurion to be escorted from the cell. Then he carried the vial to his cot, sank weakly on one end of it, and regarded the amber-colored poison. With a cynical smile, he considered the ramifications of his death. The court would be denied the chance to try him. But most importantly, his worldly goods, those received by honest dealings, would be handed down to his heir.

Christopher Stuart was about to become a millionaire, his monies held in trust for him by his attorney, Lynwood Spenser, a man sworn to keep Owen's dreams close to his heart. Not even the Culprit, who had contributed to Owen's downfall while retaining his anonymity and power, could get his hands on Owen's fortune. It would pass, in Centurion tradition, to his most promising male heir, who, with Lynwood's guidance, might one day assume his grandfather's position in the hierarchy.

With a tug of the cork, Owen freed the contents of the vial.

Allowing himself no cowardly thought, he tipped it into his mouth and swallowed, confident that his legacy would live on.

Dear Reader,

If you read DON'T LET GO, you'll remember
Lucy Donovan, the intrepid CIA agent. Lucy
is the CIA's top choice for a rescue mission to
Colombia, where American hostages are held
deep in the jungle by rebel terrorists. Thrilled to
take on an undercover assignment, Lucy hates
the fact that Navy SEAL Gus Atwater, the only
man she ever loved, will be her partner. At odds
from the start, they trek deep into the jungle as
part of a UN negotiating team. Their secret mission: to locate the hostages and summon Navy
SEALs to extract them. Confronted with deadly
obstacles and fanatic guerillas, Lucy and Gus
must rely on each other for survival. When the
tables suddenly turn, and they are torn apart,
only then will they realize how deeply connected
they've become.

Please check out my Web site at www.marliss
melton.com for an excerpt from Lucy's story.

Enjoy!

Marliss Melton

THE DISH

Where authors give you the inside scoop!

♥ ♥ ♥ ♥ ♥ ♥ ♥ ♥ ♥ ♥ ♥ ♥ ♥ ♥

From the desk of Elizabeth Hoyt

Gentle Reader,

The hero of my book TO SEDUCE A SINNER (on sale now) Jasper Renshaw, Viscount Vale, had quite a rocky road on his way to the altar. In fact, TO SEDUCE A SINNER opens with Vale being rejected by his fiancée—the *second* fiancée he's had in six months. Thus, it should be no surprise that once married Vale endeavored to pass on some of his marital wisdom to other gentlemen. I'll reprint his advice below.

A GENTLEMAN'S GUIDE TO MARRIAGE AND MANAGING THE LADY WIFE

1. Chose carefully when selecting a bride. A lady with a sweet disposition, engaging smile, and full bosom is a boon to any man.

2. However, should a gentleman find that he has been left at the altar yet again, he may find himself accepting the proposal of a lady of less than a full bosom and rather too much intelligence.

3. Surprisingly, he may also find himself attracted to said lady.

4. The marriage bed should be approached with delicacy and tenderness. Remember, your lady wife is a virgin of good family, and thus may be shocked or even repulsed by the activities of the marriage bed. Best to keep them short.

5. However, try not to be too shocked if your lady wife turns out *not* to be shocked by the marriage bed.

6. Or, even if she is wildly enthusiastic about her marital duties.

7. If such is your case, you are a fortunate man indeed.

8. The lady wife can be a mysterious creature, passionate, yet oddly secretive about her feelings toward you, her lord and husband.

9. The gentleman may find his thoughts returning again and again to the subject of his lady wife's feeling for him. "Does she love me?" you may wonder as you consume your morning toast. Try not to let these thoughts become too obsessive.

10. Whatever you do, do *not* fall in love with your lady wife, no matter how alluring her

lips or seductive her replies to your banter are. That way lies folly.

Yours Very Sincerely,

Elizabeth Hoyt

www.elizabethhoyt.com

From the desk of Marliss Melton

Dear Reader,

Sean Harlan, the hero of my latest book TOO FAR GONE (on sale now) is a killer. Surprised? I thought you might be. How could such a charming, sexy, fun-loving man with a sunny disposition and a special way with children be a sniper for his SEAL team? How could he be so ruthless and merciless, taking lives without remorse?

Oddly enough, this all began with one of my kids. I wanted to create a hero with the same relaxed and irrepressible charm as my son. So Sean was born. But I did a little research into that "relaxed" personality type and learned something that blew me away: it's the one and only personality type that makes up a natural born killer! Did you know that in battles, only 15 to 25 percent of infantrymen ever fire their weapons? And most fire over the heads of the enemy! Those who actually shoot to kill comprise less than 4 percent of those in battle yet they do half the killing!

When I discovered this, I knew exactly who Sean was, dark side and all. He was a man that was indispensable to the military. After all, without men like Sean, armies would crumble and decisive battles would be lost. But I wanted Sean to be indispensable to a woman who needed him, too; so, I created Ellie Stuart as the perfect foil. As hesitant as she is about Sean's killer instinct, she soon realizes that without Sean, she stands little chance of reclaiming her kidnapped sons. She also comes to see that her mother's instinct makes killing a viable option and that she and Sean are not so different after all.

It is my hope that you'll love Sean as much as I do. Oh, and by the way, my son is a perfectly nice young man . . . so far.

To learn more about Sean and Ellie's personalities, visit the FUN STUFF page at www.marliss melton.com.

Thanks for reading,

Marliss Melton

From the desk of Lani Diane Rich

Dear Reader,

Most often, when you write a book, people ask you why you chose that particular setting. All I can say about northern Idaho, the setting for my latest book, WISH YOU WERE HERE (on sale now), is that I drove through it once while moving with my family from Anchorage, Alaska to Syracuse, New York, and I was absolutely entranced. Given the hard-nosed business woman Freya was, I figured there would be no greater fish-out-of-water situation for her than being stuck in the middle of all those trees.

One of the challenges of Freya's story was where I'd left her at the end of CRAZY IN LOVE—on a road toward something of a mental breakdown. Like her sister Flynn, I felt it was high past time for Freya's life to buck her off like a mechanical dive bar bronco; and so, it was with great relish that I saddled her with a rare "condition" and placed her in an impossible situation. While writing CRAZY IN LOVE, Freya was one of those magical secondary characters who just begged for her own book, and it was so much fun to spend this time with her and watch her grow into her own person.

As for Nate, he was a lot of fun to write as well.

Where Freya was hardened and tough, Nate was open, sensitive, and honorable. His relationship with Piper was especially fun for me to write, especially against the backdrop of Freya's relationship with her own father. Nate's a classic cleft-chin hero, but there was a lot of depth under those still waters, which made him a pleasure to write.

I hope you enjoy reading the story as much as I did writing it. Thanks so much!

Lani Diane Rich

www.lanidianerich.com

If you like Romantic Suspense . . .
You'll LOVE
Shannon K. Butcher!!!

NO REGRETS
(0-446-61865-9/$6.99 US/$9.99 CAN)

"NO REGRETS is an absolute must read.
This is a real page-turner—romantic suspense
at its very best!"
—MARIAH STEWART,
New York Times bestselling author

"Top pick! A promising new talent who wastes
no time getting gritty has just joined the romantic
suspense world . . . Butcher is a first-rate find!"
—*Romantic Times BOOKreviews Magazine*

NO CONTROL
(0-446-61866-7/$6.99 US/$9.99 CAN)

"Top pick! Butcher is on the fast track to becoming
a major presence in the romantic suspense genre.
Chilling plotlines and layered characters add
serious punch to this thriller."
—*Romantic Times BOOKreviews Magazine*

"Explosive passion and a touch of tenderness combine
with fast-paced action and gritty, vengeful violence
in this high-speed thriller . . . it's a winner."
—*Library Journal*

AVAILABLE WHEREVER BOOKS ARE SOLD

WANT MORE BONECHILLING SUSPENSE?
CHECK OUT KAREN ROSE

DON'T TELL
0-446-61280-4

"Utterly compelling . . . high-wire suspense that
keeps you riveted to the edge of your seat."
—Lisa Gardner, *New York Times* bestselling author

HAVE YOU SEEN HER?
0-446-61281-2

"Offering heart-racing thrills . . . Rose populates her novel
with vivid characters . . . and stokes the tension
to a fever pitch, throwing in shocking twists."
—*Publishers Weekly*

I'M WATCHING YOU
0-446-61447-5

"A sensual, riveting book that kept me on the edge of my seat. I
loved this book, and if I had to rate it, it would be off the chart."
—*Rendezvous*

NOTHING TO FEAR
0-446-61448-3

"A caring women's advocate heroine, a determined, gritty hero,
and a diabolical villain drive the plot of Rose's riveting story."
—*Library Journal*

YOU CAN'T HIDE
0-446-61689-3

"Densely plotted and with amazing twists, this novel is,
in a word, riveting."
—*Romantic Times BookClub*

COUNT TO TEN
0-446-61690-7

"Takes off like a house afire. There's action and chills
galore in this nonstop thriller."
—Tess Gerritsen, *New York Times* bestselling author

AVAILABLE WHEREVER BOOKS ARE SOLD

Want to know more about romances at Grand Central Publishing and Forever? Get the scoop online!

GRAND CENTRAL PUBLISHING'S ROMANCE HOME PAGE

Visit us at www.hachettebookgroupusa.com/romance for all the latest news, reviews, and chapter excerpts!

NEW AND UPCOMING TITLES

Each month we feature our new titles and reader favorites.

CONTESTS AND GIVEAWAYS

We give away galleys, autographed copies, and all kinds of fun stuff.

AUTHOR INFO

You'll find bios, articles, and links to personal Web sites for all your favorite authors—and so much more!

THE BUZZ

Sign up for our monthly romance newsletter, and be the first to read all about it!

If you or someone you know
wants to improve their reading skills,
call the Literacy Help Line.

WORDS ARE YOUR WHEELS
1-800-228-8813